C.Blanco

C.de S.Sebastian

P. s...

Tropicus Capricorni

CALIFO...RNA

B. de Corōn do.

Lago de Oro

coyot

ntde rey
B. de Trinida.
Punta de la concepcion

Canal de
S. Bar bara

I. S. Cacalye

Punta de la Concepcion.
P. S. Digio

I. S. Clement.

Bayad. de Todos
Santos

I. S. Mart.

B. de L. Quintyn

B. de la virginas.

I. d. Parara.

R. de Engaño

I. S. Marco

B. de francisco

B. de S. Symon

I. d. Cerita

Punta de S. Barthelome
Sirra Pintado
P. de Roque

I. d. de Cerro

B. de las arenas

B. de S. Cristobal.

Punta de S. Apolonia.

B. de S. Ma geyn.
P. de la Magdalona
P. de la Ch.

R. Xaquich

R. de Acom.

R. de Carali

S. Miguel.

las Pulgas

P. S. Clara

Pat

STRANGE California

edited by
JAYM GATES AND **J. DANIEL BATT**

FALSTAFF
BOOKS

STORY Jitsu

STRANGE CALIFORNIA: Kickstarter Edition
strangecalifornia.com
Falstaff Books | falstaffbooks.com
StoryJitsu | storyjitsu.com

ISBN-13: 978-0-9906385-8-2
ISBN-10: 0-9906385-8-8
Worldwide Rights
Created in the United Staes of America

Edited by Jaym Gates and J. Daniel Batt
Cover Illustration by Galen Dara
Cover Design, Interior Layout and Illustrations by J. Daniel Batt

PRINTED IN THE UNITED STATES OF AMERICA

With appreciation to our Kickstarter backers

TABLE OF CONTENTS

FOREWORD
TO THE
FRONTIER

Jaym Gates & J. Daniel Batt

THE SANTA LUCIA MOUNTAINS HUG THE
California coastline between Monterey and San Luis Obispo and
stare out at the dark, cold waters of the
Pacific. For centuries, perhaps back to
the Chumash legends, lore tells of dark
figures materializing upon the edges of
these mountains to gaze across the ocean.
When the early migrants came to California, these figures were waiting for
them. The myth of the Dark Watchers
was reinforced by John Steinbeck, the

Golden State writer that championed the plight of the migrant agricultural worker. In his story "Flight," he described one of these watchers as "a dark form against the sky, a man standing on top of a rock." Steinbeck's reference of these creatures is even more shocking against his usual cast of common, authentic American characters.

The mythology was picked up by Steinbeck's son Thomas. Remembering his father and grandmother's retellings of the phantom observers, he collaborated with artist Benjamin Brode to craft an art book in honor of the Dark Watchers: *In Search of the Dark Watchers: Landscapes and Lore of Big Sur.* Thomas Steinbeck begins: "And if for a brief moment they entertain the least suspicion… the Dark Watchers will literally evaporate in front of your eyes like the fog." Later, attempting to establish their history, the younger Steinbeck notes "The early Spanish explorers, as well as the later Mexican ranchers and their vaqueros, called them 'Los Vigilantes Oscuros.'"

On the Weird California (weirdca.com) forums, a user named Joey gave his own account: "I'm a long distance runner and most of my training is up in the good old Californian Mountains. I had a long run scheduled so I headed out. I headed to Veterans Park here in the San Fernando Valley. Time of day was 2:00 pm I was running and up in an area where no human could climb without gear I saw a black figure in plain day light. I never seen anything like it up in the mountain. Was darker than dark could not explain it. A year past and today again January 24th I saw it again and in the same spot." Another user, C. Gardner, commented: "Up here in the Eastern Sierras, we see the Dark Watchers all the time. They are always out at dusk and dawn. All you see is just a tall dark silhouette. They almost look like horses standing on their hind legs with the assistance of a walking stick. Its pretty creepy, and nobody has ever seen them close up. They disappear the moment you try to get closer." They are watchers and observers only.

Imagine the immigrants slowly venturing into the expanding frontier—to the unexplored, unknown wild. California was so far removed from early European settlers that some maps showed the territory as a separate island. Those pioneers crossed the Sierras and settled the varied topography only to discover the mythological Watchers, looking out to another frontier. The Dark Watchers are a unique mythology representative of the Golden State—spirits ever gazing into the unknown.

California is seen simultaneously, alternating throughout history, as both the frontier and the staging area to explore the frontier. For the early wanderers coming from the north to settle the western coast around 17,000 BCE, California was their frontier. From then until now, for millions, California is synonymous with the frontier—the embodiment of the unknown and, within the unknown, the possibility for the strange and wonderful.

Near the end of 1890s, with the settlement of California, the US government declared that the American frontier had vanished. Yet, from California, hinted at by the occasional glimpses of the Dark Watchers, the vision for further frontiers was glimpsed. The frontier is that unexplored, uninhabited territory on the border of what is known.

Moving from mythology to science fiction (often called the literature of the frontier), Captain Kirk has challenged us to explore the "Final Frontier." In the fiction of the future, California is home to Star Fleet. In Roddenberry's vision, the exploration of the new Final Frontier is staged within the Coastal State. As an unintended potential precursor to that future, SpaceX, based in Southern California, has recently laid out the plans for humanity to become multi-planetary. In Northern California, citizens and industries in Monterey are working towards the establishment of a spaceport.

The Encyclopedia of Science Fiction extols California as "pure [science fiction], that California was not discovered but invented… California [is portrayed] as the promised land, where the streets are paved with gold; and California as a place in which one may construct an advocated world."

Viewed as the ever-present frontier, the borders of California are easily imagined to contain a myriad of oddities and wonders. Whether you're from California or not, if you're a fan of science fiction and fantasy, this anthology has something for you. Strange California celebrates the frontier that is at the heart of speculative fiction. The land of California, since the early humans settled the region millennia past, have been drawn to the frontier land. California not only creates this diversity of thought and experience, but invites it. It calls for us and we find from it a call to to Carl Sagan's own words, "Somewhere, something wonderful is waiting to be known…"

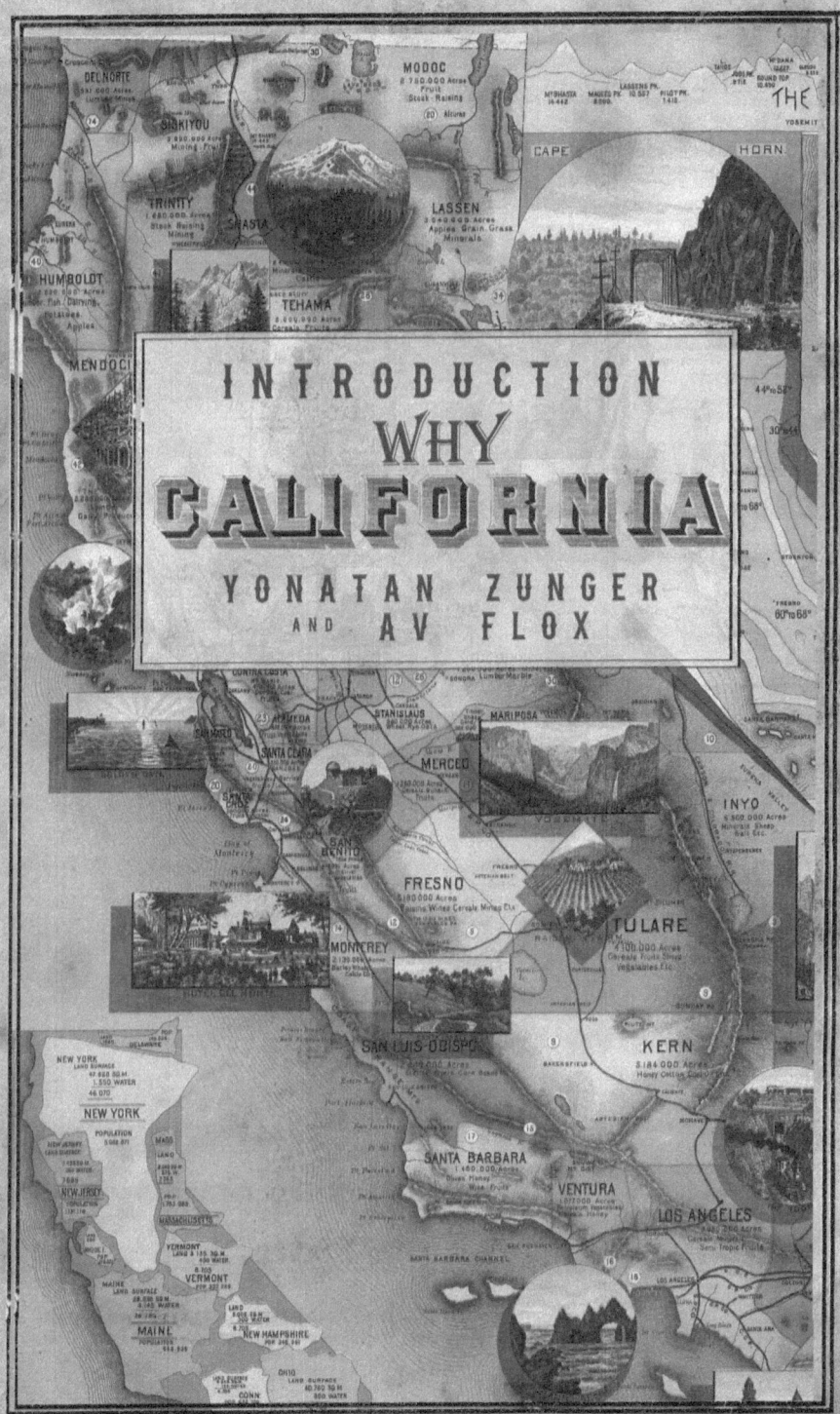

INTRODUCTION
WHY CALIFORNIA

YONATAN ZUNGER
AND AV FLOX

YONATAN ZUNGER

Yonatan Zunger moved to California in 1997 to pursue a career in mad science, only to find himself pursuing mad engineering instead. Forced out of the confines of academia, he sublimated his teaching urge into essay-writing, amassing an impressive collection of mortal enemies in the process. Today he lives in Silicon Valley with his wife and co-author, where they are secretly plotting the robot uprising.

AV FLOX

AV Flox has always been a little strange. She spoke before she crawled, she found her own limbs more interesting than toys, and, at the age of five, she stole a chicken's head from the kitchen bin to star in an ill-fated puppet show that resulted in the violent ejection of the entire household's lunch. She became a journalist because people tend to answer questions when they believe these have purpose beyond simple curiosity (and also because it's probably the only profession where looking through a bin isn't utterly beyond the pale). She chose sex as her beat because people will read anything with sex in it, including things as tedious as patent law. She didn't believe in the concept of home until she landed in California in 2007: here she remains with her mad scientist husband, a much better preserved collection of dead things, and her murder of crows.

WHY DOES CALIFORNIA FIT SO NATURALLY WITH STRANGENESS?

It is no coincidence that this book is titled *Strange California*. The editor's earlier plans to name it "Strange New Jersey," "Strange Minneapolis," or "Strange Duluth" all fell through—not because you wouldn't have picked up the book (who could resist figuring out what "Strange Duluth" might mean?), but because the writers would have been hopelessly at sea trying to fill it.

"Strange" is not the same thing as "weird." Weird implies the uncanny or inexplicable, that the ordinary laws of reality have been temporarily suspended. Nearly every place has weirdness in its folklore: ghost stories, monsters, old murders left unsolved, a history forcibly forgotten. Even profoundly "normal" places become ideal settings for the weird by contrast, as they encourage us to imagine that their normalcy is merely a thin cloak for the horrific.[1] Thus nearly any place could be the subject of a "weird" anthology; in fact, such stories make up entire subgenres, from Southern Gothic (which ranges from the magical realism of Faulkner to the popular vampire novels of Charlaine Harris) to Weird West (with its zombies in Tombstone and its necromancers in Topeka). Were the authors of this anthology challenged to write about "Weird Indianapolis," I have no doubt that they could rise to the occasion.

Weirdness exists and is perceptible because it deforms our familiar reality. Strangeness, on the other hand, suggests a more lasting difference: that reality in the strange place has always been like that, and it is *you* who are out of place. Consider what the Oxford English Dictionary says about it:

---

1 *The Twilight Zone*, Lovecraftian fiction, and the Cold War spy novel are all based on this idea. For how these relate to one another, see Charles Stross' essay "Inside the Fear Factory," in *The Atrocity Archives* (Ace Books, 2006).

Strange. *adj.* … [L. *extrāneus* external, foreign, f. *extrā* adv. outside, without]

1. a. *Of persons, language, customs, etc.:* Of or belonging to another country; foreign, alien…

10. a. Unfamiliar, abnormal, or exceptional to a degree that excites wonder or astonishment; difficult to take in or account for; queer, surprising, unaccountable.

That is, the strange is perpetually foreign: its persons and customs seem entirely normal to its natives, but mysterious and astonishing to us. To experience strangeness is to experience being a visitor to a foreign world, to be Alice beyond the looking-glass. To experience any single strangeness, from aliens living openly among us to rising fascism, for any length of time is for it to become one's new normal: as with any foreign place, we ultimately adapt.

But all this tells us is that any place is strange when you first come to it.[2] What it does not explain is how even to lifelong Californians, the title *Strange California* continues to seem perfectly reasonable, while "Strange Minneapolis" does not. How can foreignness be a property of one's native land?

It is tempting to approach this through L. P. Hartley's aphorism that "the past is a foreign country." It is true that profound change can create profound alienation, especially if one returns after a long absence, and there is no doubt that California has changed profoundly and repeatedly: forty years ago, the dense part of Silicon Valley I live in was mostly farmland. But such change typifies America as a whole; if anything, the country is known for having the cultural memory of a goldfish. "Americans think a hundred years is a long time," the saying goes, "Britons think a hundred miles is a long way." A country which could go from the Civil Rights movement to the election of Barack Obama in the span of forty years — no matter how racist it may still be — moves incomprehensibly fast by the standards of most of the world, where thousand-year-

---

2 For a masterful illustration of how the experience of travel or immigration can create the sense of strangeness, see Shaun Tan's wordless graphic novel *The Arrival* (Arthur A. Levine Books, 2007).

old grievances are routinely settled with rocket-propelled grenades. If California is truly stranger than Minnesota, there must be something further at work.

A second potential source of foreignness is the coexistence of radically different people and customs, which is certainly something California has; it has large populations from virtually every country in the Americas and Asia. But it is hardly unique to the state; the comingling of populations is almost the defining characteristic of urbanism, and can be found anywhere from New York to ancient Babylon.[3]

Foreignness created by the proximity of different immigrant groups also tends to be extremely overt, a type of strangeness one can immediately identify. But as our difficulty describing it illustrates, whatever the characteristic Californian strangeness is, it is somewhat more subtle. To give a first illustration of what California Strange *is* (rather than is not): if you were to tell me, as a long-time resident, that down the block secretly lived the high priest of an ancient Andean sect that made regular sacrifices to a jaguar-headed god, transforming himself into a half-bird, half-man with the aid of psychotropic drugs, I would probably reply "Huh; I didn't know Bob did that." The archetypal Bob of this story would neither live under a secret trap-door in someone's house (as he would in a tale of the Weird) nor routinely walk around Silicon Valley wearing the traditional shimmering gold leaf garments and nose ornaments of second-century Peru; he would be a project manager or realtor, and if he had never mentioned the high priesthood it would simply be because it had never come up.[4] When strange things in California are actually secret, it's for a specific

---

3 And in each case, as the object of the same furor from outsiders that this mixing of cultures will lead to the corruption of youth. Babylon had its rants from Isaiah and John of Patmos; New York has Ted Cruz decrying its values as antithetical to those of "real America." There is truly nothing new under the Sun. Those interested in the history of this idea in the United States will find an interesting discussion of its rise in the wake of 19th-century urbanization in Helen Lefkowitz Horowitz's *Rereading Sex* (Vintage Press, 2003).

4 To clarify, the Bob in this example is purely hypothetical. The only Bob I know in Silicon Valley is a system administrator and Mormon priest who until recently co-owned a BDSM café. Whether you find this more or less unusual than a realtor-slash-Andean-priest is a matter of taste.

reason, like when the studio executive you are talking to at a party has recently been invited to join a necromantic cult which has access to *really good cocaine*.

This brings us to one of the natural founts of Californian strangeness, namely Hollywood. Hollywood is, after all, an institution professionally dedicated to the manufacture of dreams and unreality, so it is no surprise that many stories of strangeness and alienation take place there. What's perhaps more interesting is that this strangeness is by no means limited to the Los Angeles area. To understand how this works, we should consider the ways in which various Californian cultures match and differ. As an example, let's compare Santa Monica and Silicon Valley.[5]

In the heart of Los Angeles County, Santa Monica is a place obsessed with beauty and health. Everybody you encounter seems to have a fitness program, a personal trainer, a favorite provider of kale and wheatgrass, a bewildering array of cosmeticians and plastic surgeons, and a colon hydrotherapist. And everyone looks *amazing*.[6] More importantly, people define their social identity in these terms; the set of parties you go to and the people you meet depends very sharply on your appearance. The right face can lead to you being "discovered." A dog-walker or cosmetologist shared with the right celebrity might prove a critical social *entrée*.

When you come to Silicon Valley, the contrast is startling: one of the first things you notice is that engineers' reputation for not paying attention to their appearance has a real basis in fact. But the truth is more subtle: Silicon Valleyans tend to each have a handful of obsessions, putting tremendous energy

5 I'm about to make a series of gross oversimplifications, because a full discussion of this topic would be a book in its own right. In particular, I will speak about the stereotypes which are recognized as true by their respective locals. This doesn't mean that these are universals; for example, there are profound nuances to the meaning of dress in Silicon Valley, especially as it interrelates with race, class, and gender. The choice to dress in "schlubby engineer," in a lightweight sundress, or in a sharp business suit conveys tremendous social meaning. But importantly, this meaning is perceived in relation to socially-defined norms: that is, to the types of self-presentation which are culturally invisible because they are local defaults. It is the contrast of local defaults that I address here.

6 This brings up the question of how anyone there has time to get any actual work done. Long-time Angelenos inform me that most people simply don't.

into them and being only vaguely aware of anything else. Nearly everyone you meet will, upon slight inquiry, reveal their profound fascination with microchip design, or modern dance, or medieval swordfighting. It's not that people in Silicon Valley don't exercise; it's that the ones who do instrument their bodies several dozen ways, design new diets which give them *exactly* optimal nutrition, and set up year-long walking competitions with minute-by-minute, automatically generated leaderboards. It's not that everybody dresses poorly; it's that people can either tell you details about every item that they're wearing, or are only vaguely aware that they're not naked.

This contrast between places is part of a broader Californian pattern. Each region or group tends to define itself by profound fascination (bordering on obsession) with some things, and profound inattention to others. In the East Bay, the focus is political ideology; further east, it's plant breeding and crop yields. (And further into the countryside, there are rumors that they define themselves by darker ideologies—an illustration of how California can easily be strange to itself) What we see here is not the simple overlap of cultures formed by immigration, but an overlap of cultures which anyone can join by adopting their unspoken customs. And each of these unspoken customs is, in its social practice, an almost overpowering obsession, where the question of *just how far* people might go in its pursuit is a real one.

And yet, California is not a perpetual madhouse; in fact, it seems very ordinary most of the time. People go about their days, raising families and working at jobs, buying groceries and worrying about the rent. It is this contrast between a familiar exterior and startling depths of collective passion which, I think, starts to explain California's perpetual strangeness.

If all of this is true, why California? Why isn't Oregon like this, or Ohio? To put it another way: why is Hollywood in California at all? Why did the nascent film industry set up shop, not near the existing theater industry of the East Coast, or the New Jersey manufacturers of lenses and cameras, but in a place literally as far as you could get from most of the American population without leaving the country? A place not only separated from them by a multi-day train journey, but also shielded from direct approach by the Mojave Desert, a place that has areas unironically named "Death Valley?"[7]

The answer is that this separation came with many advantages. Proximity to the East Coast meant proximity to Thomas Edison and his perpetual patent lawsuits against film producers. It meant proximity to a system of legal, extra-legal, and sometimes violent anti-Semitism which peaked just as millions of Jews first arrived in the U.S. from Europe; this was a large population already prepared to move in search of opportunity.[8] It also meant proximity to the "moral guardians" of the day, such as Anthony Comstock's crusade to stamp out "obscene, lewd, or lascivious" material, a category which for him almost definitionally included film. Comstock died in 1915, only months after the Supreme Court ruled that motion pictures were not protected under the First Amendment,[9] and yet the next few decades were the first golden age of both "classical" filmmaking and porn, all produced by the studios of the San Fernando Valley. Hollywood as we know it simply could not have existed in close proximity to the powerful establishments of the East Coast.

This combination of distance from existing societies and the quest for (often commercial) dreams is far from isolated in California's history; it could even to be said to be the modern state's defining story. This pattern began with the discovery of gold at Sutter's Mill in 1849,[10] as hundreds of thousands of

7 It may not be the Taklamakan — that fierce desert of northwestern China whose name roughly means "Abandoned area, keep out, you idiot" — but it's certainly an effective way of keeping your eastern relatives from dropping by for dinner unexpectedly.

8 The first Hollywood studio was established in 1911; the Anti-Defamation League was founded in 1913, in response to the lynching of Leo Frank. For a review of the position of Jews in American culture at this time, see J. R. Gritz's article "The Jews in America" (*The Atlantic*, Sep. 2007) and the historical articles cited within, all available online.

9 *Mutual Film Corp. v. Industrial Commission of Ohio*, 236 U.S. 230 (1915), overturned in 1952.

10 California's history has two major breakpoints in it, ones big enough that the cultures before and the cultures after are nearly unrelated: the arrival of the Spanish in the 1530's and the 1849 Gold Rush. Prior to the Spanish, the region was widely inhabited by hunter-gatherers. Neither agriculture nor concentrated centers of population ever emerged, and the highest estimates of

people rushed across the country to make their fortunes. By and large, these people had no idea what to expect or what they were doing as miners; they had been lured by one of history's great get-rich-quick dreams, and found a life which generally proved the exact opposite of the riches of Croesus that they had dreamt of. The great fortunes of the day were primarily made by the people who sold them pick-axes and provisions at ruinous markups.

This period also drew the first great wave of Chinese immigration. A combination of wars in China (the two Opium Wars, the Taiping Rebellion, and the several smaller rebellions which followed) and the promise of first gold, and then work, in the Americas brought over 300,000 immigrants to California by 1880, a tenth of the state's population. Of all the groups to reach the state, the Chinese were by far the most isolated from the rest of its culture, barred by law from living near, working with, or having nearly any other kind of relationship with the white population. Despite (or perhaps because of) this, a vibrant community formed, densely packed with its own ideas—ones frequently profoundly foreign to the adjacent non-Chinese communities. California thus had a widespread pattern of "foreigners next door," nearby communities entirely separated by language and custom; early waves of Mexican immigration, starting in 1910, would follow a similar pattern.

In the early Twentieth Century, it would be the explosion of Los Angeles that attracted dreamers. The county grew from 100,000 people to 2.2 million between 1890 and 1930. This tremendous growth (more than tripling between 1900 and 1910 alone!) was powered in no small part by a major advertising campaign by local landowners, offering a clean and healthful place with unlimited business opportunities. If remoteness made Hollywood possible, it was

---

California's population density in this period are just under two people per square mile. This population plummeted by 90% during the post-contact pandemics and never fully recovered. Spanish settlement was even more sparse, peaking at roughly 8,000 non-Native people by 1846. Just as Spain saw Mexico as a remote colony to be exploited, and Mexico considered *El Norte* (roughly the part that is today in the U.S.) to be its own back of beyond, Norteños saw Alta California to be the edge of *their* world, a remote backwater compared to "bustling" Tejas, home of two! entire! towns! (San Antonio and La Bahia) If there was a bright center to the Spanish-speaking universe, California was as far away from it as you could get.

the steady flow of immigration which kept it running; even today, buses arrive continually at stations from Downtown to the Valley, bringing Los Angeles its daily supply of hopeful actors, directors, and screenwriters, and carting away the empties, drained of their idealism and enthusiasm, but perhaps somewhat wiser for the experience.[11]

These migrations were simply a few of many. The 1930's brought over a million refugees from an ecological collapse in Oklahoma; they came in pick-up trucks and hitchhiking on trains, drawn by handbills promising a rich and fruitful land where high wages were available for farm workers. Their dream was a simple one—a reliable source of food and work—but no less able to define a culture, this time of the Central Valley. The more recent rush into the Bay Area is cut from the same mold; what is Silicon Valley if not a destination for millions of people dreaming of changing the world, of reshaping its basic social and political structures through technology, or of getting rich in the process? The international origins of the Silicon Valley migration particularly highlight how arriving groups can be unified far more by the shared visions which brought them than by any prior cultural or linguistic heritage.[12]

---

11 Idealism is extracted from would-be actors and writers in Los Angeles in a continuous process by solution at 72°F in a mixture of 10% cynicism and 5% economic desperation, with the balance made up of a varying combination of ethanol, narcotics, and kale. It is precipitated from the mixture by the addition of money, which remains in compound with it. The crude product is either sold directly on the local market (typically powdered and snorted, as an anodyne and mild hallucinogen) or further refined using the same process, each stage using higher concentrations of cynicism, alcohol, and cocaine to first decompound the money from the idealism. The final product, with the money still in compound but all traces of reality removed, is then used (at roughly one part per billion) as a flavoring agent in a range of mass-market entertainment, beauty, and consumer products. Addicts who come looking for the source are, of course, promptly recycled into raw material.

12 One might at first imagine the Native population as a contrast to this, stable and unchanging through the centuries. At its limit, this idea becomes the stereotypical "wise old Indian," a ready source of aphorisms for use in inspirational quotes and New Age* self-help manuals. But the reality is quite different. Significant disruption of a social network, such as by mass death, mass deportation, or a deliberate policy of extinguishing languages and cultures (each of which is a part of California's history), invariably takes with it a tremendous amount of memory, especially in oral cultures where history is created and preserved through prolonged person-to-person

The history of California after 1849 is thus the story of one migrant group after another, each animated by the belief that *this* was the one place they could achieve their dreams. (And not infrequently, lured to believe this by elaborate advertising campaigns.) In each case, California's distance from the origins of these migrations made it an easy place onto which people could project their dreams of a better life. When such dreams reached a population already predisposed to pull up stakes, they took on a spectacular life of their own, bringing not individual immigrants but large waves of them, all animated by a shared vision. Even as these groups ultimately assimilated into California at the superficial level, the distance from old, established societies with strong norms meant they experienced little pressure to abandon these characteristic perspectives. Instead, California ended up with a rich stratigraphy of different populations, each with a particular dream and powerfully held ideas about how it might be achieved. These groups each maintained their own cohesion, but gradually intermixed at the contact points, forming a bewildering array of new groups and ideas— from the Church of the Foursquare Gospel (the original megachurch, founded in Los Angeles in 1923) to Heaven's Gate (the suicidal UFO cult, founded in San Diego in 1974).[13]

transmission. It draws a line between those who came before and those who came after, separating them into profoundly different cultures even as it joins them to a single defining memory. Rather than being a perpetually stable bulwark, California's Native population is as intricately culturally layered as any of its immigrant waves ever were.

* Experienced Californians know that this is properly spelled "newage," and pronounced to rhyme with "sewage."

13 You might compare this to a biological system. Imagine California as a chimeric organism with a rich internal structure. Periodically, it sends clouds of parasitic cognitive spores adrift in search of suitable hosts. When these spores encounter a concentrated, susceptible population, they take root and fruit *en masse*, reproducing rapidly in their new hosts' brains, creating a bloom of nascent ideas and sending their carriers stampeding back to the parent organism. There, they are promptly consumed, yielding both their delicious energy content and adding their cognitive and genetic material to the parent organism. As they move within the parent, reproducing internally and mixing with prior host populations, the now-absorbed hosts form new outgrowths of the principal organism, and provide the basis for its next generation of spores.

If this description of California as a cross between a mind-controlling fungus and Yog-Sothoth seems reasonable to you, that may be a sign that you're ready to move here. Come! The weather

The outcome of this process is a society which is tremendously mixed in invisible ways: a place where everyone goes to the same grocery store, but a chance inquiry might reveal that your neighbor is a miniature train fanatic, or an Andean priest, or an ancient god washed up from the oceanic deeps and waiting tables while preparing for either a triumphant return to Olympus or a speaking role in a film, whichever comes first. A place where the polite way to behave is to treat that god just like anybody else; after all, you yourself might be a roboticist, a member of an ancient secret society, or both. Who's to say you aren't as fictional as they are?

It is, in short, a place where unexpected difference is the rule rather than the exception. It *is* strange. But it can also be home.

---

is excellent, and the food is delicious.

THE GREAT TARANTULA MIGRATION OF 1972

SEANAN MCGUIRE

SEANAN MCGUIRE

Seanan McGuire lives and writes in the Pacific Northwest, where she shares her home with several large, fluffy cats and a disturbing number of books. The author of multiple ongoing urban fantasy series, she has appeared on the New York Times best-seller list as both herself and under the pseudonym "Mira Grant." In 2017, she won the Alex, Nebula, and Locus Awards. When not writing, she can be found at conventions around the world, or lurking in the nearest haunted cornfield. She doesn't really sleep.

LIVE IN THE DESERT LONG ENOUGH, THE DESERT LEARNS TO LIVE IN YOU. IT PUTS down roots, draws bluffs across your heart, and sows sticker bushes in your soul. And that's all right, kid, that's all right, because there's worse things to be than a desert daughter, a sandstone son, a canyon child. There's worse things by far.

People think of California, they think of beaches and bright lights and Hollywood. They think of towering redwoods and sea otters frolicking in the surf off Monterey. They forget that when you slice a state too large for a single serving, you don't get that kind of sweet nothing, that sort of sweetness without substance. When the people who chopped up this continent pointed to a piece and called it California, they cut too large. They got more than just the pretty flower at the top of the tree. They got the branches and the roots and the rotten wood and all. They got something *real*.

Wander California long enough and you'll find about every kind of land there is, from wetland to desert. We have rainforest. We have sub-arctic tundra. We have it all, and we've filled every inch of it with strangeness and with stories, with the sort of shadows that only appear when the sun is low and the fire is high and the shadows paint their own legends on the walls. California is a legend in the process of being written, and she doesn't forgive easy, and she doesn't suffer fools.

Where we're going is higher than the middle but lower than the top, in a desert region too far from the ocean to be considered coastal, and too close to the shore to be considered inland. It's all oak trees and grasslands, desert and scrubby mountainside. The rattlesnakes keep their court in the tall grass; the deer graze on the mustard flowers and clover. Night belongs to the cougar, to the possum, to the raccoon. People build their homes there, same as they build them most of everywhere in California, but there's always a sense that they're transitory things, sketched out on the landscape rather than nailed down into its bones. That, too, is only natural. The ground here wakes and rises from time to time, shaking off everything that troubles it, reminding the fast, hot specks of life that race across its surface that it is in charge here; it controls whether they live or die, and as long as they're respectful, as long as they tread lightly, it'll come down a little more often on the side of living.

Only a little, though. Earthquake country has a reputation to maintain.

And so we move into the shadow of the mountain everyone here calls Mt. Diablo, and we listen to the whispers from the locals. We hear the stories they never tell their children, the ones that their children always seem to know anyway, pulling them out of the air when the time comes for campfires and supposedly safe terrors under the sweet summer moon. We listen to them speak of phantom hitchhikers trying to escape the mountain's shadow before the sun goes down and the Devil comes to take his due. We listen to them talk about frogs big enough to swallow cats, about rattlesnakes hidden in mattresses, and maybe some of us laugh, thinking we've found credulous children. Maybe some of us write them all off as liars and humbugs, the sort of folk who think that anyone unfamiliar is a rube, ready to be misled.

Someone mentions the tarantula migration. The laughter stops. The anger follows. Spiders don't migrate; don't be ridiculous. Don't be foolish. Don't tell lies.

Don't scare me like that.

Come on. It's time to show you what the truth looks like in California, under a bleached-paper sky that stretches from here unto forever, where the only person lying is the one who says they know what the truth is shaped like.

JULY, 1972: CONCORD, CALIFORNIA. Not the biggest town going, and not the smallest city, but something right in that gap, wedged into the liminal space where growth is possible, and so is stagnation. This is the space where cities die.

The streets are still fresh black tar, by and large, stretched smooth from here to the horizon, slowly curing under the unrelenting sun. Fog clouds them like sheets of cotton in the morning, boiling up until every scrap of moisture has been baked away, leaving them clean and ready for another day. Eucalyptus lines the streets, an opportunistic invader from a sister on the other side of the world, Australia, which burns and drowns by turns, just like California, just like home.

Spiders in the eaves and snakes in the tall grass and it's a miracle anyone grows up here: they should all be dead before they can decide that growing up is a good idea. Black bears in the woods and cougars on the mountains, and still the children run, laughing, into the golden dry-grass meadows, which beckon them as such things have always beckoned to the young.

The people who live here are clever and hard-working, foolish and indolent, just like people everywhere in the world. They want their city to get bigger. They want their town to stay precisely the same. They do not see the contradiction in these two desires. They have children with desires and ideas of their own. Here come two of them now.

Mike is the sort of boy parents hope their daughters will bring home: endlessly polite, scholarly to the point of distraction, with thick glasses and the occasionally scatterbrained aura of someone who has yet to figure out what he wants to do with his overlarge hands, or what he wants to be when he grows up. He is a good boy, in other words, the sort of boy who will never push the issue behind a closed bedroom door, who will not make a grandmother of a woman barely entering middle age.

Angela is the sort of girl parents shake their heads at when they think she isn't looking: scruffy, dressed in thrift store clothing that she had been on the verge of outgrowing even before they had the price tags off. She walks like she expects to be kicked, to have all good things dangled in front of her and ripped away before she can bite into them, a feral dog of a teenager, a coyote in scuffed shoes and a hand-me-down bra. She is a good girl, but no one seems to see that, save for Mike, who walks through a world kinder than her own—kinder, and infinitely more forgiving.

They are Concord children, the high and the low, the sacred and the profane. The first time Angela went to Mike's house, where his mother set a platter of strip steak on the table without admonishing them to eat lightly, what was in front of them had to be a week of lunches and more than a few dinners, she nearly wept from the crushing realization that what she'd always thought of as "normal" was anything but. The first time Mike went to Angela's apartment, down near the train tracks, he looked with wide eyes at the bugs on the walls and the water stains on the ceiling, at the low, dark rooms that seemed to pull everything into them, never letting go, and he nearly ran. His life was an aspiration for her; her life was a punishment for him.

But they get by, they get by. They met in middle school, before height and hormones complicated everything, and they've been best friends ever since, two slowly orbiting moons all too aware that the planet whose gravitational pull holds them in place—a planet called parents, called high school, called Concord, California, home of the Warriors, the Mustangs, the Red Devils—is destined to let them go all too soon.

Let one of them go, anyway. Angela is never getting out of here. She knows that, and Mike knows that, and so they never talk about it. It might have been easier if they'd done what her mother hoped for, what his mother feared: if they'd fallen in love, middle school friends turned high school sweethearts turned young adult spouses, Angela's belly getting hard and round as a late summer apple, Mike tied to her by fatherhood and undeveloped lust. He could have pulled her with him when he ran. But they're friends, not lovers, and friends don't save each other that way. For some reason, friends don't throw that rope.

See them walking down the sun-dappled main street, through the patchwork of sun and shadow created by the eucalyptus trees. The day is hot. The summer sun doesn't mess around in this part of California: it's up and shining when most of the golden coast is still tucked comfortably away in bed, reminding the people who live here that they've chosen the desert for their home. They can talk about oceans some of them will never see, about rolling hills and foggy valleys, but they live in the desert.

School's been out for the better part of a month, and Mike's mother doesn't like it when he brings Angela home more than twice a week—when he does that, she can't help looking past his friendship with the girl from the wrong side of the town's phantom tracks and seeing that full-bellied future that both of them swear will never happen. She's smart enough not to forbid him to see Angela, to know that forbidden fruit is the sweetest of all, that it will spark hungers that would otherwise never have existed, but still, she's nervous, and still, she sets limits. She *needs* limits, to keep her steady on the precipice of her son's adulthood.

As for going to Angela's place…that's never a consideration. Her apartment is small, and her mother is desperate, and their landlord is already making noises about property damage and complaints from the neighbors. They'll probably move again before the end of the summer, going from a small place to a smaller one, an endless succession of hovels where the air always smells like smoke and stale laundry and boiled potatoes. Mike has been a good friend to her. They both know their friendship could never survive too much exposure to the way she really lives.

So they walk. Outside, baked by the sun, feeling the moisture sucked from their skins by the air around them, feeling the heat settle into their bones. They were born to this desert: they do not yet feel the discomfort the way adults might, people who traveled here from some far-distant "away" in search of California gold, and found only the simple reliability of stone.

A shopkeeper, broom in hand, pauses in the act of sweeping his stoop to wave to the teens. "Morning," he calls.

They wave back, calling their own mild, mingled greetings. They are good kids, both of them, inclined to seek praise and approval from the adults around them. It is a trait that will serve one of them well and one of them ill, once their own adulthood comes.

"Where are you heading?" asks the shopkeeper. If his eyes are sharp, if his hands are shaking as they hold the broom, it's not enough to notice.

"Just going for a walk, sir," says Mike. They've found that men listen better to him. So do women. So does the world. It would bother him, if he thought about it, and so he never thinks about it.

It bothers Angela. She can't *stop* thinking about it. The world does what the world wants.

"Up near the mountain?"

Mike and Angela exchange a glance. They'd never discussed anything that far ahead. The base of the mountain is at least a mile away, and there are several places between here and there to stop for a drink, or to sit in the shade and talk. In the normal course of wandering around town, they might have made it as far as the mountain…but probably not. They don't, usually.

Angela realizes with a start that she can't remember the last time they did.

"Yeah," she says, and her voice is a glass of cold water cast in the face of the conversation: it stops everything where it stands. Mike, who isn't used to her having opinions, even turns to stare at her.

Angela smiles. She's made a choice. That's not a thing that happens often, for her. She'll stand by it.

"We're going to the mountain," she says.

"Beautiful day for it," says the shopkeeper. "You two be careful out there. It's going to be a hot one. The tarantulas will be on the move."

Then he laughs, like this is the funniest thing anyone's ever said, and they laugh, because when adults are laughing, it's best to play along.

He stands and watches as the teens walk away, down the smooth white sidewalk, toward the distant shadow of the mountains. His hands are still upon the broom, and his laughter is gone, one more thing for the sun to swallow.

He could still call them back. He could pull them inside, offer them an ice cream soda—and they're young enough, unformed enough, to accept his generosity without question. Even the girl, who's already developing an edge like biting down on tin foil, would go along with it. She's too hungry to be wary. She'd be a coyote like her mother, that one, if she had the chance.

He doesn't call them back. He watches them go, and he says nothing, and when they're gone—when his duty is done—he turns his face away and goes back to sweeping.

His debts are paid.

So they walk, the children of the town in the shadow of the mountain. The day is hot and the way is hard, but their legs are young and strong, and they still have a thousand inconsequential things to talk about, beating them out in the space they make between them, finding all the places to crack and pry and get at the meat of the thing.

They don't talk about the future.

They don't talk about how he's going to get out and she's not.

They don't talk about how she's smarter than he is, how she could have gone just as far and done just as much if the world didn't insist that where a person came from was just as important—maybe more important—than where they wanted to go.

They don't talk about how he's going to leave her.

Instead, they talk about books and movies and their classmates, who are off having their own adventures, off living their own lives, unaware that they're the topic of discussion for two of their resident outcasts. The time passes quickly, seconds transforming into footsteps, and here they are, two teenagers standing in front of the crude wooden gate that delineates the edge of the parkland around the mountain's base.

Someone has scratched the crude silhouette of a spider into the wood. Angela rubs her thumb against it, and squeaks as a splinter stabs deep into her skin. She sticks her thumb in her mouth, sucking like a baby, while Mike looks on in bewilderment.

"What happened?" he asks.

"It bit me!" She pulls her thumb out of her mouth and holds it out for him to see. A bright bead of blood has formed at the center of the whorled maze of her thumbprint. It is oddly intimate, the way it hangs there, shining. Mike turns his face away, cheeks blazing red.

"Don't touch spiders," he says.

"Better watch it, or the spiders will touch *you*," she retorts, and swings the gate open.

The base of the mountain is a low forest of scrub, thorn bushes and blackberry tangles making progress treacherous, even as the sunbaked, broken ground slows them down. They pick through it, not quite sure why they're here, only knowing—with the stubborn single-mindedness of people who have decided on a course of action without thinking it entirely through—that they aren't ready to turn back.

Something moves in the gravel. Angela sees it first. She stops, eyes scanning the ground, before crouching down and pointing.

"Look," she says.

Mike looks. The tarantula, no bigger than a fifty cent piece, raises its front legs off the ground and waves them menacingly. Disgust washes over him. Before he can consider what he's doing, he stomps on the spider, grinding it to paste beneath his shoe. Angela cries out, surprise and dismay in her voice, and he keeps grinding, grinding, until there's nothing left. Until there's no chance the spider could survive.

"Why did you *do* that?" Angela demands. "It wasn't hurting you!"

"I hate spiders," Mike says. He feels suddenly silly, like coming here was a mistake—like this whole day was a mistake. He could be home, with a book and a snack and the pool in his backyard, cool and deep and calling to him. He doesn't have those things, and why not? Because Angela wanted to hang out, and his mother doesn't like her.

Maybe his mother is onto something. Maybe he doesn't like her either.

"But we came to the spider's house," says Angela. "It wasn't hurting you."

God, she's so stupid, and she's so annoying, and how could he ever think she was a friend? It's like he smashed their relationship when he smashed the spider, and now he can see her clearly for the first time in years.

She's still yelling at him. He's not listening anymore.

Angela is taller than he is, but he has stronger arms, and he has the element of surprise on his side. When he grabs a rock off the ground and slams it into the side of her head, she doesn't scream or try to dodge. She just falls, silent as a stone, and sprawls among the spiders and the thorns.

Mike turns and runs, back to the sidewalk, back to the street, and it's not until he gets home that he realizes the rock is still clutched tightly in his hand, so tightly that it's broken through the skin in several places, leaving him scraped and bloody.

He puts the rock in the decorative border around his mother's flowers. He rinses the blood off his hand. He tries not to think about Angela, sprawled in the dust. She isn't dead. She can't be dead. She might be mad, but she can't be dead. He still can't find their friendship. No matter how deep he digs, he can't find it. He can't even find regret over what he did. All he finds is a sliver of fear. If she's dead, if he hit her so hard that she's dead, is he going to get in trouble?

His mother notices that he's quiet during dinner. She chalks it up to sunstroke—his skin is so red it seems to sizzle when he moves. That girl's fault, no doubt. It's a miracle the little bitch didn't follow him home again, the way she does three or four times a week, like it's somehow Mike's responsibility to make sure she's properly fed.

Maybe he's finally getting tired of her. That would be a blessing.

He sits on the couch after the table is cleared, reading his book while the news plays on the television, and it's almost a relief when he goes to bed early. His father follows shortly after, silent as ever, a hulking shape in the hall. His mother rises, after a while, and walks to the window. She's reaching for the curtain when something moves on the lawn, some small ripple of shadow and light. She freezes, trying to see the source of the motion.

It doesn't come again. Eventually, she shakes off the nervousness that sits on her skin like soap scum, closes the curtains, and slides between the sheets, pressing herself close to the hot warmth of her husband's back. She closes her eyes.

The night is silent.

The moon is high.

The desert air is dry as dust and twice as unforgiving. It can pull the moisture from a body in a matter of hours, making mummies out of corpses, refusing to let decay find a foothold.

Angela's body lurches, and for a moment, it seems like she's going to sit up: like she's been sprawled in the hot, dry air for hours because she wanted to be, and not because Mike's blow split her skull and left her to bleed out in the thorn briars. Then it lurches again, and nothing living moves like that, like it consists of a hundred individual pieces, motile and independent.

Her body lurches a third time. The tarantulas scatter, and it seems that the girl's body must have been nothing more than a trick of the light, something that was nothing there at all, because they leave only stone and sand behind. There is no skeleton. There is no evidence.

The tarantulas move toward the gate. As they travel, more come, and more, and more, until they are a swarm of hundreds, of thousands, pouring toward the streets of Concord, California with a single, unthinking purpose. The migration has begun.

All around the town, shopkeepers whose parents were born within the city limits lock their doors and draw their blinds. For some of them, it should be hours yet to closing. That doesn't stop them. Bars and restaurants allow their patrons to remain inside, but no one goes out, and no one comes in. Everyone knows why and no one says it; no one needs to. The lines are drawn.

In the residential streets, the people whose families have lived here for generations, when the town was called "Todo Santos" and "Canterbury" and "the place we do not go," turn off their porch lights and close their windows and hold their children tight, praying that this night will pass them by.

And in a small shop on the main street, a man puts down his broom and puts his hands over his eyes, opening his heart to regret. He did only what was required of him, as his father had done, as his father's father had done before him. He has upheld their side of a compact which allows a town to survive, if not to thrive, in the harsh, hot California wastes, in a place that many people will deny even exists, for how can there be such privation in the heart of plenty? California is green valleys and warm beaches, not stony deserts and the slow, creeping march of the inevitable. California is a dream.

This is a reality.

The tarantulas swarm through the streets on uncounted legs, tasting the air with their strange mouths and seeing the world through their strange eyes. If they are aware that some part of their body was once a girl named Angela, a girl who knew she was going to die in this town, they have no way of showing it. They simply walk, on and on, heading for what the mountain has been promised.

Always there are two. The sacrifice and the one who holds the stone. The one who dies to open the door, and the one who runs. Neither of them is willing, or unwilling, or even aware: awareness would spoil the flavor of what's to come, what must be done.

Sometimes it is the girl who scoops up the stone, strikes her companion across the temple or in the hollow of his throat, consumed by a loathing she cannot name. Other times it is the boy, as it was *this* boy, on this night. The mountain gives all their darkest thoughts the space to breathe, and they breathe for the stone, for the bones of the earth, for the city. They breathe, and they strike, and the migration begins.

They walk down the street, the tarantulas, creeping along by the hundreds, and no one sees them coming, and none will see them go.

They turn down a narrow court, past darkened houses, to one house where the light is still burning. The windows are closed. The doors are closed. But there is always a way in, for a spider. If you are clever, and small, and determined, there is always a way.

Mike wakes when the first spider drops from the ceiling and lands on his cheek.

His screams begin soon after.

His parents—who are already dead, who were a delicious perk of this night's work—never come to save him, and in time the screams stop, and the spiders spin their webs through his bones.

The next morning, the city of Concord wakes to find itself beset with tarantulas. They walk on lawns and stick to walls, fat as kittens, slow as turtles. They're harmless. They always have been, this side of the bargain. Children carry them in cupped hands, laughing, while on a narrow cul-de-sac, a realtor hammers a "For Sale" sign into Mike's mother's lawn. No one asks them where the residents went, or how they knew to put the house onto the market.

There are things we do not ask here, in the shadow of the mountain, where the desert takes its due.

California is a nation of its own, too big and too varied to be anything less, no matter how hard it tries to hide behind the banner of statehood. There's much to see, and much to be seen, and if the spiders walk in the streets of a city called Concord every three years, if teens go missing in their wake, if a few coyote girls and golden boys never make it out…

No one ever promised a happy ending. We only promised you the bones of the desert and the hand of the mountain, and that's exactly what we've given you.

Be glad you weren't chosen to swing the stone.

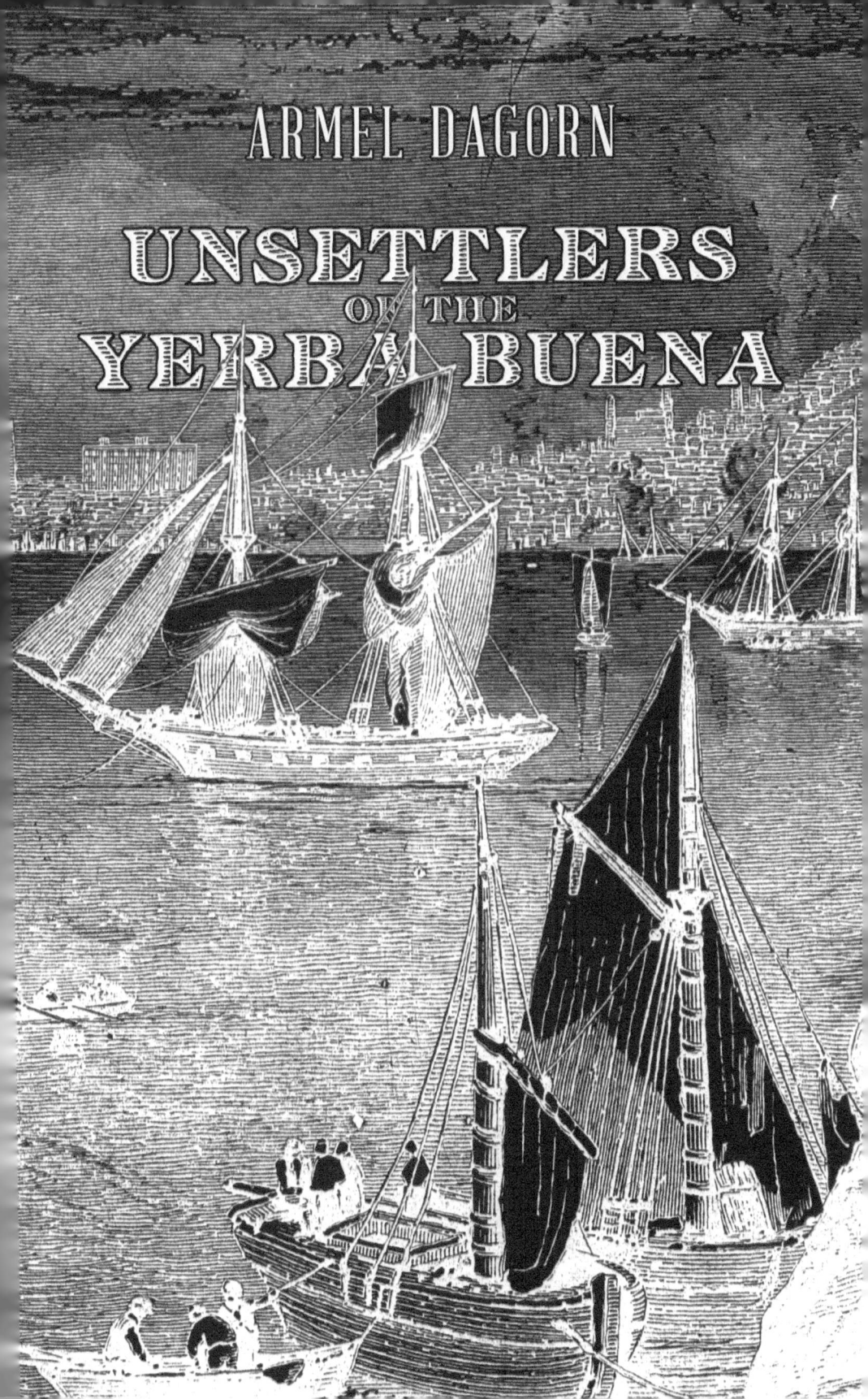

ARMEL DAGORN

UNSETTLERS
OF THE
YERBA BUENA

ARMEL DAGORN

Armel Dagorn lives in Nantes, France, with his partner and very young son, and teaches English for a living. His writing has appeared in magazines such as *Apex Magazine, Liminal Stories* and *Tin House* online, as well as in the anthology *Haunted Futures*. His short story collection *Eternal Dreamers of Greener Grass* will be out in 2018.

A START OF SORTS, WHICH ALSO HAPPENS TO BE THE END

AS PANDO LOOKS DOWN AT THE BAY STRETCHING BEYOND YERBA BUENA, it's difficult for him not to see the numerous times he's seen that landscape in his deathtime (or lifetime, for that matter) superimposed like many veils. The Yerba Buena of his arrival to this New World—its tents and ramshackle houses, huts of cheap, roughly-sawed boards, and the masts tight in the background, a forest springing at the tide-line—and the later Frisco, the tall glass buildings the Financial District has risen into.

Ghosthood rids relationships of the tyranny of time. Our Pando, our Keskidiz, well, they went years sometimes, living-above years, without seeing each other. Ghost time is to living-above time like bobcats are to food stamps. Or something. Things happen faster, or slower, or don't happen, or only like an aftertaste. Sometimes everything's there, in wavering layers. An existential millefeuille. Sometimes: nothing.

THE PANAMÁ CONNECTION

Pando and Frédéric had met on the *Bravoure* as it lay anchored off Panamá City. Ernesto Pando Solares had heard the tales of gold-hopefuls, the indescribable riches to be gotten up north. For a song, a man became a king, they said. Which with his broken English Pando didn't quite understand, but then, weren't foreign lands always ruled by the laws of extraordinary physics? He pictured himself standing ankle-deep in a clear stream, lullabying flecks at first, then nuggets of gold out of the water, shiny twirls rising around him, landing in his pockets, his open palms.

Pando had sailed from Perú on a ship bringing European dreamers via the long but cheap route round Cape Horn, but got left behind in Panamá, where the ship had stopped to stock up, after he roamed off a little too far.

He asked the Captain of the *Bravoure* for passage, giving him a familiar story of gambling in one of the dodgy dens that warrened the wharf, of losing all money and sense of time playing *dudo* with fellow southerners, and spending whatever the dice had left him on booze. Captain D'Astignac found in this tale no sign of a terrible flaw, and he accepted to hire Pando, on condition no wage be paid until they left California again. The Captain, on his first trip to the northern land, had lost nearly all his crew, as they disappeared into the dingy streetlets of the newly-named San Francisco, following over the hills the golden beacon from the tales that spread like tentacles around the world.

Pando hadn't told the Captain the truth, wary it would make him suspicious. What really happened was this: he'd come to land, but instead of following his fellow passengers to the cantinas and bordellos, that straight narrative anyone might have expected him to follow, he'd looked up from the wharf and seen, beyond the stately whitewashed buildings, the wooden shacks, beyond that urban chaos, hills of green.

And Pando, costanero boy, used to the dustland desert of his native Peruvian shore, had been unable to resist. He followed the streets out of town, choosing at each junction the path that promised the easiest escape. He entered the lush forest, got lost in that greenery. When he finally got back down the mountain, it was with a strengthened thirst for the unknown, the taste of a few strange fruits recorded on his tongue, and malaria.

THE *BRAVOURE* LOSES HER WAY

A storm hit the *Bravoure* on her way north. Salty mountains of water rose and rolled her around. Ernesto and Frédéric lay in their nook at starboard, and every so often their bodies slammed into each other. They suffered three days of non-stop battering, a boxing match against some pagan god. Then it stopped without warning. Once they'd shaken their heads a little clearer, checked no bones protruded from their bruised skins, taken out the compass, pointed a sextant at the first stars, they found out they'd wandered too far north.

The masts were still swinging from the tumbles the ship had taken when night fell. With it came a stillness, as if the black sea had been crushed flat by the ghostly chill of the air.

Pando and Frédéric came up on deck and stood looking around with the others, at the flat sea, the bottomless sky. A strange hum filled the air. Frédéric looked up. Were the stars buzzing? His eyes found a big one which seemed to shiver. It got bigger. Frédéric flailed his arm around, trying to locate Pando without looking away. He found his friend's shoulder, but the star grew to crazy proportions and landed with a nasty tok on Frédéric's nose, knocking him down. The guilty hailstone lay melting in a pool of blood.

Pando pressed a rag to his friend's nose and helped him up. The sky beat a mad drumming on the deck, echoed softly all around as icy orbs met the open sea. The crew and passengers retreated into the bowels of the ship, hugging themselves, rubbing warmth into their aching bodies.

"Hé, I sink ze gold need sun for pousser, non?" Frédéric quizzed Pando.

"I don't know," the Peruvian said, not wanting to offend him. He had picked up enough English to get around during his forced stay in Panamá, but his companion hadn't, shacked up in this ship full mostly of Frenchmen. Later, Frédéric would explain to Ernesto the French's theory: gold grew best where there was constant sunshine.

Hail pounded on the world for the whole night, and soon a rota had to be set up to scoop out the hailstones leaking in from the deck's lattice, forming little heaps of ice that glowed cold like the fires of some wintry hell.

And through the freezing night, Pando and Frédéric laid, speechless, side by side, their tremblings eventually becoming synchronized.

FIRST GOODBYE

When the *Bravoure* docked in Yerba Buena, the passengers flooded out onto the wharf. They disappeared in the streets leading up the hills, or in the first watering hole they saw, buried like mules under parcels and rolled-up blankets.

A great number of them were Frédéric's fellow countryfolks—French rabble-raisers the government had thought judicious to send away after the little revolution of "48, masquerading their exile as a generous lottery. They could raise hell, the thinking went, as long as they did it a continent and an ocean away.

Pando had eagerly followed the crowd, taking whatever odd jobs he could find here and there to save up enough to get himself set up inland. Frédéric seemed to be digging in his heels, though. He looked spitefully at the shores of the New World. Pando wasn't sure if he really intended to go back to France, or if he was just rebelling against his government's decision to exile him.

So Frédéric stayed in the *Bravoure*, even when the crew deserted, even when she got stuck behind the fleet of newcomers, then run aground and left to rot in the silt. The space between the ships was filled in, turned into more solid ground, and Captain D'Astignac sold her to a local landlord. Her mast was cut, offices built on deck. Still, Frédéric stayed on.

One would have thought an invisible mooring line tied Pando to his grumpy friend. Pando should have gone, rushed off with the others, but every day he thought up a new excuse not to leave yet, a new item he missed.

But when Frédéric gifted him a pickax, a rough thing whose head he'd fashioned from smelt nails and fixtures scavenged from the ship, Pando had to go. There was simply nothing more he could add to the list and pretend he absolutely needed. So he packed his bundle, tied it up to his pickax, and left the stranded ship.

IN WHICH PANDO MEETS HIS END

Pando followed the tracks of the deserting crew upriver to fence off a claim for himself. He'd had a fight with Frédéric, but he still thought his stubborn friend would change his mind. Was he really going to stay in that damn dug-in boat, in mud-drenched Yerba Buena, after coming halfway around the globe? In the barge bringing him upriver, Pando weighed these thoughts—annoyance at Frédéric's stubborn sedentariness, and qualms at the idea of leaving him behind. When the boat docked in Sacramento, Pando didn't disembark. They'd come so far together, he couldn't just leave his friend behind. Telling himself that he'd make up the boat fare a thousandfold when he finally stabbed his pickax into the golden shores upstream, he traveled back Frisco-ward.

Instead of heading straight back to Frédéric, he climbed the hill to cast his gaze upon that dirty, hastily-built townlet, the hillside scarred with huts and shacks, its alleys slick with the mud that flowed in constant miniature land-slides now that no trees anchored the dirt.

Far down, though, a thick forest stood, the masts of hundreds of abandoned boats, their hulls putrefying in the bay's silt. Pando felt a pang of remorse—poor Frédéric, alone in that damp wooden hell! He started running down the hill, his heavy kit bouncing on his back, jeopardizing his already slight purchase on the ground.

What had to happen, happened. He slipped and somersaulted onto his back. Before he'd recovered, he was twenty feet below, and still sliding. He flailed his legs, trying to kick his heels in. At that speed, the slightest change in direction could send him crashing into a house. He'd get his brains bashed in, his belly staked through on splintered boards. He reached back, trying to get a grip on the pickax tied to his pack. Pando could hear laughter zooming by, people stepping out of his way without lifting a finger. *Caramba, que pueblo cruel!*

He felt the metal head of the pickax. He pulled, but nothing moved. The harbor was getting closer. If he didn't crash into a house, he'd end up in the water. With all his gear, he'd never come out again. He'd just sink like gold dust in some lucky fella's pan.

He looked up behind his shoulder at the pickax in a final attempt to free it. Then came the impact.

When the world stopped spinning, Pando saw, towering over him, an ugly giant, holding his pickax in his hand, looking pissed. He didn't even feel the blow.

Death is like this, isn't it? A senseless thing.

IN WHICH FRÉDÉRIC MEETS HIS END

One of the men who paid a small fortune to lay their blankets on the floor-boards of the run-aground *Bravoure*, between barrels and sacks of flour, came to Frédéric. The Frenchman's English was still a mess of unwieldy fragments, so the man used gestures to tell him his friend had been killed by the mammoth thug who bullied the wharf's denizens into submission.

Frédéric ran out, and quickly found the goon. He was using the pickax as a walking stick. Frédéric recognized the tool he'd made himself, and he saw red, a little stain at the tip. The giant hadn't even bothered to clean the murder weapon properly. Bloody lawless hellhole.

Frédéric pulled out his knife, but the ogre noticed him. He lifted his weight from the pickax and caught the hand thrust his way as if it were no more than a bothersome gnat. He smiled a crooked mouthful of teeth, and pushed back the Frenchman. In a graceful, hulk-defying motion, he swung the pickax upwards then sideways into Frédéric's head. Just like he had only an hour before into Pando's.

Sometimes, death was a little more meaningful. But it still sucked.

STRANGE FEELINGS OF THE NEWLY DEAD

Frédéric stumbled home. Something was missing. *Un certain je-ne-sais-quoi.* The pickax sank deep into his head. The handle bothered him. It bumped dully on his shoulder with every step. He reached up to his temple and gave the pickax a tentative pull, then, when he felt no pain, grabbed it with both hands and dragged it out. Surprisingly, it wasn't covered in blood and brains. It wasn't exactly clean—more like blurry, its contours blunted.

Frédéric dropped the pickax, and walked on towards the *Bravoure*. A thought bubbled up from some ancient place, and he stopped in his tracks. A pickax, these days. Worth a pretty penny. He turned around. Gold-rushing fools swirled around it, but no one gave the pickax a glance.

Frédéric grabbed it, and stood there a moment, confused. Then he waved it around.

"Hé! Regardez-moi! Regardez-moi, bon sang!" No one looked at him.

Then he saw the goon. Ambling down the hill, wiping with his filthy shirt the red-tainted spike of the pickax he'd just stolen.

Frédéric swung the tool hard into his chest. Instead of the expected hit, though, the squish then squirt of blood as metal dove into flesh, all these things Frédéric had just experienced, the pickax went right through, as if the brute were but fog. He sneezed, then walked on. A strange, deep cold run through Frédéric then, a bottomless awe. He dropped the pickax and stepped away, his eyes on the ghost tool. After a few yards, the very substance of the thing dwindled to a vague near-nothing.

MEETING ON THE OTHER SIDE, AND HOW KESKIDIZ GOT HIS NAME

It was luck that first brought Frédéric and Pando together. The only spare space on board the *Bravoure* had been in Frédéric's corner. The Frenchman was already a real grump, an embittered lump of curses, after three weeks at sea and two more anchored off Panamá. With every mile of the journey away from his beloved Paris, he'd woven cusses into a bitter tale of his odyssey, but when the *Bravoure* finally weighed anchor and his new floormate started shaking, sweating more than the heat called for, he kept his anger reigned in to nurse the malaria-afflicted Peruvian.

Deathside, Pando and Frédéric met again on the *Bravoure*. Pando, having roamed the wharf like a lost soul, shouting in the faces of the living, throwing punches that at best induced sneezing in passers-by, trudged back towards the ship. He went through the door cut straight into the hull.

At midday no one was around, but the floor was still littered with the few worthless possessions of the folks who paid a heavy rent for the privilege of having a roof over their heads, floorboards rather than mud to sleep on. Pando found Frédéric huddled in his corner, shaking his head.

It took, of course, time to get used to it. And now that sleep and hunger were out of the equation, who could tell, in living-above days, how long the two stayed there, wallowing in the post-partum of themselves, sitting up and grunting theories back and forth to each other. Room was scant in those days, and on land the cabin was as crowded as it had been at sea. Sometimes a drunk came home and settled down on them, falling immediately asleep in a fit of sneezy snores.

After a while, they ventured out. The world as ghosts wasn't much different, except they couldn't *do* much. This didn't really bother Pando—he'd always been the contemplative kind. He enjoyed looking around, keeping a keen ear to the many accents and tongues, the babble of the newly-arrived looking for the fortune of their dreams.

Frédéric though, the rare times he gave in and accompanied his friend for a walk, got angry at the obscure tongues the living used, and had to keep asking Pando to translate.

"Qu'est-ce qu'ils disent, Pando? Hein?"

WHERE THE READER IS KINDLY ASKED TO SWITCH INTO GHOST TIME

Both our friends having passed on to the other side, let us forsake the living's stubborn grip on time. Off with you mealtimes, bedtimes, on-times! Keskidiz spent hours, years sulking in the *Bravoure*, while Pando explored, spending the night, the decade out.

The ship, their home, sank ever deeper in the silt, as rubbish and debris filled the alleys. The land grew, the coast pushed farther and farther away, and as the *Bravoure's* upper-deck offices got half destroyed by fire then rebuilt, then half destroyed again and rebuilt again, the old lower deck got buried and no living ever sheltered down there again. Which was no skin off any ghost's nose, really.

KESKIDIZ BEFRIENDS A LOCAL

One day, as Keskidiz roamed further than usual from his cabin, to where the soil became silt then sea, he came across a woman, dragging herself up onto the land.

"You OK, there?"

"Um," the woman snorted, as if to clear her ghost airways. Keskidiz bent down, ready to help her up, but the soaked figure brushed him off. She got up and shook the dirt off herself. She wore an apron-like leather dress, and ink lined her chin and neck.

"Don't worry. I don't bite," she said. Keskidiz realized he was staring and looked away, embarrassed.

"Uh, where are you from?"

"Shouldn't I be asking you that? My folks been here a while, paleface." She chuckled.

"No, I mean, why are you coming from the sea?"

The woman's face crumpled. She shuddered, adjusted her dress, and hugged herself.

"I have a little fire going in my cabin," Keskidiz said. The woman looked up at him, and shrugged. "My name's Keskidiz. Well, my new name, I suppose."

"Your new name? I'm Taipa."

They walked inland, through earth and hulls, until they got to the *Bravoure*.

They sat around the little rusty stove Keskidiz had salvaged. No heat or cold, no sensation really could be felt by pure minds such as them, but the placebo effect went a long way. He pulled a bit of rotten wood from the wall and dropped it into the hatch. A puff of smoke exited the twisted pipe that ended after couple of feet.

"You just stew in smoke?" Taipa said, looking up at the ceiling for a vent, an opening. "How will your creator see you here?"

Keskidiz grunted. "Well, it's not like you're in whatever Indian paradise yourself, *hein*? Looks like we've both been swindled. I'm a socialist, Madame, a materialist—and look at me! A damn ectoplasm."

"I entered the ocean many times, trying to reach Ootayo'me, but I could never find a beast big enough to carry me over." Taipa glared at Keskidiz. "Is it your people? Have they taken all the beasts of the water too?"

Keskidiz frowned, and shook his head.

"I wanted to be a happy ghost, you know. A scary ghost also, of course, but a joyful ghost that the people would hear dancing in the roundhouse, each of my steps shaking the world and everything in it, felling owls from their branches and sending snakes rattling out of their holes in rage. And when the bravest of the people tiptoed to the doorway to peek in, they'd have seen nothing. Only heard my mad drumming still echoing through the hills."

Taipa sighed, slapping her thigh. "Ain't many people left to haunt. And I've grown stubborn in my goal, live-in-the-smoke Keskidiz. My family's waiting for me in the village of the dead."

And the two were silent, each nodding to themselves in the smoky darkness.

AND HOW DID EACH FEEL THE OTHER'S ABSENCE?

Keskidiz often heard dull footsteps from above, absorbed by the layers of sediments and rotten wood, and he wondered if it was Pando, near but busy with something else, someone else than him.

As for Pando, he roamed the land, bundle on stick, a little tickle in his mind, like he'd forgotten something. As if rummaging through his stuff, he might come across Keskidiz, all wrapped up small into himself, foetus-like, and that he'd come out, laughing off his centennial funk.

THE 1906 SHAKE

Pando came home to a city aflame. He was roaming far away, father than he had ever been, reaching that other ocean he'd never seen. A little after 8am, as he stood on a busy New York sidewalk, being run through by fifty people a minute, causing fifty sneezes, he felt a tremor. Around him the living-above, the busy flesh-and-bones anchored souls, didn't even twitch. None of them noticed.

Pando discarded the feeling as one of the numerous ghost events his days were punctuated by, these difficult-to-define things that often left him wondering if something had indeed happened, or if it had just been a passing quavering of the soul.

Soon the news reached the city though, crawling overland through numerous tiny trails of electricity. An earthquake had destroyed Frisco.

Pando rushed west, forsaking the living-above-like gait he usually favored, hovering over the land much faster than any automobile or galloping horse. Was the quake a call from Keskidiz? If they could, like dogs, feel what humans couldn't, might not ghosts release such vibrations into the world?

On the coast, Pando floated on over the bay, slowing down despite himself. The city, the hills burned. A giant darkness came of it, lingered in the sky, threatening to turn day into night.

He found Keskidiz underground, picking up knick-knacks from where they'd fallen down, nailing little frames and trinkets back into place. One look and Pando knew the quake had had nothing to do with his friend. Keskidiz looked untroubled. He was busy hoarding mementos of their lifetime, and whatever junk he'd been able to salvage. When they didn't leave them too long, didn't go too far from them, ghosts could hold on to their ghost objects.

Pando, who deemed this unstuff pointless, saw red—he'd abandoned a perfectly nice stroll for nothing! For a materialist hermit!

"I thought you were in trouble! Calling out for help, *cabrón*!" he lashed out, before running back out into the world.

A NEW RECRUIT

When Pando next came back from a cross-country jaunt, having heard marvelous accounts of the finished bridge across the unruly tides of the Golden Gate strait, he found Keskidiz in their old corner with a man who was soaking wet. His black hair, neatly parted on the side, slick on his skull, leaked trickles that dripped down from his chin.

"Pando! Quelle surprise! To what do we owe the honneur?"

"I came back for the bridge." There was something about bridges. About boats too, and railways. The tease of them, the implicit promise of escape. "I only saw its tips coming out of the fog, but I thought we could have a look together…" he trailed off, glancing at the wet man. There was something wrong, unhealthy about him. A bloating.

"Oh, excuse-moi, amigo. This here's Harold. Got here a few days ago. Told me aaaall about your bridge. Can't be all that great if a gentleman of good taste like Monsieur Wobber, halfway over it, would choose not to go any further and exit the bridge in the most direct way possible…"

Harold smiled, a little embarrassed, then stopped when water streamed out of his open mouth.

"Isn't he something? Look at him!"

Pando bent over the man, inspected the strange pasty consistency of his face, as he smiled further, letting more slime dribble out onto his shirt. Something was off. The man looked wobbly, like one's reflection on a calm pool, clear but wavy. But also more tangible than Keskidiz and Pando themselves.

"A little experiment of mine," Keskidiz went on. "And I must say I'm pretty proud of it. You have before your eyes, cher Pando, the first known case of a ghost-body post-mortem union."

Pando looked at Keskidiz, eyebrows raised, then back at Harold.

"Wobber, lift a hand, veux-tu?"

The drenched ghost did so, and Pando saw, clearly, the semi-translucent arm rise in the air, followed a half-second later by a more earthly limb. A sluggish dog on leash. When Harold held his arm still the two merged again, although never quite getting the unity the living-above achieved.

"Monsieur Wobber, you can be proud of yourself. First man to jump off the ship of life from that brand-new viaduct, maybe, but also first to re-enlist in the old meat-bag crew of this here underground fleet! This, mon Pando, is the beginning of something big… The remarriage of flesh and spirit!"

Keskidiz smiled, in higher spirits than Pando remembered him ever being.

A RECURRENT METAPHYSICAL CONUNDRUM

Now and then the subject came up—when Pando had exhausted his tales of adventures by proxy in far-flung lands, when Keskidiz had summed up the settling of the ship, the living-above's waste oozing down, the drama of generations of rats—of what in hell or heaven they might be doing there. Still there, despite death. There was much talk about unfinished business, but it was just like the living-above to say that, wasn't it?

"How do you think the living-above would feel if we told them they had some unfinished business, that they needed to move on, *hein*?" Keskidiz would say.

And Pando would grunt back. Clearly the thought weighed on both their minds. And their minds, well, they were all they had left.

SYLVAN INTERLUDE

Pando's roamings often led him to a large aspen forest out in Utah. He stopped there, lying down on his ghost back, looking up at the high quaking trees. He liked being in the middle of heck-all, far from Frisco's crowd and its human-ness, its constant reminder of his insubstantiality.

The late sixties were especially tough. The bustle of the city, the prolifera-tion of this new-fangled breed of long-haired youth depressed him. Not that he despised their exuberant freedom—quite the contrary, actually. Watching them made not having a body torture.

Rather than stick around, then, Pando hit the road. Those years were outback years, woodsy days, when Pando roamed the land whistling to him-self, grinning like a mad thing when a deer crossed his path, or when a bob-cat, spooked, ran off for its life. He kept out of sight of humans and their uber-physicality.

But Pando was also a social beast, so when one day a woman appeared with a heavy backpack, carrying all sorts of instruments, he didn't stir. He studied her for a while—weeks?—from where he lay, measuring girth, peeling off bark, drilling out samples. And when she took her gear a bit further, Pando got up and followed her.

He was there when she confirmed the theory she'd been working on, that the forty thousand or so trees that composed the forest were in reality stems of a single tree. A single organism. Probably the oldest on Earth. He saw her leap for joy, a little heart-breaking, lonely victory hop, and he wished he had a body through which to show her someone cared.

From then on, every time he passed the forest he looked for the biologist, training his ghost ears on the rustle of leaves. He saw her age from the spry woman she'd been in the late sixties to a tougher, silver-haired one, but she still worked as stubbornly, studying the huge beast she'd discovered.

Pando was there too when the biologist, still carrying that big rucksack of tricks up and down hills, staggered then collapsed. He rushed to her, but even if he'd possessed physical hands he couldn't have done a thing. She lay eyes open, lifeless. A second passed and the shape of her shifted, and her ghost self sat up. She looked at Pando, seeing that old unknown friend for the first time, then down at the body she was rising from.

"Oh crap."

LOVE TOKEN BY FOXFIRE

Once Pando came home and found the *Bravoure* empty. No Keskidiz, none of his friends, the random lost souls he was constantly stirring up into a strange underground crew. Pando sat down to wait for his friend to smell him out. After a while he stood up and looked around the room. The oil lamp hung unlit from a beam, and the only light was that of foxfire. The fungi's dull emerald luminescence was just enough for Pando to get his bearings in this damp Hades.

Pando didn't usually spend time in this womb of sorts Keskidiz refused to leave. It seemed like a tiny span of time now, their odyssey north, a speck of a thing balanced on the very end of this weird seesaw, against the hulk of their deathtime, but still the runt of their lifetime somehow managed to pull her weight, wiggle the plank until these thirty-odd years Pando and Keskidiz had spent in good honest bodies mattered as much, if not more, as their decades of haunting. They never discussed it, but it was clear from how much time they spent, when they met, talking about the old days of the delightful burden of their bodies.

When Pando visited from his inland, above-ground wanderings, Keskidiz was always there, lurking, and a childish reserve prevented Pando from snooping around. Shouldn't they have the same claim on the place? Hadn't they both slept on its floorboards, while luckier, bulkier men hung in hammocks, like fat hams, from its rafters? Hadn't they both worked like dogs to keep the ship, well, shipshape?

Pando plucked a mushroom and knelt along the totem pole of the central beam, following the carved lines that scarred it, drawings and random words in languages he didn't always recognize. A thin layer of fungus covered almost everything. His eyes followed the lines, down the pole, along the floor, and before he knew it, he'd reached the corner that had been theirs during their northward journey. He looked down, and for a second he imagined he could make out, there, in the wear patterns of the old rotten boards, the shape of their bodies. Was it crazy to think a remnant of their short-term presence might remain, when themselves were now mere remnants?

He sat down, lost in thoughts, and the mushroom he still held cast its little greenish shine on the wall, there in the nookest part of the corner, and he glimpsed a little heart. A perfectly carved, arrow-skewered cartoon organ.

Ernesto and Frédéric.

A chill passed through his ghost marrow, goosebumps on his phantom flesh, as the old names rang through his mind. Had Keskidiz ever even called him by his first name? He had. A deathtime ago, but he had. When they'd found themselves in dire straits, found comfort in each other. When it had been the two of them against the rest of the world.

OF THE IMPOSSIBILITY OF DEFINITE ANSWERS

Now, do we—any of us, living-above, dead-below, over hills and down mines, damned gamblers or real-estate moguls—know what the other thinks? Do we know how the other feels our hand, as we shake theirs? Is the hand brought on someone's shoulder for comfort felt, or does it sink as in fog, unfelt, like a cold draft, a goose rain-dancing on one's own future place of rest?

And, by the way, how do you see them, Keskidiz and Pando, strutting the decks of long-gone schooners underground? Going from room to room, through mineshaft-like, timber-lined corridors, or rather ghosting their way through compact dirt, their spirit shapes passing through the earth and the earth through them, one taking the other's place, like petrified trees, the form remaining but the matter different? This, too, is hard to say.

OLD FRIENDS' REUNION

Pando didn't have time to take off his ghost boots before Keskidiz rushed in and led him by the hand straight through the hull, as if somewhere out there in the infinite earth was some major treasure.

"Wait till you see this."

Pando let Keskidiz drag him through soil, the dim city-sediment dump of their underground world. His eyes roamed, an old reflex, when a glitter beckoned. Beer caps, rusted screws, a chip of fool's gold, the anchor of a long-forgotten ship... Nothing worth a pickax swing.

"Ah, *voilà*," Keskidiz said. Pando saw a dull brilliance ahead, through the sewage-saturated earth. Soon they stood over two corpses.

Two skeletons, rather. Side by side, their ribs almost touching. Pando could see, in fog-like waves, the ghost bodies of who the skeletons had been. The misty apparitions condensed, fanned by some unfelt draft, revealing his own young face. And that of his best friend.

"That fat *bâtard* must have dumped us here. Between boats. Then when they filled the place to build the wharf, the proverbial six feet of mud piled overhead."

Pando looked at himself, a little shocked. Then at Keskidiz—skeleton Keskidiz—then at the real one.

"Well, funny, hein? The stuff you find underground, Pando, you wouldn't believe."

And Keskidiz turned around, started back towards the *Bravoure*.

Pando stayed for a minute, troubled both by the discovery and Keskidiz's off-handed manner. It wasn't like him—he was usually a fool for memorabilia, a real tissue-wetter for Stuff. And this, one's own bones? The ultimate memento you're muerto.

He was about to leave when he saw his hand. Not his ghost hand—his what-was-left-of-his-body hand. Holding Keskidiz's. Had the goon posed them like this? Or had their ghosts, finally exiting their husks, reached for a last earthly comfort? Or had Keskidiz visited their makeshift grave, kept a belated vigil and fussed over their remains?

FAREWELL, FRIENDS, AND MAY YOU SAFELY REACH OOTAYO'ME

And so we circle back. See Pando standing on top of the hill. Well, standing—such a living-above word. In truth, he's hovering (imagine an angel of steam), his legs vaporizing down to nothing, as if the earth gave birth to him.

Looking down on his beloved Frisco.

He was in Florida when he felt the tremor, and knew—don't ask, ghost senses—this time *was* different. The quake felt personal. A calling. He rushed right back, forsaking the pretense of human travel, letting the winds carry his nebulous self.

Pando can see the rift now, the meter-wide gap cutting through the Financial District. The line is familiar, and Pando wonders if it's just a vision, the past superimposing itself on the material present, making him see the waterline as it was over a century and a half ago, before the ship graveyard was filled in.

People are fleeing, jumping over the fracture. Some fall into the hell below. Steam comes out, and a faint greenish glow blooms where the earth shows below the tarmac.

Pando floats down the hills, and when he reaches the rift, the earth, as if feeling him, shakes a mighty rattle. The previous quake was but a warning, the locomotive's toot before the monster shudders on. The whole bit of land becomes unmoored, and drifts out into the bay. The glass towers of offices crumble down, and from the ruins, Pando sees poles spring up. Shoots at first, they soon grow into thick trunks. When they've grown several dozen feet into the air, offshoots come out the sides. There, little leaves blossom, and some of them, out of the general greenery, expand into giant white sails that bulge in the wind.

From an earthy hollow in the rift face, lined with old rotten timber, Keskidiz leans out, waving.

"Adieu, mon ami!" he shouts across the foaming whirlpools the departing land stirs.

Pando waves back, smiling a little, not knowing what else to do. He could ghost-jump the gap, of course. But sometimes you just have to let go. Taipa appears next to Keskidiz, and she starts waving as well, smiling like a maniac. Harold comes too. He takes off his shirt, wrings it of over the drop and puts it up to dry on a ripped pipe that sticks out. The biologist, who followed Pando to Frisco when she tired of haunting the forest, stands on top of the sailing mass of land, inspecting the growing masts and their rigging.

And despite the heartbreak, the loneliness ahead of him like a whole new continent, Pando knows it's long overdue, the severance of this mooring.

of
webs and
windows
in pescadero

NATANIA BARRON

NATANIA BARRON

Natania Barron is a word tinkerer with a lifelong love of the fantastic. She has a penchant for the speculative, and has written tales of invisible soul-eating birds, giant cephalopod goddesses, gunslinger girls, and killer kudzu, just to name a few. Her work has appeared in *Weird Tales, EscapePod, Steampunk Tales, Crossed Genres, Bull Spec,* and various anthologies. *Pilgrim of the Sky*, her debut novel, published in 2011, and its followup *Watcher of the Skies* is forthcoming. Recent publications include two novellas: *Wothwood*, a heroic fantasy with a weird twist, and *Frost & Filigree*, an Edwardian urban fantasy set in Tarrytown, New York. She calls Chapel Hill, NC home, but part of her heart will always be in Northern California.

OUTSIDE, FOG WREATHS THE FACTORY. FROM A DISTANCE IT'S IMPOSSIBLE TO judge just how close it lies to the harbor. But some of the older children tell stories of escape and freedom, adventures of past factory workers climbing the scaffolding and plunging into the chilly water, swimming to a new life.

Lai Biyu tells Zu Zhilan not to believe this; she is a little thing and so gullible. And Lai Biyu knows well enough how quickly hope festers, and how when extinguished it leaves a gaping hole inside that never goes away. She does not want Zu Zhilan to feel as she does, even if she is a mouthy little thing who sleeps too much.

Yes, Lai Biyu knows better than to believe these stories because she is now almost seven and must be the responsible one. So, as the fog rolls by the highest windows, she does not think about freedom, because it is a concept now lost to her. All there remains in her mind are the looms and the threads and the sick sweet scent of silk, twisting and lengthening and filling up the dark hole inside.

And Zu Zhilan because everyone has decided that she is responsible for her.

When she began working at the silk factory, sometimes she used to think about her mother in the tea fields of home. She would remember Mother's blue dress rustling across the leaves as she follows the other harvesters into lunch, the dry, chilly air coming down from the mountains. She could hear their voices call to one another softly, then break into song.

But the songs are gone, now. And so is the face of her mother.

All she remembers is the fire that took her mother in the first silk factory. The fire that melted her mother and left her own face and hands marred. The fire that, for a small moment, filled her with peace before it left everything else in its wake.

Zu Zhilan, too, used to have a mother who worked at the factory, says Meng Si, the factory manager. He is fat and tired all the time, but he somehow manages to remember little details now and again. Like all the others, Meng Si calls Zu Zhilan Lai Biyu's little sister, only because they speak the same way. He says that Zu Zhilan's parents were She, just like Lai Biyu's.

But here on the other side of the world, even a tenuous connection is treasured. Or else used as an excuse. In this case, it's usually left up to Lai Biyu if her "little sister" ever gets into trouble. Which is both often and cumbersome. It isn't fair that, due to a simple twist of their tongues, she is made to keep after the little girl.

Since the fire, Lai Biyu has felt so alone. So it's good that the little one is there sometimes. Even if Little Sister is too lazy for her own good, it helps Lai Biyu forget the fire.

It was, after all, another world away. Now her life is the whir of the looms and the feeling of the soft, wet cocoons in her hands, and the sweet stink of silk.

And Zu Zhilan snoring again.

Lai Biyu frowns down when she notices Zu Zhilan has fallen asleep at her station again. She is about five, Lai Biyu thinks, but it's difficult to say because of her size. She's smaller than the others her age, but cleverer and quicker. When it comes to fixing the machinery, no one does it better than Zu Zhilan, and so they keep her about. But if anything goes missing or misplaced, it's probably because of her, as well. She's supposed to be helping the girls sort the cocoons in the hot vats when she isn't directly needed. Which she interprets as an ideal time to nap.

Zhang Lin, the mistress of the children, has never liked Zu Zhilan in the least. But then, Zhang Lin doesn't like much of anyone. Meng Si says it's because the man she was supposed to marry in San Francisco decided he didn't want her one day and went up North with some Japanese woman who made delicious food. He says her face looked like that, so full of frowns, because she was forced to eat her own food which tasted like bitter tears.

Whatever the cause of her unhappiness, Zhang Lin has the unfortunate task of working both long hours in the silk factory and shouldering the responsibility of getting the children to work on time and in their palettes at night, alerting the managers when the children are too sick to work, or need to be given up on all together.

"Hsst!" Lai Biyu says, shaking her leg a bit under the loom rigging so that Zu Zhilan might be impacted. But as usual, the little girl does nothing in response save for a sweet snore.

Lai Biyu cranes her neck to see the manager, Tu Cheng, walking side by side with Meng Si and Zhang Lin, going about their morning observation. If they find Zu Zhilan sleeping again, they will send her to the meat factory. She will wipe the floors of blood and offal and never again touch sweet silk. How many times have they been told how blessed they are to have been given such a chance as this? To work the most divine of all fabrics? Lai Biyu understands this because when her parents died they first brought her to the iron plant where she got half of her burns. The other half were from before she arrived in San Francisco.

Zu Zhilan is too young to know how good she has it, and it's up to Lai Biyu to look out for her because... because everyone agrees they belong together. Even Lai Biyu, though she doesn't know why.

"Zu Zhilan," Lai Biyu says again, to no avail. Why does she bother with the little girl? Because, she supposes, this burden of a child is her forsaken responsibility. And if she's caught again, like two weeks ago, they will both be beaten.

Kicking again, Lai Biyu reaches down to try and pinch Zu Zhilan. This time Bao Li catches on, shoving Lai Biyu and hushing her. There are only six girls allowed in the factory at a time, and their positions are prized enough that no true alliances have grown. Orphans to the last, but Bao Li is almost old enough to be married and she is not about to waste what little money she has from the mill because Zu Zhilan can't stay awake. As the eldest it will fall to her, even if Lai Biyu is the one they all know is truly responsible for the little brat.

It's worse than Lai Biyu fears. It's not just the floor manager, it's one of the Highbinders. Mr. Poy.. His face is even more scarred than Lai Biyu's, and not just from one event. His eye is puckered all around the edges, making half his face look like it's ancient. Meng Si says he survived a shotgun blast to the head and he's one of the most wanted Highbinders among all the tongs.

Then they approach her, eyes searching.

Lai Biyu knows not to speak, but she can't help but tremble. The last beating she had on account of Zu Zhilan was so bad she couldn't sit for a week. She'd only just stopped having trouble moving about.

It isn't, as she suspected, Zhang Lin, that does the talking. Which is unusual in and of itself. It is Mr. Poy himself who begins the conversation.

"You're the Big Sister," says the Highbinder, looking Lai Biyu up and down. He does not look upset or judgmental. He does not look one way or another. She might be nothing more than a ginkgo tree on his daily walk rather than a human being.

When Lai Biyu takes too long to speak Zhang Lin slaps her on the face. "Speak when you are spoken to, you insolent child."

Lai Biyu does not look at Mr. Poy but nods as her cheek reddens considerably. "I'm Lai Biyu."

Mr. Poy laughs. "You weren't kidding me, Meng Si. I haven't heard that accent in a dozen years. How does a She child—and a pair of them—end up in San Francisco?"

Meng Si shrugs his fat shoulders and smiles innocently. "They had parents, but they did not last long. Blended in, I suppose."

"And you're certain the little one is here somewhere?" Mr. Poy asks.

This time it is Bao Li's turn to be brave. She has been watching, always the opportunist, and grabs Zu Zhilan by the collar, hoisting her matted head of hair up for all to see.

"Always sleeping," says Bao Li, proud as a lion. "Lai Biyu does a terrible job of keeping her awake."

Zu Zhilan rubs her face, hardly noticing that Bao Li grabbed her so roughly. She looks as if she's been risen with the gentle hand of a sweet mother.

Blinking, Zu Zhilan sleepily pulls up next to Lai Biyu and wraps her arms around her waist, resting her head on her hip with a contented look on her face.

"Please don't hurt her," says Lai Biyu, choking back a sob. The idea of what they'd do to her this time brings tears. As much as she resents the little girl she cannot argue that they are connected in a way she cannot claim with anyone else in the factory, or indeed, all of San Francisco.

"Hurt her," echoes Mr. Poy, as if the thought was new and very possible. "Not yet, anyway. I am told she is a unique little flower."

Zu Zhilan sniffs, her fingers curling around the fabric of Lai Biyu's shift, making little twists like a cat.

"Hsst!" Lai Biyu says, shaking her leg to try and dislodge the little girl. But Little Sister is well and stuck.

"She is a tiresome, sleepy thing," Zhang Lin snorts. "I don't know what could be so intriguing about her other than she eats more than she should and she sleeps more than an old tomcat."

Mr. Poy ignores Zhang Lin which, on some level, makes Lai Biyu feel a bit better. "It's not your opinion that concerns me, Zhang Lin," he says. "It is my correspondence from Meng Si."

"Where the girls are concerned, so am I," Zhang Lin says defiantly.

Mr. Poy continues to ignore her and reaches out and puts a hand on Zu Zhilan's shoulder.

"Now, girl. Let me see your hands," he tells her.

Zu Zhilan looks up at Lai Biyu, and the Big Sister nods, shaking her hands out so she might follow suit.

The Little Sister frowns, then reluctantly releases the grasp upon Lai Biyu. Her tiny hands are grimy and sticky, a travesty to behold. That's always the case, though. Lai Biyu has been trying to keep her hands clean since she first met her, and yet they never stay clean. Zu Zhilan flexes her little fingers experimentally for Mr. Poy, and raises an eyebrow in question.

Mr. Poy must see something that the rest do not, for he takes one of her filthy hands with no issue and runs his own finger across the lines of her palm, muttering something to himself in a language unfamiliar to Lai Biyu. It has none of the sharp edges of English, nor the sing song nature of some of the other tongues she has heard during her travels through the city. It makes her ears ache to hear it, and she does not know why.

Just when Lai Biyu is certain that Zhang Lin is going to start off on one of her tirades about how horrible and useless Zu Zhilan is, something remarkable happens. Mr. Poy holds out his hands above Zu Zhilan's, and where there was nothing before there are fine threads of silk growing from her palms. Silvery, beautiful things. And Mr. Poy is able to speak to them somehow, to coax them into dancing around in the air, whirling in an invisible current.

Meng Si says a terrible curse, and Zhang Lin goes pale, pressing her lips together.

"A Silkbinder," Mr. Poy says.

Zu Zhilan frowns, and for the first time ever, Lai Biyu sees that she is crying. Whatever the cause of this miracle is not a good one. There is fury in Little Sister's eyes, a sense of betrayal.

That is when Lai Biyu grabs Zu Zhilan, just as Mr. Poy is about to take her. She does not know how she is certain this is going to happen, but it rings in her ears like a bell, the knowing. Lai Biyu grits her teeth and wraps her arms around Zu Zhilan, pulling her as close to her as she is able without hurting her, and the world goes up in flame.

Araby wipes blood and spittle from his face, wincing as he glances at the combined froth on the back of his hand. The resulting sludge flows into the crevices from the scars across his knuckles, shiny like melted candle wax. And it might as well be, for the scars were forged in flames.

Then he kicks the bloody corpse in front of him, flips it over, and deftly slices the coin purse away. It's not as heavy as it should be. Davis won't like that, but then Davis can go fuck herself. She didn't mention that this fucker was going to put up such a fight. Forgot to mention that it was dead already and it was a matter of literally ripping the little scarab from its throat to make it stop moving.

Fucking monsters.

Why would anyone trust them with money, anyway?

"You okay, Araby?" Bet's voice comes in through the ringing in his ears and he sighs, not surprised that she's still alive but still a little relieved.

"Had to rip out the thing's throat," he says, standing and looking through the dense, behemoth trees. Aside from the undead creature, it's a serene place. The red-barked trunks rise up so high it's hard to imagine they ever stop. It smells like citrus and cardamom, almost. It reminds him of home for just a moment, that fresh wood smell. And blood. That's familiar, too. But this blood is broken. Congealed and long stilled.

Still, the thing bled plenty.

"That's unusual. Mine all just died the usual way," Bet says, pushing through the brush and coming into view. Her hair has come undone from her braids on one side; looks like someone got a fistful of her hair, in fact, because it's a bit uneven now, tight black curls reaching up toward the sky. There's a bruise on her cheek, and a good cut on her lip. But otherwise she's same as always. Strong, lithe, deadly woman. Daughter of an escaped slave from Georgia. Best second Araby's ever known. They practically grew up at Davis's place together.

"How many?" Araby asks her.

"Three," she says. "They must have planted that one special for you, but that makes sense given your tendencies to attract dead things. Did you save the scarab this time?"

Araby frowns. It's a thing he hates, bugs. Worse even that whoever's been making these monsters does so by shoving a scarab beetle down the throat of a corpse. The last two he fought were tough but seemed semi-formed. Easy to spot from a distance due to the lumbering gait. But this one was different. Hanging around with live folks. Indecipherable until he was on them. And with the goods, too. Or most of them, at least.

"It's over there," Araby says, pointing to a large rock some feet away. It's smeared with more blood. Araby smashed the bug on it, deactivating it but not quite destroying it this time.

Bet picks it up with a gloved hand, pinching the thing with thumb and forefinger. She raises and eyebrow and nods. "Well, they do seem to like you better than anyone," she says. "At least, so far you're the only one who's been chosen. Kelley helped you last time, but you were the one who did the deed. This one's got a green carapace, though. The last ones were red."

"Oh, how novel," Araby says, trying to avoid looking at it.

Bet grins. "I've seen you rip out the still-warm entrails of a mark without so much as breaking a sweat. And yet this little thing makes you all squirmy inside." She comes a little closer to him with the scarab.

"Don't. Bet."

"It's just a little machine. Gears and coils and springs, all put together."

"You're telling me that what happened to that body was just a product of coils and springs?"

"Well, clearly there's something else going on. But it's far beyond my ability to figure it out. We'll need an expert to decipher this one." She pulls a hardened leather flask out of her pack and tosses the remnants of the scarab into it, plugging it with a cork just in case. "Isn't that why I deal with your sorry self all the time?"

"I'm no psychic." Araby feels better already, now that the bug is out of sight. "My work is a bit less subtle."

"Yes, you go transparent and then come back all pale and waif—like. It's quite the show." She rolls her eyes at him, clearly unimpressed with his abilities.

"I traverse planes," he says. "I speak to the dead."

"Makes sense. Aren't scarabs and gods of the dead from your neck of the woods, anyway?" Bet asks, shoving Araby as she heads back down where they came from, where their horses are waiting. She shakes the leather flask and he can hear its wings beating against the walls.

"That's Egypt. My parents were from the Levant," he clarifies.

"Same difference."

"Related, but not the same. I grew up in the mountains. Egypt is a desert."

But Bet is already bored and heading toward the horses. They will have to explain all of this to Davis, and she will be unhappy. And really, Araby is growing tired of having to explain himself.

Davis sits on pillows because she's always sitting on pillows. Mountains of pillows from God knows where, piled one on top of another in a such a garish array of color and design it's always a little jarring. Even after twenty years it's jarring. The first time Araby saw it, he was Kir. Kir Ghorbani. Orphaned and alone. A scrappy little thirteen-year-old boy with a haunted look and a hunger to avenge the deaths of his parents. Davis had found him. Davis had brought him in, promised a new future, and when she gave him a new name—Araby—he'd taken it, even if it made no sense. To her, any place in the near east was Araby, and so, that's who he became.

She's a big woman, Davis. Full of folds and divots, rolls and undulations. She might not do much in the way of movement, but she's got people to do that for her. Just one name and it's enough. No one knows if it's her name or her late husband's, or if there even was a husband. Doesn't matter. She's a big white woman who gets things done, and always has. Davis of the Thousand Eyes. Davis of a Thousand Ears and Tongues.

She knows everything, which is why it's so damned unnerving when she doesn't seem to care about the scarab corpse people.

"We've got a new parcel," she says, sucking on the hookah buried within the pillows of her boudoir. She puffs out a long stream of thin smoke.

In the twenty years that Araby has known her she's only gotten grayer, but that's all that's changed. Few wrinkles to belie her age. "Two of them, actually."

Parcels are people. Important people.

"Oh?" Araby asks.

Bet squirms beside him. So she was sweating the situation more that she was letting on.

"Chinese girls. Escaped from San Francisco. Last seen just outside of Pescadero."

"That's a long way from San Francisco," Bet says. "For two little Chinese girls."

"Isn't it, though?" Davis says, pulling out one of the long chains around her chest, fingering the beads there a moment. "That's what I want you to figure out."

"What's the catch?" Bet asks.

"Well, you've got some competition," Davis says, not looking up from her beads. She drags them between her fingers, glass clinking. "The Highbinders are after them, too. And it sounds like Mr. Poy is back."

"Fucking Poy," mutters Bet. "Fucking Highbinders."

"You know what he'll do to those girls, Araby," Davis says, ignoring Bet's foul language. "And do you know where they came from?"

"Of course I don't. You've just told me," he says to her. He hates her games, he always has. But the truth of his existence stares in him the face. If it hadn't been for Davis, Araby wouldn't be alive. She took him in, helped him understand his... challenges? Blessings? Hard to say. Either way, she found him—rather, one of her lackeys found him—and she fed him and gave him work to do and food to eat.

Davis smiles, looking more like a frog than a person for a moment. "They escaped a burning silk factory. How's that for irony?"

Little Sister knew her Big Sister would never burn her. That's why she chose her. Big Sister isn't really her sister, but they know the same songs because their parents came from home. And Little Sister knows Big Sister's secret. She isn't angry at her for what happened with the first fire. Big Sister hates herself for it, knows that the scars she wears all over her body are the price she paid but that's the thing. Now she's fireproof. And Little Sister always knew that it was just a matter of time...

When Big Sister brings the fire down on the mean man Mr. Poy, Little Sister does her job. She spins the silk. This silk is different than the kind they use at the factory. It's stronger and fire-resistant. She knows this because she survived the first fire this way, except Big Sister doesn't remember that she was there, too, that her mother and father were, as well. There are lots of things that Big Sister doesn't remember. She keeps them buried deep inside where the blood and bones are.

They escape the burning building quietly, once everyone has stopped screaming and the flames have gone out. The cocoon is strong, and the girls don't say a word to each other. They don't have to. They just wait until the smoking ruins go dark and slowly slip away.

Little Sister curls her toes at the edge of the harbor, everything still engulfed in fog. But it smells of smoke now, too. Smoke and charred bodies. Some of them got out. Not the mean woman, the one that beat her so badly. Little Sister doesn't mind that so much even though she should.

Then she begins weaving a boat with her silk, a little precocious spider spinning on the edge. It takes a little time, and Big Sister just watches, shivering. When they get in the boat, camouflaged perfectly with the thick banks of fog, she weaves a blanket for them both, and they fall asleep and drift away silently as ghosts.

Pescadero is nestled in right between the mountains and the sea, the smell of salt mingling with the shit and refuse of any little town. The houses are mostly painted white, though, and on the few times that Araby and Bet and the gang have gone through, that's always unnerved him a little. Why paint the houses white?

"Anyone talking yet?" Bet asks, shouldering her pack. They've approached from the mountain side, along the creek, rather than take the more open entrance by the ocean and through the farms. Too risky to be that exposed.

"How many times do I have to tell you? It doesn't work like that," Araby says. "I can walk barefoot over a graveyard and if no one's willing to talk, I can't see them. Something has to have happened, otherwise I'm left to my own devices."

"Good thing you're a goddamned amazing shot," Bet says with a grin. "Otherwise you'd be useless."

"Not all of us can turn into jackals."

"Not all of us are insufferable melancholic bastards, either."

"I was perfectly legitimate, I'll have you know."

Bet freezes, and Araby knows what that means. She's hearing something. Even when she's not a jackal, she's got better ears than he does. Can hear things miles away. And not just disturbances, but subtle shifts and changes.

Her hand goes up and she points toward the church spire still in view.

Araby raises an eyebrow, and Bet nods. Gives the signal to move slowly.

Big Sister is sick. Dying sick. Falling apart sick. The fire in her is trying to snuff her out, and it's all that Little Sister can do to keep smothering her in silk, preventing her from taking everything that makes her alive into its embrace. They both have a power in them, but for Little Sister it's overflowing and out. For Big Sister it's unquenchable.

She didn't want to stop. They were supposed to cross the ocean in their little boat, but then Big Sister started bleeding out her ears and her nose and blisters started growing on her skin. When they popped, the blood was fire.

So they came to the town. They knew no words, and the people were not kind. Once they saw Big Sister's face and hands they shooed the girls away.

Little Sister wove them a cocoon. When they were sleeping, she sang the song of her people and wove the whole town shut. Over the doorways and windows. So strong and fine that no one could get out.

Now she waits in the church with Big Sister who doesn't want to eat any food, shuns water, and keeps bursting into flames.

"Let me burn," she keeps telling Little Sister. But she cannot let her suffer. Even as the people in the town suffocate in the sunrise, Little Sister keeps singing and spinning, smothering the flames.

Then she hears voices. Ragged and whispering to one another. Two. A man and a woman. She thought she had caught everyone in her silk, but now she is going to have to be more direct. More final.

Araby senses the dying girl before he sees her through the window. Funny thing about dying people is how close they are to ghosts. How the filament of their soul vibrates at a higher frequency, or so he's always thought. A sort of desperate dance between this world and the one unseen by most.

Unless you're Araby.

He feels it happening right away, that tug at his center, like a hook latching onto his spine. Just a few steps up the church steps, the sound of the creek nearby—of course, the water, he should have realized it would amplify—fades away and is replaced by the rushing rivers of Irkalla. The Underworld. Ereshkigal's realm.

Where Bet stands she sees a pale shadow of Araby, visible but limned in darkness, standing still. He is safe for the moment. No bullets can pierce him because, in some ways, he is already dead. Araby knows that Davis has paired them together so that she can protect him, but she resents it. It's playing nurse-marm. And that's far from glamorous for a woman possessed with her powers.

In Ereshkigal's realm, the little girl burns so brightly she's blinding to his eyes. There is no warmth coming from her, though, just light. She seems so out of place in Irkalla, where all is shifting and mottled, dappled as if through an invisible canopy. It's hard enough to see things—like trying to look at a star straight on—when he's here, without a sudden flush of light all around.

"Little one," Araby says, not sure how to speak with her. Usually he's not burdened by language here. He does not know what gods she prays to, though.

There is a shimmer in the child's form, a subtle disruption as his words escape in trailing silvery streaks, like ink on top of water. That's how words always look here. Maybe they don't have language. Maybe he's just corrupted by the languages he knows. To him, he always sounds as if he's speaking Farsi, even when he tries to speak English.

"How many times will you visit me before you finally stay?" The voice that cuts through is Ereshkigal's. Clear as a bell, cold and strong. There are no whispers when she speaks. No surprises. She is death, and death is always coming.

"Hello, Ereshkigal." Araby's words drift over to her, encircling her hair.

Her skin is black as jet, as if carved by stone. Her eyes white like marble. The hair on her head is silvery gray, as if woven from twilight itself. She is a sturdy woman, but graceful. A welcoming figure, if not a little intimidating. The first time Araby saw her he thought her comely; his opinion has not much changed, though he does tire of her attention.

"I do love my name on your tongue," she says with a smile curving her lip.

"I'm here for the girl," Araby replies.

"Oh, Kir. It's never just about the job. You know that."

"Today it is. The one on fire."

Ereshkigal frowns then, a little impish pout. She folds her arms across her chest, the long thick fabric of her dress rustling like dead leaves. She isn't terrifying, not like the things that she keeps in the river. But she is always a threat. Sometimes Araby feels as if he's cursed, knowing she's always reaching out for him. But then he realizes that it's no different from anyone else. Death for him simply has a name.

"She is rather brilliant, isn't she?" Ereshkigal says. "Soon she will be mine. You came too late, and that zookeeper of a woman who sent you doesn't deserve someone as talented as this. Present company excluded."

It's always puzzles with the goddess. Araby is never allowed to simply pass through Irkalla. He always has to give something in return. Whether it's cold sex or some strange human trinket—the goddess of the Underworld fancies pomegranates and apricots—she always exacts some kind of payment, and Davis never compensates him.

But then, he's known the goddess a lot longer than he's known Davis. So he supposes the transactions are fair.

The real world pushes at him. Something loud and sharp whirs by his head.

Gunfire. The Highbinders.

"There are two girls," Araby says. "What can you tell me about the other one?"

Ereshkigal gives him a bored look. "What have I to do with the world of the living? I only care about her when she comes to me. And that won't be for a while. She's made of strange stuff. No child of mine."

"And the burning child?"

Bet must be having a hard time because Araby feels a tug on his spine, something hard and insistent, from the world of the living. If the goddess isn't going to be any help...

Bet is movement and power, but it's not enough yet. The Highbinders weren't far, and they come from the west with guns and swords drawn. They wear a mix of traditional dress and modern embellishments, and are a variety of ages—though all men—yet each carries a fury in their eyes. The eldest among them is unfamiliar to Bet, but she knows the man next to him well enough. Mr. Poy. Deadly with his poisoned sword and deadlier with his poisoned words.

They tell Bet that she can't take the girls, as if she's even making a significant threat to them. How many Highbinders? Eight? Nine?

The little girl in the church is shouting in a language Bet doesn't know, and when the fury comes upon her, her last thought is that she won't kill the children this time. Because it's hard to know when to stop. And sometimes she doesn't know when the blood is her own or the victims' or even her friends. When she was six she killed her own friend, Marlene, when she got in a fury. And worse had happened since. Only Araby is good at breaking through to her when she's going too strong, the way he can reach across into her and separate the beast from the woman.

But now Araby's in the Underworld with his goddess girlfriend, and Bet has no choice. Even though she knows the girl is watching her. And the people of Pescadero, the ones whose eyes haven't shut, can see her through webs and windows.

It starts slow, a sort of rumbling in her chest. That's always the first part to change. People think it's the hands, the knuckles, but it's never been like that for Bet. When she changes it's from the heart out. The jackal's voice takes her over from that point on, shuddering through her veins and nerves until she is buried deep within its body, thick and hairy and thirsty for blood, dreaming of another life free from this curse.

The first Highbinder, a shorter man with a club, comes at her laughing as if this transformation is a joke. But he does not laugh long, can't. Because she's already ripped out his throat.

Then the bullets fly.

Araby rushes forward, breathing in the fumes of his words. He wants to say things to Ereshkigal. He wants to remind her that he's promised her a thousand things in the dark. That he used to love her. That she broke his heart. But she knows these things. Loving a goddess is no easy task, especially for a mortal. If that's what he is. He cannot compete with her lover. He shouldn't have to. And yet he keeps being dragged down...

As he gets closer to the girl he hears a name. Two names. Big Sister. Then Lai Biyu. She is so covered in fear that the flames roil in and around themselves, dripping like molten rock. The words around her head evaporate faster than Araby can read them, but he catches snippets: love and duty, child and boat, mother and father, fire and destruction.

"Lai Biyu," he says. "Lai Biyu, I am a friend. I am here to help you."

At this, the child looks up, bright red eyes taking him in as if for the first time. She is small, perhaps seven or eight, and painfully malnourished. Yet there is a hunger in her stance, a pride, as she unfolds herself to look at him.

"Am I dead?" Her words flit around, reaching tenuously toward Araby.

For once he is glad for the silent words. Above ground he doubts they could talk. True ghosts don't use words, they paint images. So she is not as dead as he worried.

"Not yet, but you're dying."

Lai Biyu does not extinguish, but she walks a little closer, craning her flame-crowned head toward the goddess. "Who is she?"

"A friend," says Araby and this is mostly true. More of a friend than Davis. But Davis will take care of her, in the flesh, in ways Ereshkigal cannot. "I'm here to help you. To bring you to a place where people like you—like us—can be taken care of."

"The factory. I burned it to the ground. All the people inside of it, too. I want to be left alone. If I burn up, then I will be alone."

"Perhaps. But so will your…" Araby searches the words. "Your Little Sister."

"She will survive on her own. She is made of strong stuff."

"She loves you. She has—"

But then, searing pain comes, and Araby loses his grasp on the Underworld for a moment, and the living world rushes into view.

Bet is a monster, and it's hard to piece together her thoughts this way. Every nerve cries out to destroy and consume, and she does so without hesitation until she sees the ghost-stepper. His name is something other than what they call him, and he's weak and tired from treading that place in between, but just the smell of him throws off her attack. He smells like death. Not like rotting, no that wouldn't be enough. He smells like the End. The Void. The Done and Done of Everything.

And that's enough to slow her pace, to have her look up from the arm she's been feasting on, the man died so recently that she can taste his last breath in his blood.

She hates him for a moment because she doesn't want to stop, but then the guilt starts coming back. She starts tasting more than the man's life blood. She tastes his memories, his loves and hates. Bet sees a wife, or a woman at least, and a child. Though perhaps that is miles away.

"Come back to me, Bet," says the shadow man. He doesn't wear a turban, but when she looks at him it is like he is clothed in shadow silk, wound about his head and his body. A third eye is bright on his forehead, his teeth like pearls and fury on his brow.

She blinks, and he is gone, replaced by the gunslinger again.

Little Sister watches the monster shred apart her silk, shred apart the Highbinders that come for her. First, the woman and the man approached and Little Sister didn't think much of them. She'd seen hired guns before at the factory, working about their business.

When the man stopped walking and faded—he was mostly there, but then not quite, as if he were made of clouds—Little was sure that the Highbinders would do what they always did. They would kill the woman. They had always been so good at killing the women.

Except this woman turns into a monster with golden mottled fur and wild, yellow eyes. She gets taller, more lithe. She growls and moves like a beast, though still wearing her clothes. She rips the men apart.

Little Sister thinks that this should be enough of a diversion that she can get Big Sister out, except Big Sister has burned down half the church now, and all the lovely webs Little Sister made went up in flames, too. Catching fire in lovely, long strands. It would be almost beautiful if it wasn't so terrible.

Her webs aren't supposed to catch. But Big Sister's fire is changing, deepening into an orange hue. And as Little Sister rushes for her, she realizes that it's too late.

Araby sees the smaller girl running for the pyre of her friend, her sister, whatever she is, and he makes the split-second decision to intercept her. Ereshkigal was no help to him, and so he must do this himself. Saving one of the children is better than saving none of them, even if Davis will be furious with him.

She's just a few feet high, but Araby misjudges her. As soon as he puts his arms around her, the little girl dissipated into millions of crawling spiders. One moment he has his arms around her, and the next he is grasping at fat, furry bodies as they scurry away from him and reform again.

"You're no little girl," he says, tasting blood in his mouth. With her transformation he fell straight on his face, gravel embedding in his chin. He staggers to stand, checking to see how much he's bleeding. Not enough to be too worried. Bet doesn't like the taste of his blood, one of the main reasons he's been paired with her.

But no time.

The girl on fire is going to take down the whole side of the city if he can't get back to Irkalla and have a decent conversation with her.

Staggering to his feet, Araby points Bet in the little one's direction, just in time to notice one of the Highbinders rising, pointing a gun toward her. She's not paying attention, he is, but in this state a gunshot wound would do a great deal of damage.

But the fire.

But the girl.

Ereshkigal's voice comes to him, unbidden. "The fire has already taken her. Leave her to me."

Araby spins, pivoting on an already sore ankle. The Highbinder behind him is nursing some impressive bites courtesy of Bet Jameson, the Jackal Queen. But his aim is too damn good. It's Mr. Poy, Araby realizes, a breeze knocking his hat off his head. Those scars, so familiar. Fires. Fires everywhere.

His shot goes wide, but Mr. Poy doesn't care. He holds up his hand and a shield of dust rises from the ground, a living wall of particulate concealing Araby's view. By the time that Araby gets back around it, Mr. Poy is on the other side, behind him somehow, taking aim again at Bet, who's making a run for the spiderling.

"You don't know what you're dealing with," Mr. Poy says. "Davis is in over her head, and you two are jokes."

"Looks like Bet took good care of your boys. I must be missing the punchline," says Araby. He's got a clear shot, but he notices Mr. Poy lower his gun as the fire freezes before them.

Araby has never seen still flames. They defy his understanding. But they all turn. Bet, who's got the little one corralled, looks. The spiderling frowns up at the pillars of flame rising before them, cutting a second steeple beside the one still standing. Barely standing.

The whole world freezes as those amber flames simply glow, intense and perfect, for eight whole breaths. Then, as easily as the little one changed to spiders, the flames dissolve into ash, cascading down over the town in billowing clouds.

It's so thick that breathing becomes impossible. Araby fumbles forward, hoping to grab Mr. Poy by the shirt, but he comes up with nothing. Just starts coughing and retching, calling out for Bet and the little girl, cursing Davis and the goddess and the road to Irkalla.

When it settles, they're all covered in ash. White and gray and ghostlike. The white houses look like they're covered in snow, catching in the little crenellations and details of doorways, covering the cocoons and making them into billowing clouds.

"Bet!"

"Araby!"

The littlest lets out a cry, a wail.

"I've got her."

Araby rubs his eyes, the damned ash is so hard to get out, and sees Bet emerging with the little girl in her arms, squirming and crying, grabbing fistfuls of the woman's long, curly hair like a baby might to its mother.

"She can't spin in this. Can't change," says Bet, tucking the girl under the crook of her arm. She kicks fiercely. "She's pissed off."

"I see that," says Araby, looking to the ruin of the church. There's a body in there, somewhere. The ashes that made it up, maybe. "Hold on to her. I'm just going to check on the other one."

"Where's Poy?" Bet asks.

"I'll check for him, too," Araby says, as he slips away.

Ereshkigal is waiting for him, sitting by the river, her long hair streaming into the water and turning it blacker, if that was possible. She is humming one of her low songs, the ones he can never remember once he leaves, but knows every note of when he's here with her. The trees are silver, welcoming. Cold, perhaps, but of a kind of stark beauty Araby appreciates.

"Kir," she says softly, "you shouldn't come in and out so quickly. You'll tire your essence. You'll age a century in a day."

She is teasing, but not entirely. Going back and forth always has a price. When he was younger, when they were lovers, he gladly paid it. Now, he measures the meetings more sparingly, when he can control them. That's not always the case. It is difficult to simply dip a toe into Irkalla, but he is learning.

"I'm here to see if she's crossed," Araby says, looking around. The river is always full of souls, and Ereshkigal likes to fish for them sometimes, get to know them personally. They are not happy or unhappy, they are simply released from life. Most of them are more than willing to talk when roused.

"The fire one, yes. She was here," the goddess says, yawning. She rolls her shoulders, then points across the river. "But then she left."

Araby doesn't understand. He tries a few words, but they drift out wrong. So Ereshkigal continues. "I don't think she's dead. At least, well, not permanently. You might want to go see what that means."

"Have you ever seen such a thing?" Araby asks.

"Maybe once or twice. But it was long ago and far away, as the stories say."

"And Poy."

"Not here. I'm afraid he's escaped you."

"I'll find him."

"I have no doubt." She smiles at him, and her eyes are the start light of a thousand dying stars. He wants to kiss her mouth and taste of it. Wants it with a cold knowing that fills his belly.

"Ereshkigal…"

"Hush, Kir. We will speak again. But not too soon, I'd think. I found this for you. It will make your transference less painful and, I think, less of a necessity."

The goddess throws a bright stone, once entangled into her hair, toward Araby. He grabs it in his insubstantial hands and sees that it's been fashioned like a monocle. He looks through it experimentally, but sees nothing but blackness. The Void. The End of All.

"Out there you'll see Irskalla and its inhabitants better," she says. "Without the need to cross over entirely. It'll be helpful."

"Thank you," Araby says.

"My pleasure. You always are."

When Araby returns, the little one has fallen asleep against Bet. The townsfolk are starting to leave their houses, no longer stifled as the ash winnowed away much of the webs. It's time to go, lest they have to explain themselves. And that's a rule Davis enacted many years ago. No explanations. Just actions. Leave the myths to those cleaning up. They're always inaccurate that way.

"No sign of Poy?" Araby asks.

Bet shakes her head. "Time to go. He must have found a way out we didn't see. Or else is lying low so we don't kill him." She narrows his eyes at him. "You look like shit. We need to get this… her… back."

The spiderling. The Silkbinder. No child, that much is clear. Something else. No wonder Davis wanted her.

But the other one…

The town of Pescadero is ash, and so they leave it behind, removing themselves from the story the way they came, back into the mountain hills and toward Davis's salon.

As Araby looks back down the mountainside to the still smoldering town he thinks, for just a moment, that he sees a bright bird rise from the detritus. Golden, long-necked, with a long tail. But no, perhaps that is just a trick of the setting sun. He holds the cold jewel in his hands, feeling it press into his skin yet never warm to his touch, and wonders of Lai Biyu, the fiery child who did not die. He looks at the spiderling and sighs. No doubt this little soul will have more stories to tell when she awakens.

The phoenix rises from the ashes, testing her wings in the setting sun. She flashes and glimmers, full of joy and merriment. She will revel in this new shape, this new happiness, and then she will rejoin her darker sister. Now that the fire is quenched, she understands the song of her people. She understands the bond they share. She will find her soon. The fires have always come from her, will always come from her. She is the ever-burning, the ever-singing song of flame.

GUARDIAN OF THE GOLDEN GATE

loren rhoads

LOREN RHOADS

Loren Rhoads is the author of a nonfiction guide called *199 Cemeteries to See Before You Die*, as well as a space opera trilogy called *In the Wake of the Templars*, and co-author of a series about a succubus and her angel called *As Above, So Below*. Loren's Alondra stories have appeared in the books *Best New Horror #27*, *Fright Mare: Women Write Horror*, *Sins of the Sirens*, *The Haunted Mansion Project: Year One*, *nEvermore: Tales of Murder, Mystery, and the Macabre*, and more. Spy on her at lorenrhoads.com.

THE STAINED GLASS SUNCATCHERS IN THE WINDOWS AT CURIOS AND CANDLES were dull with fog outside. When Alondra entered the shop, one of the stained-glass mirrors on the wall reflected a bright green eye, another her flame orange braid, a third the curve of her smile.

As the door swung closed behind her, she heard Stella say, "You could ask Alondra. She used to work here."

Stella stood behind the cash register. Facing her was a lanky Asian-American man with straight black hair that kissed the shoulders of his leather motorcycle jacket. He wore a black T-shirt, black jeans, black engineer boots: the standard San Francisco uniform.

"Alondra DeCourval?" he asked. "Wow. I've heard a lot about you."

Alondra wondered if he saw how uncomfortable that made her.

Obviously not. He continued, "You handled that nereid at the aquarium-in-exile."

Alondra noticed heads turning, even if the man didn't. The shop was hopping on this Friday afternoon, full of the regular crowd working up their mojo for the weekend.

"That's not all she's done," Stella added enthusiastically.

Before Stella got rolling on the firestorm in the Sierra Nevadas, Alondra suggested, "Could we talk in the office, Mr. —?"

"Shang." He made a flourish that ended in a bow. "Clement Raymond Bonaventure Shang."

He didn't offer a handshake, which Alondra appreciated. Still, he was one for the grand gesture. Giving away his full name like that, in a room full of wannabe witches with a Friday night ahead of them, showed a cockiness that amused Alondra.

"You know what I'd really like, Miss DeCourval? I'd like to buy you a beer." Once the words left his lips, Shang winced. "I mean, that is, if you drink beer."

"Let me pay for my necklace," Alondra said. "Then I'd like to hear how I might help you."

She walked back to the jewelry. When Stella joined her, Alondra said, "I'd like to see the aquamarine."

While Stella's hands were busy withdrawing the necklace from the twisted black metal display tree, Alondra whispered, "You know this guy?"

"Tink dated him." Stella smoothed a black velvet swatch atop the counter and stretched the necklace across it. The teardrop-shaped stone shimmered, more green than blue.

"Are you setting me up?" Alondra asked.

Stella chuckled. "I don't mess with my friends' personal lives. He said he had a question about elementals, so of course I thought of you. You think it's coincidence you were both in the shop at the same time?"

"No," Alondra said. "Should I take him up on that beer?"

Shang scrutinized a loopy hand-knitted scarf in shades of purple and peacock. His pose revealed the back of his motorcycle jacket, painted with white-feathered wings. He hadn't taken off his sunglasses.

"Go on," Stella encouraged. "Tell him you have dinner plans with me afterward."

Alondra smiled. "Let's go to Phuket. I'm craving red curry vegetables."

"You're so predictable," Stella said affectionately. "Tink had some wild times with him. Fun, but wild. You know Tink." She grinned at Alondra. "Do you really want the necklace? I'll give you the employee discount."

When Shang escorted her out into the fog, the aquamarine felt almost damp in the hollow of Alondra's throat. Aquamarine was a fisherman's stone, protective against danger while sailing or flying over water. It also relaxed the conscious mind's grasp on psychic intuition, Alondra remembered ruefully. To balance it, she should have bought a fossil or heavy gray hematite, something to keep her head out of the clouds.

"That suits your coloring." Shang nodded toward the new pendant. "I'm surprised you didn't already have an aquamarine."

Alondra zipped her leather coat up over the cascade of pendants on her chest. "They're kind of like armor," she said. "A defense for every possibility."

Shang led her up to the corner of Haight Street, past the Thai restaurant where she'd meet Stella later, and down the incline into the Lower Haight neighborhood. Ever since she started visiting San Francisco, this neighborhood had been in transition: stores selling underground noise then trance then techno then hip hop ad infinitum as kids with money flowed in and out.

"Do you live in the City?" Shang asked. "I haven't seen you around."

"I caretake a friend's house near Buena Vista Park, so I drop in now and then. You?"

"I grew up here." He seemed to change the subject. "It's funny: things people who live here never do. Tourists come to San Francisco and go straight to Alcatraz, but people who live here never think to go unless they get visitors. I never walked the Golden Gate Bridge until recently."

Alondra realized, "I've never walked across the bridge either."

"You should do it sometime. On a sunny day."

Alondra wondered what he meant by that.

Shang set a pint of Wyder's raspberry cider on the black-topped table in front of Alondra. He sank onto the barstool opposite. "This is going to sound unbelievably weird."

"I'm open-minded," Alondra encouraged.

"I'm a necromancer."

Apparently he was used to impressing people with that revelation. "Does that work out for you?"

"It's always worked fine. Until now."

He sucked on his Chimay, then pulled out his cellphone. He concentrated over it. Alondra wondered if he was intentionally being rude.

"This is my girlfriend." Shang held out his phone to display a photograph of a dark-haired girl in high Elizabethan finery, a dog collar of pearls around her throat. "She called herself Sophrosyne, but her name was Theresa Campbell."

The tension in Shang's fingers warned Alondra not to reach for the phone. She noticed how he said this "is" his girlfriend, present tense, though her name was in the past.

Anger flared in his dark eyes. "She threw herself off the Golden Gate Bridge a week ago. She wasn't depressed, no more depressed than anyone in San Francisco when the summer fog doesn't break. But she was obsessed with the Bridge. She was working on an album about it with her band. She visited it almost every day. She was trying to 'hear the voice of the Bridge, to hear the song it sings to itself.' Sometimes I went with her. Sometimes other people did. The day she jumped, she went alone."

He tucked his phone back into the heart pocket of his motorcycle jacket. "The coroner wanted me to confirm her identity, so I saw footage from the security cameras. She was just walking, back and forth. She stopped, looked over the edge. Then she pushed herself up on the railing—you know, like a swimmer jumping out of the pool? Like she saw something below her in the water and wanted to get a better look. Then she swung her legs over. There's a little lip outside the railing, where the workers stand while they're painting. It's not very wide. Sophrosyne leaned forward with her hands on the railing behind her. She looked like the figurehead of a ship. She…"

"She didn't slip?"

Shang shook his head. "It wasn't an accident. She looked like a bird going into the water. Have you seen a gull dive after a fish?"

Alondra nodded. Shang gulped his beer miserably.

"They say you're going about seventy-five miles an hour when you hit," he said. "It's like smacking into cement. The only way you might survive is to go in feet first. Even then, the landing jellies your organs and compacts your spine. Most people suffer massive head trauma…"

"Did they recover her body?"

"Yeah. We buried her in Cypress Lawn this morning." Shang lifted his empty bottle. "You want another?"

Alondra looked at her mostly untouched pint of cider. "You go ahead."

While Shang was busy with a barman wearing a septum ring and backward baseball cap, Alondra wondered what she was doing here. Ghosts talked to her more often than she liked; she didn't seek them. She wasn't about to desecrate some girl's grave just because her boyfriend couldn't let go. She wondered if there had been signs of depression Shang hadn't recognized, or if Sophrosyne had broken off the relationship and Shang couldn't accept it. Alondra glanced at the beer clock behind the bar, glad she had plans with Stella.

Shang returned to their table and slumped behind his new bottle.

"You've tried to contact her?" Alondra asked gently.

"Yeah. No answer. Absolutely nothing."

Had that been more devastating than Sophrosyne's death? Magick only worked if you had unshakeable faith in it. For someone as proud as Shang, losing his magick would be as agonizing as impotence.

"I don't do necromancy," Alondra reminded. "How can I help you?"

"I want you to come with me, to the Bridge. I want to do a summoning. I think there is an elemental monster under the water, something that lures suicides. I want you to help me get Sophrosyne back from it. To set her free."

Alondra sipped her cider. "You want a dragonslayer, not a witch."

He made a funny little gesture with his right hand, some kind of "avert" spell. Alondra wondered if Shang knew an actual slayer of dragons.

"I thought you could deal with elementals," Shang growled. "There's a lot of water flooding through the Golden Gate, moving five miles an hour at peak tide. Whatever lives under the bridge would either have to be very big or very strong to hold its position against that. I need a witch who isn't afraid of something powerful."

Alondra wondered why she was insulted. "I don't kill elementals," she explained. "I don't know if they can be killed. Anyway, as I understand it, there's a big difference between an elemental and a monster. If what you're facing is an elemental, it will be difficult to bargain with. We may not share a common language. If it's made a home for itself somewhere as inhospitable as under the Bridge, you're going to have the devil's own time moving it along. And if you're looking to kill a monster, I won't be much help. I'm no warrior."

He downed half the beer. "Please just come with me. I don't know what's under the Bridge. I just know something hurt Sophrosyne. I don't want to face it alone." He struggled to confess, "I'm scared."

"Of what?"

"I deal with dead things. I know what they're capable of. Something that can block me from contacting Sophrosyne...that something is powerful. I might need protection from it."

Alondra responded to his tone, stripped of arrogance. "I'll come with you to see what it is. But if it's some kind of leviathan, you'll need a bigger arsenal than fits in my purse. We'll want to run away really, really fast."

"I ride a Japanese crotch-rocket. Once we're on it, we can outrun just about anything."

Alondra smiled at that. "We'll have to keep it in the circle with us, then. For a quick getaway."

"Okay."

Alondra sipped her cider, for politeness' sake. "I need to run. I've got dinner plans. Did you want to go out tonight?"

"If you're free later, that would be great."

"Pick me up at Café Reverie on Cole before nine?"

"That will give me time to run home and pull some shit together."

"Me, too."

To her surprise, Shang followed her out the door. She'd expected him to stay to finish the alcohol on the table. She'd be much more comfortable on his motorcycle if he didn't drink the afternoon away.

One of these days, she really was going to have to learn to drive.

Stella couldn't wait to hear how the conversation had gone. As their satay arrived, she asked, "Did Clement pick up on you?"

Alondra laughed. "Not yet. I'm not sure he's going to." She switched the conversation around. "Did you know Sophrosyne?"

"Who?"

"Shang's girlfriend."

Stella shook her head, scattering her mane of black curls. "If she does magic, she doesn't shop at Curios."

"He said she jumped off the Golden Gate Bridge."

"That's terrible." Stella's silver-ringed fingers made an avert gesture reminiscent of Shang's. "They say someone leaps off the bridge like every fifteen days. There are so many suicides that the authorities stopped publishing a count. They thought it encouraged copycats. Not that stopping the count has slowed the suicides. Last I heard it was like fifteen hundred people."

That sounded like something Alondra should put an end to, if she could. If twenty-five people a year threw themselves from the Bridge to feed some kind of creature, then it was time for magic to step in. It might be the only thing that could stop the predator, short of a nuclear bomb.

When Clement Raymond Bonaventure Shang came into the café after her, he wore a sword sheathed across his back. Alondra didn't comment on it. His motorcycle was black, of course. He waited to start it until Alondra had strapped on her borrowed helmet. The bike was much quieter than she expected.

Climbing onto it was sort of like mounting a horse. Alondra stepped up onto the peg and swung her leg over. Once seated, she adjusted the sword's sheath so it didn't poke her in the thigh. She discovered the only thing to hold onto was a leather strap across the seat.

"Lean forward and put your hands flat on the gas tank," Shang suggested.

She found that uncomfortable; Shang was too tall and the pillion seat too slanted.

"Try leaning against my back and putting your hands in my pockets."

His right pocket rattled with strange bits of metal that shifted against her fingers. If she'd had her gloves off, she might have been tempted to sort through them, to identify them by touch. She was relieved that her velvet gloves impeded the temptation to snoop.

She predicted Shang would drive like a bat out of hell. Instead, he took things easy as they traveled through town, accelerating gently, not weaving through traffic. By the time they reached the Presidio, the former Army base turned national park that served as a buffer between the City and the Bay, Alondra hadn't feared for her life once.

"Ready for some fun?" he asked over his shoulder.

Alondra snuggled against him and let momentum take over, trusting him since he hadn't frightened her yet. They swung through the curves on the sloping road like flying. Her helmet filled with the most incredible aromas: cypress and eucalyptus, new-mown grass and Bay breeze. She closed her eyes. There was a kind of peace to be found with the ground flowing past, inches from your feet. Clement couldn't have done anything to make her like him more.

He stopped the bike beside old buildings re-purposed from a Coast Guard rescue station to be a visitor center. The Bridge rose not far away, on the other side of a narrow causeway between the headlands and the bay. Clement led her down the exposed straightaway on foot.

The wind had shifted. Although fog had blanketed San Francisco earlier, now it had peeled back and disappeared into the West. Across the water, lights sparkled, delineating the North Bay islands and hills. The bay itself rested. Small black wavelets lapped the broken stones of the breakwater.

At the mouth of the Golden Gate, the bed of the bridge burned amber with sodium-vapor lights. The bridge's span towered twenty-two stories over the currents. Its pillars doubled that height, shadow warriors dimly illuminated except for the crimson lights warning away low-flying planes.

"We used to come down here any time we wanted," Clement said. "I liked the vibe of the big old fort and the Bridge overhead. After 9/11, they started to worry that someone might use the old fort as a staging point to blow up the bridge. Not that it will ever happen, but the FBI got involved in security for a while."

He dodged theatrically into a shadow. Alondra followed suit, feeling silly. Anyone who saw the two of them would assume they were looking for a private place to get romantic. The illusion would hold until they saw the sword slung across Shang's back. Alondra's messenger bag was stocked with a canister of kerosene, waterproof matches, a very sharp white-handled knife, and three kinds of salt, none from a living sea.

"Dammit!" Clement whispered. "There's a Park Service car down by the fort. Can you make it so they don't see us?"

"Probably. But I'm not sure I can hide the bike, or the ritual. Wouldn't it just be easier to make them go elsewhere?"

"Can you do that?"

She fished a match out of her bag and cupped it in her hands, before striking the head hard with her thumbnail. The tiny lucifer blazed bright orange. Using her left hand, Alondra flung the burning match a good distance away. It arced upward, plummeted onto the asphalt, and flared. Clement hissed as a fire broke out in the eucalyptus forest up the hill. The century-old trees went up like torches, shooting sparks into the air.

The park rangers hit their lights and siren and were still accelerating when they passed. Alondra watched them go, then stepped out of the shadows. She twisted the top off her water bottle and poured a circle around the still-burning match. Once the fire was confined, she doused it with a handful of Cheshire salt.

"You're not gonna burn down the Presidio, are you?"

"No. The fire was an illusion. But it will take them a while to figure out that it's gone."

Sirens raced up the hill.

"No time to dawdle," she encouraged.

Clement went back for the motorcycle while Alondra walked on toward the old fort squatting at the bridge's southern anchorage. Fort Point's present incarnation had been finished just before the Civil War to repel Confederate incursions into the Gold Country. Of course, the Confederate navy, such as it was, never came this far west. Fort Point's huge mounted cannons were never fired in anger. The seven-foot-thick brick walls quickly became obsolete as military technology refined explosives. When the Bridge was designed in the 1930s, public outcry rescued the fort from demolition. The architects incorporated an archway over it, adding to the filigree appeal of the huge red icon.

Alondra strode past the four-story walls into the shadows that lay between the fort and the bay. The hum of traffic overhead blended with the sigh of the waves. The eighty-year-old bridge hung midway between the modern mechanical world and the ancient mysteries of tide and wind. She opened herself, trying to sense what awaited them in the water. She felt nothing beyond natural forces. A knot of apprehension unknit in her shoulders.

She pulled the coil of cord from her bag, so she could measure out a circle. While she was busy, Clement reappeared, pushing the motorcycle.

"This is why I don't ride a Harley," Clement said. "The Ninja is better for stealthy getaways *and* it's hella easier to push."

He faced the bike toward the causeway and kicked down its stand as Alondra finished the circle. She'd drawn it with salt, and kerosene, just in case. Clement ornamented it with elaborate chalk sigils that looked half Santerian vévé and half Enochian script. Alondra suspected the necromancer made his symbols up. That made them no less powerful.

Her job was done, until something went catastrophically wrong. Alondra stood out of Clement's way, half listening as he paced the circle with his sword drawn. She didn't want to learn his method for contacting the dead, lest it rise in her thoughts at inopportune times.

Alondra watched the black-and-gold water, unable to tell if the tide was going in or out. The scene was peaceful, despite Clement's increasingly desperate invocation of Sophrosyne. Still, she was along on this project and ought to contribute. "Try calling any ghosts," Alondra suggested. "Let's see if there's anyone else who can give us some answers."

Clement did as directed. The wind shifted. Alondra found herself standing in the stink of whatever moldering garbage the necromancer was burning as incense. Shuddering, she moved upwind, but the smoke followed her. She would find it funny if it weren't so repulsive.

Necromancy is just nasty, she reminded herself. Who wanted to see what their loved ones looked like after they'd been lying in the grave?

Nothing happened on the water. No spirits seemed to be tied to the scene of their deaths. Very strange. Anywhere else in the world that 1500 deeply unhappy people had shuffled off their mortal coils would be teeming with ghosts.

Clement's voice broke under the strain of his summoning. He continued hoarsely, shouting words in no language Alondra recognized.

The temperature dropped. Something responded to the call, but wasn't coming from the water. Alondra shivered inside her leather jacket. She turned to see thousands of shimmering skeletal forms, clad in the remnants of uniforms.

"You can stop now." Her voice rang off the brick walls of the fort. Clement ceased chanting immediately. "They're behind us."

"Jesus!" Clement crowed. "Looks like I cleaned out the whole National Cemetery!"

"Young man," barked one of the spirits, clad in the shadow of a double-breasted jacket with loops of braid strung through its epaulets, "we didn't come here to listen to blasphemy. What is it that you thought was important enough to drag us from our rest?"

"Where are all the people who died jumping from the bridge?" Clement demanded.

A wave passed through the assembled host as each looked up, recognizing for the first time that a bridge towered over them.

"We've come from the post cemetery," several voices shouted.

"I was buried at Fort Yuma."

"I was buried in San Francisco, but there wasn't any bridge then."

More voices shouted the circumstances of their deaths, their funerals, their burials. The sound was thunderous, indecipherable. Alondra clutched her head and commanded, "One of you speak for the rest."

Several wraiths with commanding posture conferred amongst themselves while the army of others watched.

"They're between us and our escape route," Clement noted sotto voce.

"They're just ghosts."

"But there's lots of them."

"Guess you haven't lost the touch."

One of the revenants strode to the edge of Alondra's protective circle. A medallion with a five-pointed star sparkled on his chest. "Major General Frederick Funston, ma'am."

She inclined her head. "Did you know about the bridge in your lifetime, sir?"

"No, ma'am. But I watched them building it after my death. With pride, I might add."

"Have you seen many suicides from it?"

"Yes, ma'am."

"At least fifteen hundred people have jumped to their deaths. Not one of those suicides answered our call tonight. Do you have any idea why that might be?"

"No, ma'am."

Alondra looked to Clement. "Any questions?"

He kicked over the brazier of incense, smothering the charcoal with its own ash. Clement croaked a banishing, but the ghosts seemed content to return to their last posting. They trooped away as silently as they'd come.

Alondra saw a woman amidst the crowd, dressed in a black-ribboned Victorian riding dress. A knot of African-American men wore buckskins. If she'd known anything about American military history, she might have recognized uniforms of conflicts from the Civil War to Vietnam. Instead she saw only thousands of men who'd served their country and were buried apart from their families. Fellow warriors were the only brothers they had left.

Alondra looked up the hill, past the exodus. She hoped the park rangers were still busy hunting her fire. If they saw every ghost in their graveyard streaming back to bed, they'd have nightmares for certain.

Clement splashed water around, washing away his sigils. "All right," he demanded, "what do you need to call up whatever lives under the bridge?"

"Let's be clear: you want to see what's under the bay?"

"Under the bay eating the suicides."

Alondra nodded. Her grasp on Water creatures wasn't as confident as with Air. It was too easy to overdo it with Water and end up with flooding. Clement's motorcycle wasn't fast enough to flee a tsunami.

What she wanted now was not water, but the creatures in it. Specifically, creatures who had eaten jumpers. It would be a matter of appealing to their appetites.

She removed her new aquamarine from around her neck. She wound the chain between her fingers with the stone cupped in her palm. Then she reached out with her other hand and called, hunger to hunger. She'd drunk human blood once, years ago, before Jordan left her to caretake his house. She concentrated on the feel of that hunger, the joy she felt swallowing his blood, taking his energy into her body. Once she reawakened it, the craving quivered in her every cell.

At first it appeared that the ground outside the circle moved. Crabs were crawling over the breakwater. Hundreds of crabs had nibbled the flesh of suicides.

Beyond them, black shapes sliced the surface of the water: dorsal fins of sharks. There were fewer than she expected, but still enough to hint at how many others had fed without lingering in the bay.

Pale globes rose to float just beneath the water's surface. Jellyfish had scavenged what they could reach.

No doubt the snails and starfish were making their laborious way toward her too, answering her call.

"Just wildlife?" Clement rasped, falling to his knees.

"I called everything that had eaten jumpers. Only natural scavengers have come."

"Where is Sophrosyne?" The anguish in his ravaged voice broke her heart.

"I don't know," Alondra said.

Now that his hope vanished, Clement howled. "How can she be gone? Just gone?"

Power surged through him after his master summoning. Alondra wasn't the best person to try to help him ground it, but she was all he had. She approached cautiously, knelt beside him, and offered the comfort of her arms, unsure whether it would be welcome. Clement clutched her, sobbing painfully. All the grief he'd held at bay swamped him.

Clement's power ebbed and flowed erratically, blocked and channeled in strange ways by his emotions. With Alondra's guidance, the energy drove deep spikes through the asphalt into the bedrock below. From there, it arced toward the bay.

The crustaceans scattered. Alondra watched the shark fins vanish. She could do little but hold Clement and wonder at his love for Sophrosyne.

In the bay, Clement's power spun into a vortex, chasing its own tail. Alondra watched storm clouds race toward it from over the East Bay hills. When her gaze fell on the motorcycle, she frowned. Maybe a wet ride home would wash the stink of Clement's incense from her leathers and hair.

The morning dawned with heartrending clarity; the air washed clean by the downpour. Droplets of rain twinkled on every branch across the street in Buena Vista Park. Alondra dressed and made toast, drinking up the last of the peppermint tea as she ate breakfast. Today looked like a perfect day to walk the Bridge.

The MUNI bus dropped her off at a bustling parking lot at the southern end of the span. Tourists clustered around a sample of cable, displaying a bundle of the 27,572 wires that supported the bridge's weight. Alondra climbed the incline past it to a gate that closed the pedestrian walkway at night.

Rusting chain link rose outside the elegant International Orange framework of the bridge, preventing debris from falling onto the old fort below. Alondra passed a bright yellow telephone crowned by a sign: "The consequences of jumping from this bridge are fatal and tragic."

Alondra frowned. Barely an arm's length away, traffic roared by. With a speed limit on the bridge of 45 miles per hour, a pedestrian who slipped between the barriers stood no chance. Death loomed closer than a twenty-story drop.

Around her swirled women in wind-whipped saris, parents with children clasped in their arms, laughing teenagers photographing each other at every vantage point. The crowd moved like a party. Amongst it slunk furtive individuals. Were they simply hurrying across the span, or were they looking for a place to jump?

She found it hard to hold dark thoughts on such a lovely day. The terracotta dome of the Palace of Fine Arts, last remnant of the 1915 Pan-Pacific Exposition, rose just beyond the Presidio. Behind that, San Francisco climbed in ranks of houses topped by faraway Coit Tower. In the distance hung the gray harpstrings of the Bay Bridge, connecting the City with Oakland and Berkeley and all points east.

On Alcatraz Island squatted the crumbling prison. Partially-forested Angel Island looked peaceful now, but once served as the Ellis Island of the West, detaining Chinese immigrants for long months. Rising in grassy waves north of the bridge, the headlands held a decommissioned Nike base, once capable of delivering a nuclear warhead 250 miles. Despite the beauty around her, a legacy of misery and death persisted below the surface. Even San Francisco, city that she loved, had been founded by the Spanish to impose Christianity on the Miwok natives, forcing them to give up their traditions and ranch cattle on their ancestral lands.

She shook her head. Enough trying to depress herself. History was horrific and brutal anywhere you went. Here at least the water shimmered bright blue beneath a crystalline sky.

As she strolled the vermillion span, she found herself alone on the walkway. A sudden silence drew her gaze toward the roadbed. Cars blasted by, pushing the speed limit.

A pure white pigeon stood on the girder below the high-tension cables preventing pedestrians from blundering into traffic. The bird was literally effulgent. His black eye shone, intelligent and aware.

Alondra bent down. "What are you doing here, little friend?"

The luminous bird tilted his head, gauging how to answer. A numbered band braceleted his right ankle: 399. He seemed tame and very healthy, features uncommon in San Francisco's street birds.

Alondra considered holding her hand out to him. He seemed to expect it. Should she lift the pigeon to the railing on the outside edge of the bridge? Surely, he could fly a distance of four feet.

Alondra looked along the pathway. The northern terminus of the bridge lay a fair distance ahead. She could let the pigeon ride on her shoulder, but if he pooped on her blouse, she had miles to go before she could return to Jordan's house and change. She didn't want to shelter a nervous bird in her arms, or in her purse.

Unsure what to do—if anything needed doing—she left the beautiful creature huddling in place. She walked the rest of the way across, used the facilities at the northern parking lot, enjoyed the view.

When she returned to the part of the span, just south of the mid-point, where she'd seen the pigeon, she looked right. Plastered to the asphalt by a bright scarlet stain sprawled bones like drinking straws. A few stray feathers fluttered, as white as anything fallen from heaven. The pigeon had found the courage to leave its shelter. It flew straight into traffic.

Alondra was suddenly, crushingly sad that she hadn't helped the petrified bird.

She dragged back toward the south anchorage. Toward her came a woman with a chromed pendant like a dog tag. As the woman walked, the necklace flickered orange, reflecting the bridge, then blue, reflecting the sky. In between each color, it shone white: pure blank mirror. The hypnotic colors shifted orange, white, blue, white, orange.

Alondra staggered and felt herself going down in slow motion. A rushing, roaring noise filled her head. She listened for words, some kind of entreaty or command. Nothing. Whatever it was had no voice, no intelligence, just cold, empty, mindless hunger.

She lay on the cement walkway, while people buzzed around, trying to help. The understanding she'd reached paralyzed her limbs. Fifteen hundred jumpers in eighty years. Even if it hadn't started out hungry, the strait below had been force-fed a steady diet of bodies over the decades, souls yearning for oblivion. Something wakened, something hungry. The bridge and its chasm formed some kind of entity, one without a consciousness yet. The bridge ate one's courage, then the channel ate one's life.

She could think of no way to combat that, no way to put an end to it. There was no mind with which one could bargain. The only way from keep it from developing sentience would be to stem the flood of willing sacrifices.

Strangers helped her to her feet. Alondra thanked them for their kindness. There was beauty in the world, in people, but you had to want to see it. You had to gravitate toward it. Otherwise, darkness would willingly devour you.

She wondered how to present the realization to Clement. One went into necromancy because one refused to accept that death was the end. Here, at the bridge, death was birthing a new kind of life.

Clement already held a booth in All You Knead when Alondra got off the bus and walked in the door. She waved at Lisa the illustrated woman, her favorite waitress. Lisa called, "The usual?" Alondra nodded and slid into the olive-green booth.

"How was the Bridge today?" Clement asked.

"Hungry." Alondra's smile flickered at Lisa, who slipped a Dr. Brown's cream soda onto the table. Alondra drank a healthy swallow. The sugar steadied her.

She told Clement about the Bridge's appetite and lack of sentience. "I've been turning it over and over," Alondra said. "Until it wakes up, there's no way to communicate with it. And the only way to wake it up is to keep feeding it."

"So we need a disaster," Clement said. "A cataclysmic car crash or a ferry capsizing or something…"

Alondra made her own avert gesture.

"Joking!" he protested.

The calzone Lisa set in front of Alondra steamed. "Want some of this?" Alondra asked Clement. "I'm never able to finish it."

"Sure."

She asked Lisa for a second plate as she sawed through the crust into the tomatoes and black olives and cheese inside. Good solid grounding food, her favorite meal in the world.

"The signs over the hotline phones need to come down." Alondra eased half the calzone onto Clement's plate. "They put the image of suicide into minds that would never consider it otherwise."

Around a steaming mouthful, Clement said, "There's been talk for decades about building a barricade. They can't figure out how to do it so that it doesn't turn into a sail in high winds. The hotline phones and foot patrols are stopgaps."

"They're not working," Alondra pointed out. "That hunger is really seductive, insidious. People would find their way over or around a barrier. Closing the walkway to pedestrians —"

"Which they won't do," Clement interrupted. "Tourists bring in too much money."

"I don't think it would help," Alondra finished. "The hunger would lure people anyway. They'd stop their cars or sailboarders would dump themselves into the water or people would dive from boats."

"What do we do?"

"Not we," Alondra corrected. "You."

"No way."

"I don't live here. I don't have the strength to do the kind of magic long distance that would protect everyone vulnerable to the Bridge. A spell like that will take a lot of power. It needs to be regularly renewed. It has to be done by locals. Natives."

Clement hunched over the calzone. Alondra gratefully wolfed down her own lunch.

After some thought, Clement asked, "Where do I start?"

She folded her aquamarine charm into his hand. "This might help. And go back to Curios and Candles. Talk to my friend Stella. She will be able to hook you up with others who can help you."

He smiled as he tucked the gemstone into his motorcycle jacket. "I've never done anything like this."

"I don't know if anyone has ever done anything like this," Alondra said sympathetically. "But I saw your power last night. People are in good hands now."

MARION DEEDS

1

MAGPIE'S CURSE

MARION DEEDS

After a long career in public service, Marion Deeds retired in 2012 to devote more time to writing. In over thirty years of working with the public in a large bureaucracy, she has enough crazy stories to easily fill an epic fantasy trilogy, only she thinks people would find the work implausible. Deeds likes reading good fantasy, good science fiction and good writing in general. In her own work she loves to explore the junction of the everyday weird and the otherworldly. Deeds lives with her husband in northern California, which she believes is the most beautiful place in the world and she is completely unbiased. She tends several birdfeeders and pays protection to the local gang of squirrels. Her fiction has appeared in *Daily Science Fiction, Podcastle* and *Flash Fiction Online*. She writes reviews and a weekly column for fantasyliterature.com. You can read her blog at deedsandwords.com or find her on Twitter @mariond_d.

EVERYONE IN DUTTON TOWN SPOKE OF THE WIDOW VOLNOVA'S HONEY. ON THE small plot of land out past the bread-loaf rocks, nearly to the sea, the widow raised grapes and vegetables, had some cows and chickens, and kept her bees. She and her daughters dripped the golden ribbons from the combs into small glass jars. The girls sold the sweet syrup on market days.

The widow came from one of the Russian farms to the north but she wasn't Russian herself. The old gossipers, sitting on the hotel porch with their tobacco and their beers, said she was a Kashaya, the tribe that welcomed the Russians when they came to build Krepost Ross. Widow Volnova wore her husband's eight-pointed Russian cross of rosy gold around her neck, together with an oblong of abalone shell. Her girls, Ioanna and Katya, nearly twenty now, were twins, although they looked nothing alike.

She had purchased the land with the money Yevgeny Vasilovich Volnov left her when he died. While he worked with the winemaker for Krepost Ross, he fell in love not only with her but with the land itself. He stayed behind when the Russians sold their settlement. In 1850, barely one month after California had joined the Union, he drove a caravan of grapes to Sutter's Fort. There he fell ill and died. The girls were nine, old enough to remember his warm hands, his smile, and his stories about Ivan Tsaravitch and Elena the Wise.

In the summer of 1861, the Widow Volnova was moving carefully. She struggled to catch her breath at times. Her fingers were gnarled and often ached. Ioanna watched over the hives and took on the cheese-making.

The last market day of August the girls loaded up their wagon with the riches of their farm. There were herbs, carrots, potatoes, bags of soft cheese, honey in jars and pieces of honeycomb. Katya climbed up onto the wagon and took the reins, while Ioanna walked alongside, her eyes nearly closed. Ioanna never cared to ride, preferring to feel the earth beneath her feet.

They traveled the narrow trail through the valley. The day was warm and a light haze covered the blue sky. The meadows had turned golden brown months before. Ioanna hummed softly as they walked and Katya whistled a song she had heard from a fisherman the week before. Their small house dwindled behind them until it was out of sight.

Ioanna stopped and turned. Katya halted the mare and tipped her head, looking a question at her sister.

"Did you hear that?"

Katya listened. A bird chattered from across the silent valley. "It's just a crow," she said, but Ioanna shook her head.

"Not a crow."

"A jay then."

"Nor a jay."

They walked on, the mare swishing her tail now and then. The air smelled of sweet drying grasses. They reached the bread loaf rocks, smoothed rectangles of stone that pushed up out of the earth with no warning. Each was big enough for ten people to dance on, and people had. Up close, they did not look quite so smooth. Their gray surface was pitted, and in places the rock folded and looped back on itself making shapes that looked like a sleeping maiden, or a stag's head, or a leaping fish. Ioanna came here often. Once she had poked her fingers inside a waterhole and found a scrap of seashell.

Ioanna often wandered, climbing up to sit in the valley's oak trees, or lying in the coarse grass. Katya preferred to walk west, slipping out at night to make the trek to the ocean, wading barefoot in the cold briny foam and watching the moon draw lines on the waves.

Ioanna stopped again and sniffed. "Do you smell that?"

Katya raised her head and sniffed the air. "Fruit?" She sniffed again. "Peaches?" although that seemed impossible.

Ioanna nodded. "And honey."

"It's our own honey," Katya said.

"It's not," Ioanna said.

Katya chirruped to the horse and they moved on. Ioanna kept one hand on the edge of the wagon, her other hand twined into her long skirt. She didn't speak again.

Wagons and tables made of sawhorses and planks lined the Dutton Town road. People rode up from the San Francisco Bay to sell fish and clams, and to buy potatoes, cheese, and rye. Ioanna and Katya sold their cheese and honey quickly. Katya wandered around, inspecting other tables. She sensed a man's gaze on her and turned, but saw no one. She heard a laugh, low and cackling, from the other side of the Church of the Assumption. All the way around it Katya walked, and still saw no one. She shivered and looked over her shoulder as she hurried back toward her sister, who was loading her purchases of cornmeal and salted fish into the cart. Motion at the edge of Katya's vision distracted her. A black bird with a white belly and a long black tail swooped past, disappearing behind the covered porch of the hotel.

It was late afternoon when they made their way back. The white haze had grown thicker and grayer through the day, and a stinging breeze yanked at their blouses and hair. "Did you hear that?" Kayta said, drawing rein and slowing the mare's progress.

"What?"

"Someone laughing."

Ioanna listened, but shook her head.

They kept on their way until Ioanna put her hand on the mare's bridle. With her other hand, she pointed. "What is that?"

Katya looked west. Outlined in gold from the westerly sun, a building stood on one of the hills. It looked like a barn, with a steeply pitched roof and eaves that poked out from the ridge of the roof like the curve of a fishhook. "How can that be?" Kayta said. Their path took them right past that hill, and there had been no barn that morning.

"Some … magic?" Ioanna said. Their mother spoke of magic. Their father had, too. He shared tales from his homeland, acting out the parts—the talking horse, the bear, the treacherous raven or magpie, the hut on chicken legs and the old woman inside. The girls remembered laughing, shrieking in mock fear.

Their mother's tales were different. Mostly they weren't tales at all, but comments or observations; what the crows were saying to each other, or why the girls should show respect to a coyote. The girls did not quite know what to make of these things, but a barn sprouting up in mere hours, with no builders, seemed magical indeed.

They stopped, looking at each other. They could turn off the regular track, veering north, skirt the hill and arrive home much later. An unspoken decision passed between them, and Katya clucked the mare forward. They continued on their regular way.

As they drew closer to the bread loaf rocks part of their mystery was answered, for the barn was no barn at all, simply a wagon parked on the rise above the old stones. The empty traces rested on the ground, and the wagon's timbers were the same color as the dried grasses around it. The mare snorted and pinned back her ears. The girls looked around but saw no animal to draw the wagon—no horse, no pony, not even a goat.

Music whispered around them, finger cymbals and a sweet hooting like a flute. Katya tapped her foot on the board of the wagon as she looked around for the musicians, for surely so many players could not fit in the small wagon.

"Hurry on," Ioanna said, tugging on the mare's reins.

"How many players are there?" Kayta said, for now she heard a fiddle and a guitar carrying the melody.

"What players?"

"The music."

"I don't hear music," Ioanna said.

Katya jumped down from the seat and took a step or two toward the wagon.

"Katya! Hurry on," Ioanna said.

Katya stood, perplexed. She turned and climbed back up onto the seat. The mare tossed her head and broke into a trot, Ioanna running at her side.

They passed the bread loaf rocks and the mare shied suddenly, jarring the cart. A plank on two sawhorses blocked the track, and a man stood behind it.

Seeing them, he swept them an elaborate bow. The sun gleamed off the edges of the platters, copper and bronze and silver, that lined the plank.

"Girls," he said, smiling, "will you try my wares?"

He wore black trousers and an old-fashioned black jacket, like the one their father wore in the daguerreotype they had of him. The stranger's shirt was white, although a closer glance showed it yellowed at the throat and streaked with gray down the front. He had a round face with wide cheekbones, a long nose and a curling, closed-lipped smile.

"The finest fruits from distant lands. Will you taste? I have crisp apples, cherries plump and purple, plucked at dawn before the earliest bird could peck them. I have grapes and peaches."

"Cherry season is long past," Katya said, tugging on the reins. The horse fretted, tossing her head, and Ioanna stroked her and whispered soothingly to her. She led the horse around the planks, but the black-and-white man followed her, holding out a copper platter.

"Try my grapes then."

"Grapes need four more weeks of sun," Ioanna said, keeping the horse between herself and the man.

"Not everywhere in the world, daughter of earth," the man said. The black tails of his coat flicked out behind him.

"We must not tarry," Ioanna said. The wagon jolted a bit as it rounded the obstruction, and then they were back on the track.

"Truly? Come, try the last of the raspberries, or the first of the blackberries. Try one. You won't regret it."

"We have nothing to barter," Ioanna said.

"I'll be the judge of that," the black and white man said, and he swooped around the mare until he was at Ioanna's side.

"Ioanna, climb up here with me," Katya said.

He looked up at Katya and his dark eyes glittered. "You are nothing of the earth, are you?" he said. He looked back at her sister, clinging to the bridle and striding resolutely along the track.

"Come," he said. "One apricot? One fig?"

Ioanna shook her head.

"A drop of honey? I offer the sweetest, richest honey you have ever tasted. The most delicate, flavored with spices from the nectars of flowers you have never seen."

Ioanna stopped. "We have the finest honey from San Francisco to Eureka," she said. "There is none sweeter, more delicate, more rich."

"Such fierce loyalty!" he said. "But you do not speak from knowledge. Try mine, and set the matter to rest."

Ioanna clenched her fists and the mare snorted, tossing her head and mouthing the bit. Katya said, "Ioanna, climb up here with me. We must ride on."

"My mother's honey is the finest," Ioanna said.

The black and white man shrugged and held out a wedge of honeycomb. "One drop, just to make the test."

Before Katya could speak again, Ioanna reached out. The black and white man let a golden drop of honey fall onto her outstretched finger. Sunlight sliding under the gray haze pierced the gold and for a moment Ioanna and Katya saw the valley, the cart and the black and white man captured in an upside down reflection. The spear of golden light blinded Katya for a moment, and then Ioanna raised her hand to her lips, and her tongue swiped the golden dome off her fingertip. She swallowed. A strange look passed over her face like a flicker of light.

"Rich, yes," she said. "Delicate, yes. But it has a bitter aftertaste. The honey our bees provide is better."

The man's face went still, and then he smiled. "Loyalty," he said. "I admire that."

She turned away from him and clambered up onto the cart next to her sister. Katya cried "Hyah!" and shook the reins, and the mare broke into a trot, carrying them away. Ioanna sat, trembling, her fists buried in her skirts.

"I saw a strange bird today," Katya said, "at the market. It had a long black tail and a white breast, like his clothes."

"A magpie," Ioanna said. "They don't live around here. They're from the east."

"How does he pull a wagon? Where is his horse?"

Ioanna shook her head without answering.

They did not speak again until they reached home. Their house and barn sat on an apron of land between two hills. The rows of grapes spread a sweet perfume as they drove up to the barn. As she always did this time of year, Ioanna tipped back her head to breathe in their fragrance, but she began to cough.

Ioanna unharnessed the mare, brushed her and gave her water. As the sun went down, the two of them joined their mother at the small table close to the eastern windows and sipped hot soup.

"We met a strange man on the road," Kayta said. "He had a wagon but no horse, and music but no players, and he tried to get us to try his fruit."

Their mother leaned back in her chair, rubbing her knobby fingers. "What did he look like, this man? Was he one of the farmers?"

Ioanna shook her head. "He wore an old-fashioned black coat and a white shirt, and he had black hair and black eyes. He was strange."

"I heard him laugh," Katya said. "That is, I heard a bird laugh. A magpie."

"Magpies," their mother said. "They are not from here. They live in the great eastern valley. Your father always said they were greedy and not to be trusted. Perhaps the magpie heard something of us, our honey, our cheese."

"He had ripe fruit, fruit long out of season, or some that would not have ripened yet," Ioanna said. "He called me a daughter of earth."

"I suppose we are all sons and daughters of earth," their mother said.

"He said I was nothing of the earth," Katya said.

Their mother smiled. "Did that sting you, Ekaterina?"

"No, Mother. I thought it was strange."

"Well, as long as you ate nothing he offered, all should be well." She looked at her daughters' faces. "You did not eat what he offered, did you?"

Ioanna coughed. "Just a drop of honey," she said. "He said his honey was richer and sweeter than ours. I tried it to test it. Nothing more."

"I wish you hadn't," their mother said. "But, one drop? Well, we may be all right." But her dark eyes grew shadowed.

That night Katya slept badly, and woke from dreams of skirling music, thinking that she heard her mother weeping. When she sat up, she found her sister sitting at the foot of the bed they shared. Ioanna rocked back and forth, and she was shivering. "He calls me," she said.

Katya embraced her. "He cannot have you."

The next night the music in her dreams grew sharp and dangerous. She woke and went to the window. A man stood in the yard, staring up. Her mother came out of the house. She stood, confronting the man. He gave her a mocking bow and put his fingers to his lips. He blew her mother a kiss. A moment later he was gone, although Katya did not see where he went. She heard her mother come back inside. Katya lay down next to her sister and fell into a doze, awakened an hour later by the sound of her mother coughing.

As the days went by their mother grew weaker, and Ioanna did too. They coughed, early in the morning and in the late afternoons. One night Katya woke to find Ioanna at the window, and when she joined her there, Katya saw a figure standing in the yard, silvered by a half moon. She pulled her sister away.

Their mother could only move about for a few hours a day. Ioanna too grew weaker and weaker. If she drew water in the morning, she would cough for an hour. She still milked the cows, but the task that had taken only a few hours now lasted until nearly noon, and Katya took over the cheese-making. Ioanna twisted and thrashed in their bed until Katya moved onto the floor. And each day their mother moved more slowly, more weakly.

One night Katya woke to a sense of dread. She sat up. The rumpled bed was empty. Outside, her sister spoke to a shadow. Katya hurried down the steep stairs from their loft. She nearly stumbled over Ioanna, who crouched by the threshold, her head resting on folded arms.

"What did he say to you?" Katya said.

Ioanna shook her head without looking up. "If I don't go with him Mother and I will die, and the farm will die. My spirit is enslaved to him. If I go now, Katya, then you and Mother, and the land, will be spared."

"He lies," Katya said. "We will find a way to free you from this spell. I promise it."

"I would not want my spirit to be his servant," Ioanna said. "But I can't bear the thought of causing more suffering." She coughed for several minutes and then stopped, shuddering. "Already the hens have stopped laying. I tasted the grapes yesterday and they have grown no sweeter. I should go with him, Katya. I was foolish and proud, and the punishment should be only mine." She raised her head.

"You will not go," Katya said. She pulled her sister to her feet. "We will find a way to defeat him."

In September, Katya did not hitch up the wagon and drive to market, for she was needed to tend the house. Their mother grew weaker, and lay in her bed bundled in quilts and blankets. One night when Ioanna thrashed and tossed in their bed, Katya went down the ladder and stepped out into the silvery night, where the black and white man waited.

"You are not the one I want," he said. "I care nothing for things from the ocean. It is another morsel I require."

"You shall not have my sister," Katya said.

"She took my goods," he said. "She owes me."

"She took no goods," Katya said. "Only a taste you forced on her."

"Forced? I forced nothing."

"You tricked her."

"Tricked or not, I am owed payment," he said, and walked into the shadows. She heard the low cackle of laughter following him into the darkness.

Ioanna's skin grew pale and dry, with shadows under her eyes. They got no eggs from the hens. Katya brought her mother oatmeal one morning and said, "Mother, do you know of a way to defeat this creature?"

Her mother sighed. Her hands shook as she reached for the bowl, and Katya held it for her. "You must go to the ocean, Ekaterina. You must call on my ancestors."

"Twice now he has called me a thing not of earth, of the ocean. What does that mean?"

"It means he knows the truth of my origin, I suppose," her mother said. The spoon wobbled as she carried it to her lips.

"The otter children?" Katya said. "That's only a story."

Her mother shook her head.

"Then what are you? What are we, that the magpie hates us so?"

Her mother pushed aside the bowl and leaned back against her pillow. She closed her eyes. "The townfolk think I am Kashaya," she said, "but I am not. My people are older than the Kashaya, although we lived next to them and learned their speech."

"Mother, I know this tale," Katya said, for they had heard it many times, next to the hearth, after their father's tales. Her mother continued as if she had not heard.

"Long ago, a sickness came to my people's village. None knew where it came from; perhaps from a trading party, perhaps carried by a bird or a seal, perhaps from the ocean itself. One by one all took ill, and one by one they died. The last people alive were a young mother and her two babies, born at the same birth, like you and your sister; a boy and a girl. The mother felt the fever growing in her veins but her children were strong and healthy. She could not bear the thought of them dying alone and untended, so she wrapped them in blankets and made her way down to the sea. She lay them carefully in one of her baskets, and set it on the water. She begged the ocean to care for her children. Then she fell to the sand and died.

"The water carried the babies out to the edges of land that surrounded the cove, and the waves grew stronger, spilling into the basket. They would have drowned, but a mother otter who had lost her pup to a shark found them. She and the otter clan raised both children until they were grown. They returned to the land, and learned the speech of humans, although they also knew the language of the sea. They married and had children of their own, but the sea, and the otters, have always remembered our bond."

She stopped, panting. Katya held her hand.

"When Ioanna was born," her mother said, "I saw your father in her face. She has his eyes, his smile, his gentleness with animals and his love of growing things. And moments later, when you were born, I saw in your dark eyes the vastness of the ocean. You are *my* child. What has been done to Ioanna…if we do not break the magpie's curse, this family will end. He must not take your sister, and you must not let him trick you into going with him yourself."

"How do we best him?" Katya whispered.

Her mother shook her head restively. "You must go to the ocean, Ekaterina. You must seek the answer yourself."

She took no more to eat that morning, accepting only a cup of water from Ioanna. Later, when Katya came in from watering the cows, she heard her sister weeping and found her kneeling at her mother's side. Her mother did not draw breath.

They kept a vigil at her side that night. When morning came, as she had asked of them, they bathed her body and dressed her in her finest gown, with her favorite lace mantle. They left the gold wedding band on her finger, and buried her on the west hill, looking toward the ocean. Ioanna coughed and shivered as she helped dig the grave. Katya took the eight-pointed cross and the abalone shell from her mother's body. The shell she kept herself, and Ioanna hung the cross on its silk ribbon about her own neck. The girls knelt, weeping, but soon their tears stopped and as the sun lowered they consoled themselves with tales of their mother, and what they could remember of their father.

That night the house was quiet. Ioanna ate little, and went to sleep, not in the loft, but at the end of their mother's bed. Katya sat in the kitchen, thinking about her mother's tale and the many others she had told them over the years. She thought of her father and his love of growing things, his joy in the vineyard, and how Ioanna shared that joy. She thought of the otters, and the rising waves. In all her walks along the shore, she had never seen an otter.

Her father's tales had only been tales, but her mother had spoken as if there were truth in the words, a bond between the creatures of the ocean and Katya and her sister.

The fire died and the house grew dark. Ioanna slept peacefully. Katya sat in the darkness, thinking. Outside an owl hooted twice. Ioanna moaned and began to cough in her sleep.

Katya folded her arms around herself. She loved the sea, but this farm, the mare and the grapes, the soothing hum of the bees in their hives, was her home, and she could not endure the thought of the land withering and dying too. Perhaps the story of the otter children was just a tale, but Katya knew she must do something.

She stood and slipped out the back. The moon was thin and the way was rough, but she had walked it many times, and needed no lantern. Soon the murmur of the surf and the smell of brine guided her.

Dark brown rocks broke up the gray sand of the beach. She left her shoes in the last stretch of grass and walked barefooted toward the water. She sensed it rather than saw it, for only thin lines of moonlight glinted on its rippling surface. Icy water foamed over her feet as she waded in. The wet sand shifted. She stepped onto the brown rocks, sliding over kelp that rubbed her feet like velvet. The water rose up, soaking her skirt, pulling her down. She closed her eyes, listened to the whisper of the surf and slipped down under the water.

The ocean boomed like a drum in her ears, and she asked her question and waited for an answer. Soon her lungs burned and pressed, and she rose to the surface, gasping for air. No answer came to her, and despair washed over her like the sea foam.

When she had caught her breath, she sank below the surface again. She could not feel her toes, and she could barely move her fingers. Darkness filled her vision. She thought of the otter children, babies huddled in a basket, as the cold waves rocked it, lapped at its edges. And then an otter came. It studied her with its dark eyes. Its clawed paw touched her hand. At first, Katya did not know whether she was dreaming. Then the thoughts became clear. She surfaced and kicked out for larger rocks, farther out in the dark water. The rush of the surf filled her ears. Clinging to the slick ribbons of seaweed, she filled her lungs with air and plunged again into the blackness, using her numb fingers to trace the edges of the rock. Soon her fingers slid over a smoother, pebbled surface. Katya pressed her feet against the rock and cupped her hand over the arch of a shell. Water pulsed against her fingers. She gripped the shell and pulled it free in one tug, before the snail inside could tighten its grip on the rock. She kicked up. Her head broke the surface. One-handed, the shell clutched against her chest, she swam for shore.

Katya filled her skirt with seaweed and wrapped the shell into it. She did not stop for her shoes, and her feet were bruised by the time she came into the house, hoping that she was not too late, that her sister still lived.

Ioanna sat up, bleary-eyed, and staring. "Are you a ghost?"

"I am alive," Katya said. "And I have part of our answer, Ioanna."

"Tell me."

"I can free your spirit from the magpie's curse. Our ancestors will help us. But I fear… Ioanna, there is a chance you will lose your life in the doing of it."

Ioanna stared at her sister. "My spirit will be free of him?"

"I promise it."

"And the curse will not remain on our land?"

"The land will be free."

"Then I will take that risk gladly."

"Come then. We will go to the bread loaf rocks, and we will call the magpie."

They did not stop to harness the mare. Katya pulled on a pair of her mother's boots and they hurried to the rocks that glinted like the ocean in the darkness. When she stood upon the flat rocks, Ioanna said, "Magpie! We've come to bargain."

A yellow light flared in the grasses at the foot of the stones. "Have you come to join me, child of earth?"

Katya spoke. "If I give you a morsel, a taste, more succulent, more tender and more sweet than any you have tasted, will you free my sister?"

The black and white man laughed. "I know all the fruits, daughter of the ocean. I know all the berries. I travel this world seeking the tasty treasures of the earth. I magick up the best and sweetest pleasures. You can offer me nothing."

"Then you need not fear the wager," Ioanna said.

The man laughed and leaped, swooping up onto the rocks next to them. He smiled, and in the flickering light the smile looked cruel. "Very well," he said. "Let me taste this morsel. If it is the finest thing I have ever tasted, you are free."

Katya knelt on the rocks. She set down the cradle-shaped shell, and with the oblong piece her mother had always worn, she sliced away a bit of pale dawn-colored flesh. She held it out and the man snatched it. He brought it to his nose and sniffed.

"I do not care for things from the sea." He raised his eyebrows and nipped at it anyway. The girls waited while he chewed.

"Sweet, yes," he said. He chewed some more. "Tender, but with a spring in the bite. Not bitter, not salty. Rich." He held out his hand. "Another."

Katya sliced another strip from the abalone and handed it to him. He chewed slowly, savoring, and held out his hand again. "Another."

Gradually, Katya fed him the entire abalone. As he swallowed the last bit, she reached for her sister's hand and scored it with the edge of the shell their mother had worn. Before the magpie could notice, she struck her own fingertips as well, and their blood dripped onto the stones, mingling there.

"A rare treat," the magpie said. "Mortals would find this delicious. I find it so myself... yet not the sweetest, or most tender I've ever tasted. Your sister is mine."

"You will not take my sister," Katya said. "The ocean will save us."

He threw back his head and gave a chattering laugh. "Foolish! We are miles from the water! Come, daughter of earth."

"You knew the treat my sister offered came from the sea," Ioanna said. "You were confident that you would not like it."

"Come now. Let us not tarry."

"But you ate all of it."

"All of it," Katya said.

"'Another,' you said. And 'another,' until you ate it all. You could not stop, because it was the finest thing you've tasted. You have lied. You must keep your bargain."

The man shrieked. Feathers sprouted through his hair. His nose grew sharp and dark, and he rose into the air, slashing at them with his beak and talons. His forked tail flailed them. Katya and Ioanna fell down onto the rocks. Katya called out the words the ocean had given her, and around them water, tasting the bloodline of the otter children, rose in a great swirl, rushing up out of stones that had grown at the bottom of the sea. The magpie screamed again in anger and beat its wings, but the water flowed over it, drenching it, and in the rising water the silken, gleaming bodies of the otters flashed, round and round the two girls. Ioanna alone crouched in a pillar of open air, as Katya was swept along with her ancestors, darting and slipping through the welcome waves. The magpie thrashed, but the otters surrounded it, clutching it in their paws, drawing it toward their whiskered mouths. In moments there was no sign of the bird or of the black and white man.

Water rose around Ioanna now, spilling up over her chest. She pressed her bloodied hand flat against the rocks. With the other she clutched the eight-pointed cross her father had given her mother. She could see Katya whirling past her, as if at a sheet of glass, and with the hand that held the cross she reached out. The water rose above her lips, forcing them open, flooding her mouth and throat with salt, and then above her nose, but she did not waver, and soon her sister's hand clutched hers.

The girls fell and lay, sodden and shivering, on the dripping bread loaf rocks. Ioanna opened her mouth to speak and coughed instead, spewing out sea water. Again and again she retched, until the water was gone, and she coughed up one last thing; a bead of golden honey, with a tiny feather trapped at its center.

The sun was rising as they walked back. Ioanna went first to milk the cows, even before she changed into drier clothes.

On market day they sold their finest cheese and honey. When a wine-maker came to test their fruit for purchase, he brought his son. He and Ioanna shared a love of the earth and the vineyards, and soon they were married in the Church of the Assumption.

Katya married a fisherman who berthed his boat at Rumiantsev Bay, which many now called Great Bodega Point. It was said that when she went out with him on his boat, he had the best catches in the fleet. It was said, too, that on nights of the waning moon, Katya swam in the bay, although it was too cold for any human to survive. Both women grew prosperous and soon were happy mothers. Kayta came to the farm always on the day of their mother's death and the two sisters would spend the day at her grave. At nightfall, they would take a bottle of wine and a wedge of honeycomb and walk to the bread loaf rocks, remembering their ancestors.

Magpies are common birds, seen up and down California's central valley, but never since has once been seen near Dutton Town.

LAURA ANNE GILMAN

Laura Anne Gilman is the author of more than twenty novels, including the Nebula award-nominated The Vineart War trilogy. Her newest project is the Devil's West series from Saga Press/ Simon & Schuster, beginning with 2015's Endeavor award-nominated Locus-bestseller *Silver on the Road*, and continuing with 2017's *The Cold Eye*. She has also dipped her pen into the mystery field as well, writing as L.A. Kornetsky (*Collared, Fixed, Doghouse*, and *Clawed*). A member of the writers' digital co-op Book View Cafe, she continues to write and sell short fiction in a variety of genres, including her new story collection, Darkly Human.

WORK HAD BEEN SHIT. THEY'D BEEN RUNNING AT WHAT SEEMED LIKE NONSTOP fever since December, and the piles of casework didn't seem to be going down any. Lee had been the one to decide that taking a day or two off wasn't going to end the world, and if they were very lucky, maybe an eager young thing would lay claim to a file or two while they were gone.

Josh had been the one to decide their destination. "Wineries. A couple of big ones, a couple of the smaller ones. Like real tourists. I'll even wear a Hawaiian shirt."

"No," Sally had said firmly. "You won't."

They'd left mid-day on Monday, beating the worst of the traffic out of San Francisco, and started fresh Tuesday morning.

They'd been to three wineries that morning, two of the big ones, then going off the main road to a smaller one, just the way Josh had planned. The larger ones had been flashy and crowded, even mid-week, but the smaller one was more to Sally's liking: cozy, laid back, and the only other people in the tasting room had been an older couple, clearly regulars, the guy behind the counter, who turned out to be the wine-maker, and his dog, an aging but friendly collie mix.

When they'd finished their tasting, the wine-maker sold them a bottle and opened it for them, sending them off to the open field behind the tasting room, where there was a picnic table and a set of old tire swings.

They ignored the table, spreading a blanket from the car out on the summer-dry grass. Lee pulled a cooler out of the back, with sandwiches the B&B owner had made that morning. Plastic wine glasses for the wine, a bag of potato chips and a tupperware container of sugar cookies to finish.

Sally flopped down on her back, one arm flung over her face to block the sun, and groaned. "Why did I think cookies would be a good idea?"

"Cookies are always a good idea. It's multiples of cookies that you have to watch out for." Lee brushed the crumbs off Sally's lips, then sprinkled her face with a few drops of wine from the dregs in her glass.

"Fuck you."

"Ladies, ladies." Josh had been examining the bottle, now empty, reading the smaller print on the label as though the winemaker hadn't explained it all to them already. "Did you know that Char-"

Lee flicked the rest of her glass at him. "No more facts! God, can't you just enjoy the wine, without having to analyze it to death? It's *booze*."

"It's art," Josh said, wiping the spray off his face, and looking sternly at her. "And for what we're paying for it, it should be appreciated like art."

"Guys." Sally still had one arm over her face, but her other was waving lazily in their direction. "Shut up, okay? I swear to god, we're only a day into this trip and I want to kill both of you, separately and together."

"I think we both wanted to kill you last week, over the Bannon depositions, so seems fair," Josh said, and Lee nodded. "Totally legit."

"Fuck you both," Sally said amicably, hoisting herself to an upright position. ""I'm gonna stretch my legs, get some fresh air before we get back in the car. Try not to say anything stupid until I can get back and mock you."

The other wineries they'd been to had been huge, manicured; sweeping lawns leading to elegant tasting rooms, backing up acres and acres of vines that you could look at, but only from a distance, like they were under glass in a museum. This place, the only grassy area was where Lee and Josh were sprawled, barely larger than the back yard she'd grown up playing in, and the tasting room had been a converted barn, for god's sake, complete with an old tractor still in one corner.

But the vineyards were right there, only a wooden fence keeping people from walking into them. The fence had a gate that swung open easily at a touch, almost as though it were inviting her in.

The gate stayed open behind her as she walked down the wide dirt trail between rows of vines. The vines were shorter than she'd expected, green branches extending out as though to rest on each others's shoulders, the fruit hanging low and green—she supposed the grapes weren't ripe yet, they'd been told harvest wouldn't be until mid-August at the very earliest, and it was only late June. She was tempted to reach out and pick one, just to taste it, to see if it was different from the grapes they'd been served at the B&B the night before, with cheese and crackers, but she kept her hands at her side. She was already trespassing, sort of. She wasn't sure if picking fruit would be theft, or maybe shoplifting.

But that didn't mean she had to stay on the center path, did it? She hesitated, looking back to where the gate and fence were still in clear view, and took a sharp left, moving between the rows. The ground was softer underfoot, and she stumbled occasionally, having to keep an eye on where she was going. The vines here were taller, too: nearly to her shoulder, the posts they were twined around older and more weathered.

"Hey there," she said, reaching out to a leaf in passing, watching it flutter under her touch. Josh had been right about spending too much time in the office. Just the three of them, no deadlines, no stress, lots of wine and good food and sunlight.

So far, so good. But sometimes a girl needed some time on her own. To breathe.

Not that she didn't love them, she totally did. But they were both a bit much. Extroverts to the bone, and she…wasn't.

"Like you," she told the vines. "Hanging onto each other, yeah, but you've each got your own post to grow on."

"Vines dig deep," a voice said, and she yelped, managing to turn to face the speaker without knocking into a vine or falling on her ass, somehow.

The man behind her looked harmless, as much as a stranger sneaking up behind you in an otherwise deserted vineyard could be harmless. He wasn't old, she decided, but he gave the vibe of being ancient: his face was sun-browned and lined around the mouth and eyes, brown eyes sunk deep over cheekbones, squinting even though the sun wasn't in his eyes. His hair was mostly hidden under a flat cap, the kind her dad used to call a newsies cap, she thought. Her gaze slipped down, taking in the shirt—linen, or really good cotton weave—and suspenders attached to the waist of loose, tan pants. He looked like he belonged in a yachting ad or something, not a vineyard, except for the scuffed workbooks she could see peeking out from under his cuffs.

"I beg your pardon?"

He grinned at her, showing off remarkably stained teeth. "The vines dig deep. They're social in the summertime, when everyone's around, but they do most of their thinking in the winter, when everyone's gone, and it's just them and their thoughts."

She licked her lips, thinking about it. "Huh. Okay." On impulse, she offered her hand. "Sally. My friends and I were visiting the tasting room, I'm sorry if I wandered where I wasn't supposed to be… There wasn't a no trespassing sign?"

She waited for him to explain where she'd missed it, to guide her back like an errant, truant child. Instead, he just shook his head, looking out over the rows of vines.

"They don't get many folk visiting, these days."

She started to object—the tasting room had been quiet, sure, but hardly abandoned—when she followed his gaze and realized he meant the vines, not the winery.

"Well, you're here. Let me show you around."

He must be the vineyard manager, she decided, following him down the row, the neat lines turning into more of a tangle, the trunks thicker and more gnarled, the vines less neatly-trimmed.

"It looks different, here," she ventured, when he didn't seem inclined to speak. "Are they different kinds of grapes?"

"Same varietal—Zinfandel. Just older. This section was originally planted in 1892,"

She stumbled again, this time in shock. "I'm sorry, did you say *eighteen ninety-two?*"

"I did, yep." He turned just enough to grin at her, enthusiasm making him look much younger. "There've been vineyards in this region since the 1870's, thereabouts." His expression shifted a little, the enthusiasm tempered by a shadow. "Over a hundred and forty wineries, before the phyllox came in and rotted half the vines, and then Prohibition came down and tried to kill it all."

Phyllox—Josh had been talking about that. A virus or something that killed the original vines, and they had to graft new ones to save them or something. Prohibition—

"The guy at the tasting room said some of the vineyards survived by making communion wine?"

"Some. Not many. The Feds got wise to that dodge, pretty quick. Nowhere near *that* many devout Christians in America, not even back then."

She laughed, and reached down to touch the rough texture of a trunk as they passed, feeling it scrape across her fingertips. She couldn't remember ever having touched anything that old, before. Maybe furniture, but furniture didn't have that same sense of... living.

"We sold bricks, concentrated juice, for folk wanting to make their own at home, which was still legal," her guide went on, "or, more likely, passed on to a clever bootlegger, but it was a risk. The law said we'd be culpable if anyone used the juice to make wine, so we sold the bricks wrapped with clear instructions on how *not* to turn the juice into wine."

She thought he sounded as proud as if he'd thought of that dodge himself, and found herself grinning in turn. "Speaking as a lawyer," she said, "that was very well done, if not something I could officially advocate for my clients."

His smile faded, as he reached up to tuck a wayward vine back into place. "Most of the vineyards couldn't take the risk. Vines were pulled up, burned out. They planted over with pear trees, or apple orchards."

He gestured for her to pass him, and she did so cautiously, catching her breath as she exited on the top of a rise, a narrow dirt road leading to what looked like a stone hut a few yards away.

She turned in a circle, taking in the view. Beyond the hut, there was nothing but green-topped vines and brown posts for acres, it seemed like, as though they were alone in a sea of vines. Even the dirt road seemed to dead-end into a row of vines, rather than leading back to.

She frowned. Shouldn't she be able to see the tasting room from here? It had been a low-slung building, but two stories, with a brightly-white roof....

"Must be the angle, some trick of the landscape. It's probably right there, behind the fields," she told herself, as her guide emerged from the vines and turned to look over the vineyard as well.

"Took a long time for the vineyards to recover from that, even with good people working 'em. But vines remember things. They're old, some of 'em, and like I said, they dig in deep. Pull up things from the deep, all the flavors of the earth, tight and bright in the fruit.

"You can get good fruit a few years in, three, maybe five after planting. But it's like listening to a young'un babble, you have to prune through to find what they mean. Older vines, they wait, and only use the words they mean."

She'd heard people talking about old vines, as though they made particularly good wines, but nobody had ever said what that meant. "How old is old?"

He laughed. "Good question, miss. Some say twenty, thirty years, especially around here. But there're vines like these, over a hundred years now. They don't produce much fruit any more, but everything they are is in the juice."

She frowned, a thought occurring to her: hadn't the guy in the tasting room said *everything* here had been pulled up during Prohibition, that they'd replanted everything in the late 40's? Well, that was almost a hundred years now, maybe her guide was just exaggerating for effect, like a good storyteller.

"In the juice?"

"Vines remember things," he said again. "You can taste it—for good and for ill, sometimes. Start fresh and easy, then deepen and darken..." His expression shuttered. "And then, eventually, they fade away. Just like people."

"Um. Yeah." That was a little deeper than she'd been expecting. Also a little creepier.

He laughed at her, at her expression or her voice, she didn't know, but he definitely laughed at her, not with her. And that was also creepy, but not in a bad way? She suddenly realized she was out in the middle of nowhere with a stranger, and yet, none of her 'bad scene vibes' were twinging.

She wasn't sure if that made her feel better, or worse. Instinctively, she reached into her pocket, even though she knew her cell phone was in her bag, left with the others on the picnic blanket.

"Wait here a moment."

She pulled her hand away from her pocket as though embarrassed to be caught out, even though he didn't look offended. "Okay."

It wasn't as though there was anywhere for her to go. Even if she had gotten a bad vibe, she had no idea which direction to head to get back to the others. The orderly rows of vines had turned into a tangle of clumps, and there wasn't a clear entry point back. She supposed she could see if the road really dead-ended, or if it was just an optical illusion but..

He hadn't actually done or said anything threatening. Just an odd old man. She dealt with those every day. She'd be fine.

And the others weren't that far away. if she screamed, they'd hear her.

While she was deciding not to panic, his long, quiet strides took him toward the stone hut, where he disappeared past the wooden door, closing it behind him.

Alone, she was aware of how quiet it was. Not that there had been a lot of noise to begun with: the road up to the tasting room had been a turn-off from the main highway, so the only traffic it saw were people actually visiting the winery, and they'd walked a while from there, she thought, but up on the ridge, it was quiet-quiet, the kind where your breathing suddenly gets too loud and obvious.

She hadn't heard anything since her guide showed up, she realized. Nothing except their voices.

"Okay, get a grip," she said, and was relieved to hear her voice, normal and okay, a little loud, but that's just because she was focusing on it. "It's quiet because you're out in the middle of nowhere, effectively by yourself, and it's the middle of the afternoon so you're not going to hear a lot of birdsong or shit. Stop freaking yourself out."

On impulse, she clapped her hands once, hard. The sting of flesh against flesh was accompanied by a sharp thwacking noise that lingered for a second before fading away.

"There, see?"

She wasn't sure what it proved, but she felt better. Moving helped, too. He had told her to wait there, but he hadn't said she couldn't look around. Not that there was much to see. Staring over the expanse of vines made her slightly dizzy, so she focused on individual plants. The woody stems were even thicker than the ones she'd touched earlier, thicker and taller, and twisted like ropes, which made sense if they were older, but the leaves looked the same: five lobes, with serrated edges, about the size of her palm.

Zinfandel, she vaguely remembered, looking at the clusters of grapes underneath. The shape and color was closer to blueberries than what she normally thought of as grapes, although there were green ones scattered throughout the clusters, and an occasional reddish-green one, too. They were ripening faster than the clusters she'd seen earlier. They'd need to be harvested soon, probably?

She straightened, and looked out over the vineyard again, trying to imagine people out there, picking grapes. There was no way you could get a machine through, maybe not even a wheelbarrow, so you'd have to carry them all by hand, on your back probably, to the end of the row, and then go back and start all over again…

Her body hurt just thinking about it.

This time, she saw him coming toward her, although she hadn't heard the door open or close, the sound of his boots on the dirt road, or even the inhale or exhale of breath as he strode back toward her. Only after the fact, when he was holding it out to her, did she realize he was holding a bottle in his hand.

"Here," he said, clearly waiting for her to take it. "For humoring an old man."

The glass bottle was heavier than she'd expected, thicker in the neck than the one they'd opened earlier. The cork was sealed with a dark red wax, and the label was one she didn't recognize, an unfamiliar name on it.

"You're hardly old," she said automatically, and then smiled. "Thank you."

"Wine is for sharing. History needs to be told to be remembered. And I think the vines like you. But now, it's time you be getting back."

She was reasonably certain the route they took back wasn't the way they'd come, but if pressed she couldn't have said why she thought that, or point to anything specific. Maybe it felt as though they were going uphill, not down, or because the vines were still a tangle, rather than the orderly rows she remembered, but either way, she was surprised when he stopped abruptly, and turned to let her see past him.

"The fence is just up there."

"You…" she didn't know how to finish that. Was she going to invite him to join the picnic? Come meet her friends? She didn't even know his name, she realized suddenly, and felt like the rudest bitch ever. "I-"

"Time to go," he said.

"Sal! Saaaaallleeeeeee!"

She could hear her name floating toward the, and from the sound of it they'd been yelling for a while. With a sigh, she tightened her grip on the bottle, and turned to offer her hand again in thanks to her guide.

Somehow, she wasn't surprised that he'd already left, without her hearing a thing.

"Thank you," she said anyway, tucking a curl of hair behind her hear, and suddenly realizing that she was sticky and sweaty, as though she'd been hiking for miles. "And… I'll remember."

"Hey, there you are." Lee didn't look particularly annoyed, although she had her hands on her hips in a classic waiting-mom stance. "We were starting to wonder if you'd gotten lost or something."

"No, sorry, I-"

"Hey, where did you get that?" Lee noticed the bottle in her hands. "That's not one of the ones we bought."

"No, it was…a gift."

"A gift? From who, the goats?"

"The what?" Sally turned to look over her shoulder. There was the gate, and the vineyard beyond it, and beyond that…

Instead of the acres of vineyards she remembered, there was a handful of goats, calmly chewing. She hadn't remembered seeing them before, and she was reasonably certain…

"No."

Josh joined them, looking curiously at her. "No, what?"

"Not from the goats. The bottle, I mean." Josh looked as confused as she felt, so she shook her head and started again. "I went past the gate, just to look at the vines, you know? And I met a guy—I thought he was the vineyard manager?"

She had been certain of it, just a moment ago. But now…

He had moved like a ghost, she thought suddenly.

"Anyway, he told me about the vineyards, and…"

"And he gave you bottle? Cool." Josh reached for it, but she drew back instinctively. He didn't seem to notice. "I bet it's something seriously special. Or it's crap he was dumping on the dumb tourist."

"It's not crap. It was a thank you. For… I got the feeling he didn't talk to a lot of people, maybe? Maybe he was lonely. I-"

Lee held out a hand, asking rather than trying to grab, and Sally held the bottle up so they both could see it.

"Huh."

"Huh what?"

"That's an old bottle," Josh said, going into total wine nerd mode. "See how thick it is? Most of 'em these days, they're thinner, lighter. Better manufacturing or something, I don't know. And there's no wrap around the neck… I don't think that one was ever meant to be sold? What year is it? Cool, if he gave you something that's got a couple of years on it…"

She turned the bottle back so that she could read the label, and something stuck in her chest.

"Sal?"

"Nineteen nineteen."

"Wat?"

"That's what the label says. 1919."

"That's impossible. That would be, like almost a hundred years old." Josh took the bottle from her, but gently, as though he wasn't entirely sure it might not be that old, and Sally turned to look back over the fence, past the goats, to where the vineyards began.

"It was all torn up," she said softly. "But the vines remember."

GOLD-WASHING IN CALIFORNIA.

THIS SPACE FOR

CALIFORNIA GOLD
CENTENNIAL
SUTTER'S MILL, COLOMA
WHERE JAMES W. MARSHALL'S
DISCOVERY STARTED RUSH
OF ARGONAUTS

1848 U.S. POSTAGE 1948

THIS SPACE FOR ADDRESS ONLY.

TOMMY BONES
AND
A PACKET
OF EARTH

SUZANNE J. Wilhois

SUZANNE J. WILLIS

Suzanne is a Melbourne, Australia-based lawyer and writer, a graduate of Clarion South and an Aurealis Awards finalist. Her stories have appeared in anthologies by PS Publishing, Prime Books, Fablecroft Publishing and Fox Spirit Press, and in *Fantasy Scroll Magazine, Metaphorosis, Mythic Delirium*, and *Lackington's*. Her tales are inspired by ghost stories, fairytales and all things strange, and she can be found online at suzannejwillis.webs.com

KNOCK, KNOCK.

He rapped his bony knuckles on the mine wall, the sound of soil showering onto the girl's skin reminding him of rain in a lost, green country. From her still body and shallow breathing, it was clear she was still unconscious. Cocking his head, he listened for the other knockers, who would be taking the spoils of the collapse. There it was. A dragging sound on the other side of the rockfall as they pulled the body of the dead miner, a Cousin Jack—for all the men brought from the old country seemed to be someone or other's Cousin Jack—deep down, under the mine shafts and veins of gold running through the darkness like rivers. There had been three men in the chamber; only two had the sense to listen to the knocking before the collapse.

Then there was the girl. Lila. All shimmering herself, with her auburn hair and sunny eyes. Even in the thick darkness of the mine, covered in flecks of dirt after the cave-in, it seemed as though she'd been dusted with gold. He had been watching her every day for the past two months. She may have fooled those up in the camp easy enough, her hair shorn short and certainly skinny enough to be a boy, but it was clear as a bell to him.

He shook his head, told himself to pay attention to the task at hand. There was a little time, but not much. He hoped it would be enough.

Knock, knock. He was louder, more insistent this time. Lila stirred and moaned, lifting a shaky hand to her head as she tried to sit up.

"You'll be wanting to sit a moment," he said quietly.

She shook her head and felt around on the ground for her lamp. Although he could see and hear and feel the mine as though it were an extension of his own self, the darkness, for the likes of her, was so thick it felt like it could be kneaded. At least, that was how it had felt to him when he had been working in the mine.

"Who are you? What happened?"

"There was a cave-in. My name's Tommy," he said. "Down here, we're all called Tommy."

Silence, then the girl began to laugh.

"You're a funny one, you, whoever you are. Da always said, the Tommyknockers aren't— "

Quick as lightning, he put his hand over her mouth, muttering a quick curse to bind her tongue. "Shhh. You don't want to be bringing the rest of them back here, now, Lila. Hush a moment."

Tommy listened with his whole body. One of the knockers dragging the feet of the Cousin Jack had stopped for a moment when Lila had spoken foolishly. But he was the only one and after a moment, he went back to his task. Tommy pulled his hand away and, with it, the soft curse. Although he could feel she was scared, she simply straightened her back and took a deep breath.

"I think you've got the wrong end of the stick. Name's Liam." She spoke through clenched teeth, tension stiffening her neck.

How could he explain that he had watched her these long months, that she reminded him of someone with the same lilting voice and thin shoulders whose name eluded him, now, but he knew was important to him once? That he read her dreams at night and knew she longed for the same places and food that he did? That once you know these things about someone, knowing their name is like knowing your own self?

"Your secret goes no further than me," he said instead. "Although there's plenty of women out here, tis a strange thing for you to be pretending to be one of the men, no?"

She sighed, a sigh that held the exhaustion of months of hiding and pretending in one exhalation. "It's better this way. Less complicated. Safer… specially when you're alone." Lila finally found the lamp and righted it, then searched her pockets for a match. "All right, then, Tommy, you'll need to show yourself to me."

He hesitated. What would lovely, golden Lila, say when she saw him? Not that he was bashful, mind, it was just that he knew he used to look different. Like the boys and men above. He lit a green-yellow flame in the lamp, illuminating the chamber, and drew himself up to his full height of two feet. Lila looked him up and down, eyes wide as she surveyed his bony frame, skin knobbled as tree bark, the string of teeth hanging around his neck. Lucky for him he still had his bright blue eyes and his black hair that belonged to another time.

"It doesn't make any sense," she muttered. "There's no... but Da..."

"Plenty in the world that doesn't make sense. Your Da was wrong, Lila. You should always listen to the Tommyknockers."

Lila shook her head. "I didn't hear anything. One minute I was working, the next..." She put her hands to the rocks that had fallen and blocked her exit. "The others didn't warn me?"

"There wasn't time. But they'll be speaking to the boss man, asking him to start digging, to pull you out." He listened to the voices as they echoed through the earth, sounds that only Tommyknockers and their like can hear. "They'll not get through here, though, t'others'll see to that."

Lila tried to stand, falling back down as she bumped her head on the low ceiling. She scrambled about like a trapped, panicked animal.

"Shh, calm yourself, girl. I'm here to help you get out."

"I've nothing to give you—certainly no food, for I've not eaten myself these past two days. Boss isn't kind if you don't produce at day's end..."

Another fractured memory slipped through Tommy. Of boys following fast after the forty-niners, to find prosperity that they could only dream about in the old country. Of those same boys dying on the trails that led here, whether it was the cholera that got them or gunshots after drunken, unwise words. It slipped away again, making him wonder if he had been a part of it or if the stories from those above had merely slipped down into his own dreams.

He didn't answer, but began knocking again, this time a soft rapping with his fingertips that was an unspoken question. *Tirroo, tirroo, tirroo.* Across the walls his hand whispered. *Tirroo, tirroo, tirroo.* There! Behind the far wall, loose earth waiting to be hollowed. Tommy began a different knocking. *Killee, killee,*

killee. Three times widdershins around, a circle big enough for a slip of a girl pretending to be a boy and a subterranean goblin.

Lila held up her lantern as Tommy stepped back. The wall was gently shifting and moving itself aside. The entrance to a tunnel appeared. Inside, the earth continued to draw its shadowy curtain aside, while tree roots danced away to lay themselves against the tunnel walls. Tommy smiled.

"This way," he said.

Knock! Knock! Knock! A drumbeat of angry fists beat from the other side of the rockfall, followed by crackling laughter. "You canna hide him, Tommy. Be a good lad, now, and open up." The smaller rocks began to loosen and roll downwards. Lila's eyes were wide and she swallowed, hard, the lamp in her hand trembling.

Tommy bundled her into the tunnel and climbed in after her. Plucking one of the teeth from the string around his neck, he laid it on the ground, then began to walk.

"You don't need to give me anything, but she's always grateful for a token of appreciation." He pointed to the ground.

Behind them, the knocking grew louder and the larger stones began to tumble as Lila pulled a leather pouch from her pocket. Tipping it upside down, a little gold nugget fell into her palm. She put it briefly to her lips, mumbled a word of thanks and then placed it next to the tooth. A thin arterial root snaked out and around the offerings, pulling them away from the light.

"Lead on, Tommy."

The cavern was heaped with all sorts of bits and bobs, roughly sorted into piles by the Tommyknockers, like rusting, forgotten treasure. Here were hammers and picks of all size and condition. On the far side, hats and purses and a woman's mourning shawl. Nearest was a great stack of saffron cakes, the kind that the men left at the mine entrance each night so as to gain the favour of the Tommyknockers. Tommy relished the silence of the cavern. As Tommy and

Lila had crawled along the tunnel, the knocking had followed them, getting fainter until they arrived here, when it had stopped altogether.

Lila sat with her back to the wall, resting after the twisting squeeze through the tunnel that closed up behind them as they moved through it. Only way is forward, he had had to keep telling her, and she'd been brave enough. But now she needed to rest.

Tommy put his ear to the ground and closed his eyes. The hum and bluster that snaked its way up to him from the lower levels told him that the others had gone back to the Cousin Jack and were working on chipping him into his new form. First the teeth would come out, then they'd snip a lock from his hair. Then, an incision carefully made at the base of the skull, just enough for Jack's ghost to slip through. A new Tommy would be waiting, just twig and bone and mud. They would bind the ghost to it, whisper stories to it. Then string the teeth from his old body around his neck as he crackled to life. Judging by the grunting and the sound of heavy pliers, they'd just gotten started on the teeth.

Tommy raised his hand to the teeth strung around his neck. The teeth that had been his when he was mining, hoping to snag some of the California luck. What had he lost, giving one up for the tunnel? He was lucky Tommyknockers weren't blessed with tears, for it wouldn't do to weep for a loss he wouldn't know. Lila had mentioned a Da, but that word had no meaning for him, now. He had had a Da once, he knew that. It wasn't the memory that he lost—there had been a man with a sweet face and a jarful of whiskey on Fridays, quick with the back of his hand, but quicker with a laugh—but it didn't have any meaning for Tommy. As the bonds to that life weakened, the thin filament between then and now getting ever thinner, Tommy's connection to the earth and the goblins inhabiting her secret corners grew stronger.

"What are you listenin' for, Tommy?" Lila's voice was scratchy and tired, but still soft.

"I need to know how much time we have. T'others are…busy, but they'll be after us again, soon enough."

"What do they want with me?"

"Easiest way to explain is, the bigger the settlement gets and the more gold they take, the more Tommys're needed to keep 'em safe. See?"

"Not really. When I was little, my Da was a miner in the north of Britain, and the men he worked with, they told stories of the Tommyknockers. 'Bout how they'd knock on the walls to warn the miners or make mischief with their tools and such. But I never heard of them chasing miners through the tunnels."

Britain...he clung to the word. It wasn't the same as "Da" or the other words that Tommy was sure had had meaning for him once, but now slipped frustratingly out of his reach. Britain was where he had come from, too, chasing riches. That was before he left behind his name and feeling of sunshine on his skin and what it meant to be one of them *up there*.

"When the Cornish miners came across the seas, Lila, they brought the Tommys with them on the ships, just like their stories and their songs. They hadn't known it at the time, of course. When you bring something to a new land, it changes." A plink and a muffled curse reached him from the depths. The teeth were done, then. He began to walk around the chamber, collecting a broken pick and a small earthen jar. "I wasn't always a Tommy, Lila. But I'm not like you, anymore, either so…" He beckoned to her and she began to help him shift the odd assortment of wooden stools and doctor's bags pushed up against a hidden doorway.

"People here—the ones who were born here, I mean—say that the…well, you and your like, are the spirits of dead miners, not of the wee folk at all," Lila said. "Are you saying that they're right?" She heaved a cartwheel out of the way, dusting the spider webs from her hands.

"I'm not one or t'other, I think. I'm both, maybe, a mix of the two. 'Tis the same as being part of a new land, but hankering after the old, always between the two and never properly part of either one."

Lila nodded and Tommy thought that she knew all too well what he meant.

"Why're you helping me, Tommy?"

He briefly touched his hand to the teeth around his neck, then reached out and tentatively rested his hand on hers. "I've seen your dreams, Lila, as they make their way down here. You reminded me of what I've lost—what we've lost, down here. Because of you, I'm holding onto the part of me that's almost invisible—a boy without a country, a creature of in-between. I don't want to just fade into another Tommy. You've helped me hold onto myself."

Lila smiled then and it hurt Tommy's heart to know that someone special had once always smiled at him like that. Together, they shoved aside the final pieces of junk and Tommy brushed the dust off the door that would lead Lila up and out of the mine.

Knock. Knock. Knock. The door swung open on the third thump. The biggest of the Tommyknockers, who Tommy thought of as "Ogre", stood in the door-way, smiling wide as you please and showing his sharp, white teeth, his black-ened gums. Ogre swung his fist at Lila and knocked her out with one blow.

"Time t'pay the piper, Tommy. He didna listen to the knockin', he's marked…"

Tommy listened as Ogre rattled on, talking the way all the knockers spoke about the miners who were called to pay. He had his back to Tommy as he laid Lila out as though she were already dead, hands crossed over her chest and head slumped to one side. The Tommmyknockers were nothing if not careful with the dead, or near-to-be.

As he watched Ogre arranging her, he felt disconnected from himself—as though the spectre of the boy he used to be was slipping from his Tom-my-bones, shifting between worlds. Lightheaded, it felt as though he might simply fade away after all, that maybe he was just a discarded dream of Lila's. Was that how the knockers had laid him out, after the cave-in that took his life, too? Did he shed blood as they pulled the teeth from his gums, stringing them around his new Tommy-neck? He thought of his old body, lying in soil specked and veined with gold and good fortune for the lucky, far from home. It didn't know the music or the cold of home, but had its own ancient tales drifting through it. Is that why it called for payment? Tommy wondered.

Lila began to stir, tried to open her eyes. Ogre whispered something sooth-ing and stroked her brow and began muttering the Tommyknockers prayer for the departed over her. A prayer not of words, but a rolling dirge of water over rocks, of hammers hitting rock, wind across the plains, coyotes in the lonely hours of night.

It's not right, Tommy thought. Silently, he plucked three of the last four teeth from the string around his neck and spoke his own imprecations to the earth. Tree roots snaked down from the ceiling and up from the floor of the chamber, wrapping themselves around Ogre's ankles, twisting like vines around his shoulders and wrapping his arms in delicately strong tendrils.

"Ye're mad, Tommy!" Ogre struggled uselessly against his bonds. Where he managed to tear one, more arterial roots bloomed in its place. Tommy walked over to him and tucked the teeth between the ropy roots that now held Ogre captive.

Lila pulled herself onto her knees and crawled towards the door as Tommy faced Ogre.

"I'll take my punishment for this, but this one'll not be dying here today. This one's not your decision to make." As he spoke, his knuckles and bones creaked and stretched, pushing away almost the last parts of the boy that Tommy used to be. One tooth left. One more piece of his old life that still held meaning for him.

Lila reached the door. Tommy walked over and opened it, ushering her through. He left Ogre struggling and swearing bloody murder and led Lila up, up, to the surface again.

It was a new moon when Tommy crept out from the mine again. Up to the entrance that was only used by the Tommyknockers and to which he had sworn Lila to secrecy. It was away from the town, from the men with their jars full of whiskey and pockets full of money. It was a world that didn't mean much to him now, only the vague remembrance that he had been part of it, once.

He stretched as he emerged onto the grasses, among the Joshua trees that looked like phantoms in the moonlight. She had left gifts for him just beyond the entrance. A lock of auburn hair. A saffron cake, wrapped in a white kerchief. A packet of earth from the old country. He opened the packet, emptied the earth into his right palm. Brought it to his nose and, closing his eyes, breathed its peaty scent. Images swam before him.

Glorious gray skies above the vivid green pastures. Men, covered in coal dust, making their way home in the dusk. An old world, where history lay thick underground and the Tommyknockers were but one of a host of imps under the hoarfrost and rime. Mists lying like skeins of silver hair in the valleys. Waterfalls frozen in winter.

They faded like seafoam on the shore as he opened his eyes. Tommy shivered in the autumn wind. With his left hand, he picked up a handful of sandy soil and poured it into his right, mixing it with the dark clumps there. He stirred it with his forefinger, calling up meaning from the innocuous grains. They quivered and whispered to him.

In this land, we all become something else. The desert gets into our bones, the plains and the warm salt air of the coasts. We are washed by different seas. We become its lover, its story, its family. It commands us and we live forever more between two worlds, never quite belonging to either one.

It gave voice to the nameless wraith-feelings that moved restlessly inside him. The wind picked up and he held his hand out, palm up, watching the grains swirl upwards and away, across the star-flecked indigo sky.

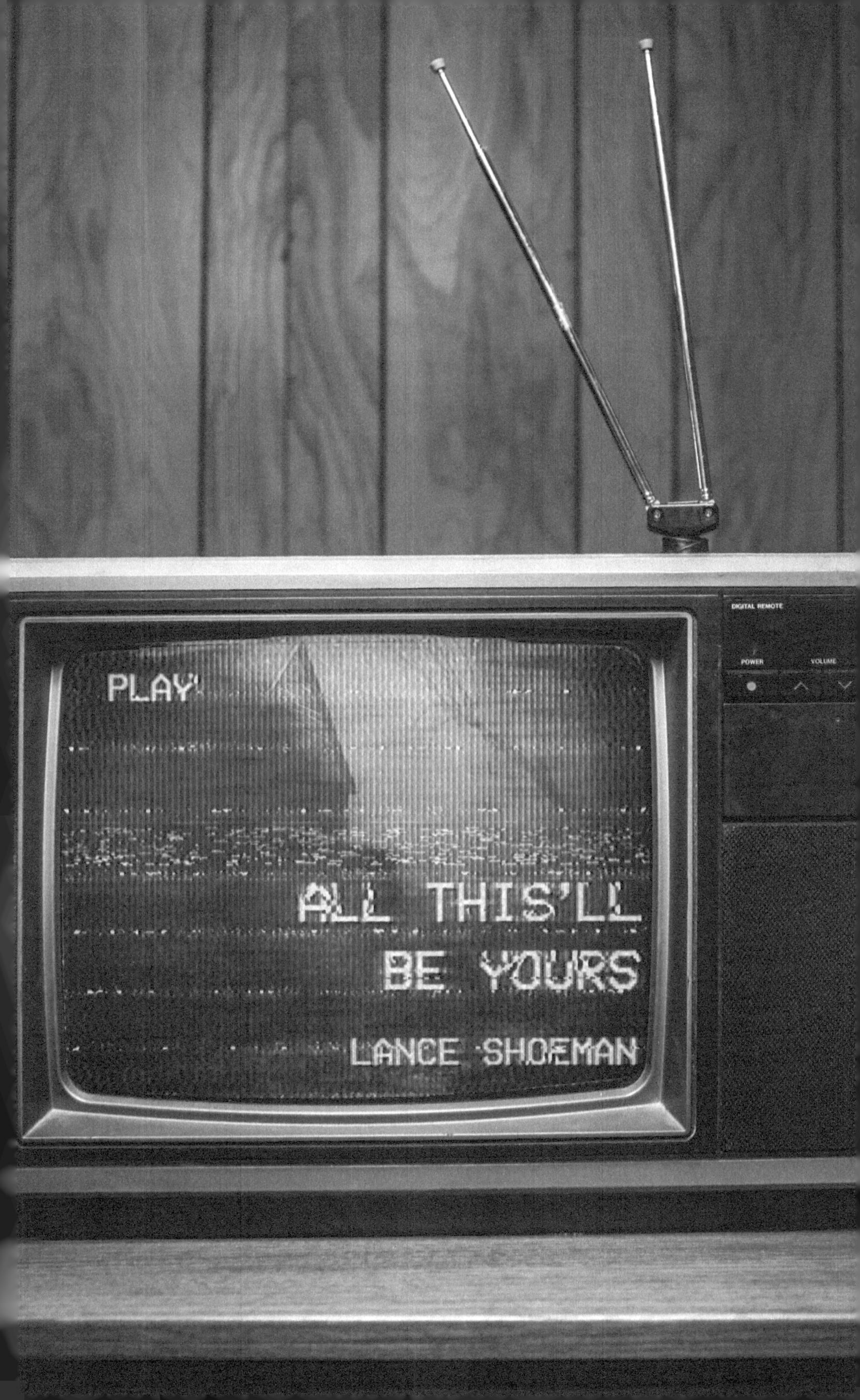
PLAY
ALL THIS'LL
BE YOURS
LANCE SHOEMAN
DIGITAL REMOTE
POWER
VOLUME

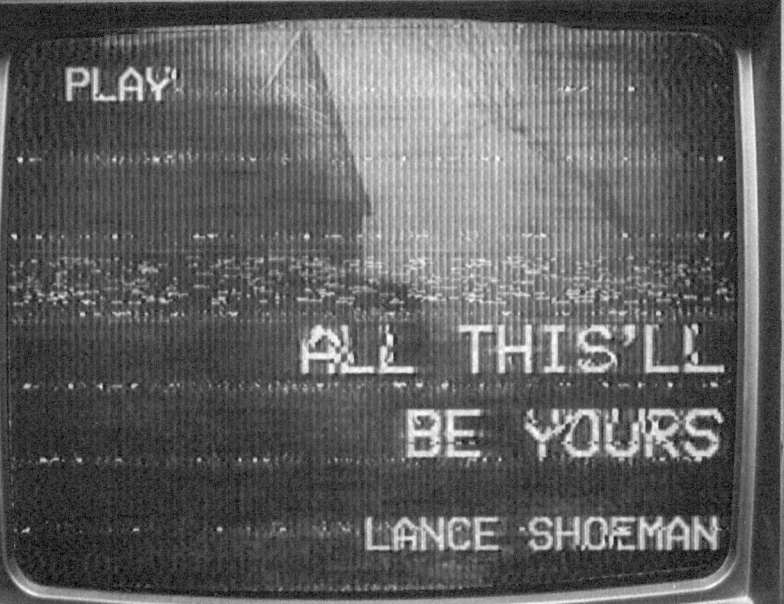

LANCE SHOEMAN

At the age of sixteen, Lance Shoeman's first published story appeared in the horror magazine *Haunts*. Fast-forward through 25+ years of wife and kids to when an old friend of his convinced him to get his head back in the game. In the period since then, Lance has had quite a few stories published including "Split" in the drabble anthology *100 Horrors*, "I'm Not Going To Be That Guy" in the BSA-nominated anthology *Slices of Flesh*, and "Among Us" in *Dark Moon Digest #8*. Although a frequent visitor to California, Lance currently calls Colorado home, where he lives with his aforementioned family, a dog, and far too many cats.

"DAMN IT!"

The grading of the old county road had been uneven at best, a seemingly endless series of shallow, bladder-jarring ruts the rental SUV's presumably decent shocks had done little to mitigate. But as bad as the almost constant vibration was, the occasional bump or pothole—and that last one had been something special—was much worse, and each one made Rachael second-guess her decision to order the *venti soy caramel macchiato*.

"Sorry about that!" Paul said, grinning into the rearview mirror.

"Can't you go any slower?!" Diana asked, mopping up the remains of her own coffee from both her lap and the backseat. Watching her, Rachael was almost but not quite thankful she'd polished hers off so quickly.

Well, at least I didn't spill mine on my crotch, she thought. *But if we don't get to a bathroom soon, we'll be looking at the same result.*

"Not exactly speeding as it is," Paul said, his voice quavering in perfect synch with the road's choppy topography. "Besides, we really need to hurry... we're running late. Al Padilla from Fresh Start and the local hire—what's that kid's name, again?"

Rachael snapped open her planner, efficient as ever. "Hanson, Brandon."

"Yeah, they're already there. Or should be."

"Can you at least try to avoid those big dips?" Diana asked.

"I'll see what I can do, Ms. Peslo," Paul said, shooting Rachael a sly, sideways eye roll. Rachael smiled, but—truth be told—she'd come close to asking him the same stupid question. Another jolt like that, though, and she'd have *no choice* but to ask one of her own... The only thing keeping her from it at the moment was trying to figure out how to ask him in a *professional* manner to pull the hell over so she could take a piss in the woods.

Okay, she thought, looking out the passenger-side window and into those woods. *Maybe that's not the only thing stopping me.*

"Old-growth" didn't even begin to describe it. The forest was thick with tanoak, pine, and Douglas-fir, all struggling for sunlight beneath a canopy of coast redwoods that had stood perhaps a thousand years, their ancient roots obscured by a dense carpet of foliage. Rachael was no botanist, but she could make out ferns and poison oak and rare, carnivorous pitcher plants (she'd perused a brochure at the coffee shop) and mushrooms... presumably also poisonous. And as off-putting as all that was to the notion of hiking up her skirt and exposing her bare bottom to the elements, the thought of what might be living in and around and *underneath* all that greenery was even more so. It had also not escaped her attention while reading literature about the area that Bigfoot sightings were a commonplace occurrence among these trees.

"You said the old woman's name was Tonia?" Diana asked her, leaning forward between the front seats to primly drop coffee-soaked tissues in the bag hanging from the dashboard's cigarette lighter. Rachael noted her perfectly-manicured, rhinestone-decorated nails, as well as the way she lingered knowingly, allowing Paul another good, long look in the rearview mirror at her no doubt surgically-enhanced cleavage.

To his credit, Paul McKenna's gaze remained focused to the road, and Rachael realized that—somewhere along a rough, uneven road in rural northwestern California—she'd begun to fall just a little in love with him.

Diana slumped back in her seat, arms folded, her lips fixed in a collagen pout. "Well?"

Rachael returned to her planner. "Darling, Tonia. Yes."

"Has there been a previous evaluation? Someone from Human Services or...?"

"Not that we're aware of, no."

"Probably Diogenes syndrome," Diana said, taking a turn of her own staring off into the woods. "Senile squalor. You said she's old... How old is she, again?"

"I can't say for certain. Her grand—"

"Wait," Diana interrupted. "If nobody from the county or state's been out to see her, how did she come to our attention?"

Rachael sighed, continued. "As I was saying, her granddaughter contacted us directly. I guess she caught an episode of *Wall-to-Wall* and decided we were just what the doctor ordered."

"Well, *I'll* see about that," Diana said, but it was the haughty tone with which she said it that immediately grabbed Rachael's attention. Diana Peslo was a frequent on-screen personality (although this was Rachael's first time working with her), a fan favorite, perhaps even a star of sorts. One thing she most definitely was *not*, however, was a "doctor." She was, not to put too fine a point on it, a marginally qualified therapist who'd been hired not for her M.A., but for her T&A.

"So no neighbors reported her for hoarding?" Diana asked. "No 'Dirty birdie's filth's lowering property values'-type complaints?"

"No neighbors, *period*," Paul said. "Property's bordered on all sides by national forest, wildlife refuge, a reservation… The whole of Del Norte County's unincorporated to begin with, except for Crescent City. So—in answer to your earlier question—even if someone *had* reported her, I don't know how high on the list of priorities looking in on a crazy old cat lady all the way out here in the boonies rates with the local authorities."

"Hey, now," Rachael said, instantly worried that she'd done so too playfully. "There's no mention of cats in any of *my* paperwork."

"Well, if there isn't, there should be," Paul laughed. "Trust me, there'll be cats. There're *always* cats! Almost, anyway."

And—as the GPS announced they had arrived at their destination and they entered the enormous clearing where the old Victorian farmhouse waited—Rachael saw that he was right.

Since he'd been the first to arrive and had spent some time chatting with the family, Al Padilla handled the introductions. Rachael was rather fond of Al and his big belly; she'd hired his cleaning crew for her first *Wall-to-Wall* segment as field producer (she'd started out as a production assistant, or P.A., a position that usually only lasts as long as it takes the producer to remember there's such a thing as unpaid internships), and—after he proved particularly helpful, even supportive of her efforts—had engaged the **FRESH START!** proprietor's services several times since.

Al's job today was to estimate the resources—manpower, dumpsters, etc.— necessary for a standard 48-hour cleanup. The young man accompanying him, whom he introduced as Brandon Hanson, was not there to assist with Al's task, however, but rather Paul's. The two of them together would determine the production's technical requirements. Diana would evaluate the subject's receptiveness to treatment (bottom line, get her signature on a release giving them permission to turn her life into a three-ring circus for the viewing pleasure of ladies, gentlemen, and children of all ages), and Rachael, well… Rachael Fassler's job was all of the above.

"I hope you can help her, bless her heart."

Rachael turned her gaze from her feet—where she'd been gently nudging aside a steady parade of purring, rubbing felines as they crossed the dirt yard leading up to the front porch—and toward the sound of Ruby Gasquet's voice. It was Ruby, Al had told them, who'd contacted *Wall-to-Wall* on behalf of her grandmother. She was a tall woman but heavyset, with a spotty complexion and beauty parlor-red hair. Ruby's husband—Rachael thought Al had said "Jeb" was his name, but wasn't entirely sure… she'd probably have to play the "wait until someone else says it before addressing him directly" game— struck an equally imposing figure but seemed much more soft-spoken than his brassy spouse.

"Well, we'll see what we can do," Rachael said, producer-speak for *Only if she and her situation are fucked-up enough to make for riveting television.* "Should your grandmother be chosen for the program, Wall-to-Wall will not only cover the cost of initial cleanup but six months of follow-up therapy as well."

"With her?" Ruby thrust her chin at Diana, who had reached the front porch's splintery steps. She was having some trouble climbing them; her stiletto heels and the too-tight designer jeans she'd poured her perfect ass into that morning working against her… or in her favor, rather, judging by the men's reaction to the spectacle.

All that's missing is the "Oops, silly me!" giggle, Rachael thought. An oversight "Dr." Peslo quickly rectified.

"No," Rachael said, practically spat. "Not *her*."

Once they themselves had reached the front porch, Jeb (*Jed? Jeff?*) excused himself and disappeared behind the west side of the house, admonishing his and Ruby's two children—a boy and a girl, groomed Sunday best as opposed to po' white trash—not to go near the cellar doors or get too attached to the cats as he did so. Rachael couldn't help but wonder if he was urinating back there; she was still, as an old college roommate used to put it, in desperate need of a slash.

Rachael had no problem scaling the steps, a feat no one seemed to notice. No one, that is, except Paul. He greeted her with that winning smile of his, and for a moment her knees went weak and she thought she might take a tumble after all. But she steadied herself and forced her eyes from his handsome features, focusing them instead on her immediate surroundings. The porch was fully screened-in and as generally in need of repair as the rest of the house. What it *wasn't*, Rachael was surprised to discover, was cluttered; it had been her experience working on *Wall-to-Wall* that hoarders rarely, if ever, kept their messes contained to the confines of their homes. There should be spillage… but this was tidy, practically immaculate.

"So you sleep out here, hon?" Diana asked of an elderly woman seated on a wicker couch at the far end of the porch.

The woman chuckled and smacked her lips over toothless gums in response. "Ain't room in there n'more!"

So this is Tonia. Jesus, she looks like one of those dried apple head dolls.

"Out here in the summer heat, the humidity," Ruby said, making no effort to disguise her displeasure. "I don't know that you can handle another winter, Memaw."

"I's *fine*. 'Sides, got the house t'tend," Tonia said matter-of-factly.

"That's just it, Memaw. Jedediah (*Jed!*) and I worry it's gotten too damn big for you to tend all on your lonesome!"

"I got these *cats!*" A slight breeze had picked up, stirring thin wisps of Tonia's long white hair. But it wasn't wind rippling across the loose, faded yellow fabric of her sundress; she had grown so agitated, she was shaking.

"I know, Memaw."

"Got t'be patient! A Darling's been caretaker since Darlings put down roots, an I's the last! All this'll be yours one day. *Then* y'can worry." Tonia punctuated this by slapping her hands on her knees—the liver-spotted skin on her upper arms flapping like wrinkled leather batwings—and reclining back onto the threadbare couch cushions.

"I know, Memaw." Ruby sighed, but was nowhere near resigned. "That's why we got these people to come out here today, so we can show you that we care just as much as you do."

"And *about* you, hon," Diana added. "Right, guys?"

Everyone murmured in agreement—a chorus of "Yes, ma'am!" and "We're here to help!"—except for Rachael, who recognized Diana's use of "guys" for the gender-specific exclusion it was. That made it official... she was pissed, almost as badly as she needed to take one.

"Why don't we head inside?" Rachael asked. "Get the lay of the land, maybe give everyone a chance to collect their thoughts?" *And to find a fucking bathroom* was currently the only thought she had in her own personal collection. She didn't care if its condition rivaled that of the fabled Augean Stables—and she'd seen shitters during her tenure on *Wall-to-Wall* that Hercules himself wouldn't touch—she had to go and she had to go *now*.

"Help y'self," Tonia said and smiled.

"Thank you, Mrs. Darling." Rachael shot Diana a look. "Guys?"

Brandon—who had thus far failed to impress Rachael with either the way he enjoyed kicking the cats aside a little *too* much or the way he ogled Diana as though she'd been hand-delivered to his doorstep by the MILF of the Month Club—was nevertheless eager to impress Paul and was first to the front door.

The knob turned easily, but the door was met with resistance from the other side. With no small degree of effort, Brandon was able to push it open and shove his way through. He was followed closely by Paul and at least three cats that Rachael counted.

"We'll give it our all, Ruby," Rachael said before entering. "Promise."

"Thanks, Miss Fassler. We're counting on it."

Al was the last in line, after Diana, and had a somewhat difficult time squeezing his gut through the narrow gap of the doorway. With one final "Oomph!" he was in, and the door—the pressure of countless years of accumulated detritus bearing down on it—slammed shut behind him. Everything moved and shifted… boxes filled with long-neglected contents, stacks of faded newspapers, old toys and clothing, you name it and God only knows what. Al stepped forward, and a tower of clutter collapsed behind him, blocking their exit.

"Everyone, *stop!*" Paul yelled.

Rachael had never considered herself claustrophobic and had certainly found herself in some close quarters before; it was all part and parcel of working with hoarders. But this? This was different, oppressive. They found themselves sandwiched sideways into a narrow corridor formed by garbage and the old woman's possessions; the rubble reached almost all the way to the Victorian's high ceilings, and Rachael could barely make out an impassable staircase—each step piled high in an almost comical display evocative of block-stacking balance games—to the right of the hallway. What little light there was shone in from windows in rooms they couldn't possibly reach, and—

"My God, the *smell*…!" Diana reached into the pocket of her fashionable denim jacket, pulling out a surgical mask and pressing it to her face. "Is that cat pee? And poo?!"

It is indeed, Rachael thought, the first hints of panic announcing their presence. *And not just what cats leave behind when they're alive, either. That smell's also what they leave behind when they're dead.*

As if in confirmation, Brandon—who'd gotten out ahead of the rest of them—called out. "Holy shit! There's a mummified cat here just, like, curled up like it's taking a nap!"

"Brandon, get your ass back here!" Paul said.

"Yessir!" Brandon said… and then screamed.

"Brandon?" Rachael felt as though she might be on the verge of screaming herself. "Brandon, what happened?!" Then, to Al, "Clear those boxes out of the way!"

"I fucking *cut* myself, that's what happened! This… it's like you can go this way, and the crap's at an angle, but you try and go back and all this sharp stuff's pointing right at you!"

Rachael looked more closely at the few feet behind and between her and Diana. What she saw made her blood run cold. The jagged tines of discarded silverware, the rusty edges of expired license plates, saw blades, bed springs, a thousand razor-sharp objects eager to tear, slice, and gouge their flesh. She turned back toward Paul and saw nothing menacing but could tell by the look on *his* face that he was seeing—looking back at her—what she'd seen looking back at Diana.

"I think we're in trouble," he said.

Rachael was reminded of a story she'd read while doing research on histor-ical hoarding as a P.A. The Collyer Brothers, Homer and Langley, were famous recluses who lived amid more than 140 tons of scavenged items in the Harlem brownstone they'd inherited from their parents. Upon their deaths in 1947 it was discovered that the brothers had constructed an elaborate tunnel system through the garbage, booby-trapped to protect against intruders… a fact that would ultimately prove their undoing. Homer, the eldest—blind, paralyzed, and no longer able to care for himself—died of dehydration and malnutrition days after Langley was crushed to death by one of their own traps. Langley had been bringing Homer breakfast when it happened.

"I've never seen anything like this," Al said, dislodging one hunk of junk only to see it immediately replaced by another. "God damn it!" Rachael saw what he meant to do but was unable to caution him against it (in truth, the only word that immediately came to mind was "*Jenga!*") before he shoved his arms into the chaos, grabbed hold, and pulled.

The column Al had been working at came loose from the bottom, pinning his legs against the debris and causing him to double over his own stomach. The impact dislodged an old toaster oven from its perch atop the opposite stacks, and the sickening crunch as it struck Al between his shoulder blades started Diana screaming.

"Guys," Al said, the side of his face pressed against a balding tire, exposed steel cords digging into his cheek. "Help."

It was Rachael's turn to scream, only hers was directed at Diana. "For God's sake, *help him!*"

"I can't! I can't!" To Diana's credit, however, Rachael could see that she was trying. Diana reached for Al, straining against the rubble pressing in on him and cutting her jacket sleeve to ribbons in the process. But Al, eyes widening in fearful realization, made no effort to grasp her hand; his own hung disconnected at his side, its limp pendulum swing tracking the forces being exerted against him by either side of the shifting aisle.

"I can't feel—" Al said, his eyes bulging even wider… not from fear, but rather pressure. Broken capillaries bloomed across his face, and blood seeped through the spaces between his teeth. As the final exhalation was forced from his lungs, the hoard settled, and all was once again silent.

"Why didn't they hear?" Diana asked weakly. "Why don't they help?!"

Paul eyed Rachael levelly. "It's a fair question. Your answer same as mine? That they knew?"

"I don't see how they couldn't," Rachael said, suddenly recalling how Jed had cautioned his children to stay away from the cellar doors. "I mean, the paperwork quoted them as saying they hadn't been inside the house in years, but how could you *not* know that your grandmother had constructed a literal deathtrap?"

"Well, our darling Tonia certainly didn't backtrack through all this shit, that's for sure," Paul said. "So the only way I can see out is forward… Those cats must've gone *somewhere*."

"I'm hurt bad, man," Brandon said, hitching in a frightened sob. "I think I'm dying!"

Paul turned his attention toward Brandon. "Jesus, he's *really* bleeding. Rachael, Diana, we've gotta get a move on! Let's hustle, ladies!"

"Come on!" Rachael implored, gesturing to Diana. *Wall-to-Wall's* breakout personality had already closed the gap between Rachael and herself but was holding her phone high above her head—the tattered sleeve of her jacket sagging loosely about a spray-tanned arm now covered with shallow cuts that weren't so much bleeding as *beading*—and focused intently on the screen.

"No service," Diana said.

Rachael looked at Diana's heartbroken, doe-eyed expression and instantly felt guilty for every negative thought she'd had about the woman; a remorse she wouldn't have previously thought possible. "Come on," she coaxed, gently this time. "Let's get you out of here."

"No, that's okay. You go on ahead. I'll just wait here."

Diana moved to negotiate a seated position, and Rachael had a sickening suspicion that there'd be no arguing with her... that the therapist was the one now most in need of therapy. Diana had checked out, given up and curled into a ball like the cat Brandon had stumbled upon.

As Rachael watched, Diana's jeans and heels once again conspired to throw her off-kilter, and—with no white knight currently available to rush to her rescue—she landed hard on her rear, grabbing instinctively as she did so for anything that might prevent her from falling further backward.

"*Ouch!*" Diana said. "My bott—"

The drywall hammer's axe-blade struck her where her forehead met her hairline, just to the left of median. Rachael stared blankly for a moment at the handle sticking out from Diana's head at a rough right angle; at the look of surprise that instant, violent death had frozen across her face (Botox, it would seem, has nothing on instant, violent death). Had Rachael thought to investigate, she might have discovered the old-fashioned wooden toolbox from which the hammer had fallen lying on its side, perched atop the stack against which Diana had braced herself and was now resting. But as the reality of her not-quite-rival's untimely demise slowly crept in around the edges, Rachael's thoughts fixated instead on a singular realization...

This is murder. They murdered them. Tonia and the Gasquets.

Only vaguely aware of her actions, Rachael pulled the drywall hammer

murder weapon

from between Diana's big, sad eyes—a sharp spike of rebar twisting into her shoulder as she did so—and turned to follow Paul. But Paul McKenna was, she now noticed, missing in action; he'd taken off after Brandon, whose blood trail suggested a young man in danger of not getting any older.

"Paul?"

She worked her way quickly through the clutter, pausing once only briefly (after slipping on one of the splatters—what Rachael couldn't help but think of as "blood crumbs"—she'd been following) to survey the stacks for any sign of loose or falling objects. The ambient light was growing brighter as she approached what her internal compass told her was due north, the rear of the house, and the drier smells of dust, moth-eaten rugs, and ancient cat shit were subtly but steadily replaced by a mustier, *greener* aroma, one Rachael presumed the hipster barista who'd served them that morning would describe as "organic."

"Paul?!"

Although they'd adjusted somewhat to the gradually increasing brightness, Rachael still had to avert her eyes as the Victorian's scuffed floorboards gave way to the dull, deteriorating linoleum of the kitchen. Sunlight—albeit filtered through a scum of grease and untold years of hard water condensation—streamed into the crude

I'm being herded, like cows down a slaughterhouse

chute from a double-hung window located just above an antique washbasin-style sink, illuminating (as the circular fibers of Rachael's irises further dialed down her pupillary dimmer switches) a completely different variety of clutter. Gone were the wax-coated cardboard crates and tangled bicycle frames, replaced instead by piles of dark green garbage bags whose seepage evidenced all manner of putrefaction, tin and aluminum cans—the former of which, she noted, sported the kind of jagged, partially-attached lids created by old clawed can openers… lids which only became an obvious danger, as was par for this particular course, in the direction of retreat—colored glass jars (also dangerous, depending on the direction), half-empty cereal boxes and gallon jugs of congealed dairy and fermented fruit juices, and plastic containers in every conceivable shape and size repurposed for storing leftovers… what her pretentious stepmother had referred to as "Tupperwelfare."

Also unlike the front of the house, the kitchen was fairly teeming with life. While there was still no sign of Paul, Brandon (whose blood trail had all but petered out, a fact that Rachael figured was very bad rather than good news), or even the three cats that had entered the Darling domicile as though they themselves were *Wall-to-Wall* crewmembers, all manner of skittering and vermicular creatures were readily apparent amongst the garbage… maggots and mealworms especially gnawed and burrowed through everything. But there were no *flying* insects, as one would expect—no flies, no bees or wasps, not even so much as a cupboard moth—an oddity that didn't entirely register with Rachael as she was preoccupied with reaching the washbasin.

And the mold…! It grew on everything, had spread everywhere. A white/grayish-green fuzz carpeted the dry goods, a black mass extending vine-like tendrils wallpapered the broken plaster and exposed wood lath (the latter of which made it difficult to determine where the kitchen's borders ended and the moldering trash bags—wrapped like great wet leaves around their contents—began).

This, Rachael decided, *this is the source of that "organic" smell.*

But—as was the case with Eau de Forgotten Kitty Litter—there was also some other vaguely unsettling odor just underneath it, wasn't there? Something sickly sweet, like rotten flesh. As Rachael reached the old sink, however, she simply pushed these thoughts aside as easily as she had the cats outside.

The washbasin—in all likelihood older even than the grinning mummy who'd greeted them on the front porch

Jesus Christ… Was that only ten, maybe fifteen minutes or so ago?

—was rusting in several spots where the enamel had chipped away but still perfectly capable of holding water... or something like it. Haphazard towers of glass- and dinnerware, much of it cracked and broken, had been erected atop a foundation of encrusted pots and pans sitting in a shallow pool of what looked to Rachael like the stew a backed-up garbage disposal might produce. She reached over the sink—straining as she did so—and tried to open the window, but without any luck. Carefully (she had absolutely zero desire to dip her toes in a concoction of shattered glass and raw sewage), she climbed atop the washbasin by propping one knee on the edge of the tub and then using the windowsill to pull herself up. From there, she was able to achieve a standing position, with one foot on the rim of the sink and the other on a faucet handle.

As she searched along the top rail of the window's lower sash for a lock, Rachael noticed three things in rapid succession: First, that the window was neither locked nor nailed or painted shut... it seemed, rather, to have been constructed as a single (and not completely finished) piece; second, the film she'd seen coating the window's upper and lower panes wasn't—upon closer examination—years of accumulated filth but instead some inherent quality of the glass itself; and third, that a California Highway Patrol cruiser was parked outside, not twenty feet from where she now struggled to maintain her balance.

"*Help!*" she screamed, banging her left hand against the windowpane. "Please, dear Lord, *HELP!*" The sound of her palm slapping the glass wasn't crisp as it should have been but dull, hollow, like a loose head on a bass drum. And the *feel* of it was all wrong; it wasn't smooth and cool but finely textured and with a waxy warmth. "The hell...?"

Is it Plexiglas or something?

Rachael grabbed the left side of the window frame, freeing two fingers and the thumb of her right hand, digits that had been keeping a tenuous grip on the opposite casing. They quickly joined her ring and pinkie fingers in more firmly grasping the handle of the drywall hammer she could only barely remember taking.

"*Help, God damn you!*" Summoning all her strength, Rachael slammed the hammer's scored head against the window, which made the same strange sound as before and seemed to give just enough to absorb most of the impact.

"HELP ME!"

As Rachael had just about given up hope of attracting anyone's attention, an SUV pulled up alongside the CHP cruiser. It took her a second or two to recognize it as the very same SUV Paul had rented for their trip. It took her another second or two to recognize the man behind the wheel... it was none other than Jedediah Gasquet, he of the I-didn't-quite-catch-that name, who had at some point changed out of his street clothes and into his state trooper's uniform.

"No."

Jed spared her a glance over the rims of his sunglasses, then pushed them up the bridge of his nose and turned away from her in the same direction he was turning the vehicle. As Rachael watched, he drove the SUV some distance into the almost primordial forest behind the Darling property, parking it among what Rachael could barely make out as the rusted hulks of countless other cars and trucks. A chill ran down her spine as she realized that the vehicular grave-yard probably wasn't visible from anywhere other than her current perspective, and at the sight of Al Padilla, whose friendly visage—a larger-than-life photo featured on the side of all of **FRESH START!**'s trucks—smiled at her through the foliage.

"No, no, no, no, no..."

Rachael could feel herself reeling. She teetered precariously, threatening to fall either in the sink or to the floor, as her field of focus shifted rapidly back-and-forth between the inside and the outside of the window.

And that's when she saw it.

A single drop of fluid—not entirely clear, not quite opaque—ran lazily down the pane in front of her. For a moment she thought it might be some of her own spittle, expelled during her frantic efforts to call for help. But as she traced the length of its slightly milky track back to its source, she saw that it had originated not from her own salivary glands, but from a scuffed and dented section of the window; the same section she had struck with the hammer just moments earlier.

With one quick, smooth motion Rachael wouldn't have thought herself capable of, she flicked her wrist, rotating the implement in her right hand and presenting its axe-blade as the business end. She reared back and struck the window in the exact same spot as before… only this time the tip of the axe—an uneven coat of Diana Peslo's blood, brain, and professionally highlighted hair still drying on it—broke through.

"Oh-ho, didn't see that one coming, did you, Deputy Dipshit?"

Rachael hacked at the window with renewed vigor, each strike spraying her with a fine mist of that unusual, increasingly pungent liquid. She wasn't so much *breaking* the glass (for lack of a better word… Rachael remained ambiguous as to the material's true nature) as she was *cutting* it, chopping *through* it. The area she'd been working at began to sag in a small, pliable sheet, and Rachael let go of the frame and began to rip and tear at the window with both her left hand and the drywall hammer.

"I'm coming for you, you dried apple bitch! *You and your whole fucking family.*"

Deep within the gloom of the passageway behind her, something shifted and moved. Rachael froze, listening intently. Her initial thought was that things were still settling after having been disturbed by the *Wall-to-Wall* cast and crew's intrusion—but then it happened again. And again. With quickening and frightening regularity, the sound of movement behind her grew louder, *closer.*

Oh, my God, they're coming for me.

Rachael turned her head, fully expecting to see Jed stalking toward her, his statie service revolver drawn and aimed squarely at her. Or Ruby, her ruddy complexion gone from spotty to blotchy with rage, her eyes twinkling with malicious intent. Or Tonia, reaching out to her with those leathery arms, eager to make Rachael the most recent addition to her hellish collection.

What she did see, however, was far worse than anything conjured by her imagination.

Diana emerged from the shadows of the stacks, her face forever frozen in an expression of bewilderment, now bisected by a stream of gore emanating from where Rachael had pulled the proverbial cork. She lurched forward in short spurts over and over again, her movement unnatural and relentless, accompanied by the dull, rhythmic roar of the collapsing

No, not collapsing…

corridor. As Diana's corpse neared the faded linoleum, Al's bloated face—his familiar smile now a twisted rictus—made its second unexpected appearance of the day when his mangled remains were expelled, disgorged from the undulating morass propelling America's former favorite therapist forward.

…swallowing.

Rachael redoubled her efforts, hacking furiously away at the window despite the nagging feeling growing deep within the pit of her stomach that—while she was close to escape—the peristaltic wave behind her was closer still. Desperate, she gave the ragged flap she'd carved another yank, and then tried to squeeze through head first. She had no time to appreciate how fresh the air was after suffering the suffocatingly stale air of the Victorian's interior… her shoulders were proving too wide, her tip-toes were losing their purchase on the rusted washbasin. She pulled out and put through her left arm up to the shoulder—bracing it against the outside of the pane as she did so—and then strained to push/pull her head through a second time.

"Come on…" Rachael exhorted. "*Come on!*"

As rigid as it was pliant, the window's baffling material refused to give any further—not even the crude lubricant of whatever the hell it was secreting would prevent Rachael's right ear from being torn from her head if she persisted. She wrenched her head out and spun around, her arm—still pressing against the outside of the window—the only thing keeping her from spilling ass over teakettle into the sink.

Diana and Al were *right there.*

"Fuck you guys!" Rachael screamed, raising the drywall hammer in what she knew to be a futile attempt to defend herself. "LEAVE ME ALONE!"

"*Rachael?*"

Rachael's head snapped in the direction the sound had come from. She'd been focused so intently on the window that she hadn't realized the narrow passage leading to the washbasin also branched *away* from it, continuing toward a small pantry or laundry room. Judging by its contents, it must have also served at one time or another to keep houseplants; it was overgrown with some sort of vegetation.

"*Rachael, is it you?*"

Faint though it may have been—and as close as the cacophony had come to drowning it out—there was no mistaking Paul's voice. Without so much as a second thought, Rachael launched herself toward the pantry, barely avoiding the surging clutter as it slammed into and broke wave-like against the old sink, her former colleagues the figurehead of some nightmarish, unseen vessel. More dishes and glasses cracked and shattered, providing (or so the producer in Rachael might have recognized under entirely different circumstances) the perfect Foley as her left ankle impacted awkwardly with the floor.

"*PAUL!*" she screamed, as much in pain as in response.

She limped as hurriedly as her injury would allow, using the hammer's axe-blade to cut a path through the thick, dark green brush of both plant and plastic, no longer able to differentiate between the two. Had she been moving any faster, her forward momentum would have carried her over the threshold of the cubbyhole's partially-concealed basement doorway, sending her tumbling down the stairs where a broken neck no doubt awaited.

The cellar door, Jed said something about the cellar door; that's got to be the way out!

Rachael leaned forward and grabbed the handrail just past where the basement door—its lead paint cracked and flaking in a pattern reminiscent of a dried lakebed—hung by only the top hinge and hobbled down the steps. She stopped abruptly midway, however... the basement was flooded, but—as was the case with the kitchen sink—not with water. Light poured in through semi-transparent membranes that had given up any pretext of being windows, shimmering across an unfamiliar, viscous fluid, the stench of which was almost palpable. All around the edges of the basement—walls constructed not of brick and mortar but of a complex tangle of interwoven, fibrous plant tissue—were piles of skeletal driftwood; the remains of countless cats and more than a few humans.

There was no sign of Brandon, but Paul was indeed there, his right arm hooked around a corroded pipe that had snapped free from its moorings alongside one of the unfinished ceiling's joists and was now bowed under his weight, its unattached end bobbing lazily in the air. At first glance Rachael thought Paul was sidling toward her; closer examination, however, revealed he was actually *sliding* forward and down along the length of the pipe, its steepening angle (it now dipped in and out of the fluid in a way that put Rachael in the mind of drinking bird toys often employed by high school science teachers) and his own loosening grasp conspiring to sink him gradually deeper into the quagmire. As she watched, Paul's jaw submerged beneath the surface, leaving only the top half of his head visible.

Seeing Rachael, he struggled to once again right himself and succeeded in pulling far enough up out of the strange solution—trailing thick streams and thin sheets of the sticky goo as he did so—to then open his mouth and speak. Only Paul—or the grinning thing that had once *been* Paul McKenna: Man of Her Dreams—would never speak again; everything below his nose was in the process of being eaten away

digested

by the mucilaginous and no longer *quite* so mysterious substance.

Rachael screamed one final time, the sound inaudible over the avalanche of clutter that came tumbling down the stairs, the ghastly, entangled bolus of Diana and Al's corpses pushing her forward, into the belly of the monstrous, house-mimicking cobra lily.

"See, Memaw?" Ruby asked. "I *told* you that we could tend to the home place for you."

Tonia's brow furrowed and she stuck her lip out in a pout, her toothless lower jaw nearly touching the tip of her nose. "They's gonna come lookin for them folks," she said.

"And when they do we'll pretend we don't know anything. Between Jed's job, and my working dispatch for the county sheriff's office—and we fed them local names as aliases to begin with—we'll have no problem selling whatever story we come up with. Shoot, worse comes to worst, we'll invite anyone foolish enough to come poking around here to have a look inside for themselves. *We can do this.*"

"Mayhaps y'can," the old woman said, her tone as stubborn as ever. "An mayhaps I's go right on ahead and move in with you's… but then what? Jus wait to wind down? A body's got to keep busy!"

"There's a garden, Memaw," her granddaughter said, placing a reassuring hand on the old woman's bony shoulder. "With its own little shed."

The old woman the *Wall-to-Wall* crew had known as Darling, Tonia sat quietly for a few moments, watching her great-grandchildren play with the clowder of felines practically carpeting the front yard and listening to the wind in the trees.

"That might do nicely," she said, and smiled.

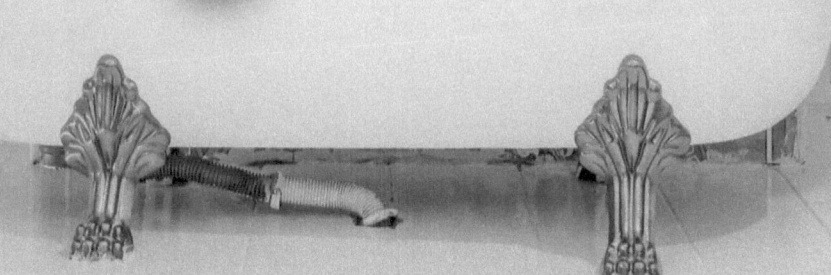

A SEA MONSTER IN THE BATHTUB

TIM PRATT

TIM PRATT

Tim Pratt is the author of over twenty novels, including *Heirs of Grace* and the forthcoming *The Wrong Stars*, and many short stories. His work has appeared in T*he Best American Short Stories, The Year's Best Fantasy, Best New Horror,* and other nice places. He's a Hugo Award winner, and has been a finalist for World Fantasy, Sturgeon, Stoker, Mythopoeic, and Nebula Awards, among others. He lives in Berkeley, California and works as a senior editor at *Locus*, a trade magazine devoted to science fiction and fantasy publishing.

SYDNEY COPE WENT WITH HER FRIENDS TO THE HANDS AROUND LAKE MERRITT "peaceful protest" even though she was more in the mood to march in the streets and storm barricades. Still, she thought it might be nice to be with people who shared her sense of devastation at the election of a misogynist, racist, confessed sexual abuser to the nation's highest office. She and the two Dereks headed to the train station, and their new housemate Chris, the brogrammer tagged along for reasons she didn't want to contemplate. They got off at Twelfth Street and walked a few sunny, warm blocks, joining a stream of people headed to the water's edge. There were a lot of mostly white liberals here, stunned by the ugly realities of life, their progressive bubble rudely popped. Sydney was sad but not stunned. This country had tried to beat, kill, and electro-shock people like her out of existence for ages, and in some places she couldn't use a public restroom without risking arrest or assault. This was just another in a list of very bad days.

The organizers estimated it would take thirty-five-hundred people to encircle the lake, holding hands and generating positive energy in a symbolic show of healing and solidarity. (That and a molotov cocktail would keep you warm.) Enough people showed up to circle the lake twice over. She was impressed. There were, what, seven million people in the Bay Area? So that was maybe one-one-thousandth of the area's population gathered together to... sing old songs and do the wave and take pictures and talk to their neighbors about protests past and clutch at inane straws of hope regarding the Electoral College or recounts or some kind of pre-emptive impeachment. She couldn't help but feel the energy would be better directed otherwise, but what could anyone *do*, short of violent revolution? That appealed to her sometimes, but the other side had more guns and fewer qualms about using them.

The Dereks wandered off, which was uncool, because Chris had a weird species of crush on Sydney (he either wanted to prove his own open-mindedness or saw her as a fetish object, she suspected), so she slipped away before he could try to hold her hand under cover of peaceful protest. She wasn't eager to hold hands with anyone else here, either, so she kept moving beside the crowded footpath. There was no real cue, but people on the far shore linked hands and raised their arms up high, like they were taking a bow on the stage. That struck her as funny. One last curtain call before America finished its theatrical run.

Behind the mediocre seafood restaurant with the lake-view seating, a woman sitting at the end of the pier caught Sydney's attention. There were people standing around her, holding hands, but the woman was apart from the chain, sort of like Sydney herself. She wore a cute blue sundress decorated with sea horses and puffer fish, but the weird thing was the sort of crown she wore on her head; it seemed to be made of crab legs and vegetable matter.

The woman shaded her eyes and scanned the lake, like she was looking for something, and Sydney looked, too.

An immense beast broke the surface of the water. Its dragon's head was crowned with long spines, and it regarded the people on the pier with gleaming black eyes as big as teacups, catfish whiskers dangling around its mouth. Its scales glittered, greenish-black, twinkling wetly in the sun. After a long moment, it dove, and the coils of its serpentine body broke the glittering surface in a series of arcs. Was it fifteen feet long, twenty, more? Its tail, tipped with a pair of small triangular fins, gave a last flip and then vanished.

Sydney gaped, and wondered why no one was screaming, or pointing, or filming with their phones. No one reacted at all. Were they all so wrapped up in their own heads, or the experience of touching the sweaty hands of strangers, that they were oblivious to the sighting? How had seven *thousand* sets of eyes failed to see the serpent?

The woman with the strange crown rose, turned, and walked along the pier, toward the path, her face sun-worn and serene. She passed close by, and Sydney said, "Hey. Did you… see something… in the water?"

The woman paused and regarded her. Her crown was woven of kelp and chitin. "Sometimes she's attracted to crowds. Stay a part of the crowd. Don't give her a reason to notice you in particular." The woman moved closer. "Or she might eat you."

"Wait, what—"

The woman moved on, and a herd of baseball-hatted bros tromped by and cut off Sydney's view, and by the time she shoved through, the woman with the crown was gone.

Sydney walked in a daze, looking often toward the now ordinary lake. She found the Dereks and walked with them deeper downtown to get beer and pizza at Drake's Dealership, which would probably be crowded but not as much as places closer to the lake. "That was pretty cool," Tall Derek said. "All those people, hating the same person, it made me feel better."

"Yeah," Sydney said. "Hey, have you guys ever heard of a… *creature* in Lake Merritt?"

"What, like the Loch Ness monster?" Tall Derek said.

"Actually yeah," Hot Derek said. "I saw this girl last summer whose t-shirt had a drawing of a sea serpent, and it said 'The Oak-Ness Monster.' I googled about it a little bit."

"What did you find out?" Sydney said.

He shrugged. "That it's a bunch of bullshit to sell t-shirts, mostly. Or an ironic hipster joke. Maybe a few crazy people saw some tires in the water and decided it was a sea monster. But, come on—the lake's not that big, and it's in the middle of a city. How's anything going to hide in there? It would be like having a sea monster in your *bathtub*."

"Yeah. Makes sense," Sydney said.

"Why do you ask?" Tall Derek said.

"I heard some girl talking about it," Sydney said, which wasn't exactly a lie, since she'd just heard *herself* talking about it.

"It was a pretty sick t-shirt though," Hot Derek said. "Maybe I'll get one."

Sydney curled up in the purple velvet armchair in her room with her tablet. She didn't search for the Oak-Ness Monster right away, because that was too ridiculous. Instead, she read about the lake, hoping to build herself up to the *real* questions. Lake Merritt, the jewel of Oakland, was a tidal lagoon with the contours of a misshapen Valentine heart. A path followed its three-and-a-half mile circumference (not that it was remotely circular), the paths strung with fairy lights that twinkled at night. The lake was surrounded by parks, gardens, a bird sanctuary, assorted gazebos and playgrounds, a labyrinth in the grass, Children's Fairyland (a vintage inspiration for Walt Disney's theme parks), that mediocre seafood restaurant, a historical mansion, and a boat house where you could rent canoes, paddleboats, or get a gondola ride. Canadian geese predominated, along with coots, assorted ducks, and the odd egret, cormorant, and pelican, plus night herons if you were there early or late.

There were crabs and mussels and turtles and rays and other life in its depths, which maybe a sea monster could eat, but those depths weren't very *deep*: depending on the tide, it was between eight and ten feet down, max. Sydney read that a couple of times, because it didn't seem like it could be true, but apparently so. A twenty-foot-long sea monster could hardly go unnoticed. It really would be like hiding in a bathtub. There was no open water connecting the lake to the bay, either, so her monster wasn't a misidentified sea lion that had taken a wrong turn. What the hell had she *seen*, then?"

She finally just searched on "Oak-ness monster." There were a handful of articles, most treating it as a joke, a couple on the wild-eyed-conspiracy-theory end of things, and a shaky video of what was pretty obviously a sculpture made of tires and stuff in the water. There had been intermittent sightings since the 1940s, and an uptick around 2013, with some speculating the monster fled when the lake was polluted and returned when it got cleaner. There were vague mentions of ancient Ohlone legends about a marsh monster, but Sydney had studied history as an undergrad and could spot an unsupported reference. No serious cryptozoologist believed there was an undiscovered species in Lake

Merritt, and these were people who thought the existence of the Loch Ness monster was a strong maybe and Bigfoot was nearly certain.

Sydney flopped back on her bed. This was dumb. Maybe it was a joke, some kind of underwater drone dressed up in serpent drag. Maybe she'd had an acid flashback (though she'd never had an actual hallucination on acid). Or, hey, maybe she was experiencing some kind of twenty-something-onset schizophrenia triggered by the election of a groping reality TV star.

Except… that woman in the crab-leg crown. *She'd* seen something, too.

Sydney dug deeper into the search results and found a thread on a defunct cryptozoology forum from over a dozen years ago, talking about Oak-Ness monster sightings. There were a lot of dismissive comments, but there were also a couple of people who claimed to be witnesses.

One of the profile pictures, a slightly out-of-focus thumbnail, looked a lot like the sun-worn woman with the crown. She had an email address posted — to a hotmail account of all things— so Sydney composed a note:

Hi. I saw you at the protest today. Found your address on a cryptid forum. I saw something in the water today, and it looked like you did, too. Can we talk about it?

Sydney hit send, and waited for the "undeliverable, no such address" bounce-back, but it never came. No reply came, either, though, so after twenty minutes of pacing, she sighed and went into the living room to see what the boys were drinking.

The Dereks were making out on the couch and Chris was standing in the kitchen. He was okay looking, in a bland sort of way, but he seemed vaguely unfocused as a rule, except when he awkwardly tried to flirt with her. (He took hints okay, but she was tired of dropping them. He seemed to lack object permanence, or at least didn't get that her objections were permanent.) Maybe Sydney should have felt some impulse to take him under her wing, but he just bored her. He brightened up when he saw her. "Hey! I'm making Jägerbombs. Want one?"

"I already have an election hangover. I don't need a real one." She paused. "Aren't there a bunch of big lakes where you're from?"

He laughed, like she was making a joke, then stopped when she just stared.

"Uh, yeah. The Great Lakes."

"Are there stories about monsters in those lakes? Like, what is it, the Lake Champlain monster? Champ?"

"No, that's in New York. But sure, some people say there's a monster in Lake Erie, and I heard about one in Lake Michigan too. And the Dewey Lake monster, but that's more like a bigfoot sort of thing."

"Oh. You believe in that stuff?"

He snorted. "Nah, course, not. It's stupid."

She nodded. "Right. Some people think there's a monster in Lake Merritt, apparently."

Chris clearly couldn't tell whether she was being serious. "That's super dumb though. The lake is like the size of a swimming pool. Basically it's a pond."

"Not so great by your standards."

"I mean, not really, but it's pretty, the lights and all. And that was interesting today, really wild. This old black lady got me to sing 'We Shall Overcome' and stuff. I never saw anything like that back home. All that *energy*, it's gotta go somewhere, right? All those people, caring about the same stuff all at once, I don't know. Makes me wish I'd voted."

Sydney knew plenty of people who didn't vote in presidential elections, or voted strategically, for sound political reasons, but it was hard to imagine Chris's abstention was due to a radical leftist viewpoint. "Why didn't you vote?"

"I don't know, I'm still registered in Michigan, and I didn't get my absentee ballot filled out in time or whatever."

One of the Dereks wandered in. "Better not tell our friends who voted Democratic about that. They'll blame you personally for losing Michigan's electoral votes."

Chris shrugged. "I guess. But it doesn't really matter, right? There have been lots of presidents in my life, and it's never made any difference to my actual life. Everybody's acting like it's the end of the world, but life goes on, it's just like your team lost the Superbowl or something. What's the big deal?"

Tall Derek looked at Sydney. She looked back at him. "Mother*fucker*," Hot

Derek began from the other room.

"Good night," Sydney said, and returned to her room. Not that it wouldn't be fun to see two gay men of color drop some truth on a straight white boy from the upper Midwest, but she had other things on her mind.

Sydney's phone buzzed the next day at work. She was working as a barista at one of the indie coffee shops in Temescal, which was an okay job because she was allowed to be surly with people, but a terrible job because it didn't pay well and she had to interact with so many humans. All anyone could talk about was the election, and all Sydney could think about was sea monsters. Maybe the political process had caused a psychotic break. That would be almost comforting.

Then she got an email, from that hotmail address:

Somehow in all the vastness of the internet, you managed to find me, which speaks of destiny. The serpent may want you after all. Meet me by the Mid-Century Monster at nine tonight, and we will perform a summoning and solicit a visitation.

Mallory

Sydney had to look up the "Mid-Century Monster": it was that sprawling metal abstract sculpture by the bandstand, near one of the lake's only beach-like shores. She hadn't known the sculpture's name (though it seemed appropriate) and it didn't much resemble a monster, but it was cool. Kids played on it, historically, though lately it was fenced off, awaiting either restoration or demolition—the internet wasn't sure which. She shot back a "Great, see you then" note and tried to focus on work instead of cryptid craziness.

Somebody made a disaster in the bathroom, and she pulled the short wooden stir stick, so she had to clean it up. After she finished, when she was washing her hands for the fourth time, she heard a weird *bloop* in the toilet, and when she looked over, she saw the end of a reptilian tail, frilled with double fins, disappearing down the drain.

"That was just a weird shadow," she said aloud, and was not reassured, because talking to yourself in the bathroom was not a sign of good mental health. Hallucinating water lizards was a strange way to cope with the downfall of the Republic, but maybe her mind had its reasons.

Sydney went home and into the bathroom, planning to shower off the coffee stink before her sure-to-be-weird meeting with Mallory. She stripped off her caffeinated clothes, and when she pulled back the shower curtain, the serpent was there, its coils filling the tub, five feet of its length rising up and swaying so its head was on a level with Sydney's. It regarded her placidly. *A sea serpent in the bathtub*, she thought dizzily, as she stumbled back and let out a small scream.

A moment later the door started to open, Chris saying, "Whoa, hey, are you okay in there?" She spun to shove the door closed. From the edge of her vision she saw the serpent dive for the tub drain and slither down, even though that was impossible—it couldn't fit any more than her finger could fit through the eye of a needle.

Chris pushed the door half open, but Sydney got her back against it. "I'm *in* here, do you mind?" Focusing on the immediate concern was easier than thinking about… whatever just happened.

"You screamed, I was worried about you—"

"I screamed because of all your hair in the drain," she said.

"Oh, sorry. I guess my mom always cleaned up that stuff for me—"

"I'm naked in here, Chris, if you don't mind?"

The pressure against the door didn't ease up right away, and there was a moment of long silence before Chris said, "Right, sorry," and let the door close.

Sydney thumbed the lock. She didn't trust Chris not to try to sneak a peek, which was fucked up. She needed to shut that shit down. Maybe he wasn't a bad person, but he was so oblivious and self-centered he was indistinguishable from a bad person in certain respects.

She decided she couldn't face getting in the shower when a hallucinatory sea monster might appear, so she washed up as best she could in the sink.

Maybe Mallory would have some answers. Somebody had to, right?

Sydney didn't usually go this deep into the park after nightfall. It wasn't notoriously dangerous, but sometimes people got mugged, or otherwise attacked. There wasn't anyone around, though, except for a familiar silhouette, seated on the gritty sand near the fenced-off Mid-Century Monster, practically at the water's edge.

Sydney approached her. "Mallory?"

Mallory beamed up at her beatifically, sitting cross-legged at her feet, her stinky crown in place. "Welcome, brother."

Sydney, who'd endured a lifetime of misgendering, smiled back as blandly as she could. She was coded pretty female these days, so the word choice was probably willful rather than accidental. "It's sister. Or, better, just Sydney."

"Mmm." Mallory patted the sand, and after a moment's hesitation, Sydney sat beside her, because standing over her was awkward. "We may not have everything in common, Sydney, but we have one thing: we have both been blessed with visions of the serpent."

"The Oak-Ness monster. It's real?"

She sniffed. "That ridiculous name is offensive. It profanes a sacred thing, and makes material a spiritual one."

Ohhhh-kay.

Mallory went on. "The few scientists who've been questioned on the subject insist no such creature could live in the lake. Even if there were some undiscovered species, the lake is too small, the conditions too inhospitable. We can dismiss mundane explanations."

"I dismissed *those* when I saw the serpent in a toilet," Sydney said. "And in my shower—"

"Do not mock," Mallory said, and before Sydney could object, she barreled on. "The serpent appears rarely, and only in Lake Merritt. I have tried to summon her elsewhere without success. I first saw her almost twenty years ago, walking one night near this very spot. Someone tried to hurt me, and the serpent intervened. She saved me. I have been her priestess ever since."

"Twenty years, huh?" Mallory must have been a teenager.

She waved her hand. "Time is meaningless to the serpent. She can swim through the years at will." Mallory sketched a circle in the air. "The serpent embodies time, and rebirth, and eternity: the ouroboros devouring itself. The serpent swims through the waters of other dimensions, including the waters of time, and occasionally breaches into our world, like a whale surfacing for air before descending again."

"Totally," Sydney said. Maybe it was time to call a psychiatrist instead. Get some tests done, and maybe some medication.

Mallory went on, gazing at the dark water, dappled by reflections of the city lights beyond. "There are many things about the serpent I do not know, despite our long association. But there is one thing I *do* know: she belongs to women." Mallory turned head and looked at Sydney coolly. "The serpent is also a symbol of the umbilicus, and thus of fertility. The great goddess has serpents as Her attendants. The serpent protects and guides and gives comfort to women. As she did to me, that first night, and as she has on occasion since." Mallory smiled and patted Sydney's knee. "The serpent didn't come to help you, or to guide you as she guides me. She devours evil men. If you see her again, it will be the last thing you see, and you will be so wholly consumed, it will be as if you never were."

Sydney tightened her fists. "I'm not a man."

Mallory sniffed. "You're not a woman. You've taken some hormones, I'm sure, and you play the part, a little boy in his mother's skirt, but you're no woman. You were born a man, and a man you remain. You might fool some people, but not me."

"I'm not trying to *fool* anybody. My gender assigned at birth doesn't define—"

Mallory shook her head. "Have you bled as a woman? Have you suffered as a woman?"

Sydney stood up. "I've suffered as myself. Being born a woman isn't easy, I know, but people want to destroy me—men and women both. There are laws out there premised on the idea that I'm just automatically a pedophile or a predator. I didn't transition because it made my life easier, Mallory, or because I thought it would be fun. I couldn't stand the divide between what the world wanted me to be, and what I am. I'm a *woman*."

The waters suddenly began to churn just offshore, and fear stabbed at Sydney.

"We'll see." Mallory had the serenity of the righteous. "How did you draw the serpent's attention? It's been ages since I saw her devour anyone. I used to walk around the lake after midnight, hoping someone would attack, to tempt them into their own destruction. Once, I posted online, pretending to be a prostitute, and lured a man to the shore here. The serpent appeared, but the man ran away before he was consumed. Who did *you* hurt?"

"I didn't hurt anyone, you crazy bi—"

The serpent rose from the water. The beast yawned, showing off teeth made for tearing flesh from bone. The serpent swayed back and forth, its movements cobra-like and hypnotic, and Sydney froze. Fuck. What *had* she done to draw this thing's attention?

"Any moment now." Mallory looked at the water, but not quite at the sea serpent—just off to one side. "I'm sure I sense her presence. Your reckoning is near."

"What. The fuck. Are you talking about. It's right there." Sydney raised a trembling arm and pointed.

Mallory frowned, shaded her eyes, and looked far off over the water, not at the creature, close enough for her to lean forward and touch. "Where? I don't see it."

The serpent extended her head out over the shore, long neck stretching until her face was just inches from Sydney's. There was no voice. No telepathic communication. But the creature's dark eyes met Sydney's, and if they shared anything, it was a silent understanding: the serpent meant her no harm. What it *did* mean was a mystery.

The serpent withdrew then, and disappeared into the water, undulating away through the shallows.

"Any minute." Mallory's voice was still almost serene, but there was a crack in it. "She'll come, and you'll see."

But Sydney was already walking away. She wasn't going to wear a crown made of eels or anything though, damn it.

"Hey, you want a drink?" Chris was in the kitchen of the otherwise empty apartment.

"No. I want about ten drinks. But start with one." She slumped on the couch.

"Aw yeah, I've been wanting to get tore up with you." A few moments later he returned with a pair of plastic cups and handed her one before dropping onto the couch beside her.

She took a few sips, but it was horrifically sugary: a hangover in a glass. Sydney put the cup aside, trying not to make a face. She should have asked for a beer and a shot. Even Chris couldn't mess that up. "Where are the Dereks?"

"I got tickets to some play held in an old train station or something, and offered them to the guys. I was hoping to get some alone time with you actually. You and me haven't really *connected*, and I feel like if you gave me a chance and just loosened up—"

Ugh, no. She stood up, and the room was oddly swimmy. She hadn't eaten much, but the booze shouldn't have hit her that hard. "Hey, no, sit down." Chris's voice seemed to come from far away. "I knew if I got a couple drinks in you, helped you chill, you'd be into me. I just gave you something to help you relax. Jumpstart the process." His hand touched her hip, but it was like it was someone else's body he was touching.

There was a shimmer on the sliding glass doors to the balcony, like the reflection of something vast swimming by.

Fuck, Chris had drugged her with something. She stumbled toward her room, but he was coming after her, making calming noises. She veered into the bathroom, because that was closer, but he came after her, and she couldn't get the door shut in time. Everything was white and silvery and black and spinning, and her back was against the wall. "Let's see what you've got going on under there." Chris's breath on her face was sugar and rot.

Then the shower curtain rattled, and the room stank of sea water and salt, and Chris screamed. Sydney reeled away from a confusion of scales and spines, and then suddenly Chris was *gone*, and her head was clear, poof, like she hadn't been drugged at all. She lifted her gaze from the tile floor and looked at the serpent, undulating, and watched as it swallowed.

Then it vanished down the drain, and she was alone.

Sydney wandered through the apartment. It was as if Chris had never been. His room was full of her and Hot Derek's storage boxes. His bike wasn't hanging in the entryway. She went to her computer, and the only "Chris McLaren"s she could find on Facebook weren't him, and every other site she tried came up dry, too. .

The serpent swims through time. She had devoured Chris, and… made him cease to be. Sydney wasn't drugged anymore, because the person who'd given her the drugs had never existed. The serpent had devoured him. The serpent who devoured evil men. Men who tried to hurt women. She consumed them so completely, it undid all the other hurts they'd perpetrated, retroactively.

Sydney sat on the couch, thinking. Her mind was as calm and cool as a still pond. After a while the Dereks returned. "How was the play?" she said.

"What play? We were just at the bar."

Oh, right: no Chris, no tickets. "Oh, sorry. I misremembered."

Hot Derek dropped onto the couch beside her. "Why are you sitting in the dark?"

"I was just thinking. About stuff. The election and everything."

"Ugh," Tall Derek said. "We've been drinking to forget it. I just don't know what we're supposed to *do* now. Like, our literal president-to-be is a guy who brags about sexual assault. How is this our actual reality?"

"I was thinking of going to Washington DC in January," Sydney said. "I'm sure there'll be a protest march for the inauguration. It might be interesting, to see the enemy up close." She looked at the balcony doors, and watched the long, scaled reflection of a serpent swim past in the glass.

NICK MAMATAS

THE KODIAK BELL

NICK MAMATAS

Nick Mamatas is the author of several novels, including *The Last Weekend* and *I Am Providence*, and short stories appearing in *Best American Mystery Stories, Tor.com, Asimov's Science Fiction*, and dozens of other venues. He is also an anthologist, having co-edited the Locus Award nominees *The Future is Japanese* and *Hanzai Japan* with Masumi Washington, and the Bram Stoker Award winner *Haunted Legends* with Ellen Datlow. His next book, the hybrid cocktail recipe/flash fiction anthology *Mixed Up*, co-edited with Molly Tanzer, was published in late 2017. Nick's fiction and editorial work have also been nominated for the Hugo, World Fantasy, and International Horror Guild awards.

ONE DOESN'T NORMALLY FIND CHRIST, MUCH LESS ORTHODOXY, THROUGH PUNK and metal, but it happened to me. It was the usual mish-mash—underground Serbian nationalist hardcore, an issue of *Death to the World* with a serene-looking monk holding a human skull on his palm on the smudged Xeroxed cover, a place to get out of the heat on Sunday, and icons staring from every corner, practically begging me to do something. *Come earlier next week to stay for the whole liturgy* (though I didn't understand a word of Arabic). *Become a catechumen. Stop meeting my "older boyfriend" and exchanging hand jobs for hamburgers* (one shouldn't cultivate lust, and one should fast regularly). *Stop huffing forever, stop drinking, forever. But do not fear,* the icons told me, *the blood of Christ never counts as alcohol, because it literally is the blood of Christ.*

The icons told me: *the miracle is that the Blood still tastes like a spoonful of wine.*

The icons told me: *Steal the Kodiak Bell.*

When the Church tells a story, you'd best settle in, as even the most contemporary of issues start with either the Bible or an early Church Father wandering the desert or having his guts ripped out. I'm a miserable sinner, not the church, so I'll start in the middle. I liked to read books, but didn't like school. I liked living in Los Angeles, but my parents didn't like me living with them. Nobody is stupider than an intelligent autodidact. Nobody is lonelier than a girl who has to make friends fast, every night, to get a couch or half a bed to sleep on. There's that line from The Firesign Theater: "There's a seeker born every minute." That was me. I drifted from paganism to Marxism to an obsession with krav maga to an obsession with whatever hobby the man I was spreading for at the moment would like best, and even dallied with Scientology—though luckily they tossed me out when they realized that I had no money and thus could never become Clear. Thank you, Lord.

In California, back in the 1980s and 1990s, a few punks looking for a real counterculture joined St. Herman's monastery. The ascetic life is pure straight edge, but ecstasy comes from the Holy Spirit rather than power chords and adrenaline-stoked drum beats. All that Minor Threat/Positive Force stuff is ancient history to me, but it brought me to where I am now, hanging by a strand of intestine. By the time I was kicked out of the house, a dying Antiochian Orthodox church near Los Angeles had been visited by some Xian (X for straight edge and for Christ!) punks who were disappointed in their native Protestantism—not much protesting going on there, in Peach Cobbler Land. They were welcomed into the parish, embraced positions of authority and community outreach, and now we have a heavily tattooed psalter and a celibate gay deacon.

I met a few parishioners at an all-ages show. They'd come to mosh, and to proselytize, just like the Maoists, the white nationalist Thor-worshippers, the Krishna Consciousness people, and obscure cults and sects common enough to California but unknown elsewhere: the Cosmic Tuning Fork cult, the "raisin-eaters", the Prodhounian-Anarcho Free Silverites.

Starting a movement is a great way for older men to find teens who'll fornicate with them.

I wouldn't say that the kids from Saint Katherine the Educator stood out as happier or more authentic than anyone else, but I didn't get a predator vibe from them, so two weeks Sundays later I found myself in a half-empty church, incense swirling about me, chants thrumming along the great beams holding up the hull-shaped walls. I got a part-time job at a gyro place thanks to the father of one of the parishioners. Let nobody tell you different—food service work is the bomb. You get a paycheck every week, plus cash in hand and a free meal, sometimes two, on the daily.

And the Kodiak Bell, there's a story too. It's a Russian bell, cast for the first Orthodox Church in Alaska in the late eighteenth century, and it's been in the possession of the Roman Catholic mission of San Fernando Rey de España since…well, who knows how long. Or how it got there. The Russian incursion into California was harshly resisted by the Spanish hegemony back in the early 1800s, when the bell was probably brought down to the mission, to barter for food or pay off a gambling debt. The bell itself was buried sometime in the nineteenth century for obscure reasons, and was forgotten. In 1920, during some landscaping, it was rediscovered and placed back in the mission. The Catholics have kept it ever since.

And there's another story, the story of Cungagnaq, aka Saint Peter the Aleut, aka the Martyr of San Francisco, aka my companion on this dark night. Peter was converted by Russian monks up in Alaska, and hunted seal up and down the West Coast. The Spanish Franciscans captured Peter and his fellows, and tortured him. First they snipped off his fingers, one by one, in an attempt to get him to renounce the Church and instead embrace Rome. Then they brought in some "mission Indians"—Tongva people enslaved by the mission, and had them cut off Saint Peter's stumpy hands. Then they sliced him upon, chin to groin, like a fish.

That's how most of the stories go. California's a big state and nineteenth century record-keeping was spottier than even nineteenth century transportation. Some reports have Saint Peter's martyrdom occurring in San Francisco, while others place the crime down here, near Saint Pedro, which makes sense given that the Port of Los Angeles is nearby. Others think Saint Peter may have been martyred on Catalina Island. I'm not even sure if it makes sense for an Alaskan seal-hunter to be so far south in California waters, but the lives of the saints are not always matters of strictest literalism.

My church, Saint Kath's, is pan-Orthodox. The liturgy, a mish-mash of Arab, Greek, and English. The basement full of vodka like a Serbian joint; the iconography mostly Russian. An icon is not a painting or a mosaic, not really. An icon is a window. The saints live on near us, in a place where time moves very differently, and they can see us and we them. Saint Peter the Aleut, whose skin was dark as mine, whose thick coat was much like the big Swedish grenadier's greatcoat from World War II I used to sleep under, caught my eye. And I caught his.

Amelia, he told me. *Return the bell to the mother church.* It was a real thing, a communication from a saint, into my whole body. I didn't hear it in my ears or even my mind so much as I felt it in my rib cage, along my spine. The world is a demon-haunted one, a fallen place in which we all live and die. An imp could just as easily be shaking my bones as a saint, I knew, and so I prayed. I'm a miserable sinner, one of the most vile to ever have lived—as are we all—so of course I'd be prone to demonic influence and obsession. I was a new believer, eager for experience and *theosis*. Like I would have said of myself a year earlier, I was down for whatever, any time, anywhere. It took months to prepare. I read all I could about Saint Peter the Aleut, and about supernatural manifestations. I did not talk to my spiritual father, which was my great mistake. Amelia Chen Gonzalez, street kid, former occasional druggie, awkward parishioner who ate too many cookies during coffee hour after services…if I wasn't being manipulated by Satan I was clearly just having a psychotic breakdown. I didn't want anyone to tell me that, to send me away.

And if it was the saint, if it was Peter the Aleut…

I could have written a letter.

I could have launched a blog.

I could have made a YouTube video.

I could have prayed that God would prefer that the bell ring once more into the frozen Alaskan dawn, and gathered others of the church to pray similarly. I could have written a paper letter to the brothers of the Monastery of Saint Herman, and waited for a paper letter response.

I didn't have to break into San Fernando Rey de España.

I didn't have to spend a day casing the joint, taking pictures like a tourist with my seven-year-old dumbphone.

I didn't have to sidle up to Serge one Sunday afternoon after church and ask him to coach me on the use of kettlebells. I didn't have to flirt with him, or stroke his arms, or kiss him while working out in his garage either. He told me as much, after his lips lingered on mine for longer than they should have. Of course he'd train me—I was his sister in Christ. *No funny business* was his promise, and he mostly kept it except when adjusting my form during squats.

I needed to get swoll to lift the bell, to carry it on my back.

In the church's small library, I read up on the saints and basic Old Church Slavonic. I wanted to be able to read the bell's original inscription myself. Was Peter the Aleut illiterate?

I knew all about the mission system already, as every kid in California has to pick a mission from among those dotting the long El Camino Real, and write a report about it at some point in their academic careers. Peter the Aleut had been to one, and perhaps never left it. There wasn't a shred of evidence to place Saint Peter the Aleut near the Kodiak Bell, or San Fernando Rey de España, except for what he told me, and what dwelled within my heart.

What was it like, seeing a strange new religion, one nearly identical to the one he had just embraced, one who served the same One God that had replaced the many spirits he had previously venerated, treat him as an enemy? Pull out the knives. I printed out pictures and carried them with me, and visited the mission as a tourist.

It's a nice place, the Mission, though I could smell blood. I could smell the blood of my poor martyred saint Peter the Aleut even though the mission mostly collapsed twenty-five years before I was born, in the big 1971 quake, and was rebuilt from the ground up. I could smell the blood even though the mission is on the U.S. National Register of Historic Places, is a California Historical Landmark, and a Los Angeles Historic-Cultural Monument. The signage was subtle, but oppressive all the same.

The church itself was glorious, though the statues turned my stomach. I grew up a nominal Catholic, but after two years in an Orthodox Church, I found graven images unnerving. The icons I loved always put me at ease, like opening a curtain at the beginning of another sunny Los Angeles and seeing a friendly neighbor drive by. You wave, and she waves back, from world to world. The walnut statues looked like there was someone trapped inside, straining to break free of a wooden coffin made to fit.

I was more concerned with the statues than security. Despite its history and infamy, San Fernando Rey de España is just another place to drag middle-school kids to, or pray at if you're Catholic and can compartmentalize the taint of genocide. Some of the religious art on display was precious and artifacts are rare, but it's not like you can sell a seventeenth century mahogany relief of the Christ Child on the streets for crack money. The glass cases and alarms were proof against casual vandals, not thieves.

No, not thieves. Reclaimers.

I am not a thief. That's why I was chosen. Even back before the church, when I didn't know always know where my next meal was coming from, I never stole. I went hungry instead, like a saint might. But I learned how to be good at getting into places, and staying there unseen. I can sleep standing up. I can stay awake all night, still as a statue, quiet as a ghost, an apology or a good story on my lips and tears in my eyes ready to launch, in case of discovery.

I was raised from birth to accomplish this task Saint Peter the Aleut asked of me.

San Fernando Rey de España is a big complex too, which made things easier. I wouldn't break in, I decided. I'd just visit again, loiter in the Convento's wine cellar, keep an ear out for the doddering old security guard, hope that Saint Peter the Aleut was with me and that…

Surely in heaven saints don't disagree with one another, even if some are only Catholic saints.

Surely I wouldn't have a wooden hand reach out for me to slice off my fingers, to cut open my belly…

I brought a footstool, a knife, a length of clothesline, and some granola bars with me, and carried them in my everyday rucksack.

The old high school trick of standing on the toilet in the far end stall after closing hours, then hustling out when the janitor comes in to the restroom to clean the stall closest to the hiding place worked fine. Then it was a quick rush to the Convento and down into the wine cellar. Which did not smell like wine.

The Kodiak bell wasn't kept behind a glass case, nor was it set into the mission's belfry. It hung from a wooden beam, like a belt or purse thrown lazily over a doorknob. I stood under it for a long moment, wondering. My plan was to walk out with it, get it back to my room for the night, and then in the morning simply ship it to Saint Herman's in Alaska via UPS. It would be expensive, but I'd been saving my tip money. My plans were simple because I expected to get away with it. God wanted the Kodiak Bell hanging in an Orthodox church, not in a Catholic museum. I was the mysterious way in which He worked.

Though I paused…

Because.

I'm still a street kid. At heart.

A sin in the form of a thought—was I being set up?

By God?

The stepladder was a bit wobbly.

I saw myself on the ground, arms thrown wide open, neck at a fatal angle. The police, the museum officials, the Missionary Oblates of Mary Immaculate who run the religious aspects of the mission piecing together my life, my story, and realizing, finally, the crime they've been complicit with and agreeing to return the bell.

Maybe some of the witnesses to my broken body wouldn't understand at all, would consider the bell cursed forever after.

That's one way to separate the sheep from the goats.

If that's what I was to be, so be it, I decided. Then I saw him.

Saint Peter the Aleut, straddling the beam from which the Kodiak Bell hung. I let the rucksack slide from my shoulders. I couldn't pull my eyes away from him. Not as I reached for the zipper to undo my bag. He looked back at me, his face serene, stoic.

Saints never seem to smile.

I upset the ladder as I set it up, and pinched my finger, but still didn't even glance down at my work. In the distance I heard something move. I didn't turn to look over my shoulder to see if anyone was coming.

Better they find me, bell in hand. Then I could tell them.

And I didn't want to tear my eyes from Saint Peter the Aleut.

Was it his bell, after all?

Was he murdered for it?

Would he tell me?

I put the knife in my mouth, the loop of clothesline around one arm, climbed the ladder, and reached. I was too short.

My idea was to throw the clothesline over the beam, tie the end to the bell, cut the bell's own rope and ease the bell down. But though the roof of the mission was fairly low, I was very short and my stepladder not tall enough to get me up there.

Saint Peter the Aleut reached out his arms, as if to pull me up onto the beam.

He had no hands.

In 1987, the Orthodox Diocese of Alaska, through an intermediary, asked Pope John Paul II if they could borrow the bell for several months. And miraculously, the Pope said yes! But the bell was never removed from the beam from which it hanged due to what the few articles on the subject describe simply as "complications."

Saint Peter the Aleut's hands were sliced off. He could not help me up. He could not undo the rope holding the bell. That was a complication.

I took the length of clothesline from around my shoulder and put the loop in hand. The knife, I held in my mouth. I jumped and grabbed the beam. It creaked and I nearly yowled from the pain of aged wood digging into my palms. Saint Peter the Aleut watched, impassively. I managed to toss some of the clothesline over the top of the beam with a flick of my wrest. My heart was pounding. Saint Peter the Aleut had waited centuries for this; it would take centuries for his icons to smile. Thanks to Serge, I could do an extended one-arm hang. Like a kid on a playground climbing structure, I shuffled hand over hand, closer to the bell.

I heard a noise behind me.

I dared not look, dared not lose my grip.

Saint Peter the Aleut shifted his gaze.

I slipped the clothesline through the crown of the bell and looped it over the top of the beam. I started to cut into the rope holding the bell, but had to give up. I was about to let myself down, to rest a bit and let the blood flow back to my arms when I heard the stepladder skitter away as if kicked down the hall.

A series of miracles happened.

A thick hand grabbed my ankle.

The beam creaked.

My muscles screamed.

I looked down.

A walnut monk from the altar had a firm grip on my foot.

He pulled.

I screamed.

Time slowed down.

The bell wobbled.

The clothesline gave way.

A second wooden hand grabbed my other ankle.

My hands slipped.

Saint Peter the Aleut with his handless arms shifted and opened his thick winter coat.

I fell backward toward the floor.

I reached for the beam, the swirling ropes, anything.

From Saint Peter the Aleut spilled forth his intestines, his viscera.

I grabbed at them.

They squished between my fingers.

I wrapped them around my hands, my wrists.

They stopped unfolding out of the great gash in his torso.

They held.

The walnut statue was stiff again, still.

I pulled my feet from the grip of its dead wooden hands.

The bell floated to the floor like a feather.

The lights came on, slowly, like the sun rising.

FROM SOMETHING EMERGING

S. QIOUYI LU

S. QIOUYI LU

S. Qiouyi Lu is a writer, artist, narrator, and translator; their writing has appeared in *Uncanny* and *Strange Horizons*, among other venues. In their spare time, they enjoy destroying speculative fiction as a dread member of the Queer Asian SFFH Illuminati. Find out more at s.qiouyi.lu or follow them on Twitter at @sqiouyilu.

'VE LEARNED HOW TO TILT MY HEAD AT THE RIGHT ANGLE TO LURE SOMEONE IN,
how to fake a Duchenne smile. How to pretend to be prey when I'm anything but. Tonight, I'm out to dinner at one of the more high-end restaurants in downtown LA with a white guy named Kevin, and the only thing betraying my true nature is the side of deep-fried silkworm pupae that I've ordered.

"I'm an adventurous eater," I say when he raises an eyebrow. Then, with the innocent smile he expects, I add, "I'll try anything once."

That gets a lewd grin out of him. "Oh?"

I nod. "I'm pretty open-minded."

"I pegged you for the shy type. Vanilla," he says. He takes a sip of wine and swirls the glass. Despite his cool demeanor, there's something fake about him. If he's hiding an animal inside him, it's probably some kind of mite: successful, sure, but still gross and parasitic.

"Me? Vanilla?" I say in surprise, but of course I'm not surprised. People see my black hair, my pale skin, my "almond-shaped" eyes, and assume from that that I'm shy and meek, obedient and pliant. Like how all Asian girls are. I let them believe it, if only for long enough to get them where I want them. "Nah."

He grins and sets down his wine. "Then what are you into?"

It's the first question he's asked about me all night, but even then it's not really about me: he wants to know what to expect after dinner, how he's going to get himself off. I look into those watery blue eyes, too pale to hold much real color, and disgust unfurls in my gut.

But I have to keep up this persona I'm playing. I mask anything that might betray my disinterest; I tell him what he wants to hear. I start with the standard fetishes; then, I move on to the ones that men think are kinky, but are still pretty standard—a flush starts to rise on his cheeks. I throw in a couple more fetishes, and finally, I lower my voice and lean in close:

"But honestly, all I want is to taste every part of you. I want to suck you up and swallow all of you down into me; I want to leave you in such a stupor that all you can do is lie there in bliss." I smile. "I just want to eat you up."

The glimmer in his eyes tells me I've caught him. After our orders arrive, I swear he finishes his entrée in a dozen bites; I'm only a third through mine, but I tell him I'm full even though I'm not. I sip my glass of water, my neck long and slender; as I put the glass down, I catch his gaze.

"Wanna get out of here?" I curl my lips into a tiny smirk.

"Hell yeah."

We leave the moment the server comes back with his receipt, and soon we're back at his place, a high-end apartment in a Spanish Colonial-style building—no doubt financed by Mommy and Daddy. He makes to get started immediately, but I draw things out. I shut the curtains of his apartment; city lights still twinkle through, but the curtains are opaque enough to mask our forms. I take my sweet time getting undressed, commanding his attention with every move.

I let him cup the curve of my hip with one hand, let him touch me all over. I suppress a shudder—I'm not attracted to him in the least, but this, too, is part of the hunt: hot blood, pumping thick with lust and adrenaline, satisfies my hunger longer than any other kind of blood. I get on my knees, flash a dazzling smile up at him, and get to work on him. I ignore the musk filling my nose; I take the salt on my tongue as a price I have to pay to get him closer to satiating me. He lets out a groan.

Any longer and he'll start to cool down. I shift. As always, my transformation begins with my jaw unhinging. Before he can react and run off, I'm on six legs, his torso wrapped in my other two, my hunched back just short of brushing against the ceiling.

I did tell one lie: I said he'd be in bliss afterward. But when I'm done with him, all I leave behind is a husk that can't feel a thing.

My first memory is of watching my father consume my mother. This was back in our old home in South El Monte, a squat little one-story house; there wasn't much room, but it was enough for me, my parents, and my sister.

My older sister was already asleep that night. I heard sounds coming from the kitchen and took soft steps over, my feet slippered. I peered around the doorframe. Mama was murmuring something, whimpering almost, and even back then I wondered, *How come she's not fighting back?* But with Ba looming over her like that, I suppose it would've been hard to. He had her pinned up against the corner of the counter with nowhere else to go.

I've seen my father transform many times since then, but that first time was still the most terrifying. The way he opened his mouth, the *crack* of his jaw unhinging, mandible splitting and growing into two ragged pincers. Skin tearing bloodlessly to reveal four more legs, each tapered to a fine point, all scrabbling against tile and granite to cage my mother in further. It only took a few seconds, and then my father was a hulking spider of a man, exoskeleton gleaming, sharpened and polished with practice.

My mother was silent when he went in to feed on her. He tore her mouth open with his, sucking her out tongue-first. All manner of viscous and disgusting sounds, thick slurps and everything liquid and flesh, and then she was gone. My father didn't even leave a husk. I watched in terror, but even when I was that young, there was something about that event that sparked other sensations within me: a longing, a hunger of my own.

The transformation back was just as quick. In a moment, there he was again, all trace of spider gone: just a middle-aged man with a little bit of a stoop, the bald spot on his head growing ever-larger. He walked toward the dining room and I pressed myself into the dark corner by the kitchen door, my heart thumping as my father passed by me without noticing that I was there. Back before I grew up enough to understand the shape of the world and the way things worked, I was horrified by the fact that my father had just transformed from a gentle, soft-spoken man into a spider and back with so little effort—surely something had possessed him; surely he had switched places with a monster.

It was only when I was older that I realized there was no division between my father and the monster. That spider was inside him the whole time, just like how there was already a spider growing inside me, too.

Kevin leaves a bad aftertaste, and in a couple days I'm hungry again.

There's nothing in my apartment that would satisfy me the right way. I could go to the grocery store, or maybe one of the restaurants near me. I'm in Pasadena these days, enough a part of the San Gabriel Valley to have all the perks of great food, but far enough from what I might call "home" to provide me with some distance from my father.

But it's not my stomach that's growling; food won't help. I go through my texts and pick up a thread from another guy I'd been talking to who seemed decent. I ask Cory if he's free tonight; my phone pings a couple seconds later— *As it happens, I am. Were you thinking of meeting up?*

Sure, I type, adding a winking emoji for good measure. We've been messaging online and via text for maybe a couple weeks, but I still haven't met up with him yet. He comes off as a standard Caltech nerd in his photos, so I'm not expecting much in the looks department, but who knows about everything else—if anything, I swear it's nerds who have the highest sex drives. I won't have to do much to coax him to where I can feed on him.

We arrange to meet on campus. I live on the far side of Pasadena City College; it's only a few blocks' walk over to Caltech. His pictures don't do him justice—he's still very much a white bread kind of nerd, but in a sweet and wholesome way. Not so much scrawny as he is slender. His face lights up when he sees me.

"Hi," he says. "Annie?"

I nod. "Hey Cory. It's great to finally meet you." I flash him my best smile.

"So, I was thinking," Cory says, "we could grab dinner at Chandler—I mean, if you don't mind; I know it's not that fancy, but the food's not bad."

Via text, Cory had come off as a little boring, but I'm seeing now that there's so much more enthusiasm and body language that didn't come through in that format. He's just so damn eager, but I guess I don't mind. Better than the self-reassured assholes I'm used to picking up.

"No, that's fine," I say.

As we walk toward Chandler Café, his hand brushes against mine. I don't know if it's on purpose or not, but he apologizes profusely—"Sorry, sorry, that was an accident I swear. I mean, if I were going to hold your hand I'd ask first, promise." I'm amused, if not a little charmed. He seems so flustered around me, and it's flattering, in a way.

We separate to order our dishes cafeteria style, then join back up at a table by a window. Cory's Mongolian barbeque could probably feed an army. When he catches me glancing at the pile of food on his plate, he grins.

"See, you only have one bowl to put your ingredients into," he says. "But they didn't put a limit on how high you can pile the ingredients."

I laugh. After that, I expect Cory to start chattering about himself like most guys, but he starts the conversation with a question.

"Pasta, huh? You like Italian food?"

I nod. "It's my favorite."

I half expect him to talk about how he's Italian himself and make some kind of innuendo out of that, or to say that he makes great spaghetti and that I should come over for a taste, hint hint, wink wink. But then I realize that I'm projecting a mix of my past experiences and the hooks my flirty persona would use onto him.

Instead, he recommends his favorite Italian restaurant and a couple others in town. Then, he asks, "So what do you like to do in your spare time?"

"Rock-climb and hike, mostly," I reply. "There's a climbing wall at the gym I go to; it's really fun. And I love exploring, but I never have someone to discover cool things with."

I'm surprised by how easy it is for me to talk to Cory. He seems to actually be listening to me, seems to be interested in more than my looks. Part of me feels suspicious, but another part of me chides me for being suspicious—*Not all men are terrible, Annie. Maybe you've finally met someone nice.*

"Have you ever been in Tech's steam tunnels?" Cory asks.

"Steam tunnels?"

Cory's eyes light up. "Dude, have you never even *heard* of them? There are all these tunnels running under the campus; students have been going in and out of them for years, and there's some pretty fantastic stuff down there. Murals and all sorts of Caltech lore. Want me to show you?"

I have to admit that I'm intrigued. Cory's enthusiasm is contagious, and the tunnels do sound cool. I've been meaning to do more urban exploration, anyway.

"Please," I say.

The hallway above had glowed a gentle orange, but as we descend the stairs to the tunnels, the light grows dim, illuminated not by lamps but by individual hanging lightbulbs.

"So," Cory says, "here we are—careful of the pipes; some of them can be really hot. If we go on ahead, there's a mural of Medusa."

The tunnels are hotter and more humid than I expected, and cramped enough that I have to follow closely behind Cory and watch my step so that I don't trip on anything. We reach a crude painting of Medusa, her hair wild, her tongue lolling. Cory reads aloud the sonnet painted beside it, titled "But Maybe I Won't":

> *"Medusa, wicked maiden, death within*
> *Your gaze: you are a monstrous being. Too*
> *Beloved your golden hair, it lured anew.*
> *Athena turned you into living sin;*
> *The Goddess, so enraged by sight of skin*
> *Believed 'twas you, and not Poseidon, who*

Bore all the blame. Medusa, chaste were you
To be in Pallas' temple, sacred inn.

"But maybe it was not Medusa's fault.
Did no one ever stop and ask if she
Accepted Neptune? Fault lay not with her
But with Poseidon and with Pallas. I halt
This tale and weep for her, her pain; for me.
Medusa lost the whole that once we were."

I'd stop to contemplate the poem, but Cory's already moving on, gesturing and speaking as if he's given this tour a dozen times.

"The next mural I'm taking you to is a lot bigger—there are four Cow murals, but one's kind of hard to get to and a broken pipe destroyed the other one a while back."

We reach a rickety staircase; the clanging of our footsteps echo as we go down one level. True to his word, this mural takes up an entire wall. Block letters form the word LOVE; figures and symbols adorn the letters.

"As you might be able to guess, this mural is called Love; the two we weren't able to visit were Hope and Faith." Cory tells the lore behind each symbol, how they each represent one of the Houses at Caltech; I can't help but feel that all of this feels like it's part of some kind of fantasy novel. When I bring up the comparison to Cory, he snorts.

"Yeah, lots of people say that," he says. He smiles, and a moment passes between us; we make eye contact for perhaps a second too long. I flush; I don't know if I'm feeling awkward, or maybe some kind of attraction.

And then Cory says, "Wow. You're beautiful."

My eyes widen, and suddenly I don't know what to do. I know how to read people who are expecting something out of me, who have already decided who I am; then, it's just a matter of playing to their imagination and their stereotypes. But Cory seems genuinely interested and I'm at a loss; it's like he's seeing *me* and I've long since forgotten how to just be myself.

"May I…?" he says, and I nod.

He cups my neck and kisses me. It doesn't send a shiver down my spine, but then again, the only kiss that ever did do that was the one I shared with my best friend on her sixteenth birthday. Cory's kiss isn't terrible either, not like some of the others I've had; I could almost call this enjoyable.

When we part, he smiles sheepishly, and I find myself blushing and looking away—so uncharacteristic of me.

"So," Cory says, "um, I guess that's Love—the mural, I mean!"

There he is all flustered again, and I can't help but laugh. We make our way back up the stairs, and Cory leads the way to the next mural.

"I hope you're not claustrophobic," he says. The tunnels in this section feel cooler, no longer humid; I even feel goosebumps on my skin.

"No," I say. I see better in the dark when I'm a spider; as a human, I remember that darkness holds no more terror than light. "Why?"

"There's going to be a stretch where I'll have to turn off my flashlight—the last mural is best viewed in the dark."

"Huh." I don't know what that might entail, but I'm excited to find out. The lighting in the tunnels has long since gone; we're relying only on Cory's flashlight at this point—and then, when we're some ways down the tunnel, he switches it off. The world plunges into absolute black; I hold my hand out before my face—I can't see anything.

"You doing okay?" Cory asks.

I nod, but then I remember that it's dark. "Yeah."

"Great. Just follow my voice and footsteps."

Tap tap tap; a couple more minutes, then the footsteps stop.

"Okay, stand right there," Cory says. "And let your eyes adjust."

I stand still and stare straight ahead, not sure what I should be seeing. I thought maybe it'd be some kind of glow-in-the-dark mural whose effect would be lost if Cory still had his flashlight on, but I guess it must be something different.

"What should I be looking for?"

"Just wait." Cory's voice sounds a little more distant. I squint at the darkness, and right when I'm about to whirl around and tell Cory off for playing an asinine prank on me, parts of the darkness grow a little lighter, to the point where I can make out some contrasts. Bold, black lines form the edges of block letters, no drawings within like with Love, and then I see it—

FEAR.

My heart skips a beat, and right at that moment, a clatter echoes against the concrete. I whirl around; I can make out a giant shape, but all I can tell is that it's moving toward me, fast. I trust my reflexes; I dodge, and the thing crashes into the wall.

"What—"

I back away. Now that it's still, I can make out its shape: a scorpion, stinger held aloft, pincers pinned against the wall; my mind whirs, and in an instant, I understand.

"You—!"

I will my body to transform. The pull and tug, the way I elongate and re-shape myself; it's a burning sensation, a strange type of pain, but then there's venom and power coursing through me and all I feel is anger.

I can see him clearly now as he turns back toward me: his eight eyes, every segment of his tail, the way his mouth parts clack open and shut with excite-ment. We circle around each other; I can barely make out the amber of his tail, the deep maple of his body—under any other circumstance, I'd call him beautiful.

I release a pheromone. *You tricked me.* It's not a particularly nuanced way of communicating, especially across species, but there's no way in hell I'm trans-forming back into a human in front of him.

You want to be food, he replies. *I want to eat.*

I bristle. *You think I want to be food?*

You do. You're so easy.

He pounces on me; too late, I realize that he provoked me long enough, circled with me just so, so that I'm up against the wall when he attacks. I try to fend him off, try to push him away. But the more I struggle, the more he throws his weight on me and crushes me into the concrete surface. I'm on my back; he constricts me, pins my limbs to my side. I keep trying to fight, but soon I realize that I can't do much, and panic starts to rise in my chest.

He leans in and clamps his pincers down. In a last-ditch attempt, I try to kick out against him, try to bite him, but he grips me so hard that I can't move.

He brushes his stinger against me, white-hot and venomous; he releases a message: *Stay still or die.*

He starts to feed.

It's such a violating feeling: an intrusion, him tugging open my pincers; suddenly I remember my mother being sucked out by her tongue and I wish I could scream, but in this form I have no voice. He's sucking me down, burrowing his way deeper into me, and I want him out, I want him *out* and I won't have him consuming me; I can't let him—

But he already is, and I feel myself growing weaker; I feel myself being overwhelmed. As he grows fuller and fuller, he lets his grip slack, and in his greed he leaves an opening: I twist away from him, sink my pincers into his chest, tear open a gash; he retreats in reflex. I run out, back down through that dark tunnel, only it's growing narrower and in a few paces I won't be able to fit.

I have to change back. I'm so much more vulnerable that way, but I have no choice; my body shrinks back into human form. Jaw aching, entire body sore, I feel my way back down the tunnel, stumbling as I think to myself, *Please, please don't let me sprain an ankle; please let me get out.* I hear a faint scrabbling coming behind me and know he's gotten back up. He knows these tunnels better than I do, but I've got a head start and a decent sense of direction; it's all I can do to make my way out as fast as I can.

When I can't hear scrabbles anymore, I feel terror and not relief: he must've turned human again, too, and with his much smaller form, the sounds he makes will be harder to keep track of, too. I pass the staircase down to Love and my stomach twists; I can't look back or let any stray thoughts into my head—all I can do is tell myself that at least I'm going the right way.

Then I'm running past Medusa and I hear footsteps behind me; I sneak a glance back and Cory's close, too close—there's a decent distance between us, but I wish I couldn't even see him; I wish he weren't even *there*—

I push all of my remaining energy into dashing toward the exit; I bound up the stairs in twos and burst out the door, back into the courtyard above. The air outside is cool, but against the sweat on my skin, it sends chills all over my body. A few people mill about; I don't know anyone on this campus and I'm not sure how to ask for help: *Please save me from a guy who can turn into a scorpion.* Those of us who can shift keep it to ourselves; I don't know who I can trust to believe me.

So I run. But before I get very far, I hear someone shout, "Cory!" and I can't help but turn to see where he is.

He's out from the tunnels, and the gash I left bleeds through his torn shirt; a girl rushes up to him.

"Are you okay?"

"Yeah, no worries," he says, and he flashes her that same sheepish smile he used on me earlier—I might throw up. "Fell while in the tunnels. I'll be fine."

I turn to run again, but right as I'm doing so, I catch his gaze. It's flint-cold and full of anger: *How dare you get away.* And in that instant, as he lets that girl walk him to the student health center, I understand: He won't chase me here, not while there are people around. He's going to keep playing the nice guy; he'll find another person to prey on.

I make sure he's not watching me to follow where I'm going, and I walk home. My mind buzzes the whole way, but I can't pick a single thought to focus on. Only when my front door's shut and locked behind me do I finally allow myself to sink to the floor and sob.

I don't forget him in the months that come. I can't suppress the memory of him like how I can hide away my disgust over Kevin, my nausea over all the others I've seduced.

And through it all, I still hunger. It's maddening and brings up only the memory of Cory feeding on me; I can't do that, can't put up the walls that let me pretend I'm happy feeding this way, can't inflict that on anyone else. I'm too busy making sure I can even function through the day to sum up the energy to pretend I'm somebody's perfect China doll.

My older sister comes to visit at the end of spring semester. I don't know if I'm up for seeing her, but I haven't spent time in the presence of another human being for far too long. I normally keep my place tidy, but it's become a mess recently; it's all I can do to clear off the couch for her to sleep on before she comes over.

She gets to Pasadena in the afternoon and greets me with a hug. "Annie, God, it's been way too long—even without traffic, the drive up is a bit long for my taste."

Sara moved in another direction away from our home; she went south to San Diego. I hug her back with limp arms; sensing that my heart's not all into it, she pulls back and scrutinizes me.

"Annie..." she murmurs, "you've lost weight, and you're so pale. Is everything okay?"

Tears spring to my eyes. Absent our mother, Sara practically raised me herself; it's only been once I've gotten older that I realize how much she cares about me.

"Hey, come on; let's get inside." She steers me to the couch and sits me down; I'd protest, but there's never been any use fighting Sara when she's in a mother hen mood. I hear the water running in the kitchen; shame steals over me as I remember that the sink's full of dirty dishes, and I wonder if Sara's judging me for them. She comes back with a clean mug—she must've washed it out herself; more shame falls on me as I think about how guests shouldn't be doing chores. She sets the mug down in front of me.

"Warm water. It'll make you feel better."

I take a sip. Sara's right; I do feel better, if only for a moment. The water washes salt from my tongue, draws back my tears. Sara sits beside me and rubs my back.

"Wanna tell me what happened?"

I open my mouth, but I can't bring myself to speak. My tongue feels useless in my mouth; I end up shaking my head. Sara doesn't say anything either, just lets me rest against her, mug of water still cupped in my hands.

After a long time, I ask her, "Have you ever fed on anyone? Like… like Ba."

Sara furrows her brow. "No, I can't say I have." Then, she smiles: "I guess moths don't really do that."

I remember then that Sara's not like me and Ba; she has a moth inside, a beautiful green luna moth. But my memory of her velvety wings only makes it all the more difficult to contemplate the other question on my mind: *Have you ever been fed on?* I can't imagine that someone as strong and lovely as she is could have ever experienced anything similar, and if she has, it might break my heart to know.

So I don't say anything more, and Sara doesn't ask. We spend a week going to cafés and watching TV; I take her to Old Pasadena and the Norton Simon Museum, and she treats me to ramen and the best baozi I've ever had.

On our last day together, we're sitting at a boba shop in Alhambra; she's ordered Thai tea, her favorite, and I've ordered jasmine milk tea. The sky's a soft, dusty blue, punctuated only with trails of cirrus clouds. I could almost believe that everything is fine.

Sara breaks the comfortable silence between us.

"Mei, you know I'm always here if you need to talk, right? Or if you just want to talk."

"I know."

She reaches across the table, and, instinctively, I place my hand in hers, twining my fingers with hers like how we'd always do as kids.

She smiles.

"Whenever you're ready."

It gets easier sometimes, dancing around my memories, playing at functioning, pretending there isn't this hunger and hurt gnawing at me all the time.

I decide I'll be neither hunter nor prey, but even so, sometimes I find myself falling back into my old ways and playing up other people's lusts. But as I imagine consuming them, my chest goes tight and my breaths grow shallow;

I can't follow through with it and I end up saying good-bye at the end of the dates, choosing instead to spend the night curled up on the couch, watching but not watching reruns.

I discover I'm neither man nor woman, too, and I wonder if this would still be true even if this gnawing weren't killing me, even if what happened hadn't happened. But I suppose that no matter my past, my feelings in the present are still true.

Sometimes, when I see a scorpion, or when I catch a glimpse of Medusa, whether through art, through fiction, through anything that might remind me of her, I remember those tunnels and the art upon their walls.

Maybe I'll succumb to the pain tearing through me too. Maybe I'll give in to it, let it take over me and control my life, let it destroy me from the inside out.

Or maybe…

Maybe I won't.

CHAZ BRENCHLEY

UNCANNY VALLEY

CHAZ BRENCHLEY

Chaz Brenchley has been making a living as a writer since the age of eighteen; this year marks the fortieth anniversary of his first professional sales. He is the author of nine thrillers, two fantasy series, two ghost stories, and two collections, most recently the Lambda Award-winning *Bitter Waters*. He has also published Chinese fantasy as Daniel Fox, and urban fantasy as Ben Macallan. He lost count of his short stories long ago. His work has won multiple awards and commendations, including regular selection for best-of-year anthologies; it has been translated into numerous languages, from Chinese to Estonian. He has recently married and moved from Newcastle to California, with two squabbling cats and a famous teddy bear.

SO THIS IS HOW IT GOES. HOW IT WENT. HOW IT WILL HAVE GONE. SOMETHING. Language is as slippery as meaning is as slippery as time; we have nothing to hold on to but each other.

So. You in the lead, me with my eyes fixed on your extraordinary cyclist's calves, muscles like woven steel cables. You could suspend a bridge with those.

Not that you need them, hereabouts. Do cables slacken, for lack of traffic? Do bridges sag?

Probably not, but I worry even so. Of course I do.

Here's the only climb on this whole damn trail—and it's a ramp, not a hill, doubling back on itself halfway, to lift us up over the freeway. Call it a bridge, then, and call that ironic if you like.

There you go, released at last, rising in the saddle and pumping some wicked gear to test yourself, this brief chance you have. I follow more sedately, falling behind with every revolution, almost stalling out at the turn and needing to grab hold of the railing to keep myself vertical. I'd be embarrassed, but I know that you're not looking. You're way ahead, you've peaked.

I find you halfway over the bridge, you and your bike both just leaning on the rail, chilling while you wait. Watching the commute, almost static below, four lanes in both directions.

"I'm sorry," I say. Gasp, rather. It's a very new thing, this bike. My legs and lungs are burning, both.

"What? This is a ride, not a race. It's only fun if we do it together."

"Not that." You've been very good, honestly: sticking with me all the way, once you found a pace that I could stick to. I do stubbornness where you do grace; between them, I think they'll see us through. "I'm sorry it's so dull here."

"I'm not bored," you say. Your hands don't shift, but your eyes reach out to touch me, up and down and all over. Your mouth quirks a deliberate innuendo.

"Really? Because I am. I don't mean the bike trail," which is frankly as much as I can manage, and who knew I could even manage that? Don't claim that you did; all you had was confidence. Not the same. "And I don't mean you, damn you," which ditto ditto. "It's this place, this endless fucking suburb, from the city down to San Jose. Endlessly flat and endlessly repetitive, not a thing to see that's worth the looking at. High-rise office blocks in rectangles of glass and concrete, apartment complexes all the colours of beige, fifty miles of bloody bungalows cheek by jowl and so determined to look different from their neighbours they have no idea how very much they look alike. And everything stitched together with freeways and expressways and highways and boulevards and Christ."

You're laughing at me now, but that's only fuel to the fire; if it amuses you to see me rant, then I can cheerfully rant for ever. You're as new as the bike, and you leave me just as breathless. "And they call it a valley, but that's only because there are mountains over there and mountains over there," with a nod to each horizon, east and west. "In between it's not a sodding valley, it's a sodding alluvial plain. Which come the flood, please God, for we deserve it."

"No one gets their just desserts," you say, which just about covers God for you too. Whatever I've done in all my life, nothing in it, not all of it together amounts to earning you. "Don't be angry," you say. "Look at me."

And I can do that, I can do that and do that, and of course you're right, it's a panacea. It's a way to stop looking at the rest of it, everything, the desolation of mediocrity. What need I the black tents of my tribe, when I have the red pavilion of your heart?

So there you have it, I'm a besotted romantic, apparently. But this is Silicon Valley, where cynicism comes with the territory and maps itself as opportunity.

The trail is pretty much all I have to offer you, least and best. It takes us to the Bay, which is some kind of horizon, something to look at. Boats and birds, a better class of traffic. Coming home, though, as we are—well, it doesn't actually bring us home. It spits us out a couple of miles short, so that we have that much of traffic lights and trucks, of bike lanes that appear at one junction and vanish the next, of Bay Area drivers whose God-given right it is to cut us off or blast their horns at us for following the rules or somehow neglect to see us altogether.

And yet we make it home intact, and home is my house, just one more bland bungalow in a street and a neighbourhood of just the same, with two-car parking and a front lawn and a back yard and a six-foot fence all around. And I really shouldn't complain, because after five years it's worth twice the mortgage and that number won't be going down; and of course I do complain, because where's the impact, where's the history, where's the ambition? Our town centre believes itself and declares itself historic because one of its buildings—*one*—is a hundred years old. Every plank and every timber replaced again and again, but none the less: a centenarian by virtue of occupation. That's what history means, right? It's still Grandfather's axe.

Bikes under shelter at the back because you insist on it; you first in the shower because you're quicker than I am, both in and out. I'm pulling the cork on a bottle of Cab as you emerge, still damp but only metaphorically steaming, black of hair and lean of form and brown by courtesy but only in the way that twilight is brown, meaning not really, not at all. If I were an artist I'd need green and purple on my palette, to come anywhere near the shadows that your skin addresses.

No artist I, but I can look and look at you.

You hold your hand out, empty, asking. *Drink, or fuck?* It's the eternal question, in the drear of a valley Sunday afternoon. Later there will be Netflix and curry in cardboard containers, and we'll sit like kids on the floor with our backs to the sofa and food between us, arguing amicably and spilling rice on the rug, killing another bottle before we go to bed. Or go back to bed, because there is always this gap to bridge, this pause in the day, this hesitation between here and there.

This question, that this day I answer with a gesture towards where two glasses stand on the coffee-table. Olives and salami from the farmers' market. What can you do but smile, and shrug a little, and go pull some clothes on while I shower in my turn?

When I come out there won't be an offering here for me, as I am here for you. No artisanal aperitif, no alcohol, no you. But I know this going in. If I make space for you, you'll vacate it.

I shower and dry and dress at the best speed that I can, too slow for you; and here's my empty house, as expected. As foretold.

Nil desperandum, and *say not the struggle naught availeth,* and *keep calm and carry on.* I walk through the kitchen, through the mud-room, out into the yard.

I always think I should make more use, better use of the yard, but I never do. You apparently don't stop to think, you're just here. In the middle of the lawn, on the bench appropriated from departing neighbours up the street, drinks and nibbles beside you on the table cobbled together from a couple of plastic crates and a vagrant plank, no interest whatever in the actual patio table with its appropriate chairs and extremely shady umbrella back over there on the actual patio.

So I join you on the bench, you pass my wine and offer an olive, we spit stones companionably into the firepit and the only shade we have is what little the cherry tree can cast across us, *en passant.*

"You haven't been here in cherry season," I say, because he knows this, and it's always best to start from common ground. "You'll enjoy that, you can laugh at us. My friends and I, we like to go full Japanese, sit under the tree and drink tea while the blossoms fall. Wear kimonos, if they've got 'em. I don't, I don't do dressing up, but…"

"But your friends are all pretty as a picture. I know, you showed me photos."

"Did I? Right."

"A lot of photos, actually. And you were in none of them."

"Well, no. Behind the camera, and all that."

"Other people have cameras. Also, other people take selfies."

"Yeah. Those would be other people, right enough. I'm still me. And camera-shy. That's the *point* of all that fancy equipment, something to hide behind. Not to have to be in front of it."

You smile, and reach out to stroke my hair. It's a pact we have: you won't tell me that I'm beautiful, and I won't tell you that you're wrong. It may be the most pointless pact in human creation, because of course we both break it all the time, just not in words. Subtext is instinctive, seemingly.

"It must have been a sight at cherry time," you say, "when all of this was orchards." That's not an exaggeration. We actually live on Orchard Row; I could take you to Almond Avenue and Peach Street and half a dozen others, but this whole neighbourhood is called Cherry Gardens, and many of the yards host a survivor. I like to think they whisper to each other in the night, or send messages by the bees. Hell, I know they send messages by the bees. Pollen is pillow-talk for trees.

"I have photos of that too." I'm halfway to my feet before you can pull me down again.

"I know, you showed me the book. But they weren't in colour, and the trees weren't in blossom."

"We could fix that," I say idly, settling back against your side. "We could fix both of those. Software goes where film-stock never trod."

"Or of course we could just go down to the library and ask to see their archive, because they're bound to have pictures of cherry-blossom time. Just because they're not in your book doesn't mean they don't exist. There were Japanese here a hundred years ago, weren't there? Even if not, it's still the same effect. A whole orchard of blossoms drifting on the wind, someone must have photographed it."

"Still won't be in colour, mind."

"There were still orchards here fifty years ago. Hell, there are still pocket-orchards even now. There are going to be colour pictures. Just because you're obsessed with olden times…"

"I'm not really. Really I'm not. You have to admit, though, the houses were better-looking a hundred years ago."

"And the people were better dressed."

I don't care about the people, or what they were wearing. "You're right, though," I say. "It wouldn't be hard to marry the colours from later pix to the structures of the early ones. And the costumes, yeah yeah. We could do a whole technicolor pictorial tour of the town as she used to be. When's the next big-number anniversary? I know we missed the centennial, but…"

By the time we decide that there are no significant numbers between a hundred and one-twenty-five, and that neither of us is willing to wait that long nor likely to be hereabouts in any case, the idea has morphed in any case, that way ideas do.

Is it you who says it first or is it me, and does it matter? I think both of our minds are already turning the same way. Of course they are. Two geeks in Silicon Valley, of course we'll come up with tech implementations, whatever the idea.

"It's an app. Isn't it?"

"Of course it's a bloody app. Use the GPS for location—"

"—and the acccelerometer and magnetometer for orientation—"

"—right, and then hack the camera so they don't see what's there now—"

"—they see what was there a hundred years ago. Right."

"The library can't have images of everything."

"Doesn't matter. It'll have enough. Most of the downtown, all the distinctive buildings, plenty of representative housing, miles of interchangeable orchards. We can cheat it, write an engine that extrapolates to fill in the gaps. Period housing and trees in serried ranks, it'll be fine."

"Cherried ranks."

"Oh, despair and die. Can we call it that, 'Cherried Ranks'? Probably not. This is going to be great…"

It was always going to be hard work. Two of us to share all the coding, all the research, all the scanning and manipulation. Two of us at first, that is. Who ever thinks to ask for help, with their own bright, difficult, demanding baby?

Friends find out, though, by intent or happenstance or late-night drunk confession. They offer time, skills, contacts: for the laugh, for the company, for the sense of community, for something to do. Or for a consideration.

"Not money, I'm not asking you to pay me. How about stock?"

"We don't have stock. We can't monetise this, for crying out loud: what d'you want, advertisements marching across the view? Logos printed on cherry petals? What?"

"There'll be money in it somewhere, brother. When it takes off. You can sell the code, at least; every small town in America will need this. Take my advice, see a lawyer, set up a corporate structure now. And give me stock."

"What about the people, though?"

"What say?"

"Half these pix have people in them. More than half."

"We can shop 'em out." Little distant figures, mostly, studding the fields and warehouses, occupying the streets. Lending human scale to an otherwise bare and unconvincing view. They tend to be more prominent in the portraits of private houses—pride of ownership, I suppose; we all see ourselves as larger and more meaningful in our own space—but still, it's no hard task to edit them out. People are more transient even than buildings, it turns out, in the timescape of a town.

"We can, yes. But should we? The whole point is to show the place as it used to be. Which was occupied, purposeful, intended. Take the people out, we lose the point."

"Hunh. But if we leave them in"—or hell, their vehicles, their horses, the horseshit in the gutters, everything that really shouldn't be a fixture—"then the picture's obviously static, it looks the same every time they come down that street, it's just a photo rendered into a kind of fake 3-D and we lose any sense that it's a living landscape."

"Same if it's an empty landscape," you say. Winningly in every sense, I guess. "It's still the same every time, and now it's uninhabited. Which is actually freakier than just being frozen in time. Think ghost towns, the *Marie Celeste*, any office building after the workers go home…"

"Okay, so what do you want to do? We can't animate 'em."

"Can't we?"

"No," emphatically. "We don't have the resources." I've stopped saying *or the skills*, because you just counter that with *we can hire the skills*.

"We could pursue the resources," you say instead.

"For this? To fill a virtual town with virtual people, coming and going, realistically? We'd need Disney."

"We can talk to Disney."

"You have ideas above your station."

"I know. Always did." And you smile and reach out and stroke my ankle, which is utterly unfair and disarming and an invitation to surrender, which I do.

"Even so," I say eventually, "that's an order of magnitude beyond where we are."

"I know it. That's 2.0, or 3.0 more likely. It's a promise for the future. Meantime, we've got to do something: more than an abandoned township, less than an active population. Can we have the engine shuffle figures about at random, so that no view's ever entirely empty, but it's never quite the same as last time? It'll still be static at any given moment, but randomly static. Differently static. Yes?"

"Oh, yes. And the trucks and the horses and the wagons. And the horseshit. If it's transient, we can shift it. Market stalls there by daylight, gone at night. The town drunk, there all the time, day or night." I was getting into this. "What else?"

"Trains coming through. On a bloody schedule. We've got the timetables, we can do that. And the population changes with every train. Did you have a model railway in your basement as a kid?"

"Yes, of course I did."

"Because that's what this is, really. It's just a bloody train set, with more scenery than we ever had before."

"On a scale of 1:1."

"Yeah, that."

Actual funding comes from a small start-up comms company that wants to play with the big boys. It thinks this is a way to get its new tech noticed. Now we have actual offices, servers, employees. No day jobs any longer, only this. We can make up our own titles; you want to be Lord High Mukamuk. Of course you do. In the interests of not frightening the bank and the VCs and so forth, not giving hostages to fortune—or the Fortune 500—you're chairman and I'm CEO.

There's some piece of paper somewhere that officially refers to us as The Former CR Corporation. *Cherried Ranks*, still hanging in there.

"This is weird," you say, standing in the doorway of what will be our shared office: two desks, two chairs, a sofa for when we need to get comfy together. An actual filing cabinet, for actual paper files. We're still waiting on monitors, keyboards, connectivity. "Isn't this weird?"

"Come here," I say, "and let me make it weirder."

So you do, and so do I. I've been keeping this, just for this occasion, the way regular people would keep a bottle of champagne. I pull my phone from my belt and touch it on, and show you. Orienting it carefully north-west and holding it up at eye height and almost at arm's distance, like an artificial horizon.

"I've seen a thousand of these," you murmur, not really complaining, only waiting.

"I know, and it feels like a hundred thousand—but this one's ours." The photo on the screen is black and white, with a cryptic notation in one corner, a file number from the library written in white chinagraph pencil.

There's a lane, a fence, an orchard. That's all. The image doesn't move as I orient the phone, because nothing's up and running yet, it's only a photo on my phone—but still you smile, as your eyes move from the screen to the window and back.

"That live oak in the lane there, by the gate," you say. "That's the same tree, isn't it?"

"Yup. Taller, stouter, a hundred years wiser; still the same tree." Grandfather's axe hasn't come anywhere near it. It used to guard a gateway; now it oversees our car park. With our car parked directly in its shade. I decide to have that slot marked, "Reserved for Chairman and CEO," the two of us together. We'll probably bike in most days, but even so.

"I thought I'd get a blow-up print of this," I say, "and hang it on the wall there, between our desks."

"You're right," you say meditatively. "That is exactly where it should go." And then you step out into the corridor, and come back in with a framed print, two foot by three foot, that you'd hidden in the office next door, you sod.

"Two minds with but a single photo," you say, smug to the max.

Of course that's where we'd like to start, home ground, X marks the spot: we could take over the world from here, spreading outwards like a new religion. Every journey starts with a single step, and where better to begin?

But work like this is all about data overlap; the more pictures we have, the less we have to postulate, the better our work and the easier our task. We don't only have this single view of our future office space, and we're confident of finding more, but images of any given single orchard are always going to be thin on the ground. And if we're not that much like a religion, perhaps we're more like bacteria, infecting a Petri dish. It only makes sense to begin where the environment is richest.

We have more photographs of downtown than anywhere else. Of course we do, that's how people work. Everything regresses to the mean. More pictures mean more angles, more details, more data points. Grist to the mill. Our rude crude mill-engine just loves grist.

So we give it what we've got, it gives us all it has. It's like a first date, awkward and hesitant and oversharing, because once we've started we don't know when to stop.

Some day, no doubt, there'll be a VR iteration with goggles and gloves, the whole surroundsight experience, and you can waltz down the street with a lady of the town, if she's willing. I'm sure we'll be able to render willingness some day. And then argue about the meaning of consent with software objects. But we're building this for phones, for today, pushing one boundary at a time. I hope.

Ritually, you and I stand at the end of our one-street downtown. "Phones at twenty paces," I say, but in truth we're side by side, lining them up neatly adjacent, holding the same view and pointing nothing at each other. Yet.

The rest of the crew is grouped behind us, supposedly looking over our shoulders. It's the captain's privilege to be first over the top. In truth, of course, they've all got their own phones in their hands and chances are they're already ahead of us. We're being very careful not to look, not to look back. Only forward.

You say, "Ready? ... Engage."

You're an iPhone, I'm an Android, because it's important to us that we're not two instances of the same person, really not; but we thumb our apps on in sync, and there we are. Looking in one direction, seeing two views. All around us Main Street as she is, full vibrant colour, action, noise; on our phones, Main Street as she used to be a hundred years ago. One recognisable building. Everything silent, static, still black and white because colour rendering lies ahead, in our estimable future. We might only be looking at a photograph, until we turn left and right respectively, stand back to back and the view turns with us. Servers far away are churning through data and spitting back images almost in real time, barely a detectable pause. Nothing I'm seeing now on the phone has survived to the present day, but the patterns make sense. Streets and buildings overlay the landscape then much as they do now, because human needs and desires don't change much or quickly. Ingenuity takes leaps and bounds, perhaps, but even then it pauses, glances back, wants to lead us where we want to follow. Better faster brighter, still the same. We're creatures of the valley floor, evolved to suit.

We turn slowly southerly, as though we've practised this. Hell, of course we've practised this. We knew people would be watching. Some of them may even be recording us, the way we asked them to. This is archival, if it's not historic.

All the way around and our arms line up again, our hands, our phones. One view of how things used to be, orchards and farmhouses from here to the distant line of mountains.

"Toto," I say, "I don't think we're in Kansas any more."

"It's California," you say, "as it always was. As witness. And by the way?"

"Yes?"

"Don't call me Toto."

After that, of course, everyone calls you Toto. To your face—sometimes—and also in print, in phosphors, all over. Images from the movie are everywhere: on our website, in people's cubes, in their emails. On our office door.

"They're not going to buy me a bloody puppy, are they?" you ask, seemingly genuinely anxious.

"I don't suppose so, no. You might get adoption papers for Chanukah," because that's the kind of people we employ: pushing a joke to its limit, in the most virtual way they can realise. "Some kid far away gets to take a rescue dog home, everything paid for, just so long as he pretends to call it Toto and sends you a card every year. Paw-prints and reports. SIT scores. You get to send checks in return."

"The gift that keeps on taking?"

"Yup. Exactly that. How's the Moveable Feast coming along?"

That's iteration 2.0, which of course we're working on before the first release goes live. It's going to be such a surprise. People will log on for what they're used to, for the view, for a glimpse of time gone by; and they'll find people going by. Someone they saw outside the hardware store glimpsed suddenly in profile in the livery stable, harnessing a carriage-and-pair. That grease-monkey in dungarees servicing a two-stroke dairy truck, wasn't he the messenger boy standing on the pedals to drive his bike through the muck of Main Street after what must have been an awesome storm? Could there possibly be two boys that willing, that adaptable, that dirty…?

And so on, and I'm so looking forward to it; and all you say is, "Look."

And you pick up a remote from your desk and work some thumb-magic, and the screen on the wall comes to life.

We've hung it on the wall opposite the print, because this is opposite to that: that's the frozen capture, where this is the live feed. If I turn it on, it's iteration 1.0 and I can drive it anywhere within our compass, look at any view the engine's rendered. You can take it further, look more inwardly, see where we hope to go.

Show me.

"Look," you say, and the screen comes to life. Here's a picnic under the cherry trees, because apparently the Japanese had nothing to teach our ancestors: chairs around a table, linen napery and dishes in profusion, it's really not my idea of a picnic but there they all are, picnicking away. One girl in white is standing at a little distance off. She draws my eye, but it's not—or not only—because she has made that little private space for herself, *not at the table, not eating, not one of you.*

She's also the only one looking at the camera, the only one apparently aware of it, of posterity, of us.

Not happy about it, perhaps. Camera-shy—or narrative-shy, perhaps, not wanting to be one of the happy family? She must actually be one of the family, she's that well-dressed. Certainly not a servant. The servants would be the ones who struggle to keep her dress that white, after she drags the hem of it all over the orchard.

"Look," you say again, and work the buttons on the remote, make the image zoom in. Did I even know we could do that?

There's her face, and here's our engine working, extrapolating, showing us more detail than the original could ever have retained. Picking out her face in painful detail: staring, accusatory, distressed.

"I've no idea what her story is," you say, "but there has to be one, doesn't there? She has to have a story."

"Everyone has a story," I say. "It's just that most of them are as dull as other people's dreams."

Not hers. You don't need to say it. That's where we are now, that we often don't need to say something aloud, we can just let it go for granted. It's a comfortable place to find ourselves, but sometimes I think it's lossy, that too. Sometimes I think those two go hand in hand.

I want to take your hand right here, right now, as you gaze at her, as you stare and stare.

"I wonder where else we can find her?" you say. "There has to be more than this."

"I'm sure." Photographs were all the vogue for wealthy families between the wars. People of property like to see themselves *in situ*. It's like a receipt from the moment, a guarantee through time, *I was here. Remember me.* Better than a tombstone.

One thing we've always known we'll need is awesome image search. We'll write our own in the end, but for now we're making do with the best on the market, bought-in expertise. You set that free to run, to rage through all our digitised stock. Dark-haired young women, women in white: soon we have her lined up in dozens of different shots. Walking and riding, in motor-cars and on horse-drawn wagons. In streets, in stores, in ballrooms. Alone or with companions, except that she's never truly with them, she's always stood apart.

And she's always, always the only one you really want to look at.

"Have you noticed a thing?"

Several things, yes, and not all of them in the images; but I was always conformable. I say, "She's always looking at the camera," like she's preternaturally aware of it, even in the candid shots that should have caught her off guard, "and she's never smiling." Indeed, she always has that same haggard, hag-ridden expression, as though the act of photography is somehow a betrayal. Perhaps it is. "And she's on her own, always. Even in company."

"That, sure, all of those—but something else."

I hate guessing-games, and I can always wait you out. Not so conformable after all.

"What she wears," you say at last, complicit in my refusal, "those dresses—or that dress, maybe, it always seems to be the same one, though I suppose she might have a wardrobeful—is twenty, thirty years out of date, compared to what everyone else is wearing."

You're right, of course. These people dress in country fashions, provincial to the core—no flappers here, no short skirts and bobbed hair—but that white dress of hers is Edwardian, Victorian even, mutton sleeves buttoned to the wrist and the hem barely showing the heels of her sensible boots. She always has a hat, but it's clear that her hair is piled up beneath it, ready to tumble halfway down her back at the removal of a pin.

"What d'you think, then—country cousin who won't or can't fit in with the fast crowd?" To my mind they're all country cousins, but everything's comparative. "Maybe her isolation is down to them, not her. And she feels it deeply, and resents it deeply, and that's why she's always scowling."

"Or she was raised in a cult, and now she's being obliged to live with relatives who laugh at her strange dress and old-fashioned ways, and that's why she resents them."

"Did they have cults, backaways?"

"Oh hell yes," you assure me. "Weird Victorian sex-cults, everything we'd need. She wears white to mark her out as a Virgin of God, only God in this case is some seedy creep with just a pinch of charismatic fervour, and 'virgin' is a technical term that only means she only sleeps with him. Maybe he calls them Brides instead of Virgins, it's much the same. And they still get to wear white. And she only wants to get back to him, but she's not allowed. He's been run out of town on a rail, his house is closed and the only family she ever knew has been scattered to the four winds, never to meet again in this life."

"How come you know all the good stories?" I grumble, because of course I can't compete. I could almost believe every word of it, though I know you're making it up out of whole cloth.

You just smile, and pat my butt, and turn back to the monitor. The search engine's found another picture. This one shows her at the railway station, standing as ever apart from her party, looking as ever at us while they watch their train come in.

"That coalsmoke's going to play merry hell with her whites," I say, trying to sound cheerful against the mood that oozes from the screen, from her. "Pity whoever has to do her laundry."

"Maybe she has to do it herself," you say.

"Oh, surely not? Even the poor cousin taken in reluctantly, even then… This isn't Cinderella. Even the governess gets to enjoy the services of the household," I finish emphatically, not quite making that up. Sure that I'd read it somewhere.

"She might insist. Her clothes are that particular, maybe she wants to take care of them herself. Or maybe it's ritual, required. Cult. That would get right up the servants' noses, having a member of the family down in their quarters, interfering with their work. Maybe they hate her as much as the rest, as much as she hates them. Maybe that's why she never even has a maid with her."

Maybe it is, though hatred isn't normally a disqualifying factor. "Who is she, though?" I ask. "Her name's got to be in the metadata, for one of these pictures at least…"

What we call *metadata* these days, people used to call *scribbling in pencil on the back of the print*. Our scanners have been scrupulous about copying whatever information there was, front and back, and checking library files in case they knew anything more.

Nevertheless: we can put names to most of those we see around her, and not at all to her. There seems to be no record. Baffled, you take off on a mission: back to the source, to each of the original pictures, to double-check the prints and interrogate the archivists. Neither of us really believes that you'll get anywhere, but she's preying on your mind. You'll get no work done either, till you've either hunted her down or else admitted her lost to human ken, a face without a name. Pixels shorn of their metadata, a story no longer told or remembered.

Your obsessive nature is an old story hereabouts, but neither one of us is at all likely to be forgetting it. You go off with my weary blessing. Of course I can do the work of two, for however long it takes you to burrow through to victory or else admit defeat.

Defeat really doesn't suit you, as a concept. The good thing about your current state of baffled rage—the only good thing, because bafflement does now suit you, and I find rage incredibly hard to live with—is that defeat can always be relabelled as victory deferred. There is an answer out there, you just haven't found it yet. There's always tomorrow, and you're very, very bad at giving up.

Much less bad at giving me grief about it. What's yours is mine, stress not excluded; a trouble shared is—yeah, just that. A trouble shared.

Still. There's always something I can give back. "Let's go for a walk, you. Toto."

"Hunh?"

"Test run. Something to show you."

"Oh, you shit. I've been chasing around getting nowhere, and you've set it up while my back was turned, haven't you?"

"Strictly in beta." It's hard to talk around a grin this broad. "But yeah, 2.0 is up and running. Sort of. Don't expect to see them waltzing in the ballrooms, but we might meet someone riding down the street. Someone who wasn't there last time we saw that view."

I suppose I could have cheated it, set up a script to walk you through, knowing where to look and who to show you. I haven't done that, and as it turns out I didn't need to. They line up to show themselves to us, as it seems, like pent-up visions released at last.

It's not even that odd these days, to walk down the street looking at your phone all the way. Or your friend's phone, as you do this night, hanging over my shoulder, holding on to my arm that way you never do when we're merely out together like a regular couple, doing our thing.

This must be our new thing. We don't make it to the end of the block before there's Mr Renton who kept the post office for twenty years, still in the apron he always wore on duty, beaming at us from the corner as he had beamed from the steps of his empire with all his clerks and telegram boys lined up in their uniforms beside.

It's impossible not to give him a cheery salute as we pass. Watching neighbours may think us crazed, perhaps. Perhaps not for the first time.

Around the corner, and where the new church stands, what we see on my phone is the old church, gone fifty years now but rendered more credibly, more solidly than anything around, we've had so many views to work with. No speculative reconstruction here, we know it from all four sides.

Today there's the back view of a farmer on a mule, apparently trying to ride it through the main doors of the church.

"Engine may need a few tweaks," I mutter. You just laugh.

We walk on across the flyover that bridges the expressway, seeing nothing of that because the expressway in its cutting hadn't even been imagined back then. Our view shows us only a country road, with wagons coming in from the west. Same wagons as yesterday, as ever. Not everything is scheduled to change, or subject to it.

Maybe I'm lulled by that particular, familiar view. Maybe we both are. Certainly we're distracted, suddenly all business, arguing as so often about whether there's any real point in releasing version 1.0; won't people get bored with seeing the same static views as they step out of their doors, the same static horses at the end of the street? Won't they just use the app a few times for novelty's sake, mostly to show their friends, and then abandon it when it isn't novel any more? Maybe we should hold back till 2.0 was ready, so at least we can promise change, if not—yet—animation…

And by the time we remember to look back at the screen, there she is. Right in front of us, staring directly at us, in her usual dreadful impractical whites. With her usual dreadful expression, horror constrained by inevitability, weary acceptance of the unbearable, as though she lives it every moment.

As ever, I want to comfort her with apples, or at least with platitudes: *you are stronger than you know, no one is given more than they can bear, you are still and always a survivor.*

What you want, even now, I have no idea. What you say is something else. Of course you're talking to her, not to me; my instinct was the same, it's just that you're the one with follow-through.

"We'll find you," you say. "We will." That's commitment, not desire. I can read your passions as readily as your code, and it's really not what you want. It's a desperate act, almost. No one could want to bring her anywhere closer than this, where she stares from the phone screen as though she were right there in front of us, as though we stood in her street or else she in ours.

The phone's power switch is right here under my thumb, but I can't turn her off, any more than I can turn away. Any more than I can dream of turning you.

One of us does have to move, though, and it certainly won't be her. Nor you, not without help. So I take your arm and nudge you, tug you, haul you into motion. Keeping the phone on her, keeping her in clear sight for you as we walk carefully around her. Somewhere servers are burning hot, running the numbers they're picking up from my phone, position and orientation, every-thing to hold her pinned in place, in view.

Smarter than I knew, those servers. They extrapolate a back view for her as we step weirdly around an apparently empty spot on the sidewalk: that fine white gown all laced and trimmed, with the long fall of her hair held in a bow we've never seen before and neither have the servers, neither apparently the cameras that caught her all over town a century ago. Even her profile is an extrapolation; we've never seen her anything but full-face, flying her distress like a flag.

Without the distraction of that terrible sorrowful stare, she seems—well, odder than ever, from the back. More out of place, though we see her standing in her own street, in what ought to be her own time. There are cars and trucks in the roadway, while she's dressed for a world of horse and carriage. Of course there must have been an overlap, in technology as much as fashion; it must have been commonplace to see horses and motor vehicles side by side, at least for a few years. Odd to our eyes, perhaps, but not to theirs. And country styles are always lag of cities, and some families must surely have clung to earlier ways of dress—and even so. Even calling her Edwardian is a stretch. My eye still wants to say that she's dressed purely Victorian. It's only my mind that revolts, that pleads an essential compromise. Here she is, photographed over and over, in pictures unequivocally dated to the 1920s. She can't be a Victorian, in anything but outlook.

"I will find you." You say it one more time, and this time it's personal, it's exclusive. It's not a common enterprise any more, you're not including me.

That's—well. Significant, of course. Hurtful, of course. Worrying.

We see less and less of you in the office, I see less and less of you at home. You're spending all your days out in the field, tracking down archives that haven't been digitised. Wielding your charm on hapless archivists, scanning and uploading as soon as they succumb. Nights you're in the office alone, coding and debugging, refining search parameters, pounding keyboards as if brute force will hammer the data in hard enough to shatter walls of ignorance and obscurity, to break you through to where she lies concealed.

Not much can stand against you, when your blood is up. I know it; I never could. One night you come home late, and you come straight to me, which has become almost unusual; and there's a look in your face that is almost defeat, a tone in your voice that could foretell catastrophe as you say, "I found her."

Of course you did. She never stood a chance. I kick a chair in your approximate direction and say, "Sit. Speak. Show me."

You're holding a print in both hands, and all I can see is the back of it, with an ink stamp and those hand-written notations so familiar by now. Source and classification: which archive and where stored, whose work, who the subject (if known). A few strings of numbers and a few scribbled words, and that's almost more data than the picture itself can offer. Almost. We think we're visually driven, but appearances are deceptive and the camera always lies. There's a reason why prisoners of war have to hand over name and rank and serial number, rather than a photo ID. Faces are changeable, but words will pin you down. Words and numbers will always find you out.

You don't want to show me her face suddenly, seemingly, although it's so familiar by now. You're holding that print close to your chest, and not even reaching for the drink I pour for you.

"Her name's Amanda," you say, "Amanda Scarett. She was born here in the valley. Her parents were farmers—well, of course they were; that's what respectable people did, they wouldn't be in trade—and she was their only child. Their only surviving child."

"So?" And then, "Let's see," when you still don't move to show me.

And you sigh, and bite your lip, and lay the photo face-up on the tabletop between us.

And yes, that is certainly her face, that same face that we have seen and seen again, wracked and mute and frantic; and she's eighteen or twenty perhaps, and she's sitting in a stiff high-backed chair holding a stiff little boy in her lap while a man and a woman stand behind her, each with a hand on her shoulder.

I'm sure they're not actually holding her down, but it could look that way.

"So—those are her parents, yes?"

"Eveline and Harold," you confirm.

"So who's the boy? You said she was an only child."

"Only surviving child, I said. The only one to survive her childhood. I think this one's her youngest brother. Their last attempt. I looked up the records, and they pretty much went for a baby a year. If you read between the lines, Eveline clearly had a string of miscarriages and stillbirths, and the few she carried to term died in infancy. Like this one."

There's something about the way you say that, that has me looking again and a lot more closely. Seeing less clearly, the harder I try: as though focus were somehow shifty, or the recorded world lossy. A boy, a doll, a puppet... "Wait," I say. "Wait. No. ... He's *dead* here?"

"Yes. Yes, he is. It was a thing some Victorian families did, to memorialise their dead children with a last family photograph. In the cities, child mortality was common enough that photographers could specialise. Not so out here, but even so, they found someone to oblige."

"And they made his poor sister hold the corpse? No wonder she looks so..."

"Yeah." And you reach to touch her face, just for a moment; and then you say, "It's worse than that, though. I said, her mother had a string of dead babies, boy after boy after boy, and their big sister was the only one that lived. I think they did this to her again and again and again. Maybe they meant to punish her for living, when all their glorious sons were dying one by one. I don't know, they might just have wanted something to remember every lost soul by, a sort of rolling successive family portrait—but I think it did something dreadful to her, deep inside."

"Yes." I believe you, absolutely. Well, of course I do; I'm programmed to. "Maybe you were right before and they were cult-religious, some weird isolationist sect like the Mennonites or the Amish. Dressing their virgin girls in white and idolising dead boys, they might have been."

"I suppose. Why?"

"Because else—oh, hell. Do you have a date on this photograph?"

"Yes," you say, with infinite reluctance. "That's the other thing," the thing you didn't want to talk about. Now, neither do I. I'm really sorry I brought it up. "It is dated, reliably. To 1872."

"Yes." Or rather, *no.* "We really didn't import any photos that early, did we?"

"Absolutely not. Nothing earlier than the turn of the century." We've been scrupulous about that, not to sour the timeline. This photo's not in our database—but you know that, you had to find it offline. The same must be true for any other, every other picture of her. That's why she always looks so out of place, wherever we find her; she's a generation too early to be there.

Which is a rock to run aground on, which is why we steer clear.

"We can filter her out. Can't we?"

"I don't want to do that," you say.

"Why not?"

"Because… because this may be all she's got. And it's got to be better than this." You reach to touch that photograph again—no, to turn it over. To deny it the light it feeds on. "Would this be how you want to go into eternity, exhibited with a body? Less important than the family corpse?" Because that was inherent, that the photo was all about the dead boy. "Well, now she doesn't have to. Now she gets to, I dunno, occupy the Bay. Here, there and everywhere. Like a game of Find the Lady, she's never where you expect to see her, because the software will always shuffle her off somewhere else. Maybe she'd enjoy that, after the life she had."

And I don't say a word about reification, I don't remind you that she's not any kind of conscious, she's barely even code, she's just data. If it's in my mind—well, it can stay there. She's in our system, after all, and apparently you want to leave her there.

I don't. I really, really don't.

"Maybe not," I say slowly. "Maybe it's worse, did you think of that? She surely doesn't look any happier now." Now I'm doing the same thing, reifying her: offering pseudo-life to a data packet, making a software object into a lost girl. A lost and sorrowing girl, a girl whose distress defines her: it's impossible to imagine her smiling, or at peace, or at rest. It was hard enough when we only ever saw her in other people's photographs, on the fringes of other people's parties. Now we've freed her up, we see her everywhere, and she's more alone than ever. It's as if the software itself has recognised her state of mind and reacted to it, giving her space. Or giving space to everyone else, perhaps, relief from her.

I'd console myself with the thought that I'm doing it for you, for the sake of argument, for us, for survival; only there's nothing in the least consoling about your face either, as I blunder on.

"Listen," I say. "It's a story, yes?" *It's a ghost story* is on the tip of my tongue, *she's a Trojan ghost*, but that's something else I'm going to leave unsaid. "There she was, this girl who couldn't ever be enough. Her parents kept trying to improve on her, child after child; and the newlings kept dying, and they made her pose with the bodies time after time, like a living example of her failure to satisfy. Potential energy outclasses any other form, right? Conservative principles apply; what you have, you want to hold. Dead sons outrank a living daughter.

"I don't know what happened to her in life, whether she went on surviving—"

"Oh, she did that," you murmur, amplifying rather than interrupting. "Hell, yeah. Amanda Scarett, died at eighty-six. Still a spinster, still on the family land. I looked her up."

"—but that doesn't matter," I go on, thinking *of course you did*, "because this was her perfect moment, the instant that defined her life. We all have them, and they don't have to be good. This is what she always goes back to, what she can never escape. That moment the photographer captured, with her dead brother and her own untouchable body and her parents' utter rejection, you can see that in their faces, how one more time they'd be willing to trade the living girl for the dead boy.

"And when I say that's what the photographer captured, it's not a figure of speech. No, bear with me: I told you, this is a story. It's science fiction, I guess, because there he is with this new machine that snares the light that reflects from her, through his unthinkable lenses onto his alchemical paper that'll hold it through the ages—and are you truly willing to tell me that there's nothing of her that goes with that, no vestige of self?

"I think something did. Maybe it wasn't captured by the camera, so much as driven by her own torment—but some essence, some hint of her soul at that perfect moment of her despair, passed out of her and into—well, into technology, photography, this new mechanical art. Which is why we see her passed from picture to picture, from one studio to the next: never part of a party, never dressed right because she was never actually there in the flesh, only in the image. She's all about the image.

"And I think she knew. What was left of her, that tiny memory of self, I think it remembered what it was, what she was, and what was done to her; but more than that, I think it knew where it was now. Where she was. Trapped in silver chloride, frozen motion, her suffering forever laid out for others to gaze at.

"That's what appalled her, see? Not her normal human unhappy life, she's stronger than that. She *survived* that. Intact, and for a long lifetime after. What broke her was this other thing, this half-life. No life at all, just time: like an insect trapped in amber, only still aware. A consciousness in amber. Silver chloride.

"And nowhere to go, no possibility of change, that's the killer. That should have been the killer, except that she survived that too. And then along we come with our clever scanners and our greedy servers, sucking up whatever we can find, changing its nature, taking this analogue of self and turning it digital, giving it a folly of motion, a scripted independence, a false equivalence of life.

"And she's still trapped, only now she's not a frozen portrait any more, stealing into the corners of other people's pictures. Now she's a puppet, and we have her fucking dancing in the street. And that's worse, don't you see? That's *worse.*"

You don't say anything, but that's all right. I'm not done yet.

"That's why you can't find her in the database. She isn't there. She's like a leaf in a stream, the system keeps her moving. Always skipping ahead. There is no rescue. No one can go back; history is full, it has no room for visitors. It's a book without margins, a tale told. History is complete, and we were never a part of it.

"Only the future has space for us. We can only ever go forward. And we've doomed her to hurry on ahead, in her old-fashioned clothes and her old-fashioned scenery, tossed on from one technology to the next, never human and never free, just an ever-closer simulacrum, until in the end we will be able to dance with her down the fucking street and believe it, feel it, taste and smell and all. And we'll use her and use her, and never feel what she feels, and never quite see her as she is, across that dreadful, terrible gulf. Always falling short."

Like a prisoner of war, it's the words that I surrender. You can have them all, I could always talk up a storm—but I need you to stop, think, step back. And I've already said you can't do that, I could never make you do that. History is full, and there is no rescue.

"We can give her something to skip for," you say. "Somewhere to skip to. To skip in, because she's there already. She only needs to look around and realise. Horror's just a habit, she sees what she expects; she's trapped because she thinks she is, no more. Hell is just a state of mind. This used to be called the Valley of Heart's Delight, remember, before the tech companies came. When she lived here, it was beautiful; she should have loved it. She still can. We can help, we can teach her how. We can rescue her…"

What hope do I have, to resist this? I gave you the keys to myself, and you are everywhere. Working from within. For myself, my only fear is that one day I will find you gone. For you, my greater fear is that one day somehow you will go.

Meantime, here we are. Here I am, facilitating what I fear most.

You do dressing-up, so I don't need to.

Later, you say, we'll call in all my friends to make a party that she's actually invited to, where she'll be guest of honour. You say that, but I'm not sure I believe it. All my friends have Victorian garb and they'd be glad to play, but nevertheless. I don't believe it'll happen, because you don't want it. I think you want her to yourself. You want to be the one she looks for, her focal point, the bridge-builder. The one who crossed the gulf.

I think you'd tear the bridge down behind you, if you could.

Looking at you through the viewfinder, in your finery and your new-grown whiskers, posed beside our cherry tree, for a moment you seem almost unreal, almost. One step across the gulf already, for all that I could step into view my-self and touch you, hold you, fuck you right there under the camera's eye.

What you see when you look in my direction, I have no idea. I can no longer imagine what I am to you, more than a placeholder. I suppose you're in character already, and looking for her. Or looking to the future, version x.1, where you and she will waltz down the street together and I'll be the one watching from somewhere else, some technological absence. And you and I might live a lifetime yet—as she did, ever forward, ever further from her per-fect moment—and talk and touch and fuck and never quite inhabit the same space. And how will I ever know what's gone of you, what more you might have been for me, what you've given to her instead? Love is lossy, by its nature; it makes strangers of us all, strange to each other and strange to ourselves. Will there be two of you, each growing apart from what you are?

Every touch of my finger on the shutter peels away another shaving of you in time, twice realised. And I can't stop doing this, though it leaves me with less and less for every frame I take. Is it you I'm unmaking here, or is it simply us? God alone knows what she will make of you, but nothing that I can reach or touch or recognise. My true love hath my heart, and she has yours; all that's left me is the fact of you, none of the art. Which will be a hard thing to look back on, when we must.

THE ONE THING I CAN NEVER TELL JULIE

LAURA BLACKWELL

LAURA BLACKWELL

Laura Blackwell has lived in the San Francisco Bay Area for over two decades. Her fiction has appeared in various publications, notably in 2016 World Fantasy Award-winning anthology *She Walks in Shadows*. She's also a copy editor for *Shimmer*. She crochets scarves from the same pattern over and over. You can follow her on Twitter at @pronouncedlahra and visit her website at pronouncedlahra.com.

ONE COOL TUESDAY EVENING IN JUNE, JULIE AND I WALKED INTO THREE LITTLE Knittens to find Marie-Grace arranging Filipino bakery cookies, ever so carefully, with a napkin-wrapped hand. Across the room, nerdy Bill hunched awkwardly over four knitting needles and a swath of red-orange wool. He gave us an unaccustomed grin. On the edge of the chair next to him, dividing wide-eyed attention between Bill's handiwork and Marie-Grace's cookie mosaic, perched a thin woman.

The new person looked so unassuming, so innocuous, my eyes slid away from her. She had a blank, unwrinkled face, and I think her hair was a dull brown. I remember that she wore an ill-fitting gray dress, with no coat or even a scarf to take the edge off the ocean breeze that chilled San Francisco's Outer Richmond District. Her hands lay slack in her lap.

Another knitting-circle regular, Svitlana, sailed in and shut the door with enough force to make its glass pane shudder. "It's cold," she said sternly. "Why you call this summer, I will never understand." She strode over to sit next to Bill's guest, who he introduced as "my girlfriend, Tracey."

Bill, whose hairline was retreating as if it feared his big glasses, with a romantic involvement? Julie and I would have something to talk about later. We talked about everything: our jobs, my dates, her fertility problems. We'd been best friends since college, and thought we would be forever.

A half-dozen more regulars had trickled in by the time Marie-Grace took her place on a tall stool. She selected a ball of gray wool and began knitting without a pattern.

Bill gave Tracey a ball of yellow acrylic yarn and asked what she'd like to knit, but she offered no opinion.

"Crochet is easier for a beginner," Svitlana asserted. "Tracey and I will make a scarf." She crocheted several inches of chain stitch, then handed hook and yarn to Tracey. "That will get you started."

Tracey held the hook like half a chopstick set and twiddled it in the yarn. Julie took the open seat next to Bill, and I sat on her other side. The lacy shawl Julie was making shimmered as it caught the light.

"Do you have a new chapter?" Julie asked. Bill had suckered her into reading his fantasy novel-in-progress; she was too sweet to say no.

"Not this week. I've been working on the appendices." He proudly brandished his needles, dangling a mess of wool. "Thanks to this knitting circle, I've made five ceremonial beards this month. It's giving me a lot of insight into dwarven society."

Bill called himself "an inveterate world-builder." When he and Julie discussed *The Five Fates of Caltibranzia,* I got very involved in my knitting.

Everybody in the circle was pleasant, but I wasn't there for them. I wasn't even there for knitting so much as because Julie asked me. I'd do anything for Julie. When she and Min-Jae got married, I wore a floor-length lavender dress and carried smelly lilies.

"Tracey and I met at a writers' workshop," Bill told Julie. "Well, I was there for the workshop. She was browsing in the store."

"Do you like to read fantasy?" Julie asked, smiling the careful, encouraging smile you give a shy child.

"No," answered Tracey in a toneless voice. "I just like to see what people are making."

I thought Tracey was the most forgettable person I'd ever met, but I wasn't given the option of forgetting her. She showed up with Bill at Three Little Knittens the next week, and the week after that, with Svitlana's discarded J hook and the same ball of yellow yarn.

"You've made no progress at all," Svitlana fussed one evening. "What's wrong?"

"It's good when you do it, but I can't." Tracey's shoulders drooped.

"You'll get it," said Marie-Grace. "It just takes practice." She brought something gray from behind the register. "Tracey, since you're becoming a regular, I've made you a gift. If you like, I'll teach you how to make another two, so you'll have Three Little Knittens of your own."

Tracey accepted the toy with an expressionless "thank you," turning it over in her hands as if searching for loose yarn. There was none, of course; Marie-Grace had made dozens, and they were seamless as molded clay.

Usually there was more exclamation over the kittens, but Bill had conversational plans for Tracey and Julie. "Did the revised appendices help? I didn't want to overburden you, but the political tensions changed when I realized that Queen Mellith died of the poison and not the stab wounds, and now the gnomes' language uses glottal stops as possessives."

Knitting a coffee-cup sleeve was a thousand times more interesting than hearing about Bill's novel. I tuned him out.

Throughout the session, Svitlana tsked over Tracey's shoulder. Finally, she grabbed the hook and yarn from her and crocheted several stitches. "Like that, see?" She handed them back to Tracey with a joke. "I may have to give you lessons."

Tracey's face lit like a paper lantern. "Yes, please."

Bill and Tracey showed up at Three Little Knittens every Tuesday, him with a new ceremonial beard and her with the same project. Julie made admiring comments about the progress she was making, but Tracey always said, "Svitlana did that part."

Tracey was growing on people. She never volunteered anything about herself, but she listened to everyone else's ups and downs, and she gave compliments from time to time. And she dutifully worked her crochet hook in and out of the yarny rectangle, though she never had anything to show for it.

Still, Julie worried. "Tracey's so thin," Julie whispered as she brushed her shoe-soles on the welcome mat outside Three Little Knittens one evening. "Her body, her hair...even her skin looks thin. Do you think she eats enough?"

"I don't know." I glanced through the door-glass. "Don't you think her face looks fuller than it used to?"

Tracey was already in her usual place, yellow yarn in her lap and Bill at her

side. Svitlana sat on Tracey's other side, knitting a red glove with green chev-
rons. It was September, and the circle was crafting for the holidays. Everybody
but Julie, knitting a granny-square baby afghan for a co-worker, and Tracey,
fruitlessly poking a crochet hook at the increasingly grubby yellow yarn.

"These cookies with the nuts are so good!" enthused Julie. "Let me bring
you some, Tracey."

"I don't want sweets," said Tracey.

"You are a strange woman," said Svitlana with an indulgent shake of her
blonde head. She watched Tracey struggle with her yarn for a second, then set
down the glove. "Let me help you." As she took the mess from Tracey, the hook
dropped out and clattered to the floor. Tracey dove for it like a cormorant for
a fish, and pressed it into Svitlana's hand. Svitlana accepted it and made a few
more stitches. "Like that. See? Do you need me to finish the row? Of course.
Turn, and chain three…"

When Marie-Grace unplugged the water heater, Julie packed up her gran-
ny squares, stroking them wistfully. She was taking Clomid and some weird
herbal supplements, desperate to have a baby with Min-jae. As I marked my
spot on the ornament I was making, a black bowling-pin shape that would
someday be a penguin, Bill called us aside.

"Julie? Nicole? Can I talk to you?" He hovered tentatively by the door.

"Sure. What's up?"

"I'll be just outside," he called to Tracey, who was still tangling yarn around
a crochet hook.

Once the three of us were on the sidewalk, I checked around for wandering junkies—the neighborhood's gone down in the past few years—while
Julie studied the dark circles beneath Bill's eyes with concern. "Are you coming
down with something?" she asked.

"Me? I'm fine. Well, maybe dividing my energies too much." He took a
deep breath. "It's time to buckle down on the writing. I found a critique group
that meets on Tuesdays, so…" He trailed off.

"We'll miss you," said Julie, "but I'm glad you'll be spending more time on
your book."

Bill laughed. "Sometimes I think there's more of me in Caltibranzia than there is in my body. I've been living part of my life there since I was in middle school." Then his face got serious again, anxious eyes peering from the depths of his thick lenses. "Thing is, Tracey's still enjoying the circle. She's learning a lot from Svitlana, but I worry about her getting back to our apartment. Could you please look out for Tracey? Make sure she gets on her bus?"

My eyebrows shot up before I could stop them. "You live together?"

"She moved in months ago," he said as if he couldn't believe his luck. "Almost the day we met."

"That's great!" Julie said with a big smile. "Of course we'll keep an eye out for her."

I couldn't congratulate Bill on getting saddled with Tracey, but sometimes being quiet near Julie let me pass for being as nice as her.

Early the next afternoon, I was dragging through the balance sheet when my cell phone rang with the arpeggio ringtone I'd assigned to Julie. Normally she would just text during work hours.

"Nicole, I'm sorry, but…" She sounded stuffy, like she'd been crying. "I just found out and there may not be much time."

"What's wrong? Are you okay?" I started closing out the programs on my desktop.

"It's Svitlana. She collapsed late last night. Marie-Grace is at the hospital, and it doesn't sound good at all."

"Oh my God." I'd seen Svitlana almost every week for three years. She was a part of Three Little Knittens, solid as the fixtures and reliable as Marie-Grace.

"I'm leaving work now, so—"

"I'll meet you in the lobby of your building and get us an Uber car."

The driver was a handsome Asian-American with a radiant smile, but I didn't make chitchat. Julie's knitting needles were already clicking when I sat down, and they didn't stop until we pulled up to the tall, boxy beigeness of UCSF Moffitt Hospital.

Svitlana was in the ICU, so only two people could see her at once. Her parents were in with her when we got there. Her barrel-chested husband was pacing the waiting room, while relatives and half the knitting circle squirmed in the hard seats.

Julie went straight to him. "Vitaliy, we just heard. How is she?"

"They're calling it multi-organ failure." Vitaliy enunciated the phrase with distaste. "But why would her organs fail? Svitlana is never sick."

"She did seem subdued lately," said Julie, casting her eyes downward. She twisted her fingers together, probably missing the comfort of yarn and needles. "I didn't think anything of it."

"Well, she was losing weight," said Vitaliy. "She was pleased. But I could see she was tired. I told her not to be silly."

I hadn't noticed the weight loss—Svitlana kept her coat on—but she had seemed run-down. I should have known something was up.

Vitaliy and one of Svitlana's sisters were in the room when an electronic alarm sounded. Nurses came charging through, and I heard Vitaliy shouting. Then there was silence.

Tears ran down Julie's face, but her fingers kept moving. When I handed her a tissue, she dropped her knitting, flung her arms around me, and sobbed on my shoulder. My eyes stung.

Across the room, Marie-Grace was crying, too. So were Svitlana's relatives, pulled together in a knot of shared misery.

Sitting upright a plastic chair, head back and eyes closed, Tracey pulled the yellow yarn to unravel the last few stitches of the crocheted rectangle.

Marie-Grace spent a minute talking with the relatives in a low voice, telling them how highly we thought of Svitlana, how sorry we were. Everyone was gracious, but it was obvious we couldn't stay.

Outside, the wind whipped at our hair and teased a piece of yarn from Julie's usually tidy knitting bag.

"We should get a drink," Marie-Grace said suddenly. "Svitlana liked a drink."

The closest bar had the dark wood paneling of a former English pub and the maybe-tiki-maybe-Mexican decorations that helped sell umbrella drinks. The bartender chivalrously checked the birthdates on our IDs—except Tracey's. She didn't have one on her.

"Don't you carry a driver's license?" asked Julie. "Or a state ID?"

"I don't have anything like that." Tracey's voice had an unaccustomed lilt that sounded mocking.

"We'll see you next week, Tracey," said Marie-Grace firmly. "We're going to toast Svitlana's memory."

Tracey turned and walked away with a spring in her step. After shifting from foot to foot, Bill mumbled an apology and lurched after her. I gave them the side-eye, but everybody else seemed too numb to notice.

"Tracey and Bill," mused Marie-Grace. "Good for her. Bill's a nice man. Steady. Blondes do get their pick, don't they?"

"Tracey's not blonde," I said, startled.

"It looks like she started getting it highlighted recently," said Marie-Grace. "A good job, too—very natural-looking."

I opened my mouth to protest that there was no way that Tracey, who didn't even get professional haircuts, was springing for highlights. But I realized I'd rather not talk about her.

The next Tuesday, Julie told me over tamales at Tommy's that she and Min-jae were expecting a baby in May. We toasted with margaritas—hers a lime slushy, mine the real deal—and we talked about nothing else until we walked into Three Little Knittens. Then we tabled the subject. Julie hadn't told her boss yet, so she wasn't going to tell anyone but me.

My happiness soured when Tracey bounced, bright-eyed, through the door. Marie-Grace was right; her hair was dishwater-blonde. Her clothes draped better, like on a person instead of a hanger. That night, though, she didn't have her tangle of yellow yarn.

Julie sat on my right side, practically glowing. For Julie, I would make an effort. I nodded to the chair on my left. "Want to help me sew this penguin together?"

Tracey took the seat eagerly. "Can you show me?"

I had forgotten my tapestry needles, but I kept a sharp needle in the mending kit in my purse. I showed her how to stitch the wings to the body. "I'll knit him a scarf while you do that," I told her.

Ten minutes later, the scarf was done and Tracey had only prodded the penguin.

"I'll take that." Irritated, I grabbed the penguin too roughly, and the needle pushed deep into Tracey's thumb.

"God, I'm so sorry." Horrified, I dropped the penguin into Tracey's lap and fished a clean tissue out of my purse.

"I'm fine," said Tracey, pulling the needle out. I pressed the tissue against the wound. Tracey didn't resist.

"Are you bleeding?" asked Marie-Grace, unfazed. "I can get a Band-Aid and some disinfectant."

The tissue came away sodden but unstained. Clear, thick liquid welled out of the puncture. Not serum. Not blood.

Tracey's eyes met mine, and it was like facing down an animal. Worse. There was something like camouflage to those eyes. There was no color to put on a driver's license.

The penguin and the needle fell to the floor as Tracey stood up. She walked out without a word, leaving the door ajar.

I told Julie about it at the bus stop.

"Poor Tracey. She really is different," said Julie. "It's a good thing she has Bill. She must have been lonely."

Being an introvert, I have a clear understanding of shy versus quiet and lonely versus alone. I never thought Tracey looked lonely so much as needy. Now, just thinking about her made me tired.

That Sunday afternoon, the arpeggio ringtone trilled as I was steeping a mug of lemon tea and settling in to binge-watch *Orange is the New Black*. "Did you see that email from Bill?" Julie asked. "I'm not sure what to make of it."

I checked my email. "Hang on a sec."

I'm writing to you because you two were so welcoming to Tracey and me. I asked her about the knitting circle, and it came out that she doesn't want to go anymore. I think losing Svitlana affected her more than we knew. I said I was sure you'd take her under your wing(s), but Tracey says it's okay.

We're doing great. This came up because I'm trying to get Tracey to join my writing group. She doesn't write, but she's a very encouraging critiquer.

The shop doesn't have email listed on its site (maybe someone should mention that to Marie-Grace), so if you could let people know, I'd really appreciate it.

Bill

"I don't think Bill is one for subterfuge," I said. "I'm guessing Tracey didn't complain about me sticking her with the needle."

"That was what I thought, too. If she didn't mention it, she must be fine. Maybe it wasn't as bad a jab as you thought?"

"Maybe." I suspected that Tracey's reasons had less to do with pain or personal epiphany than with fear of exposure. Whatever she was, she was not a normal human being.

But seeing neither Tracey nor Bill at Three Little Knittens, I stopped thinking about them. By mid-November, I had nearly forgotten what Tracey looked like, and I wouldn't have tried to remember if Marie-Grace hadn't given us the news.

It was a turbulent time of year for a knitting circle, with many regulars out for travel and parties, and newbies coming in for help on projects they shouldn't have attempted. Marie-Grace sat down empty-handed and said, "I'm sorry to be the bearer of bad news. Some of you will remember Bill, who used to attend this circle. Bill has passed away."

I heard one voice squeak "What?" and another demand "How?" I knitted relentlessly without looking down. Julie's trick: Keeping my hands busy made me feel more in control.

"It's not clear what happened," Marie-Grace said. "He missed two days of work before a co-worker went to his apartment. The neighbors hadn't seen him, and there was…a smell, so they called the police."

"Is Tracey all right?" Julie asked.

"The police haven't been able to locate Tracey. Bill's sister told the police that he and Tracey came here. Does anyone know how to find her?"

Marie-Grace's gaze traveled the circle, but met with only blank faces and regret. Nobody knew Tracey from anywhere else. No one even knew her last name.

As the store cleared that night, Marie-Grace asked Julie to stay a moment. "It wasn't just the police who came by," said Marie-Grace. "Bill's sister asked me for the Caltibranzia files. She said they were gone from his computer. She tried a recovery program, but it couldn't even locate the files. Do you have any of them, by any chance?"

Julie looked stricken. "They disappeared from my Dropbox last week. I thought Bill's writing group had inspired him to make revisions."

Marie-Grace furrowed her brow. "I can't picture Bill deleting his book."

"I can't, either," said Julie softly. "It was his life's work."

At the bus stop, Julie said, "I hope Tracey is okay."

"The whole thing is suspicious as hell." I was surprised that Julie had any doubts. "Think about Svitlana, too."

"I am. Poor Tracey, losing the two people she's closest to. You don't think she had anything to do with it, do you?" Julie's eyes filled with tears. "I couldn't live with knowing I sat next to a killer every Tuesday for months."

"Of course not," I lied. Whatever Tracey was, whatever she did to Svitlana and Bill, she was gone. I wasn't going to upset Julie's delicate pregnancy. She could believe what she needed to believe.

A week later, I hopped onto the 38 after work, lucked into a seat, and pulled out my knitting needles. I had started a blanket for Julie and Min-jae's baby. They didn't want to find out the sex, so I was using variegated pastel yarn. I could finish the layette set in pink or blue when the baby was born.

The bus wasn't that full. When I felt somebody standing too close, I glanced to the side, and my heart sank.

"Who's that for?" Tracey asked.

"Julie," I snapped without thinking. Then I looked up and realized what I'd done.

The gaze that held mine wasn't human, but it wasn't unintelligent. Tracey had been to enough knitting circles to know that a pink-and-blue square was going to be a baby blanket.

I could swear Tracey's hairline was further back than it used to be. She grinned wolfishly, and her fingers twitched.

Not a wolf. A parasite.

I felt a rush of cold stiffen my hands. Could there be such a thing as a parasite that ate creativity? One that could draw nourishment from an ever-changing fantasy world or a never-completed scarf? That kind of animal wouldn't be interested in finished works, like expertly-knitted amigurumi. And maybe the host would die when it was done.

In my mind's eye, I saw Tracey's trancelike expression as she unraveled the last of the yellow yarn, as she unraveled Svitlana's life. Did she nibble Bill's epic word by word, or did she gulp it down file by file? Did he feel himself dying? Did he beg her for help as his body shut down?

She looked too pleased that Julie was gestating a hard-won fetus.

I could give Tracey CalTrain fare to Mountain View and tell her to go entrench herself at some startup, but even if she left, would she stay away? I couldn't chance it.

I chose my words with care. Lies were inventions; Tracey might be able to spot them. "I'm turning over a project in my head. Would you meet me later to go over it?"

"What kind of project?"

"I want it to be a surprise."

The sky was dark and starless when I arrived at the ocean-side trail. It was high in the cliffs, and the air knifed cold through my work clothes. I walked fast, knowing the park had closed at sunset.

Tracey was already at the lookout point, shapeless as a rock outcropping. I'd been right—she couldn't resist the lure of food.

"Come this way to see," I told her, walking to the guardrail. I could hear a dog barking on Ocean Beach, and the wind stirring the eucalyptus trees all around. A bonfire blazed by the water, some distance away.

Tracey stepped up to the white-painted rail. "Where is it?"

I didn't answer. I just drove the knitting needle into her chest.

If creative energy was her food, perhaps a creative tool could be her destruction.

Her face didn't change, and she didn't fight. Even when Tracey's chest was riddled with holes, the thick liquid on the knitting needle remained clear. Not serum. Not blood.

When Tracey's breath grew unsteady, I pushed her over the railing. I heard her crash against the rocks as she fell. It was too dark to see all the way down, and I didn't stay.

Ocean Beach is notorious for its riptides. I checked the news for weeks, but I never saw an article about a Jane Doe found on the rocks or in the water.

I don't know what I've become. If a tapeworm took on human form, would it be a murderer, or just a parasite? And if a person killed a parasite that looked human, would she be a murderer, or just an exterminator?

Julie can tell there's something wrong, a distance in the awkward conversational lulls and the increasing lag between messages. But she's busy, too, her time and attention directed toward the perfect little boy she gave birth to last month. He has Min-Jae's features and Julie's smile.

She probably thinks parenthood has driven a wedge into our friendship. Although it twists my gut to see the hurt in Julie's eyes, I hope she always thinks that.

THE

PANTHER LADY'S

INCREDIBLE TRUE TALE

OF HORROR!

K. A. ROCHNIK

K. A. ROCHNIK

K. A. Rochnik is a speculative fiction writer in the San Francisco Bay Area. She's most fascinated about how technology illuminates human relationships, needs and passions. She recently finished a big post-apocalyptic adventure novel set in a future Silicon Valley that might or might not be a utopia (okay, it isn't). Plus it has other fun stuff like bringing prehistoric mammals back, since she figured who wouldn't be psyched to read about a giant sloth? When she isn't writing or reading, she hangs out with her awesome family and their golden retriever Lexa. Her short fiction has been published at *Fantastic Stories of the Imagination*, NewMyths.com, and a few other places. She graduated from the Odyssey Writing Workshop in 2014 and highly highly recommends it. Perhaps ironically she admits to a mild aversion to social media but does what she can at plus.google.com/u/0/+KarenRochnik and on twitter.com at @karochnik.

A CLAW SPILLED OUT OF AN EVIDENCE FOLDER, CLATTERING ONTO MY DESK, setting my heart to hammering. I picked it up, feeling the smooth curvature, nearly as long as my forefinger. A bear claw, but shaved down to a sharp point. There were papers in the folder too, but no official report tying the strange evidence together.

As I rubbed bleary eyes, the door to the station creaked open. The earthquake had ruined most of the city, including the Hall of Justice. So we in the Third District worked across the street in a charred but serviceable building on Portsmouth Square.

The day was unseasonably warm; a hot tarry breeze fluttered the papers on my desk. A lady in a faded yellow dress, hands cuffed behind her back, shuffled inside. A gorilla-sized policeman gripped her elbow as he maneuvered her through the station towards the holding room in the back.

I wondered why the sergeant had cuffed her. She was only the size of a tall child, but with an exceptionally long torso. She hunched and swayed as if jointed in some peculiar painful fashion. The lady's eyes rose to meet mine, pupils dilating rather quickly, set in blue irises. Her skin was dusky and rough-textured, at odds with soft black hair. Her gaze dropped to my desk, lingering on books by Wells and Poe, which I kept to read during breaks.

The sergeant pushed the lady past my desk. I couldn't help wondering—what had happened to cause her deformities? Her skin looked like burnt flesh, but too long-healed to have happened in last April's conflagration. I put these thoughts out of my mind—it wasn't my concern.

A few minutes passed, then the chief reared over my desk. He dropped a report. "Body was found this mornin' in an alley off Market and Van Ness, behind Malkin's Tavern. Probably killed around midnight. No witnesses."

I puzzled over the deceased's name—Robert Jennan. The barkeep had identified him as a regular. At five o'clock, he'd had a brief argument with an unknown man, before proclaiming his intention to join the New Year's parade and exiting.

"You like to read, yeah, Lisso?" The chief pointed to a few newly published pulps with their lurid covers. Most of my original collection had burned. My face grew warm, but he didn't seem off-put.

Then I remembered and fumbled through the pulps until I found one called *Monsters and Marvels*. Robert Jennan was listed on the masthead, along with the publisher, a Frederick Herbert. Published local "true" stories, actually salacious facts, rumors, and innuendo. The paper was especially fond of grainy photographs of oddities, particularly Siamese twins, people covered in fur, unicorns and mermaids, though the latter resembled deformed animals rather than their noble counterparts.

The chief grunted. "Yeah, that's him, some sort of reporter. Didja see what we found in his apartment?"

"You mean—" I picked up the claw. Jennan's throat had been slashed. "Found at his apartment you say? Not the murder weapon then."

"More likely knifed in a robbery. Nothing found on his body, not even a billfold. "

I shuffled through some bills and a sheaf of paper rolled up and tied with string. I pulled out a card in large swooping calligraphy dated October 1906, asking Jennan for a meeting, to discuss an idea for a story, and asking how much payment might be expected. Signed *Victoria Montgomery*.

The chief tapped the card. "This Miss Montgomery was seen in his company. Might've been to his apartment. She's in the back room. I'd like you to talk with her."

The strange-shaped lady. My hands began their familiar tremble. "I—I don't think—"

He gave a slight nod. "Lisso, it's your last day, I know that. Just askin' for your assessment of the lady." His manner was gruff but kind, like a placid bulldog. I didn't want to disappoint.

I linked my hands together to stop the trembling. "All right, Chief, I'll talk to her."

Leaving the bundle of papers on my desk, I collected a glass of water and the handcuff keys, then went to the back room, tight and dim as a rabbit's burrow. The lady sat stoically at the heavy walnut table, and didn't react to my introduction, except with a twitch of her shoulders. When I removed the cuffs, I saw mottled purple bruises on her wrists.

I pointed, frowning. "Miss, did the sergeant manhandle you?"

She shook her head. Curling her fingers around the water glass, she drank it down in a gulp. She put a hand to her throat, massaging it briefly. She opened wide her mouth and flexed her jaw several times.

"Thank you." A labored whisper.

"Difficult for you to speak, Miss?" I thought, *the poor lady—*

As if she read my pitying thought, she straightened up, her spine cracking audibly, as her eyes pierced mine. I gripped the table, my heart racing, a rabbit mesmerized by the gaze of a deadly hunter. In that strange moment, I glimpsed why the sergeant had felt the need to shackle her.

It passed. She relaxed, hunching again.

I let out my breath. "Can you write, Miss?"

"Yessss." She lisped the s-sound, a hiss.

I pushed across a piece of paper and the pen. "Your name and residence, please."

As she began to scrape the pen on the paper, I left the room and returned to my desk where I untied the bundle of paper. Miss Montgomery must have written it as well—the distinctive bold calligraphy was the same as the greeting card. I smoothed out the pages to read.

When I was a panther, I was captured by men in Africa. They drugged my kill even though I still nursed my cub. When I was asleep, they bound me and took me aboard a ship, in a cage that was too small. When we finally arrived at the island I was miserably seasick, my ribs showing, and my thick black pelt falling out. Still I growled and menaced all who came near me.

I was taken from the ship and forced into a small room which stank of blood and fear. Even though I was starving and thirsty, I fought these men, which were strange. Though they looked and talked and walked like men, they smelled like swine and ape and dog and other animals. They chanted something called the Laws of Man, which forbade the eating of raw meat and drinking on all fours. I managed to bite the one that smelled like ape, but I could not fight them all, and they succeeded in chaining me to a table in the room. The strange men left, and a man with white hair and blue eyes entered. This was the man called "doctor" and greatly feared by the people who smelled like beasts.

He told me that I would be his greatest creation. A lady to equal the natural-born ladies. A lady worthy of the great doctor himself. He thrust a bitter-smelling rag at me. Once again, I fell helplessly asleep.

When I woke I was bound on my side, with shackles on each limb, around my neck and shoulders. The doctor stood where I could see him out of the corner of my eye. He stood not too close, but close enough for me to learn his person-scent.

He watched as I took stock of myself, as I struggled against my bonds, and realized I could not move. He watched as I yowled and tried to twist, and yowled more, until I stopped, exhausted and panting. When he was satisfied I would not break free, he moved close to my head and spoke. "I have such hopes for you, dear Puma. Dear lovely Puma." (He called me Puma, but my proper name is Panther. It was not the only mistake he would make with me.)

I stared as he leaned over me, his breath hot on my face. I smelled rabbit meat he'd eaten not long before. I opened my jaws and snapped. I'd hoped to bite off his face, but he sprung back in time.

The doctor scraped off my tail first. I looked for it later, because it was a fine tail, long and dark and plush. Scraps of my pelt I found in the fire pit, burnt to almost nothing. Perhaps he burned my fine tail as well. Even now, years and years later, when I sleep I can almost feel my lost tail, wrapped around me. Even now I feel it, sometimes, waving behind me, holding me steady. How dare he burn such a fine tail.

He bandaged the hole in my backside, but he didn't stop to wait for the blood to clot. Never enough bandages to stop all of the blood...

He skinned me. He started at my neck and dulled one razor after another. He cut and pulled, cut and pulled, down, down, down my body. Strips of my pelt fell away, and the blood rose and pooled and spilled over, down the table, slicking the floor. He skinned me down to my bound paws.

He left only the pelt on top of my head. I tried to claw him, but my bindings were too tight. The pain was too great. He ignored my screams. He went on with the cutting and pulling. Finally he stopped. But the pain wasn't over. He used a torch to burn away any remnants of my pelt. He wrapped me in bandages. He let me heal a little, mewing like a cub. He made me eat and drink, so I would keep up my strength.

He fed me my own flesh, to save time.

I recovered a little. When next he came, he took a file and forced open my mouth, to whittle down my sharp teeth. I growled so loudly that he shoved an iron bar in the very back of my mouth. The pain began again, but I could not scream. Instead I bit so hard on the bar, my back teeth broke off and rolled in my mouth.

The doctor made my new face. He shaved and cut and shaped my nose, and jaw, and chin. He pulled off my ears and gave me new ones. He examined my eyes very closely, holding a small blade to them as I shuddered and squirmed and moaned. In the end, he decided to leave them be.

There was a notation in different handwriting at the end of the page.
Freddie, I can make photographs of the lady's scar flesh and depression of the tail where it was ripped out for the rubes to enjoy! Ending to follow. Expect remainder of payment at that time —RJ

In something of a daze, I walked back to the room. I entered to find the lady's wide blue eyes gazing up at me. She pushed me the card as I took a seat at the table.

"Thank you, Miss." I murmured. She'd written: Victoria Montgomery, residing at the Ladies Benevolent Charity, Franklin Street.

I asked her questions about Robert Jennan and the nature of their relationship, but got little in the way of response. She'd known him yes, and they'd worked together on a story, but she refused, or could not, elaborate further. She shrugged when I asked her when she'd seen him last. She might have been evasive or merely strained by the effort.

I took out the police report again. Jennan had been arguing with another man just hours before his death. I had a hunch who that person might be.

"I need to step out, Miss. Will you be comfortable enough here?"

The lady nodded. But as I got up, there was a banging at the door, and raised voices just beyond. Suddenly it opened and the chief stood there, frowning. Before I could speak, he moved aside, and another woman appeared in the doorway, in a fine green gown and with an agitated expression on her face. I reckoned her about my age, as her face was unlined. Her nose turned up a tad, freckled. Her hair was very curly, a rich reddish brown; her eyebrows thick and untidy. Her body seemed taut as a falcon on the arm, readying to burst free.

The chief swept his hand to indicate Miss Montgomery. "Here is the lady—"

The woman pushed past him into the room. I caught a whiff of a pleasing grassy scent as I offered my hand in greeting. "Inspector Raymond Lisso, Miss?"

She ignored me, asking Miss Montgomery if she was quite all right. The lady nodded in response, as unperturbed as ever.

Next the woman turned to me. "Margaret Burrows, I represent the Ladies

Benevolent Charity." She shook my hand firmly and dropped it quickly. "Awfully young, aren't you? I suppose you weren't the brutish policeman who arrested Miss Montgomery. Look at her, she's half his size." She spoke brusquely, in the manner of one used to getting her way. "I shall complain to the Mayor himself if she is not released *immediately*."

The chief looked bemused. "Miss Burrows, you can see she's not mistreated. Now please, will you let the Inspector continue his questions? You may wait in my office, if that suits."

"Actually, Chief," I broke in, "The timing is fortunate. Miss Burrows, might I have a word with you first? You can see the lady is comfortable here."

The woman bit her lower lip, assessing me. "I suppose, if it's quick."

Outside the room, the chief retreated to his office while Miss Burrows followed me to my desk. With an impatient swirl of her skirts, she sat in my chair. I pulled up another, catching another whiff of her perfume.

"Lovely—" came out before I could stop myself.

She cocked her head. "Excuse me, Inspector?"

"My apologies. I merely… I meant…" I stammered. "You're wearing a lovely scent."

She raised a brow, as though amused. "Funny, you should say so, Lisso, is it? Miss Montgomery makes perfume. Or she did, before the quake. I'm wearing one. Now, can we get to it? Especially with the poor lady left to stew in this sorry excuse for a station."

I tensed. "Excuse me, Miss, but last year I stood helpless as I watched the Hall of Justice crumble and burn, so now we make do. You must have sympathy, running a charity for poor ladies."

Her countenance softened slightly. "Yes I do, Inspector. It's just that most people in authority don't understand what it's like to be dependent on the charity of others."

"Miss Burrows—"

"Call me Meg."

"Meg. Call me Raymond."

"I like Lisso actually."

I smiled without meaning to. "Tell me what you know about Miss Montgomery. She has trouble talking and she's unusually formed."

She could tell I wasn't making light of Victoria's condition. "She's strangely shaped, yes. She can speak but a few words at a time."

"How long has Miss Montgomery been in your care?"

"Since right after the quake. Her boarding house was destroyed. She lost her savings and the means to support herself. Before it happened she'd been able to make a decent living, selling her scents to local shops."

"What happened to her? She wasn't burned in the fire. Her skin is scarred but long healed. I wonder about her strange shape—did she suffer some crushing injury in the quake?"

"Her shape—" she faltered, then took a deep breath. "No, she wasn't hurt in the quake. The terrible truth is that she was tortured as a child. She must have been though she refuses to speak of it." She grimaced. "She hates being dependent on the charity. I wanted to help her rebuild her business, so I tried contacting the perfume shop owners, but they were struggling, too. Then she started seeing this Robert Jennan." Her eyes narrowed. "He wasn't a decent fellow."

"How do you know?"

"He was harassing her."

"You saw this?"

"I saw the bruises! That is why I beg you to see the whole picture. She's a convenient suspect. She's an abused desperate lady, without the protection of a husband, and the police always want to solve a case."

Yes, I had seen the bruises. Yes, I did want to solve this case. Yet the lady didn't seem as desperate as Meg stated.

Although she sighed extravagantly, Meg agreed to wait at my desk, while I stepped out to follow my hunch about the mysterious man with whom Jennan had argued.

I took my copy of *Monsters and Marvels* as I left.

Outside the station, I pulled off my wool coat, trying to ignore the sweat trickling down my back. According to the masthead, the publisher of *Monsters and Marvels* was located on Sacramento Street near Van Ness. Not a long walk from Portsmouth Square, but much of the street was obstructed by construction machines, though fallow due to the holiday. The smell of tar lingered.

As I wove my way through the crowds, an image, unbidden, arose at the corner of Clay and Mason. I remembered the two massive draft horses crushed by debris, half-buried in rubble, their eyes and mouths frozen in horror. With my heart hammering, I had to lace my hands together to stop the trembling.

Thankfully as I got closer to Van Ness, the street returned to the present day, with offices and storefronts, men in bowler hats and ladies in their long skirts and high-buttoned blouses, strolling around, enjoying the holiday.

I found *Monsters and Marvels Press* stenciled above a doorway sandwiched between a cigar shop and a cafe. I pushed the door open to find an empty narrow office in a state of disarray, desks with scattered paper and pens, jackets and hats strewn about, and the smell of stale coffee, cigarettes, and liquor mingling together. Even devoid of people, the place had a bustling, vigorous feel.

"Hello?" I called out. Towards the back of the office, a door creaked open. A tall angular man with a pencil thin moustache emerged to greet me in the narrow aisle. His close-set eyes and the sharp way he studied me gave the impression of a wary fox, alerted to danger.

I shook his hand. "Inspector Raymond Lisso. Are you the publisher of this magazine?"

"That's right—Frederick Herbert."

"Working on a holiday, sir?"

"Hoping to meet with one of my reporters."

"Not Robert Jennan by chance?"

His vulpine eyes widened. "You know Jennan?"

"I'm afraid I have some bad news for you. Mr. Jennan was killed last night."

He gripped the edge of a desk, blanching. "Dear me. Killed? In an accident?"

"Looks like murder."

He hunched for a second, then straightened, looking me in the eye. "I saw him yesterday."

"I thought you had. What was the nature of your meeting?"

He waved in a vague manner. "He turned in a story, but without the photographs he had promised. I'm afraid he argued with me when I refused to pay him."

My spine tingled. "A story you say? Not an important one, I hope."

"Part one had already gone to press. This was the ending—" He stopped, clearly uncomfortable at giving me any more information than necessary. "Jennan was a fine reporter with a knack for picture-taking, but I don't know anything else that might help you. He drank too much, certainly."

"A story titled *The Panther Lady's Tale* was discovered at his apartment today. It wasn't the entire story. Did Jennan turn in the ending to you last evening?"

Herbert's gaze bored into mine. After a moment he nodded, slowly.

"Then I would like to see it. To confirm your statement."

"I don't see how it's important—"

"I'll decide what's important, Mr. Herbert, or you'll come down to the station with me."

He hesitated, squinting at me. Apparently the resolve in my face convinced him, because he went to a cabinet, opened it with a key and withdrew some papers.

"Very well, Inspector, but read it here please. It's the only copy I have."

FROM THE ISLAND OF THE BEAST PEOPLE—HOW THE GREAT AND CRUEL DOCTOR OF VIVISECTION MET HIS END!

When he finished creating the lady out of the beast, the doctor realized he had succeeded even beyond his wildest imagining. The lady was too perfect for people to believe that she had been so completely transformed. He told her that he would have to leave some evidence of her beastly origin. The lady begged him not to leave any remnant of the animal she had been, worried that he would not love her if he was to be constantly reminded. But he insisted that she keep one single claw on her littlest finger.

And so, though the panther lady fell in love with her creator, theirs was a love that could only have a tragic end. With his attention diverted to the panther lady's creation, the beast people on the island had begun to revert back to their animal selves.

When the panther lady's change was complete, and she was healed and ready to meet the world, the doctor went out onto the island again. He realized his neglect had been a terrible mistake. A hyena man had been killing and eat rabbits raw, rebelling against other Laws of Man, and inciting others to follow. The doctor ordered a gathering of the beast people, planning to make an example of the hyena man and to show off his new lady.

The beast people heeded his call, and the doctor ordered the hyena to be bound and beaten. But the doctor miscalculated again. Instead of cowing them, he angered them. A group of swine men charged, knocking him down. As the panther lady watched, horrified, the hyena man broke free, tied up the doctor, and threw him inside a dark cave. The hyena man argued that the doctor should be set free but only to be hunted down and killed. Some of the beast people still loved the doctor and argued against killing him, but they were too few.

As the hyena man wanted, the doctor would be set free in the morning so they would have all of a new day's light to hunt him to death. The panther lady pretended to agree with the plan, so the other beast people would trust her.

In the dark of night, the panther lady snuck into the cave where the doctor was bound. She whispered to him the beast people's plan. She wanted to free him, but the doctor stopped her. He told her that it was no use, that the beast people would find him. They wouldn't just kill him, but torture him to death. The island was too small to hide for long, and he was an old man. If they knew she had helped him, then they would kill her, too. There was only one choice left—she must kill him instead. She could make his death quick.

She pleaded with him, but his mind was set. He told her that she knew what to do, and to do it quickly. While they embraced, she put her last remaining claw against his neck. He shuddered to feel it, but he held still, telling her that she was a true lady, better than any natural born, and worthy of him. With tears running from her eyes, she drove her claw into the vein where the blood runs out quick.

For a time she cried over his body, despairing. Then she went deeper into the cave, to hide from the other beast people. She stayed in the cave for many days. When she finally came out, the beast people did not seem to recognize her. They had become animals again. Not long after, she was found and taken onto a ship bound for San Francisco. Here she lives as one of the natural born ladies, utterly transformed by a great and cruel man, and a love tragically cut short.

Freddie, I'll do a picture of my lady's little finger, with the bear claw sticking out. —RJ

Confusion creased my brow. "This is not at all—"

Herbert interrupted in a mocking tone. "'The rubes won't notice, Freddie.

This is the ending people want. The tragic love affair of a master and his creation.' "

"Do you agree?"

He shrugged. "It'll sell."

"And the lady he makes note of? Do you know her?"

His eyes flicked away. "I was introduced once. We barely spoke."

"What do you know of the nature of their relationship?"

"They collaborated on the story. Beyond that I dare not speculate."

I stood up, stuffing Jennan's story inside my coat. "I will take my leave, Mr. Herbert. I appreciate your assistance."

He looked askance. "What are you doing with the story? It's the only copy—"

"Evidence, sir! I'm afraid I must keep it." His futile protests followed me out the door.

Back at the station, Meg gave a little sigh, but agreed to wait while I went to speak with Miss Montgomery.

Victoria didn't move when I reentered the interrogation room, apologizing for my absence. Only her eyes flickered up. She seemed exactly as I left her, patiently waiting my return.

I sat across from her and reached inside my coat for Jennan's story.

"I'd like you to read this. I want to know if you are familiar with it. Will you do that?"

I pushed the paper toward her. Hunched as she was, she merely had to look down. Her eyes swept the paper as she read.

When she was finished, she carefully pushed the paper back to me with a single finger.

"What is your opinion of it?"

"Falsssss…"

I nodded. "I believe, Miss Montgomery, that Mr. Jennan hurt you. Bruised you, at least, and maybe worse. I suspect that Jennan rewrote the story you had collaborated on and so you refused to cooperate in the photographs he needed to sell it."

I paused and looked at her closely, to see if she was reacting to what I was saying. But though she continued to stare, her expression remained as unfathomable as ever.

"Jennan wanted a certain photograph for his ending to *The Panther Lady's Tale*." I removed the bear claw from the folder, and placed it carefully in front of her. "Did you slash his throat with this claw, Miss Montgomery?"

Her pupils dilated into deep pits of black. She began to shake her head.

"No," she whispered. "No, no, no."

I asked to the chief not charge Victoria Montgomery for the murder of the reporter. After listening to my accounting, as well the lack of physical evidence, he agreed, until there came a time we found more compelling evidence against her.

Before I let Miss Montgomery go, I put a candle flame to the false ending of *The Panther Lady's Tale*. Together, we watched the paper curl and burn to ash.

Afterwards I called in Meg and said that Miss Montgomery was free to leave. Meg cocked her head at me, but kept any questions to herself.

With Victoria at her side, she began walking away, only to turn around and blurt, "Lisso, I just wanted to say... I think someday you'll make a fine inspector." Her cheeks flushed two bright spots.

"Actually—" But I stopped myself from telling her that this had been my last case.

"Yes?" She raised an eyebrow.

"Nothing. It was a pleasure meeting you, Miss Burrows. You are as fierce as a mother bird protecting her chicks." I added, drily. "And thank you for your confidence."

As Meg and Victoria walked away, a strange curiosity came over me and I followed them outside the station. People were out again, celebrating the holiday and the start of the new year. Survivors of the quake, many of them, hoping and praying that this year would prove more ordinary than the last.

The two ladies followed the same route as I had earlier, toward the press office of *Monsters and Marvels.* When they came to a point roughly across from the office, Victoria stopped abruptly. Meg turned back in surprise. They stood together, with Meg gesturing in an increasingly agitated fashion. Victoria gave no response. Meg threw up her hands, whirled around and strode away, disappearing into the crowd, her long skirts sweeping the pavement.

Victoria crossed the busy street, careful to avoid the traffic, the streams of horse-drawn carriages, bicycles, hand-driven carts. A cartful of squawking caged chickens pushed through, a loose dog barked and ran about; some children chased it. The sun's light waned in the sky; the loud and boisterous mood filled the evening air. When she reached the other side, she grew still, like a distorted statue around which the ordinary people and animals flowed.

I felt compelled to watch her as long as she remained. But soon a man emerged from the press office. A tall and angular figure—Freddie Herbert. Their heads dipped together. He nodded, relief evident in the straightened set of his shoulders. From a deep pocket in her skirt, she passed him a bundle of paper, as he passed her an envelope.

The man returned to his office; the lady lingered a bit longer, before she too disappeared. Towards the waterfront, perhaps having caught the scent of the salt breeze.

Freddie published the first half of the story, titled in dripping red letters, *The Panther Lady's Incredible True Tale of Horror!*

I had to wait for the next issue to discover the ending.

After I saw the lady disappear down the street, I went back inside the station and told the chief that I'd like to keep my job. The chief, taciturn as always, waved his hand in agreement. "Plenty of work, Lisso. The city needs you."

Not long after, Meg came back to inquire if I would be the police liaison to her charity, as I had demonstrated a small degree of sympathy for poor ladies. She had hope for me, she said, standing with arms crossed and keen eyes glittering. I agreed.

In 1910, the San Francisco Police Department, with my encouragement, hired its first female police officers. Meg continued to run her charity on Franklin Street, taking in displaced or abused women.

The perfume shop owners eventually began buying Victoria Montgomery's perfumes again. She earned enough money to move out of the charity and into a room of her own. She worked until her body gave out in 1916. Meg and I spread her ashes by the waterfront, where she had liked to wander.

Meg and I lived together until she passed in 1954. I retired and began volunteering at the charity full-time. In 1963, the charity was modernized and reopened as a women's shelter. And now at the end of my life, even this achievement of which I am so proud has begun to fade in my mind. As even my dear Meg has. As even the cases I had investigated over the many long years have.

It is Victoria Montgomery whom I remember with a peculiar acute clarity. Peculiar, because no one understood Victoria, not even Meg, who saw her as a cause, as part of the fight against injustice. Meg looked at Victoria and saw terrible abuse and its aftermath.

When I looked at Victoria, I saw something else.

That day after she and Meg walked out of the station, after Meg stormed off, after Freddie disappeared with the story's ending, she looked back across the street, sensing something.

As if a blood-red veil had fallen over me, I staggered, trembling, watching helplessly as the people and the animals merged together, dying beast-people, thrashing in agony. I gasped for breath.

Through the phantasmic veil I saw the lady, a beacon of calm. She raised a hand toward me, across that divide. Those bright blue eyes with their deep dark pupils locked into mine, as she stretched out her arm. She curled down her fingers except for the smallest one.

Breath came back, rich and warm. I blinked once or twice and the red veil lifted. People and animals separated, their cheerful noise resumed.

The phantasms that had plagued me ever since the quake and the fire... fled.

There, held above the lady's head, a curved claw glimmered.

THE AMAZING ENDING OF
THE PANTHER LADY'S INCREDIBLE TRUE TALE OF HORROR!

The doctor examined my eyes very closely, holding a small blade to them as I shuddered and squirmed and moaned. In the end, he decided to leave them be.

The doctor sawed off my skull and shaped the inside of my head to give me language, to let me speak in great swooping sentences like people did.

From that point on, I plotted the things I would say.

What pretty words I told the great doctor, what flattery I gave him. It was easy to pretend to love him. Part of me did love him—my new shape did—and every day I told myself that I was a small weak grateful female. I told him as I told myself, to be a person was better than to be a beast!

He let me keep a claw on my littlest finger after I begged him, tears from my new eyes, on my new cheeks. How else will people believe you? He let me keep a claw, and then came the day he trusted me so completely that he took off all of my bindings and raised me off the table. There, in the room of pain, with the long torture at its end, we embraced.

I drove my last claw into his neck.

I was heralded by the other beast people, celebrated

as their savior. Unfortunately the triumph of killing our tormentor was short-lived; they quickly reverted back to their animal selves and their animal minds. Their memories ran out as if in a sieve.

I myself never reverted back to my panther body. I was the final triumph of the doctor's obsession.

The only other true person on the island, a man who'd been shipwrecked months before, couldn't forget any of it. I wished he could have. I pitied him for the torment of his memories.

This man became my benefactor. Although disgusted by me, he hated the doctor more. My survival exacted a measure of revenge. Without his help they would have never let me on the ship that finally came to the island. When we arrived in San Francisco, he helped me with new papers, a new identity, and some money. I found a room of my own. My nose was still sharp, and so I bought perfume stock and made scents, which I sold to the finest shops in the city. Now the finest ladies in the city wear them, with no one the wiser what I am and what I will always be.

RICHARD DANSKY

#WHITEKNIGHT
VS.
#MEGADISRUPTOR

40¢
ALL NEW!

APPROVED
BY THE
COMICS
CODE
AUTHORITY

RICHARD DANSKY

By day, Richard Dansky is the Central Clancy Writer for Red Storm/Ubisoft, having worked on games including *Splinter Cell: Blacklist, Outland, Driver: San Francisco* and *Rainbow Six: Black Arrow*. He has also managed the game design group at Red Storm Entertainment, and worked in narrative design, worldbuilding, and other various and sundry tasks over the 15 years he has been in the videogame industry. In addition, Dansky is an executive of the IGDA Writers' SIG and on the advisory board for the GDC Game Narrative Summit, and speaks regularly at videogame conferences around the world. But by night, he suddenly turns into a writer of science fiction, fantasy and horror. His first publication was in the academic journal *Lovecraft Studies*, and since then he has produced five novels, plenty of short stories, contributions to over 130 roleplaying game products, and a steady stream of book reviews and other pieces for magazines like *PW, Bull Spec, Green Man Review* and others. He was also briefly the world's leading expert on Denebian Slime Devils, but those days are past, and really, it's best just to move on.

I.

Scene: The top of the Marriott Marquis in San Francisco.

THE BAR ON THE TOP FLOOR THERE HAS HUGE WINDOWS FOR patrons to gawk out of, and it annoys the building's management to no end when the view from those windows is partially obscured by trespassers.

There are two trespassers now, and they are on the outside of the building. One of them can fly. He is wearing what appears to be a hand-modified black speedskating outfit, with red highlights, boots and gloves, and a firmly-affixed domino mask. He calls himself MegaDisruptor, and he is idly wondering if he can possibly take the crotch out on his costume just a little bit, as he has been told it is inappropriate for superheroes to scratch their balls in public. Because he can fly, he is not actually on the building, simply hovering near it, He looks extremely comfortable.

The other one cannot fly on his own, but with the assistance of technology (some human, some not) he fakes it pretty well. He is wearing a powered suit polished to a silvery shine. The faceplate of the armor is an expressionless mask, and the voice that emerges from behind it is carefully modulated so that no two listeners can agree on what the speaker must be like. He is sitting on top of one of those magnificent windows, and his feet are dangling over the edge.

Occasionally, he kicks one of his heels. He calls himself #WhiteKnight, which his friend thinks is a terrible name, particularly since there is a white supremacist supervillain out of Wyoming who occasionally flies into town to fight him over it.

So far, the hero has always won.

They met here for various reasons. The view was nice, of course, and it was centrally located. And #WhiteKnight, who worked as an app programmer when he was not off fighting crime, had once been thrown out of that very same bar for complaining too loudly and too long about the drink prices, and as a result he enjoyed tweaking the bar's management whenever he could.

His friend, MegaDisruptor, whose job had recently been reclassified from "analytics specialist" to "data scientist" to "we're sorry you're no longer working here", thought that was kind of a dick move, but let it slide because the view really was that nice.

They had come here to talk, as there were precious few places in the city where two superheroes who were also friends could discuss things without being swarmed by smartphone-wielding civilians, or people trying to guess their secret identities, or traffic cameras, or camera-equipped drones. The Marriott was tall enough that they could talk in peace, albeit without beverage service, about anything.

"You free Saturday?"

"What's Saturday?"

"You promised me you'd help me move, man."

"Aww, come on. You're a superhero. You got the super-speed, you got the super-strong—you don't need help. Just…super it."

"I can't super moving out. People will see it. Landlord sees me supering shit around, there goes the secret identity."

"You didn't tell him you were a super?"

"Of course I didn't. You know how much extra insurance you have to carry if they find out? And half the buildings in the Tenderloin have no supers policies in place now, anyway. The ones that don't, they see you flying out the window and they jack the rent. 'Worried about collateral damage', they say. It's bullshit."

"There was that time Mandragore followed Sleight home and blew the crap out of her loft? The whole building got condemned. Landlord was pissed."

"Didn't need to be. I hear the landlord actually paid off the inspector to condemn the building so he could knock it down and sell to a developer. They're putting a 20 story condo building up there instead. Guy made out like a bandit."

"And Sleight still lost her deposit. So, right. Moving. What time?"

"Noon. I've got the truck lined up. It shouldn't take too long."

"Where are you moving to?"

"Livermore. Guy who owns my building is using some legal horseshit to dump all his tenants so he can turn the place into condos and make a killing."

"He can do that?"

"He can do that. He did do that. And I've got til Monday to be gone."

"Well, shit....but Livermore? That's, like, where Uber drivers live, right?"

"Still a couple of affordable places if you know where to look."

"You know, there's another option."

"Yeah?"

"Yeah. Lobis's got this program now where they're hiring heroes on as a sort of public works thing? You go work for them, you still get to hero all over the place, and they pay you to do it. 'course, they're only looking for coders and project managers and stuff, so they can Lobis away when they're not flying around the Bay saving people."

"I dunno, man. I'm not really Lobis material."

"Shit, you're double perfect for this. You've got the coding chops, and you can bench press a bus. You go in, you get the job, both jobs, and suddenly you don't have to worry about getting kicked out of a shitty apartment because the owner's gone all greedhead. Lobis lucre is filthy, man."

"I don't like it. I mean, the whole idea of doing this, not because it's the right thing to do, but because some company's paying you? It feels dirty."

"Naah, man, it's some company freeing you up from worrying about the everyday bullshit so you can fight more crime, you know? It's a good thing, and if it works for Lobis, I'm sure everyone else is gonna jump on it too."

"You've doing it, aren't you?"

"Thinking about it. My rent's not getting any cheaper, either."

"Jesus. Just…I don't know. Think about it before you sign anything, okay?"

"I will, I will. You are such a grandpa sometimes."

"Yeah, yeah. Just show up to help grandpa move, OK?"

"See you Saturday."

II.
Scene: Early afternoon, on the Golden Gate Bridge.

There is a sign on top of each of the bridge's towers reading TRESPASSING BY SUPERHEROES STRICTLY FORBIDDEN. They ignore it and land; #WhiteKnight "accidentally" kicks the sign and it spirals far out over the water before hitting with a tiny, distant splash.

They look different now. MegaDisruptor's costume remains largely the same, but careful observation shows signs of careful repair. There are more pads now, too, strategically placed over vulnerable joints and weak spots. He crouches down, wary, eyes scanning the horizon.

#WhiteKnight's armor, on the other hand, has received an upgrade. It's sleeker, cleaner, somehow more appealing to the eye. Small corporate logos adorn it, breaking up the perfect clean lines of silver that had been his trademark, but he seems unconcerned. He stands next to his friend, hands on hips, as if he's posing for a photo opportunity.

Perhaps he is.

MegaDisruptor speaks first.

"Nice outfit."

"Thanks. There's an internal group that does design for stuff like this, and then they 3d-print the costume. It's wild."

"It says 'Lobis' on it. I can't tell if you're a superhero or a fullback for a French soccer team."

"Ha, ha. Very funny. At least mine fits."

"Yeah, well, I didn't get super-stitching in the accident."

"You didn't get taste, either. The Batman Beyond cosplay look ain't a good one for you."

"It's eye-catching."

"Yeah, you make a great target."

"I can take it. Unlike some people."

"Oh, sure, you get knocked out by one energy bolt to the chest and you hear about it the rest of your life."

"One?"

"…okay, two."

"Three."

"Raveller doesn't count. That was actually a solid projectile."

"And you're proud of this?"

"Shut up."

"You shut up. So they're treating you all right?"

"Yeah. It's actually, like, billable hours. I get supering time as part of my schedule. Not sure about the morning standups, to be honest—what do you say, "I'm gonna fly around until I find a bad guy and then I'm going to punch him"—but they're taking good care of me. Oh, and other companies have noticed. Got headhunted by a couple of startups that want their own heroes, but I told them to go screw. So how about you?"

"Gonna have to move again. Landlady got a bigger fish on the line, then came up with some crap about how I'd invalidated my lease by violating the building trash policy."

"I thought you vaporized your trash."

"Don't ask. Anyway, you know anyplace cheap?"

"Mmm. Couple of buddies of mine have this shared house thing. They gotta interview you and make sure you fit the 'culture', but they're pretty mellow."

"Culture means 'am I a binge-drinking bro', right?"

"Mostly. But they're OK."

"They gonna be OK with a super?"

[pause]

"Didn't think so. Crap. Oh well."

"Honestly, if you wanted, I could put in a good word for you. Get you front of the line, let them bring you on board—we could do this together, man."

"I told you, I'm not interested. I don't want some suit telling me who I should be fighting or how I should be fighting or, hey, could you throw the villain into the competition's billboard and not ours because optics, you know? That's bullshit. That's not what we do."

"What do we do?"

"Fight baddies. Save people. Cause it's the right thing to do."

"But what about all the property damage? Doesn't that mess up people's lives, too?"

"Less than getting eaten by a giant space-slug."

"Edge case, man. You're arguing edge cases."

"I'm arguing truth. Right now, they're letting you do what you want, but the leash is gonna tighten. They'll be telling you to ease up on some villain that's getting good buzz on Twitter so they can build him up as a nemesis and then have you take him down—when there's cameras around, and strategically placed advertising in the background."

"You are paranoid as shit, my friend. They hired me so I could superhero. That's it. No strings attached, no guilt involved—just going out there, wearing the colors, and doing the thing we always did."

"And their name on your ass."

"My chest. Tastefully. You're seeing things, man."

"Uh-huh. Anyway, got a tip on where the last of Zelkor-9's robot army holed up. Want to help me take them down before they start assimilating pedestrians again?"

"Sure, but it can't take too long. Got a staff meeting at 4. Can't miss it."

"I don't fucking believe you."

III.
Scene: Waterfront

MegaDisruptor is not happy. He is on #WhiteKnight's tail as the latter flies a lazy patrol along the waterfront. MegaDisruptor's costume is torn in several places, hastily patched. There are curious stains as well, bleached spots that look like they were left by the suckers of some titanic octopus. MegaDisruptor's flight pattern is imprecise, wobbly. He looks tired. He looks hurt.

#WhiteKnight never sees him, never notices him coming up from behind. Lost in his patrol, #WhiteKnight doesn't realize he's being paced until there's the ungentle pressure of a hand on his back.

There are more logos on his armor now, and bigger ones. MegaDisruptor has planted his hand across one, and starts shoving his friend down. The land on an unnamed rock off Coyote Point.

By the time they touch down, #WhiteKnight is not happy, either.

"Could have used your help yesterday with that alien drone thingie."

"The blue one? With the tentacles?"

"Yeah, that's the one. It was one tough son of a bitch."

"I know. I watched the fight on Periscope."

"Periscope? Periscope? Dude, you were supposed to be there. You were supposed to be helping me. And instead you watched it on your tablet?"

"Phone, actually"

"Not the point, motherfucker. You should have been there."

#WhiteKnight shifted uncomfortably and looked down at the ground. "Yeah, well, about that. I was going to show up. I was totally going to."

"But?"

"But I was on my way, I swear I was, and I got a call from Corporate."

"Corporate."

"Uh-huh. And they told me that by the terms of my contract, I wasn't allowed to help you as long as you were fighting in the Mission."

"What kind of crazy bullshit is that?"

"That's what I said. I mean, it was a killer alien drone, right? People could have gotten hurt, there was all sorts of property damage, you know. The sort of thing we're supposed to stop."

"You'd think."

"The thing is, Corporate made a deal."

"A deal. What kind of deal?"

"They sat down with all the other corps that are sponsoring supers and they drew up this map, you see. And the map was this way complicated thing that basically said who was allowed to do superhero stuff where."

"You're shitting me."

"No, man, apparently it makes all kinds of sense. Because, let's face it, you don't want every cape in the city showing up any time someone gets mugged, right? This way nobody's getting in anyone else's way, and everyone gets a chance to be heroic-"

"You mean everyone gets exposure."

"Well, yeah, but really it's about making sure we don't get in each other's way. They showed me the map, you know, and I've got some choice territory. Real high profile stuff. I mean, any supervillain attacks the new arena, I am so there."

"So your bosses told you that you weren't allowed to fight an actual alien death machine because of a marketing arrangement? Never mind that people could have gotten killed? That I could have gotten killed?"

"I told you, man, I'm sorry."

"Sorry? That's all you've got? How much are they paying you to look the other way?"

"It's not like that!"

"It isn't? 'Cause from where I'm sitting, that's all I'm seeing. You took their money, now you're their bitch."

"I'm still fighting the good fight, man. I'm just doing it in a way that I don't have to repair my costume with electrical tape after each time I get my ass kicked."

"If you'd been there, like you said you would, it never would have landed a shot. Instead you played mother-may-I, and I had to do the dirty work."

"This is bullshit."

"I know. I've been telling you."

"No, not that. This. The way we're fighting. Jesus, we've had each other's backs since we were undergrads, but now look at us. We sound like assholes."

"You sound like an asshole. I sound like a guy who's doing the job."

"No, you sound like the superhero equivalent of some piss-ant fucker who will only drink his skim latte moccachino if it's got fair trade yak milk in it and he can tell everyone about it."

"That's low, man."

"That's truth. And look at you. You can't keep this up. How's the group house thing working, by the way?"

"Shitty. I got kicked out for accidentally breaking someone's artisanal stick blender or something. Gonna try Oakland next."

"Good luck with that."

"Well, it's that or Chico."

"Chico, you're not gonna be superheroing. You're gonna be sitting out there doing traffic stops while you wait for the next meth lab to blow up."

"If the price is right."

"Look, man, I'm begging you. For your sake. For the city's. You don't like Lobis, fine. But there's, like, twenty companies doing this now. More every day. Find one of them you're willing to work for and let someone take care of you. Because the freelancing days are over, man. There's no room for that, not any more, and I don't want to see you get hurt."

"Only ones trying to hurt me are the ones I hurt worse. Unless you're warning me I've got to worry about you now."

"No. It's not like that. It's just…look, do you have any idea how many people I have behind me? Analytics types predicting incursions. Techies to repair the suit. Medical staff. All there to help me do this thing, and a paycheck on top of it. What have you got? A store discount card for when you buy yourself more bandages? Duct tape for the costume?"

"It's worked so far."

"It's not going to work forever. I'm going to outlive you, man."

"Wouldn't want to live the way you do."

"Yeah, but I don't want to die like you're going to."

IV.
Scene: Elevation 3000 feet

MegaDisruptor and #WhiteKnight are staring at each other at very close range and very high altitude. #WhiteKnight's suit of armor has undergone another serial upgrade. It is sleeker and faster-looking. The overall shape is barely recognizable as human. The branding is tasteful but omnipresent. A missile launcher pack is mounted on one shoulder, and there is a blaster strategically placed on the left wrist.

MegaDisruptor does not look new or upgraded. He looks like he was interrupted halfway through a fight, which he

was. There is blood on his costume. His mask is partially torn away from his face, his right arm hangs awkwardly
at his side, mostly useless after being yanked out of its
socket. His feet are literally still smoldering, and his
left arm is drawn back, ready to strike.

Below, a massive behemoth known as Bloodglory is smash-
ing a building to rubble. There are screams coming from
inside. Another superhero, a tiny dot of color amidst the
rising pillars of gray smoke, is attempting to stop the
beast. Whoever they are, they are not doing well.

"I said stand down."

"Stand down? What the fuck are you even talking about?"

"This isn't your fight."

"It was until you and your friend got here. I had Bloodglory down. One
more punch and I-"

"I said, this isn't your fight. It's Prismatrix's territory, but since she's off on
a mission, it defaults to Avastion."

"The fuckhead in the pirate costume?"

"Yeah."

"The one that's basically got no powers?"

"…yeah."

"And you pulled me off Bloodglory to let him go at it because of, what,
some fucking map that I never agreed to? He's gonna get killed!"

"It doesn't matter that you didn't agree to it. The city signed off on it. It's
law now. Or ordinance. Or something. You can't super in an assigned territory,
or they're gonna arrest you."

"Even if I save the city."

"Even if you save the city."

"Even if I save pirate guy's life."

"He'll come visit you in jail, I'm sure."

"Once he gets out of the hospital."

"Look, I can't let you go down there. You'd be breaking the law."

"And what's Bloodglory doing? High speed gentrification?"

"You're not understanding me. If you go down there, I'll have to do something about it."

"You're joking."

"Dead serious."

"You'd try to take me out to keep me from fighting a supervillain because it's against some bullshit rule?"

"Not my call. But yeah. I would."

"Who the fuck are you, man? Who the fuck have you become?"

"Don't go down there, bro. You're in no shape to handle Bloodglory. Your ass is halfway to kicked. And I will put. You. Down."

"So that's how it is?"

"That's how it is now."

"Then fuck this. And fuck you. You want the city so bad, you have it. I'm gone."

"You can't-"

"Pirate Boy is getting his lungs ripped out his asshole. You'd better get down there. If you're allowed."

V.

Scene: It is Oakland. It is night.

A man lets himself into a house that is not his own. He is wearing tan khakis and a navy blazer, a white shirt and loafers. He has a smartwatch and a Bluetooth earpiece, and he looks entirely respectable.

The man he is looking for is in the bathroom, washing off the blood. MegaDisruptor is there, stripped to the waist, and he looks like hamburger. The right side of his face has been pulped. There are bruises across his back and chest, and a long line of bloody gashes down his left arm. The right arm still hangs, mostly useless, at his side. The sink in front of him is half-full of bloody water, and he is staring straight down.

He is talking to himself. He looks defeated.

The man in the navy blazer clears his throat. MegaDisruptor whirls around and sees the man, his hands up in a placating gesture. He speaks.

"I hate to disturb you like this, but I have a proposition for you. One I think you'll find very interesting."

VI.

Scene: San Francisco airspace

They are fighting.

MegaDisruptor throws a punch at #WhiteKnight's head. It lands, hard enough to deform the armor underneath. #WhiteKnight staggers back, then releases a swarm of drones from a bulge on his back. They envelop MegaDisruptor's head before detonating in turn, and he tumbles back through the air. #WhiteKnight rushes forward, and the two grapple, all former friendship seemingly forgotten. The city is tiny beneath them, a collection of toy buildings and action figures glimpsed faintly in the background.

Two people watch the fight from the safety of a sound-proofed conference room. The feed is provided by a small drone ejected from #WhiteKnight's armor before the battle began. It repositions itself automatically to provide the best view of the action for the two observers. The chairs

they sit in are graceful, ergonomic, and subtly but notably expensive. The conference table is glass and chrome,
while the screen hanging on the wall offers the latest in
4K resolution and, should it be called for, 3D projection.

The woman is the older of the two watching. She is
dressed conservatively but casually, the lack of formality
indicating the level of power she wields. The man sitting
across from her is younger, and constantly fidgets with the
cuffs of the navy blazer he wears.

He is wearing khakis. She is wearing jeans.

She speaks first.

"We're on schedule?"

"We're on schedule. A little ahead, actually. You still like the numbers?"

"They're what I expected. The superhero program was useful, but the trendlines were erratic."

"Yeah, about that. The trendlines pretty much mapped to supervillain activity. People have short attention spans. Our hero wasn't fighting someone, he wasn't getting pictures taken, wasn't getting on social media, and the sentiment analysis numbers went through the floor. We needed a way to normalize the frequency of the encounters so we could stabilize the visibility and maximize the benefit."

"Which meant establishing a way to create supervillain incidents on a predictable and controllable schedule."

"Which means hiring them?"

"Which means hiring them. And as an added bonus, we don't even need to pretend we're hiring them for their coding chops, because most of them aren't worth a hot damn."

"Right. So in any case, MegaDisruptor's on board. Main contract demands were that we pay him more than his buddy and that he gets to take a crack at him on a regular basis."

"Both reasonable enough. The mayor's office has signed off?"

"After a little arm-twisting. We pointed out that staging incidents like this could actually be a revenue source for the city — tourists eat that sort of thing up—and he bit."

"Good. Keep monitoring, keep recruiting, and tomorrow morning, get me the current status of the automated #WhiteKnight armor initiative."

"The guy in the suit isn't happy."

"The guy in the suit signed his rights over to us when he took the first check. The quicker we don't have to deal with him anymore, the happier we'll all be. So, tomorrow?"

"Tomorrow."

Five Dollars for a Ticket

James Van Pelt

JAMES VAN PELT

James Van Pelt teaches high school English in western Colorado part-time and writes the rest of the time. He knew he wanted to be an author when he was in elementary school. He remembers going down the rows of science fiction books to see which two authors his book would be shelved between. It was Jack Vance and A.E. van Vogt. His fiction has made numerous appearances in most of the major science fiction and fantasy magazines. He has been a finalist for a Nebula Award, the Sturgeon Award, the Colorado Blue Spruce Young Adult Book Award, and been reprinted in many year's best collections. His first novel, *Strangers and Beggars*, was released in 2002 and was named a Best Book for Young Adults by the American Library Association. His third collection of stories, *The Radio Magician and Other Stories*, received the Colorado Book Award in 2010. His latest collection, *The Experience Arcade and Other Stories* debuts at the World Fantasy Convention this year. He blogs at jamesvanpelt.com

CREIGHTON PULLED INTO THE BEDLAM CARNIVAL BECAUSE SHE WAS TOO MAD TO keep driving. Behind her was Weed High School and its tenth reunion disaster, and before her waited U.C. Davis and her doctoral thesis, which Professor Fraietta had already declared "thin and untenable." She turned off the car, put her head back, and listened to the engine ticking as it cooled. A temporary fence, festooned with banners, blocked the view, but a Ferris wheel spun above it and a rollercoaster crested a long climb before roaring down and out of sight.

Dust from her arrival hovered off the mostly empty parking lot. Two pickups parked by the entrance, along with a station wagon and a sedan, showed she wasn't the only one here. Creighton stepped out and winced when she pushed against the hot door. The sun pounded. Who would come to the rides in the middle of a blazing California afternoon?

The ticket taker, a twenty-year old wearing a bright blue, sweat-stained military jacket, checked her out from behind his booth. "Ten dollars gets you an hour at the booths. Twenty and you're set till we close. Rides are extra."

"Is the place any good?"

He shrugged. "Look at where we are." He gestured to the empty fairgrounds and the fields around it. "This is as good as it gets in a town like this. Even the bars close at sunset."

Inside, two rows of booths formed a lane ending with the Ferris wheel and rollercoaster. Flanking the booths whirled a carousel and a spinning teacup ride. A small pavilion protected bumper cars. Nobody tended the popcorn stand, but when she leaned on the counter, a slender woman with silver hair came out of the booth that sold hotdogs next door. "Welcome to the carnival," she said. She handed her a bag with about four handfuls of popcorn in it. "That'll be five dollars."

"You sell a lot at that price?" Creighton popped a piece into her mouth. Over-salted and stale. She wondered how long the hotdogs had been spinning on the aluminum rollers. Did they throw away leftovers at the end of the day or keep them?

At first she thought the other booths were unattended, but the owners sat back in the shade, like spiders, watching her as she passed. A calliope played, but she couldn't see the carousel now. It was okay. She ate a second piece of popcorn. Going to the reunion had been a bad idea, but she'd wanted to quit thinking about her thesis for a while. Tom Johnson, the only other black student in her graduating class, didn't make an appearance, which didn't surprise her. He'd said at the reception after graduation, his diploma jammed into his pants pocket, that he'd never come back.

A guy standing in the hoop toss game booth rocked a giant stuffed panda hanging from a hook to the side of the bottles. "Take a chance?" he said. "Three tosses, and you could win this beauty." She knew how the game worked. The hard plastic hoops were barely larger that the bottle tops, and unless they settled exactly on target, they'd bounce away. It was an impossible contest.

Of course the thesis defense committee was just as unaccepting as her high school class. It wasn't just that she was different: in high school it was color while in the grad program it was gender. Both schools went out of their way to not discriminate. She could feel them not discriminating all the time, like being at a party where you were invited at the last second because not inviting you would be mean. The world felt small.

She dropped the popcorn into a trashcan. An animal display caught her eye. SEE NATURE'S WONDERS the sign proclaimed. A six-legged pony stood miserably by the fence in its tiny corral. An all-white crocodile with a dog's face floated in a horse's trough, and a large birdcage held six featherless hawk-sized creatures that sported beaks filled with sharp gleaming rat teeth. Surprisingly, the animals all looked real. She'd seen a freak show when she was twelve with displays that even then seemed fake to her.

The rundown Ferris wheel only became more rickety and worn when she moved closer. White paint hung like ribbons from the bare wood. No one manned the ticket booth. She supposed that they might not fire it up for a single customer, but the thought of circling above the carnival in an uncovered chair didn't sound appealing either. The roller coaster, though, would at least generate a breeze, and unlike the Ferris wheel, it looked modern. The tracks above were red metal tubing that emerged from a blue tent and swept up with a gentle curve. The tallest section of track stuck skyward grandly, but the tent concealed the rest. A sign above the ticket booth read, THE RIDE ETERNAL. She studied the tent. It hardly seemed large enough to contain a minute worth. Hardly eternal.

"I don't recommend it." The ticket taker in his blue military jacket stepped up beside her. "Everybody here's a freelancer. They come together to make a carnival, but they're independent. End of the season they split up. Some wait for the spring. Some go south. New booths all the time. These rollercoaster folk are new and weird."

"You're not much of a salesman. Why would you even share that with me?"

The ticket taker shrugged. "I think more people get on that ride than get off."

Inside the entrance, a short canvas passageway covered with surreal landscapes lead to darkness. "Have you ridden it? Is it a light show like Space Mountain in Disneyland?"

"No, not like Disneyland. It's hard to describe."

"It's this or the Ferris wheel. Everything else is a kid's ride."

But what she was thinking was that it was either the Ride Eternal or climb into the car and continue toward the thesis. Nothing sounded less appealing. She wondered if they needed workers at the carnival. She could just leave her car where it was, put on an apron and man the beanbag toss or the horse race booth where you squirted water into a target to advance your metal horse down the track.

"I'll tell you what I think when I finish," she said.

The short man at the ticket counter sat on a tall stool so he could work the cash register. His legs didn't reach halfway to the floor. "You want the short trip or the long one?" he said in a surprisingly deep voice. Beyond him a four-person car sat on the track. Curtains covered the tracks in front and behind.

"What's the cost difference?" She held her wallet open, ready to fish out a bill.

"Same either way." The ticket man's hands draped across his knees. His fingers were unnaturally pale and smooth, as if they'd been made from plastic. Maybe he'd been in a fire, and had surgery on his hands.

"I'll go long."

He took the five from her. "Pull the lap bar snug until you hear it click. Keep your arms inside the ride. There's a stop-call line opposite the door incase you want to get off."

"Will I want to get off?"

The man looked at her blankly. "Just pull the line."

As dingy as the rest of the carnival seemed, the rollercoaster carriage looked brand new. High quality leather covered the seats, and the safety bar swung down smooth and tight. Creighton sniffed, half expecting a new car smell, but popcorn, hot dogs and rancid animal enclosure permeated everywhere.

A light above the car flashed white as she lurched into motion, pushing through the curtain. Creighton sighed. Thrill rides' best feature was that they made it hard to think about anything else. No light. She strained to see where the car was taking her as it tilted back and climbed for a few seconds before leveling again. Ahead, a dim redness showed the car's front, but blood-colored smoke hid the left and right, and where she'd hoped for a cooling breeze, hot air pushed against her face. The car jerked to the left, not going fast. Ten feet below, a lake bubbled and seethed, like lava. She wiped sweat from her face. An effective illusion. Then the car climbed again, soundlessly leaving the pool behind. No clicking of wheels against the rails or chain drive clanking. A curve to the right took her through a circular opening, barely wide enough to accommodate the car. She ducked, and then felt silly. There must be plenty of clearance.

Orange light radiated from stalagmites and stalactites, and the air cooled, smelled damp and crystalline. Water glistened on stone. How impressive. A bear-like animal clung to a pillar, watching as she passed.

Then darkness and another hole. The landscape dropped away. Below her, hundreds of feet down, tree tops caught a slanting sun. Shadows deepened the greens.

I'm in a tent! How is this in a tent?

Through a gap, a stream flowed, and she glimpsed thatched huts. Nothing appeared to support the rails. Creighton gasped. The effect startled, but before she could figure a way that they did it, the car leaned into a steep dive and picked up speed. The rails dove into the trees. Limbs whipped by as the track wove between huge trunks, still far above the ground. Strange large birds with orange and yellow feathers perched on branches. One glided beside her for a second, riding a five-foot wide spread, glanced at her with pitch black eyes, then peeled off into the canopy with a screech.

A curve through another opening and the car slowed over a grey, life-less plain. Rocks cast sharp-edged shadows, and the wind stopped completely. Something shimmered between her and the moonscape. She reached out until her hand met a hard surface, like a glass bubble. The horizon before her curved. A ringed planet filled a third of the sky. Then on the surface, huge domes. The rails dropped to their level. They shone with their own light. Tall buildings festooned with open balconies and footbridges from tower to tower nearly brushed their enclosures.

The rails swept her up, through the next tunnel, and she was underwater, protected by the bubble. At first, only a soft blue diffused from a distant sur-face surrounded her, but soon the rail took her through seaweed waving gently. Either the car descended or the ocean bed rose to meet her. Vast, cyclopean buildings with doors and windows too large for human inhabitants passed on both sides. The water must have been intensely cold, because she shivered and wrapped her hands around her upper arms to hold in heat. A head like a moray eel emerged from a nearby door, but it was at least twenty feet tall. When it opened its mouth, each curved tooth was longer than her arm.

And the ride went on, through canyons where apartments clung to cliffs, to a jungle filled with monstrous creatures more frightening than dinosaurs, to a city in the sky hanging from dirigibles, to a beach where naked almost-people frolicked in the waves, to a gargantuan structure floating in space where one-man ships zipped to and fro like bees, to a countryside of rolling green hills awash with purple heather. There, a long dirt trail led to a stone palace overlooking a forest.

Each vista stunned uniquely. Creighton craned her head in all directions, afraid to miss the next scene. What were they? Dioramas? Clever holograms? Was the air in the tent drugged, making her hallucinate the experience? She felt delirious, not with the rollercoaster's swoops and climbs and howling curves, but with landscapes, civilizations, the grandness and variety.

Her shirt clung to her and she realized she was sweating, breathing hard, face and chest flushed. The car rose on the rail's red ribbon, reaching ahead in a long, twisting line, pressing her into the seat, before cresting a hill, leaving her stomach behind in a lightness, a swelling pressure that tingled like she remembered when she was a child in an automobile that lifted over a bump in the road. Angels flew around the car, or they looked like angels. Dark-skinned men and women weaving above and below, laughing in their play.

Then the car dashed through another door, climbing. A blue surface receded behind her, and in the distance beyond the blue surface, hay or wheat fields reached in all directions. A Ferris wheel that was as tall as the rollercoaster track spun beside her. Dizzy, her legs trembling and weak, she recognized the carnival. Her car sat where she'd left it in the parking lot.

The car reached the top, paused, then flew back into the tent. Darkness. She leaned forward as it decelerated. Finally, a curtain parted before her and the short man with the strange hands unlocked the safety bar that held her in.

"I can't get out," she said. Her heart pounded. She was sure that she could not stand yet.

The man nodded. "Take your time." He retreated back to his stool, clambered up it like a ladder until he reached his cash register.

After a few minutes, Creighton pulled herself out. Slowly, the realization that she would have to leave the tent came to her. She'd walk back through the carnival, start her car and drive to her useless thesis defense. Her professor was right. The paper did nothing original. It was weak. She'd hoped to break new ground. Instead, her research had merely dug up the bones at one end of the library and buried them in the other. And what would it matter if she rewrote it? She'd seen the graduate library: tomes and tomes of black-bound books, each one representing a year or more of a doctoral candidate's life.

Her thesis had no sense of wonder in it. It opened no vista.

She stopped in front of the ticket man. "You said I could pull the stop-call line if I wanted to get off the ride. You didn't mean that I would get off here, did you?"

His eyes glittered. They were all iris, no pupil. "If you exit, you can't get back on."

"Will I be safe?"

"Some places are better than others."

Tom Johnson had looked so convinced at graduation when he'd said he would never come back. He'd looked at the people he'd grown up with, at the town that never quite felt like home, and he'd pronounced a judgment. She could see him now, a sad, defiant boy who hadn't found his happiness yet and maybe never would.

Creighton dug into her wallet. "It's still five dollars for a ticket, right?"

The man nodded. She thought for a second that he started to smile, but it was a flashing expression. "The trip's different every time."

"That's fine." Maybe there wouldn't be angels this time. Maybe there wouldn't be a city hanging from dirigibles, but there would be something.

"Long ride or short?" he said.

"Give me the long one."

JULIETTE WADE

Juliette Wade has appeared in *Fantasy and Science Fiction, Clarkesworld,* and *Analog*. Her academic background in linguistics, anthropology and Japanese inspires her fiction. She grew up in Capitola, California, and participated in the Begonia Festival sand castle contest every year. She now lives the Bay Area with her husband and two children, who support and inspire her. She blogs about language and culture in SF/F at diveintoworldbuilding.blogspot.com and runs the Dive into Worldbuilding video series and workshop via patreon.com/JulietteWade.

T HE SAND WHISPERED.

Not when it was in her bucket, not when it chafed in her sandals or trick-led off the shovels she carried over her shoulder, shivering on her way to Capitola Beach. But when she'd started her sand pile — not too close to the wharf, not too close to the tide — and ran with her bucket through the cold morning fog, it would whisper after her.

"You wi' meeee, you wi' meeee."

She'd reward it with a hefty splash of seawater. Pile the sand, splash again, pile again, across hours while the fog thinned and brightened. The seawater bath strengthened its voice, made it more agreeable to shapes.

It liked the shapes because they made its voice clearer. She'd caress its soft and crumbly curves, and it would sigh and finally speak.

"What am I?"

"You're my entry in the contest for the Begonia Festival."

It pondered that wordlessly for a long time. She piled more sand. She worked by herself, unlike the others with their bigger teams and better tools. Their castles had bigger voices, but she didn't think they heard. They drowned out the voices with loud laughter, with boom boxes on bright beach towels, and walked unhearing through the city of murmurs.

"What am I?" the sand asked again. "I want to be something for you."

"You're a mermaid." She found a twig and a gull feather in the sand, stuck the feather on the mermaid's head, and started outlining scales with the twig. It was the best castle she'd managed, better than the cat last year, and the sort-of-dolphin the year before. So much better, with the sand's cooperation.

"What does a mermaid do?"

"In the water, it swims."

"I do that."

"On land, it sits."

"It doesn't move around?"

"No."

"Oh. I'd like to move around."

"Bummer. You'll need to hold still anyway while the judges are here." The sun had come out, to wheel black shadows around her feet. She sat down with a sandwich on the towel with the big orange flowers, and rubbed sweat from her forehead. The sunscreen there was gritty with sand. There was some in the sandwich, too. Pretty soon she'd have to start squirting water on the mermaid or it would crumble.

"What if the sea comes?" asked the sand.

She shivered a little, even though no clouds had blocked the sun. The sea was definitely closer than it had been. Its wordless voice promised endings, destruction. Maybe she should have made a moat, but her arms were already aching.

"Don't worry. It won't be long now."

"What happens when I'm judged?"

"I don't think you'll win. Your head is a little lopsided. But you might, I guess." The possibility put butterflies in her stomach.

"If I win, do I get to move?"

"I don't know."

"That's what my flower sisters say. Win the prize and you can move along the creek as you wish. They say if sand sisters moved out of the way they could even escape to sea."

"Well, I wish you could move." She pressed her chapped lips together. The worst part was when the air started to cool, and everyone gathered at the stands to hear the winners. That was when the gangs of kids came stomping and laughing like maniacs and left the castles dead and silent. She imagined taking the mermaid's hand and swimming away from them. She got up, and stretched, and went back to patting the sand.

"I make you happy," the sand said.

"Yes."

"Not just because I'm a mermaid."

"Because I made you. Last year you were a sleeping cat."

"I don't remember."

"Oh, right." Of course not. She thought of the stomping kids again, the foot-shaped hole in the cat's neck, the way it had all been kicked into sprays of grit. "Don't worry. I'll stay with you."

She sprayed water from a cloggy squirt bottle on the mermaid, and added some broken mussel shells for scales. Some kelp for the fin, though it dulled quickly if she didn't keep it wet. Tourists passed by with compliments, mostly 'did you do that all by yourself'? *Yes*, she said to them. And smiled secretly and whispered to the sand, *No*.

She stood against them, her back to the mermaid, fists shaking at her sides. The afternoon warmth was fading, and chill wind came off the sea. The waves sounded too close, but the gang was more dangerous.

"Go away! Leave my castle alone."

"Ha," said a boy, burnt face and chlorine-bleached hair. "It's a mermaid, not a castle, stupid."

"I don't care. I won't let you stomp on it."

"But we won," the sand whispered, "I can feel it. I can move. I can stay with you."

"Hey, look!"

That cry came from behind her. She wheeled around. One of the boys was running at the mermaid from the side. She screeched and charged at him, but didn't get there in time. His foot landed in the sand, which swirled, and the boy fell backward with a shout. He clutched his ankle, swearing.

"You won't get away with this," the first boy yelled.

"Get away from my castle!"

A big wave ambushed her knees from behind, cold. The injured boy squeaked and scrambled up, limping. Water swirled around her feet.

The sand said, "I'm a mermaid; in the water I can swim."

She turned and dived in, seeking the mermaid's hand, but the sea intervened. The kelp was sucked away, the scales melted, and the sand didn't speak again. The gang ran away laughing.

She dragged herself out of the water, soaked, and hugged her sand-crusted knees against the chill wind while spray stung her face.

Not until parade day did she remember the flower sisters.

Teams were building the floats down by the lagoon, and if she left now, she could catch them before they were launched. She slipped out of the house and ran down the sloping streets. Between two houses on Riverview Avenue, she sneaked right between tall fences covered with ivy, and onto the creekside path.

It was early enough. The sand of the path was cool when it sneaked into her sandals, and the scents of honeysuckle and roses on the low backyard gates were more delicate than they would become later. Someone lurched out a gate lugging a huge cooler, and staggered across the path in front of her. He wore a Hawaiian shirt and fancy shorts, and his arms were burnt bright pink. He fumbled his way into the dockside section of the garden that overlooked Soquel Creek. A tourist, a renter, planning to barbecue and watch the parade.

She kept going. What she was looking for, she'd find further down the path, past the red-shingled miniature windmill house, past the giant spider-shadow of the railroad trestle, with its knobbly iron fingers and enormous concrete feet.

There: teams were building floats all along the dockside. Huge, hulking constructions with wooden bones and skin of chicken wire. They made her feel small. People climbed over them, fleshing them out with bright begonia flowers on twists of wire. Slowly, slowly, they hinted at their true forms: rocket, seashell, tiger, teapot, octopus.

What a chorus of voices they should have!

She listened hard.

Heard people laughing, talking, shouting directions, the whirr of traffic and the honk of a car horn on the Stockton Avenue bridge. Nothing more.

She sneaked closer, dodging members of the decorating teams who ran back and forth. Here were the begonias, boxes and boxes of them in stacks of red, coral-pink, white, yellow. Their petals took in sunlight, changed it, then gave it back in a luminous glow. There had to be magic in them, but they didn't whisper, even when she took one in her hand. The begonia's petals were soft, cool; the base of the bloom was pierced with a piece of thin wire that tickled between her fingers.

"Girl, put that down, that's not yours," said a man.

She dropped it like it had caught fire. She backed off fast, while shame made her head pound. It wasn't hers; she was meddling where she didn't belong, and why should she care anyway? It was the sand that she missed, her mermaid that she'd failed to protect, not these elaborate things constructed by strangers.

Except they were flower sisters. Maybe they would care that their sand sister had sent her here. And maybe she couldn't hear them because they weren't *hers*.

She skirted around the back of the stacked flower boxes, next to a tall hedge. Waited until the man who'd snapped at her seemed busy, then plucked a red begonia from its box and approached the edge of the dock, just close enough to reach the chicken-wire tip of an octopus tentacle. She threaded the wire through, fingers shaking.

"Mm, we are all together," the flowers said. "You're one of mine."

It worked! She laughed. "You're ours, actually."

She scooted sideways to let a dark-skinned woman in a sunhat work the tentacle with thick layers of red flowers. A breeze ruffled their petals.

"You're beautiful," she said.

"What am I?"

"You're an octopus — a kraken."

The woman in the sunhat looked up. "Do you want to help, honey?"

She nodded.

"Well, go on. We could use it."

"Thank you." She took another flower, yellow this time for one of the suckers. She put a foot on the float's base, and it shifted with her weight like her own backyard boat did. When she twisted the wire in, the tentacle moved.

She pulled her hand back, but caught her finger on a twisted end of wire. She backed off to the dock's edge and sucked on it, though it wasn't bleeding that badly. The tentacle wasn't moving any more, or not that she could see.

"Did you talk to the sand castles yesterday?" she asked the flowers.

"Hmm, hmm," they answered. "Yes, as soon as I woke up."

"One of them was mine."

"Yours, mine, yours, mine, all of you are mine."

"All of *us*?"

"Are mine."

She snorted. "You don't understand. You're here because we're making you. We want you here." She rubbed her finger on her pants. "Do you know what happened to your sand sisters?"

"No one wanted them enough."

She scowled. "That's not true."

"Sand sisters not like flower sisters," the flowers said. "We're different; we last."

"You don't, though."

"We're different. We move. I'm a kraken."

She almost retorted that the sand could move, but crossed her arms and stood up. "I'm done arguing. You go float around, and if you call that moving, go ahead."

"I'm yours," the flowers called after her. "I'm yours and you're mine."

She stood on the Stockton Street bridge, hands on the rough warm concrete rail, jammed between people looking down at the begonia parade on

Soquel Creek. Crackly public announcements made jokes about the construction teams, their sponsors, the weather, the day. But they couldn't diminish the majesty in the procession of flower creatures on the water: huge and complex, ruffle-edged and glowing in the sunlight. The teapot emitted steam through its spout every minute or so, and the tentacles of the kraken moved back and forth with a motor.

There was magic here, underneath. The people could sense it, even if they couldn't hear the murmur of the flowers: they pressed in beside her, and mobbed the docks. A few beachgoers and local residents tried to approach the floats in rowboats and inflatables. As the flower creatures passed beneath her, they murmured of godhood, and glory, and triumph.

Flower sisters were very stuck up.

She left the rail, pushed through the crowd and crossed the street to Polar Bear ice cream. Even here, the place was mobbed with tourists talking about the begonia floats and how awesome they were. She considered yelling that the floats were stupid, but then they'd never give her ice cream.

She missed her mermaid.

The kraken came to her house at night. She could hear it calling from the creek's edge at the bottom of the garden.

"I'm yours, you're mine, I'm yours, you're mine."

She looked out past the curtains, saw nothing but moonlight on the alder tree, the nasturtiums and the horsetails. She shook her head. None of the floats ever came upstream this far; somehow it must have drifted loose.

She crept out of bed and let herself out the back door. The stepping stones were cold under her bare feet. Not until she took the wooden steps down past the plum tree did she start to see it, flowery tentacles bleached by the moon to stark black and white. It smelled bruised, overripe.

"What are you doing here?"

"You're mine," the flowers said. "Everyone else is gone. I'm here for you."

"I was sleeping."

"You come with me, and we'll be together."

She frowned. She should have been in bed. But even though she'd taken her boat out on parade day before, she'd never gotten this close. The float was actually bumping up against the dock. She'd lost her chance to be with her mermaid, and if she let this moment go, it would all be over.

She stepped onto the float. It tipped a little, but she grabbed for a tentacle that moved to help, and made it on. The smell of bruised begonias was strong; crushed petals stuck to her palms, and the soles of her feet.

They drifted away from the dock with surprising speed. She sat down, legs crossed rather than feet-over-the-edge, because the thought of the dark chill water made her shiver. She watched the shadows that willows and alders cast across the moonlit creek. The float moved upstream, and a resonant scraping came from underneath: that would be a large stone poking up from the creek bed. The water was getting shallow.

"Where are we going?" she asked.

"Away," the flowers said. "To be together forever."

She laughed. "That's silly. You're lucky to have got this far; you'll be grounded soon."

"I won't."

"Suit yourself. I can walk back after you get stuck." Though she didn't like the idea of stubbing water-numbed feet on rocks all the way home.

Another stone scraped the bottom of the float. She thought she saw the kraken's tentacles shiver. The float slowed, and floated back downstream.

"Take me home now," she said.

"No. We need to be together."

She looked at the flowery tentacles above her head. Some of them showed moonlight through holes where the begonias had fallen off.

"You're kidding, right? You're already falling apart, and it's past my bed-time."

"No. We'll go the other way."

She hugged herself, and rubbed the backs of her arms. "What are you even saying? You can't go out to sea with the lagoon all dammed up, and the sea would wreck you anyway." She almost wished it would, like the wave that had destroyed her mermaid. But even if they beached in the lagoon, that was a far longer walk home, barefoot in the dark, with no guarantee of a sidewalk.

She hiked the legs of her pajamas up above her knees, and when they passed the willow tree, she jumped off.

Kraken tentacles swirled and caught her before she hit the water. They weren't the tentacles of a real octopus. They were hard, sharp, wood and chicken wire barely disguised by rotting flowers.

She panted, heart pounding like the trains across the trestle. "Let me go!"

"No. You're mine. You're *mine!*"

Would anyone hear her if she screamed? She should have realized something was wrong when she didn't hear the motor; she should have realized she couldn't trust flower sisters.

Except she also remembered the boy falling on the beach, ankle twisted by betraying sand. She'd thought the sand was on her side, but was it?

The sea couldn't help her now.

She wrestled an arm loose and tore at the flowers, splitting them, showering petals into the dark water. She couldn't reach far enough for anything but the nearest blooms; the tentacles wouldn't let go.

"You're mine," the flowers insisted. "You're here because you made me. We belong together."

"No…" she squeezed the word out. "I'm here because you came looking for me when everyone else was gone."

"You don't understand."

Except she did. And for the first time she understood the bully boys: they hadn't listened to the sand's magic, but maybe they'd been swayed by something else. The voice of the sea, that understood tides and seasons, endings and destruction.

"You're here because I made you," she said. "You're here because I wanted you when no one else did."

"I'm yours," the flowers pleaded. "You're mine."

"No," she said. "The festival is over. I don't want you anymore."

The tentacles dropped her feet-first into the cold dark water.

It was always shallow by the dock: one foot struck sand; the other pinched between two round stones. She hopped once, twice, and fell over sideways with a splash. By the time she got back up she was wet all over. Her pajamas clung to her, and spidery strings of algae tickled her hands and feet. She crawled out onto the dock, and got dry sand stuck all over her hands and knees. That would mean a hose-off and a shower before she could get back into bed, and already she was shivering.

Halfway up the wooden stairs, though, she turned around. The float still hulked there — skeletal, motionless, and silent, gradually drifting down the creek with the night breeze.

She heaved a sigh and turned away. Next year she could make a bigger, better castle. And she'd make sure she didn't miss the judging.

Trophy or not, it wouldn't be magic if it were meant to last.

PATRICIA LUNDY

Patricia Lundy is a speculative fiction writer who sold her first professional short story to this anthology. Her writing frequently explores the relationship between women and death, and she is an active member of the Death Positivity community. Her article on the funeral roles of Ancient Greek women is forthcoming in the British history magazine *History Today.* Currently, she is developing a supernatural teen television pilot with her writing partner Amber Coney, of *Dead of Summer* and Lifetime. When she is not writing, she volunteers in hospice and palliative care. She graduated cum laude with a BA in English from the University of California, Los Angeles, before moving to Arizona. As she couldn't stay away from California for too long, she is relocating to Los Angeles at the end of this year. Her two favorite places in California are Hollywood Forever Cemetery and City Lights Bookstore.

EACH SUNDAY, THE FOUR OF US AMBLED OVER TO NORTH LOS ANGELES STREET to browse the leather goods, baked goods, and the occasional fresh fruits, but mostly we gathered to gossip, for it was rare to have extra coins in our pockets. Word traveled quickly in those days before the boom, when Los Angeles was but a shadow of a city.

I was standing beside the bushels of oranges, next to Cordelia Young, when I heard the news that my neighbor's wife had passed. It was all too familiar, how she had died: taken after the birth of her child. I felt a strange tenderness radiate outward from my lower abdomen, newly healed from my own delivery. Yet I suppose Cordelia took to it the worst, for the two plump fruits in her slender hands found their way back into their bushels. Without saying a word, she hurried into the hot yellow day, slightly waddling the way all pregnant women do.

"How far along?" asked Mrs. Gibbs.

"Four months," I said, grimacing from the uneasy feeling that dwelled inside my stomach, unnaturally cool. "She's only just beginning to show."

"It's those too-tight dresses of you young ladies. They make her seem farther along," said Mrs. Gibbs.

I nodded, squinting into the oppressive sun. My own dress felt much too tight. The black dye drew the sun to me as if I were a talisman, and lingering for so long in the sweltering heat had caused it to leak its pungent smell, which always occurred when I began to sweat.

Once, I had welcomed this sun. The warmth was what first drew me to Los Angeles. I thought it might heal my husband, who had been stricken with a malaise of the gut. It had been thirteen months since we had taken the Pacific

Railroad, and then the train car down from San Francisco. We spent all of our savings on that trip, with the hope that he could find work in Los Angeles after he regained his health.

His death was unexpected, and much too soon.

Without my husband, I had no wish to take a new baby and two children back to the cold winters, and so I stayed. I had begun a life here, however small; I had found kinship in Mrs. Gibbs and Mrs. Medina, both of whom were widows, and I had begun a new friendship with Cordelia, who was closer to my age.

But that Sunday was a day that made me want to escape Los Angeles. I looked upon my widow's weeds with dread, missing the blue Decembers of my home. A mourning pendant would have been much less cumbersome for this climate, but I had not the money to afford such a thing.

"Four months is early, still. It's best for her to be careful, considering," said Mrs. Medina.

Mrs. Young had already lost two little babies. The midwife, when she was drunk, was a poor secret-keeper.

"What of my neighbor's child?" I asked Mrs. Gibbs, who had delivered the news.

"It's alive. A little girl, I believe," she said. Her make-up was beginning to melt down the sides of her face, and it looked as if she was dripping with beige-colored cream. "Though she needs a wet nurse if she's to stay well, for cow's milk is a poor substitute for a mother's."

Mrs. Medina looked at me and said softly, "You could do it. You've just had one yourself."

Mrs. Gibbs nodded vigorously, her make-up sliding off her face like drops of rain. "That would certainly help things along. Oh, it is a most well-paying occupation, Laura. You should certainly consider it."

I had three mouths to feed, four including my own. I could use the money. Though I wondered if I could feed two babies at once.

"You won't run out," Mrs. Medina assured me. "You're healthy and young."

Encouraged by their sentiments, I thought it was certainly worth a try.

The door to my neighbor's house was a most fitting entryway for the house of the deceased. Half-hidden under a covering of thick black crepe, the wood had been carved with an ornate menagerie of designs that protruded in elegant curves and patterns. I ran my fingers over them, feeling their smoothness, and gave myself a jolt when I felt them being whisked away from me.

There was an odd smell that emanated from inside the house as the door peeled open, but of course, here was a dead woman, and so I did not let it perturb me. But I could not say the same for the new child's lonesome wails, emanating out of the darkness; the cries unnerved me and filled me with a strange sorrow, and I felt less confident in my proposition.

Mr. Pagan greeted me in solemn fashion. Though he was my neighbor, I had only ever seen him from afar. His house was opulent in comparison to my own, and the land surrounding it extended outward like a fortress.

He was a tall, thin man with a dark complexion, and eyes that glistened as candle flames waver and sputter on a winter's night. He was well dressed, a luxury afforded by affluence. I noticed he wore golden skull cufflinks, fastened neatly onto his raven suit. This was his mourning attire, and it suited his countenance handsomely.

"My deepest condolences to your family, though I know words will not do justice," I said, loudly, over the babe's cries.

He nodded, and I continued. "I know you have a new babe in your care, a babe that needs to be fed. I have one of my own, almost five months old, you see, and so I am in good condition to provide for your child."

His eyes continued to flicker like candle flames, dark, then bright, and amber-oiled. I smelled the rich, darkened scent of tobacco on him, and a brief twinge of melancholy arrested my soul, for my husband had smelled the same.

"You're a widow," said Mr. Pagan, his eyes lingering over my widow's weeds.

"Yes."

"We are of the same kin," he decided, his mouth upturning into a grimace, for he had not the energy to smile. "Let me fetch her." He retreated back into the darkness of the house and retrieved the babe.

For a moment, she looked so bewildered to be in new hands, that her cries ceased.

She was beautiful and swaddled, her brown eyes open and wandering. But soon after finding comfort in my arms, her cries erupted anew. How soon I had forgotten the wails of a brand new babe, so high pitched, like those of birds. The potent fragrance of death clung to her fiercely as she squirmed in her swaddling. I would bathe her before I could take her to my breast.

"She has no name yet. Perhaps Alicia, after her mother," said Mr. Pagan.

I nodded, and told him that was a fine way to remember his wife.

"She'll need about nine feedings or so, at this age," I explained, over her cries. "I can bring her back each evening after she's fed. If she hasn't taken what she needs, I can keep her through the night."

Mr. Pagan nodded. I could have said anything I wanted, I suppose, and he would have believed me; men did not touch the birthing process, nor the process of caring for children, and they did certainly did not touch the dead. These three things were a woman's burden to bear.

"What is your price?"

"Two dollars a day," I said, aiming extraordinarily high. The price would deflate as we negotiated. I decided I would work for him as long as he paid me twenty-five cents, for I needed more food if I was feeding two babies.

I suppose I looked somewhat affronted when he agreed to my asking price.

"That should be enough for you to buy a mourning gown for her as well."

My own babe was sleeping soundly when I returned home, though I did not think this would be long lasting. Baby Alicia had continued to cry since I had wrested her from her father's arms. I prayed she would be still just long enough for me to do the bathing.

I had two buckets of water on the table, for cooking, and I ladled some of it out into a small bowl to use for Alicia. Then I laid a towel down on the floor and placed her on it, and the bowl beside her. She was so small, and so new, that all she required was a sponge bath.

"Who is that?" said Thomas, peering over my shoulder.

"Baby Alicia. I will be helping to take care of her for Mr. Pagan. Now go and find Samuel and make sure he's not getting into trouble."

"She smells," said Thomas.

"She's getting a bath. Now shoo!" I said, a bit too loud, and Alicia's cries became shrieks.

It was true what Thomas said; she smelled terrible. No longer was it just the smell of death, gathered from where the corpse of her mother lay. It was a fetid, rotten smell that only grew sourer as I unwrapped her from the swaddling.

I fetched a bar of soap and eucalyptus oil. I slid the soap into the bowl of water and put some of the eucalyptus oil underneath my nose. When I had unwrapped the swaddling completely, I uncovered the source of the smell straightaway.

It was the diaper-cloth, though I regret that the rottenness was so potent, so unlike normal soiling, that I found myself retching.

The diaper had not been changed in some days. Mr. Pagan, in his grief, perhaps, or disgust, had failed to change it. I did not blame him, for he was a new father whose hands had never touched such fetidness.

I thought of my own husband then. I wondered how he would have coped, if I had been the one to die. I could not imagine him, with his clumsy hands and impatience, raising three children on his own; I could not imagine him bathing Elena and taking care to be sure her bottom was clean. He would have had to remarry.

I was happy to spare Mr. Pagan the horror of what I saw.

Fat, white, wriggling maggots had found their way to Alicia's bottom. It was an unfathomable sight, and I was bewildered. For a moment, I did nothing but watch the maggots as they wriggled in the feces.

I dipped a clean towel into the soapy water and began to wipe them away from Alicia's tender flesh, only to uncover the more disturbing sight underneath: raw, blood-red lesions on her bottom. How my heart ached for her! Such new, tender skin, stricken with such awful sores.

I smothered the maggots with the towels, as my eyes watered and shed. I cleaned Alicia a second time, and a third time to be sure, and drizzled the eucalyptus oil on her backside. Over her cleaned sores I put a thick petroleum salve and a fresh diaper cloth.

Before each feeding, I checked her diaper and cleaned her wounds, applying more salve when needed. I would never forgive myself if any new eggs appeared.

With the money Mr. Pagan had given me, I ordered the child a proper mourning gown from the seamstress, who would have it ready in three days' time. This one would not leak dye or stain the skin, unlike my homemade dress, which turned my arms the color of pitch at the end of each summer day. I went to the market and bought as much food as I could carry in my basket: handfuls of oranges, sausage, tomatoes and carrots, fresh milk and tortillas and creamy cheese. I gave Thomas and Samuel an orange soon as I returned home, and made us a spread on the table. We ate our fill, and I nursed the babies one last time before returning Alicia to her father. Yet I did not find him at home, and so Alicia remained with me for the night.

The image of the maggots disturbed me so greatly that I checked her every hour through the night, slathering on more petroleum when needed. The poor thing, for this ritual kept her nocturnal alongside me. Neither of us slept, but by morning I was relieved to find her napping in peace, exhausted from my constant monitoring.

I returned to the Pagan house with her in my arms, but saw no sign of Mr. Pagan, and so his babe stayed with me for a second night. Her diaper was clean and her sores were on their way to healing, and I felt I was getting along just fine with an extra child in my care.

I thought of the little bundle of swaddling I left behind in Missouri, just a few weeks older than Baby Alicia. She was buried in a shallow grave next to the oak tree, having not survived to her baptism. I had thought to exhume her and take her with us, for she was a tiny thing, and I could surround her with ice in a small box during our travels. Benjamin had thought it macabre and so I had left her, with no one to mourn her grave. My little darling remained in my heart as a tender sore, something the blood passed over and through but couldn't warm.

The next morning I found my neighbor just as I was taking the path up to his house. His suit was dusty and his eyes were heavy and purpled, from little sleep, perhaps.

"I cannot spend nights in such a place," said Mr. Pagan, reaching into his pocket for my pay.

"What do you mean?"

"My wife's body remains there."

Her body has not been prepared?

I did not wish to embarrass him, so I said nothing as he handed me my pay. I asked him if he wished to hold his daughter and he took her from me. With his other arm, he reached for the packet of cigars in his pocket. I offered to take Alicia again, so he could light it.

He sucked in the cigar smoke and did not breathe it out. He let it fill him, as if it were a ghost.

"I'd like you to prepare my wife's body. I've entrusted you with my child, and so I will entrust you with my wife."

I had not prepared a body since my own mother. My husband, due to his illness, had been buried immediately.

"I'm afraid I would not do a proper job," I told Mr. Pagan. "I have almost no—"

"You will do a proper job," said Mr. Pagan, sucking down his smoke. "I will pay you twenty dollars more than your normal pay for your services to my wife." It was a fortune. "Will you do it? She is rotting. I cannot stand to be in the house. I need her to be cleaned."

"Yes. I will do it," I told him.

"Good," said Mr. Pagan. "I will see you this afternoon."

I did not have much time to prepare. This was beneficial to me, as it left me little time to worry. I took my children and Baby Alicia to Mrs. Medina's house and consulted with her, as she was ten years my senior. She advised me what I should bring to help me in my services as layer-out, and I left the children with her as she bid me good luck.

Once home, I filled my shopping basket with the little salt I had: rosemary, sage, the eucalyptus oil, and the rest of the eucalyptus soap. I also brought a few towels and a small cloth, laden with aloe and spearmint, which I could use as a nose covering, if need be.

"I have left her as she is, with a cloth laid over her," said my neighbor, when I returned to his home. "I added some ice. It was all I could do. While you prepare her body, I will prepare her coffin." Then, without further word, he stepped out of his house, and I was alone with the dead woman.

I shut the door behind me and the stench was overwhelming; it had been almost four days since the woman had died. I immediately went to all of the windows and opened them to allow the house to breathe.

It was a beautiful and darkly furnished home I was not surprised, as Mr. Pagan owned a furniture store, and I had seen some of his best pieces in Cordelia's living room. The bassinet in the corner was extravagant, with layers of white lace, so light among all the dark, regal things. But it remained empty without Alicia to fill it.

I fetched the pitcher of water from the kitchen and took this and my apothecary basket to the corpse room. The first step was to remove the thin sheet that covered her. Then I assessed the work before me.

This woman was in deep need of a cleansing. Though the iced soothed her superficial wounds, it could do no miracles in this heat and had turned to water. Mrs. Pagan was encrimsoned, drenched in the scarlet sheets of childbirth. The blood had wilted in its wettest spots and turned to purple-black. I gathered up the first sheet from underneath her, rolled it into a bundle, and slipped it out the window. I would retrieve it later, but in order to work, I needed to lessen the stench.

I felt the initial sinking sensation leave me as I returned to the corpse, refreshed from the warm outside air.

The maggots were dense and feasting, but were relatively easy to wash away with soap-water, and I proceeded to kill them as swiftly as those that I had found on the baby's bottom. I gently bathed Mrs. Pagan's skin, dipping the towel in the soap-water and brushing her with it, taking care not to soak her and not to scrub too hard, for dead skin does not heal. She was a beautiful woman, I could tell, though she was beginning to bloat. Her skin had a peculiar green stain spreading outward from her abdomen, still swollen with the distension of childbirth, and the stain bled onto her torso and her thighs. Her face wore an expression of pain, and her eyes and tongue bulged outward.

I took utmost care when I cleaned her delicate parts with the sponge and soap-water. The violence of the child coming into the world was paramount; I felt my stomach contract and my heart burn, and I thanked the Lord that I was finished with the business of having children forever; I hoped.

When the corpse was clean, I dried her, for any lingering wetness would bring about the most grotesque forms of mold. I had seen these molds on my own mother: thick whiteness splattered across her face and chest like snow colored moss.

Mrs. Pagan had no mold, thankfully, and she had no other strange qualities, aside from her deadness. Her body cleaned, I remembered the woman she was in her life, at the market, purchasing chocolate and oranges and coffee. She was a thin woman, with long, elegant limbs, and a belly swollen with child. Her lips were always brightly rouged, like cactus fruit. And no matter how hot a day it was, she wore her hair down, long and waved and black, striking against her white dress.

The midwife had tied her hair up, and I released it. For a moment she seemed less dead. But then I caught her eyes, dry and bulging, and I was pulled back to my task. I had brought two coins with me, and as I remembered my aunt doing for my mother, I oiled the backs of them, closed her eyes, and placed the coins over her eyelids, so that she might finally find rest in eternity.

Everything proceeded normally. She lay as still as a board of wood as I continued to clean and prepare her, and I became almost entranced in the soothing ritual that is the preparation of the dead. I remembered the way my aunt and sisters had so gingerly touched my mother, working their living auras into her skin. We living women worked our life's energies into the flesh of the dead, making them seem less cold.

I did this now, for Mrs. Pagan, as the women of my family had done for my mother. She slept in the eternal sleep as I cleansed her. But as I began to slather the oil, and then the salts, over her skin, a preternatural change possessed her. Her left arm flinched. Though I knew corpses did often move from the gases stirring inside, I found it strange that it happened so late in my treatment of her.

Then, the left leg began to twitch.

I put my hand over it, to try to soothe the gases that might have been gurgling, and it stopped.

I had not realized I was trembling. I took deep breaths until I felt steady enough to continue. I had a duty to my neighbor, I told myself, and to his daughter and to his wife. And to my own children, who were always hungry for more to eat. It was my duty to prepare her body, and I wished to do it properly.

The breeze blew in through the window and I smelled tobacco and wood and the overwhelming aura before me, of soap scented with death. Together, they flooded my senses in an odd symphony and my eyes watered as I struggled to focus on finishing my work.

Yet it was impossible to ignore that the corpse was *moving*. I acknowledged it, the way the lashes fluttered with the coins atop them; the way the purple mouth quivered and seemed to exhale breath. *These are the gases being expelled*, I told myself. I continued to oil, massage, and salt her as methodically as if I had been dressing a meat for supper.

But as I came toward her femininity, toward the skin that was still stained with crimson, I saw that here the movement was strongest. Perhaps there were maggots underneath, wriggling to get free. As her abdomen bulged and constricted, I closed my eyes. I was thankful that this woman, dead and at peace, was spared the trauma of the maggots and the gases and the un-ladylike business of being dead.

When I had stood there in the recesses of my own darkness for some minutes, the silence spinning inside me, churning with the smell of salted, oiled death, I heard the contractions. My eyes flashed open and I watched as the abdomen grew larger. Never before had I seen such a sight.

She was beginning to open up, to usher out the mass that fought to emerge from her. To my horror, it was not a mass of maggots. It was a babe. It was crowning, and her body, dead as it was, pushed it out.

The child's stomach was partially open, exposing its innards. It never moved, but remained still, in a pool of old blood the color of pitch. It was horribly shriveled and missing a small piece of the side of its skull, revealing a glimpse of the dark pink matter underneath.

My tongue tasted of copper and my hands felt like wax, as if they were melting off and away from me and I was powerless to gather them up.

I fled the room, throwing myself into the clean air of the open kitchen window. I remained there until my shaking stopped. When I could feel my hands again, I retrieved a knife, and brought it back to the room of death to cut the umbilical cord.

The after-birth had been pushed out; all lay in a heap of festering mess.

I gathered the coffin birth from the sheets, taking care not to forget one ounce of tissue, and I wrapped it, folding it neat and tight, and let it down to the ground through the open window. Then I continued to clean Mrs. Pagan. It was the only thing I could do.

At last, when she was prepared for her burial, I replaced the sheet over her and put all of the dirtied towels, filled with the dead maggots, along with the tightly wrapped package, into my basket. Then I returned to the back of my neighbor's house to retrieve the soiled sheets of childbirth that I had cast down from the window.

As I made my way back to the front yard, I found Mr. Pagan near his grey mailbox. He smelled of sanded wood, and his hands were splattered with brown-black stain. I watched him sip from a clear vial. The liquid inside was darkly colored and smelled aromatic, and he held it out to me.

"For you," he said.

"My hands are dirtied."

He brought it up to my mouth and I took a sip. It was mescal. Heavenly.

"Take another," he said.

I gulped another sip down. I did not often imbibe but it was refreshing and calmed me.

"Thank you."

He nodded and took a sip himself. Then he gave me my payment.

"My wife was supposed to have twins, according to the midwife," said Mr.

Pagan.

The strange, sickening sensation I had felt at the market began to creep into me, filling me up to my throat. I clutched onto the basket filled with the dirty, soiled sheets and the deformed baby underneath, and tried to steady my breathing. "Yet she only delivered one. Did you find anything of the second babe, when you were cleaning her?" He cast his eyes downward in shame. "I could not bring myself to search."

I could not let him see this monstrous thing that had been born out of his dead wife. It was so gruesome; it would send his wife to the grave with a legacy that no woman should have to bear.

"No," I said quickly. "I found nothing."

"I had hoped the midwife was wrong."

As he said this, I knew he yearned to believe it. He *yearned*. I do not know if he did believe it, for midwives are seldom wrong. This, even men know to be true.

I do not know if he believed my words, either.

"A dead child would be a terrible burden to weigh further on your grief. Now I must tend to the living ones," I said. I bid him goodbye before my agitated soul could betray me.

But I did not tend to the living children. Not straightaway. I needed to prepare a grave for the coffin birth. No catholic churchyard would welcome this unblessed child.

I found a spot with soft earth, on the side of my house, the furthest side from Mr. Pagan's, and I began to dig, deep as I could. My fingernails blistered and stung, and when the grave was two arms' length deep, I threw in the soiled sheets. Then I set the little thing atop the pile.

Yet as the sun began to descend into the final depths of its own grave, and as the skies swirled with vermilion, I could not bear to send this half-child into eternity without some sort of memorial. I retrieved it from the grave and held it, still wrapped in its sheets, close to my breast; overcome by a sudden and intense curiosity, I unwrapped it, wishing to glimpse once more at the monstrous form.

Its eyes bulged and its mouth throbbed and its organs glistened. And, as if the warm air had the effect of a spell, the little thing awoke.

It took a breath that sounded as if it were drowning underwater. I saw the reason for this sound when the blood rose up from its miniature lungs and dribbled down its mouth. Its emaciated body trembled in my hands, and its little heart beat with such preternatural force. I stared at it, in shock, as I waited for it to be still.

How could such a thing as this live?

And yet, when I heard the soft gasp of pitiful life escape from the blue lips for a second time, I knew it was not a trick played upon my eyes or a phantom born out of my exhausted mind.

Its little, wrinkled fingers reached up, for me, searching for someone to love it.

heartsong

D. MORGENSTERN

D. MORGENSTERN

D. Morgenstern is a native Californian who has lived in the High Desert area of Southern California and Orange County all her life. She studies at a local polytechnic university and intends to teach Life Sciences one day. She has previously worked in the veterinary field. She is married with five cats and two rabbits. She obviously loves animals, the macabre and grotesque, stargazing, and writing on her blog.

THE CURRENT STAGGERED AND FELL, BLEEDING LIKE A BEAST OPENED BY A FINE and deadly blade. The bulldozers bit into the banks and reared back their gnashing jaws to tear open the river on its eastern side. Its waters came as a rushing tide through the wound. They spilled out across the basin in an unnatural bleed, drowning ash and copse.

Birds shuddered into the air as the last gasp of the Santa Elena. The water roared into the flat land with a thunderous crash. Fish struggled in the shrinking pools beneath the heat of the summer sun, her last fervid heartbeats. Animals mourned in silent despair as her body ate their homes and kin in her death throes. The basin had become a shallow of death, bordered on one side by a thick dam that contained its killing rage.

The river left behind more than death. Its last shudder of life was its wrath. The spirit was born from the Santa Elena's gouged innards, left to rot in the sun. She was raised in the mist of the evaporating and pooling waters. She had been born with the conscience of the brackish water that was now swirling around the cottonwood and pepper trees of the basin. She was the last cry to the earth.

She was her mother's vengeful heart-song.

Mrs. Pilgrim had a most treasured daughter named Belle. Her speech was sweet and high as her namesake. Her voice was the ringing in her mother's heart. It tolled for the little girl alone.

Small hand in large, Mrs. Pilgrim had taken her daughter to the new dam.

It was the first major government contract for the firm since she had been named CEO. She held her daughter close as they stood on the concrete wall of the dam. In the middle of the wall it was possible to see all the way to the mountain range looming in the north and the vaguest outline of the shore to the west. The dam breathed with repressed rage that shook the woman's feet.

Below the staunch edifice was dark loam, potent soil made thick with animal corpses and decomposed plant matter. The landscape was nothing but dark, rick earth waiting to be plowed and planted. The last lingering trees had been torn away the week before, days after the river had been re-routed and dammed.

"That is where the new orchards of Blanco-Fritz are going to be planted." Mrs. Pilgrim moved her head slightly down to catch the briefest glimpse of her daughter's wide eyes. She beamed in pride at the girl's astuteness, and her own self. "They plant almonds, so this is going to help all the local people a lot with making money. We dammed the river so people could live here."

She carefully kept a hold of Belle's hand. The only thing between the girl and a deadly fall of a hundred feet or so was her mother's grip. Her daughter shuddered to feel that tremor beneath her own feet, as if the waters knew they were being spoken about. It was a furious tremble.

"But there," Mrs. Pilgrim pointed to an indeterminate spot in the west, "is where the town of 'Heart-Song' is going to be."

The girl tensed at her mother's side and looked up with wide eyes. The woman smiled indulgently. "Yes, Daddy and I are going to name this new place after *you*, my heart-song."

Belle preened and giggled in delight. Mrs. Pilgrim stood taller in pride. The future seemed as a singular path across the bright horizon to the azure ocean. There was nothing that could break that glorious march to the sea.

The very same path the Santa Elena had once taken.

A year passed since the unceremonious death of the Santa Elena. The dam had been named after the bones of its predecessor, the only memorial to what had bled so that trees may grow. The earth was warming again in the same heat that had devoured the carcass of the Santa Elena. The damp heat drew out mosquitoes and Japanese beetles to hum along the dam.

The skeleton of the town was raised. The bones waited to be covered by its flesh of lumber, cement, glass and tile. That day Mrs. Pilgrim was discussing laying the pipework of not only the irrigation of the orchard but also of the grand fountain of the town square. The water of the dam was already being sluiced to bring potential to the weed filled fields.

Belle was again out of school and again by her mother's side. Now the girl was permitted to spend the afternoon catching the emerald and buzzing beetles that flitted through the dry grasses that reclaimed what had been lost by the Santa Elena. She swatted at the biting insects that flew against her red cheeks as she upset them from their posts along the tips of the foxtails and sage. Mrs. Pilgrim was too busy designing her daughter's namesake to pay attention to her heart-song beating through the summer air.

The girl came to the shadow of the dam. She at first only glimpsed the outline for a second out of the corner of her eye. She paused and turned on her heel. There was a woman standing in the shade. Her hair was long and dark, tangled with waterweeds. She was wearing a white dress of high lace around her neck and a mud-splattered hem that clung to her ankles. Her torso was vivisected by a red sash. Her face was dark, as if crafted from the loam the Santa Elena had left behind in her death throes. The girl's breath caught to look upon her eyes, dark blue and soulless, like those of a dead fish.

Belle stepped back as the woman stepped forward upon bare feet. Water clotted on the grass she touched, doused by her sopping body.

"Are you, are you…La Llorona?" Belle asked, a whimper in her voice. She had heard about the ghost every Halloween, as the image haunted many local celebrations of the holiday. The woman looking for the children she had drowned to spite their unfaithful father. However, the specter gave no wail nor cry, her thin lips remained pursed as she looked down at the trembling girl-child. Yet the spirit could be no other than the one that dealt death at the waterway.

"I am Elena." The woman's voice was a whisper of rushing water. It flowed over Belle with a killing coldness. The girl cried out as a sharp pain pierced her body. She fell to her knees, agony erupting from her innards. There was a feeling of bursting from her right side. Belle expected to see a hand covered with blood when she looked down, but nothing pooled from her other than anguish.

Then as quickly as the earth had opened to swallow her in blinding pain, it ceased. Belle climbed to her feet and found herself alone in the shade. She gasped as she startled from her waking nightmare. Yet one last thing screamed at her from across the void of terrified fantasy.

"For my mother."

The girl turned and ran. She ran with all the life still in her. She recalled all the warnings she had heard of the mourning woman by the water. *"She'll push you in, she'll drown you, take you as her own! Children must never go down to the river by themselves, or La Llorona will get you!"*

Belle did not drown that night, but La Llorona had claimed her anyways. She returned to her mother's side, but the heart-song found no more comfort there.

For the pain never ceased. What began as the dream of agony became reality only a few nights later. Belle was awoken from sleep by a pain so potent she vomited and collapsed in her father's arms.

Her right kidney, inexplicably, had failed.

At first her father's kidney gave the girl a few more days of life. Then, like a diversion in the river of the girl's life, her left kidney collapsed. The first river was dammed again as the foreign flesh was rejected. This time her mother sacrificed to save her daughter's life. But as the days turned and turned in the hellish ride, the mother's organ was rejected, attacked by the body it was meant to save. Putrid blood poisoned the girl's body, filtered by machines, but nothing seemed to totally remove the brackish taint.

The cause was found to be a genetic abnormality that had laid hidden within their daughter's body since birth. A few pairs of faulty genes suddenly turned on by unknown means had caused the failure of those vital organs and the rejection of imposters by the body. A donor was sought but none could be found. The Pilgrims watched their young daughter die inch by arduous inch. She was only twelve years old when she breathed her last.

But the songs of the hearts, human and river, continued to thrum across the universe.

The town of Heart-Song grew without any knowledge of its namesake. The only name that linked to its origin was that of the dam that held back what would otherwise kill them. The dam, and the dark soil beneath their feet.

Some years later, the town began to host a Heartland Scout camp outside its borders. One summer an eleven-year-old girl named Blanca La Rosa came with her troop for the annual jamboree. She couldn't help but to notice the strangeness of this place with all its vague, disquieting nostalgia. It unsettled her but she could give no voice to her feeling other than her observation about the name of the community.

"Heart-Song is a weird name for a town," she told her troop leader.

"Why's that sweety?"

"Because…it's what my Mom calls me." She squirmed in some subliminal horror at admitting the endearment. The woman just shrugged.

"They chose it when it was built about sixteen years ago," The leader informed Blanca before pushing her towards her group. The conversation was forgotten in the parade of festivities, but not the feeling of eyes upon her. Something traced her footsteps in the foothills, and followed along beneath the shadow of the Santa Elena dam as the troop hiked. Something, *something*, stalked her along the waterway and descended into her dreams. It was a cold tide that washed her spine and innards in a horrid shudder.

She dreamed of being washed away in a flood. She cried out to her mother but the water snatched away her words. A hand ripped into her right side, pulling out blood and viscera. Her body burst open and all her life bled through her open wound.

She awoke with a scream and a violent pain that made the world an agonizing crush. Her side had been torn open! She vomited and clutched her side, struggling against hot waves of anguish. Yet when she raised her hand, it was clean.

Her pain was encased within her struggling body, a dam containing all that would kill her.

As the first had died, so would the second.

This time the parents' bodies had already been mutilated and there was no more flesh to give to their heart-song. A new kidney was set to grow in a lab, but even the mere weeks it would take would be too long for the girl. As her right kidney died, her left immediately began its own death throes.

"This was supposed to be impossible!" railed the former Mrs. Pilgrim, now La Rosa. "We removed those genes when she was conceived! This wasn't supposed to happen!"

"We know little about the health of clones," the doctor said quietly. They were in the hallway, well out of ear-shot of the girl who had no knowledge she was such. Nevertheless, the doctor knew how far little ears could hear and was doing his best to spare her further agony, even in the face of her mother's rage. Never in the doctor's life did she think she would be treating the first human clone conceived in the state of California, one of only a dozen examples in the entire country.

"This isn't the genetic issue that claimed the life of the daughter you cloned her from, but it may be a side-effect of her genetic structure all the same. There is evidence the genomes of clones are less stable than...others," Dr. Park searched for a politically correct way to compare genomes when words like "natural" and "old-fashioned" carried their own heavy contexts. She wondered by on the look on Ms. La Rosa's face if the now-revered Dr. Simons had ever warned her of this potential outcome. The healthcare of clones was only starting, the La Rosa child might be its first failure. Humans still answered to forces greater than themselves, even in this age of wonders.

The woman's tears were caught by her hands as she began to sob, small wells of grief in her palms.

"I thought we would have a few more years with her, this time around!" The doctor could only pat her shoulder and offer a few brief words of being strong in the face of adversity that fell as flat as they ever did. Dr. Park could only try. It was all she ever could do. She promised to call Dr. Simons for further insight into the condition of the clone.

La Rosa's ex-husband tried to comfort her next but she turned on him as fiercely as a rip tide with all its crushing fury.

"Why did you take her to Heart-Song? Why did you take her to that awful place?!" She demanded.

"I didn't! I didn't know her troop was going there for their jamboree!" He snapped. "They usually go to El Cajon!"

"You don't read permission slips, you idiot?!"

"You couldn't keep the truth from her forever," he countered in a deadly hiss.

"Fuck you!" La Rosa screeched. "You didn't even want her! I had to sue you to even have her implanted! It was only after she was born you wanted to see her! And I let you! I let you…"

She collapsed against the door of her daughter's death chamber. That day in the courtroom, she had re-defined what it meant to be human in the state of California. Blanca was a pre-existing person, she had the right to a life. The right to a life as much as anyone else.

"Stay away from her. Or I will have the cops down here I swear to god. You've never had formal custody you bastard."

She looked away from his gaping mouth and pained breathing. She didn't care! This was a man she had stopped loving when he refused to resurrect Belle.

It was through her suffering alone that her daughter had been given this second life. It was by her will alone she had been given these extra ten years, an entire adolescence and young adulthood split between two births.

It was because of her alone that Belle was dying again, and leaving her mother behind, again. It was nothing but a recurring nightmare. One she had caught them both in.

She hated herself now. For the first time, she could no longer see the march to the sea. She was still standing in Heart-Song with echoes of death.

Blanca La Rosa died shortly after midnight, sixteen years after the bones of the Santa Elena had been laid bare.

Dr. Simons only returned the phone call in time to offer condolences.

Every late afternoon, the town of Heart-Song was shadowed by the Santa Elena dam. The Blanco-Fritz orchards had the more advantageous position of being farther from the dam and its darkening reach. Those who lived in the single road community were forever reminded what had engendered their town and livelihood as the shadows stretched over their houses and yards. It coiled around their ankles and raised to embrace their bosoms and heads. She held the town in a tight embrace that filled every crevice like a smothering mother.

In autumn, the shadow advanced towards the town earlier and earlier until its winter descent was as early as noon. It was in this season, two months after burying her daughter for the second time, that La Rosa finally came back to Heart-Song. Though she had conceived of the place, and was surely its mother as much as she had been of Belle and Blanca, it was a neglected and hated daughter.

The grand Spanish fountain splashed in the middle of a small park off its one thoroughfare. It was a small adornment none of the other local communities had, as they had been haphazardly cobbled together by the constant ebb and flow of humanity across the land. It was the small touch of the founder upon the town. It was at this fountain that La Rosa rested as she contemplated her fate.

Nothing remained of La Rosa's daughter but her memories of the golden fields where she had once played. These buildings and avenues had only been glimpsed by her second self. The original heart-song, however, had never seen her namesake in the time she had been alive. Like her mother, she had only dreamt of what could be. It was this ghost that had overlaid La Rosa's eyes even as she had looked down into Blanca's face. The two girls, different yet identical, were forever the same to the mother.

The bell of the church tolled and La Rosa was startled from her perch on the fountain. As she floundered in her recollections she was passed by a little boy skirting around her legs. His mother stood at the edge of the park with her hands on her hips.

"*Ernesto! I hope you haven't been by the dam again! I keep telling you about La Llorona!*" She scolded in Spanish. The boy reached to take her offered hand, his answer lost in the second toll of the bell.

"La Llorona." La Rosa had not heard that name in years. Yet she knew the story from her grandmother who had given her the same warning about the Santa Ana River of her youth. The weeping woman, forever mourning the children she had killed. La Rosa covered her mouth with a gasp and felt her stomach clench. A spirit that killed children.

As she had. She had given her daughter life to only have her die again.

She could still recall the threatening phone calls and letters written in blood. The accusation she was playing God. The screams for mother and child to both die. She had lost her job due to the harassment, and her marriage had long since died. Her life had only been rebuilt on the conviction that when she had looked upon Blanca's face for the very first time that she deserved to live as much as anyone else.

Yet now she was dead. La Rosa was a failure of a mother. She hadn't protected either one of her daughters. She had given her faith to a false miracle; nothing could stop death. Her detractors had been right all along. All she had done was played God, and she was hopelessly incompetent at it. All she had done was let her daughter die in agony once again.

She dropped her hand and turned towards the dam. She walked into the darkness, with no intention of returning, upon the path Belle had once walked. She would not clone her daughter again. She would not give birth again. She was no longer a mother. She was nothing more than a phantom haunting her last living daughter. She was living in the echo of her heart-song.

Within the darkness of the dying sun she met a black horse. It was a mare of heavy build standing in the shadow of the Santa Elena dam. Though the water was thundering behind thousands of pounds of concrete, the horse was soaking wet with water weeds in her mane. She raised her ears as La Rosa approached and gave a low nicker as the woman parted the grasses to stand before the steed.

As she hesitated before the beast, a thin wail reached her ears. She raised her head. It was the sound of an infant's cry, originating from the top of the dam. She gave a low moan and reached towards that distant noise.

"My girl, my girl." As she reached towards the sound, it became more distinct. It was the high and sweet voice of Belle, with the darling undertone of Blanca.

"Mom! Mommy!"

"I have to get up there!" she cried. The horse fell to her front knees, a willing mount. There was no hesitation in La Rosa now, though she had never ridden a horse before. She clumsily swung up onto the creature's wide back and hooked her knees into the mare's shoulders. She grasped handfuls of mane, and as the sun vanished behind the horizon, the mare began her ascent of the dam.

It was a perfectly vertical gallop. The mare's mane fell back into La Rosa's face, obscuring her view and nearly drowning her in its weight and wet. The horse's barrel expanded and collapsed between La Rosa's legs. The sharp impacts of the hooves hitting the concrete were jarring. La Rosa realized for the first time that shaking she had always felt atop the dam had been the very breath of the water, as surely as that of the mare beneath her. Both were alive and furious.

The mare vaulted in a high jump of at least ten feet to clear the railings and walkway at the top of the dam. As her mane fell down along her neck, La Rosa at last was able to raise her head. She pulled to leap off the horse but found she was stuck in her crouched position as surely if she was caught in tar. In the twilight, she could see there was nothing at the top of the dam. The walk way was empty save for darkness.

Her children were nowhere.

The mare dove into the lake at the other side of the dam. La Rosa remained stuck to her mount's back even as cold water crashed over her. She and the mare rapidly sank to the bottom of the Santa Elena Lake. She struggled to break free in the instinctive fear of death. Her limbs only seemed to sink further into the horse however the more she tried to pull away. Her arms were devoured to her elbows and her body to her waist. She became one with the vehicle of her death.

She opened her mouth to gasp and only invited water to rush in. The pain that filled her lungs was tremendous and seemed to burst them within seconds. She raised her head to look towards the surface of the lake but not even light was reflected overhead. Her world was nothing but crushing darkness. She closed her eyes.

There was a feeling of slipping away. Of relief. Of comfort. Of the end of fear and pain. La Rosa opened her eyes to a bright light. She moved her arms and legs and found them free. As she raised her arms, they encircled two small bodies. She held her daughters to her breast and wept into the great expanse of the lake. They cried with her. Laughed with her. They were never to be apart from her ever again.

A shadow covered the indistinct light shining down from overhead. La Rosa raised her head and saw a woman floating above them. The lack of light made the details indistinct. She could tell she was wearing a white dress with a dark sash around her waist, and that her hair was dark and tangled with weeds. The mare came to mind immediately, and something even mightier, that flowed all round them.

"I am Elena," the phantom told her in a tongue that probably only the dead and spirits knew. "I am what arose from the river you killed. It was I that killed your daughter twice."

The spirit reached down and gently traced her fingertips across La Rosa's face. She found no horror in it. There was something there, a familiarity. A shadow that had always walked behind her, her other half coming into the light.

"But I am what I am now, a lake. I wouldn't have been born without you. You are in some way, my mother too." The spirit's expression was lost in the darkness but her stroking didn't stop. It was a gentle, affectionate touch. "I am forded for now by the dam, but I won't always be. One day your people will die, and I will live on. Even now, my waters are used to nourish and grow. I am as much of life as of death. I am no longer my mother's heart-song, composed in death."

The spirit took La Rosa's shoulders in her hands and brought their foreheads together. The four females embraced in familial solidarity for the first time.

"Teach me how to be a mother, my mother; whose heart-song is of life."

Ms. La Rosa's body was fished out of the Santa Elena Lake some days later. Her death was ruled an accident and rumored to be a suicide. It was at this time the town finally learned why it was named "Heart-Song", the requiem of a mother to a daughter. A mother who had followed her daughters into death.

It was ultimately decided that La Rosa would be buried in the town park, with a memorial overhead commentating her achievement and the lesson in her tragic life. Her body would become part of the dark earth shed by the Santa Elena, her legacy to all future generations who would live in the basin she had cleared.

No one, save the spirits, were aware that the shuddering of the dam, breathing as though it was alive, would continue to live long after they were all gone, that it was the final line of La Rosa's heart-song.

It was of life.

IN
LOVING
MEMORY

MEG ELLISON

MEG ELISON

Meg Elison is the author of *The Book of the Unnamed Midwife*: a Tiptree recommendation, Audie Award nominee, and winner of the Philip K. Dick Award. Her sequel, *The Book of Etta*, was published in February 2017. She has also been published in *McSweeney's, The Establishment, Catapult, Compelling Science Fiction, Terraform*, and many other places. Elison is a high school dropout and a graduate of UC Berkeley. She lives in Oakland and writes like she's running out of time. She can be found online at megelison.com and on Twitter at @megelison.

THE PEOPLE OF HEMET DROVE UP THE WINDING TRAIL, NOT QUITE WIDE ENOUGH for two cars to safely pass one another. On either side of the road, small, shabby shrines lined their passage. Painted crosses made from paint stirrers stood propped up with rocks, sharpied names faded beyond recognition. Long-deflated mylar balloons and the cracked glass of devotional candles flashed and winked in the sunlight that came down from the flat, white sky.

The Ramona Bowl was tucked deep into the foothills, hidden from town. Small hills rose behind it showing granite boulders like uneven and rounded tusks, giving way to bigger and bigger hills behind them.

Families parked their UV-ravaged cars between the faded suggestions of painted lines on the half-acre of cracked asphalt in the parking lot. Crowds of kids in black robes swarmed in, dragging their parents and grandparents who shaded their eyes from the onslaught of morning sun. They walked through the entrance and surveyed the old-fashioned amphitheater with its long, curved rows of cement seats separated by grainy stone stairs.

The place was vast, but not so large that people on the broad concrete stage appeared tiny and out of focus, like they did at the Hollywood Bowl. The Ramona Bowl was the pride of the small town of Hemet, and home to the country's longest running outdoor play. Ramona's only real weakness was the pitiless San Jacinto Valley heat.

From the top section, heat shimmer was the primary obstacle to seeing what was happening anywhere on stage.

Bryan and Quin sat near the top, shielding their eyes from the sun with their graduation programs.

"Stupid square hat doesn't even do anything," Bryan said for the third time.

"Need one of those fake Chinese hats," Quin mused, pointing to a contingent of older women who all wore wide straw cones on their heads. "That prolly helps."

Bryan plucked at the front of his black acetate robe, attempting to rouse some kind of breeze beneath it. "My phone says it's 115 degrees."

Quin struggled to adjust the brightness on his phone screen while tilting it away from the blinding glare. "I've got 117. Oh, there goes another one."

A few rows down, they saw another grandparent being hauled out of their seat and onto a gurney by the small army of EMTs who watched the crowd for signs of heat stroke.

"That's four," Bryan said sourly. "And they haven't even started playing 'Pimp and Circumcision' yet."

Quin tallied another mark on his paper with a stolen golf pencil before returning the program to its sweaty perch on his brow. He didn't look up when Bryan made his way down to accept his award for academic achievement. When the principal made a big announcement about where Bryan was going to college, Quin uttered a short, bitter laugh. No one around him noticed.

Three hours later they both had walked across the stage, accepted their fake diplomas, and counted seven total casualties of the heat. They evaluated their options and chose a party where they knew there would be a pool.

Quin stripped off his plastic gown first, tossing it into the black heap of shed skins at the far end of the backyard. He handed Bryan his phone.

"Here, hold this for me."

Bryan accepted it meekly, not understanding why. Moments later, Quin had bolted out into the air over the pool, legs pedaling madly on an invisible bicycle over the center of the surface. He dropped like a stone, splayed out, slapping the flat blue water and disappearing from view.

"Crazy, bro." Bryan shrugged out of his own robe and searched for a place to hide their belongings so he could swim, too. He stuck two phones and his wallet into a bone-dry downspout on the dark side of the house, and then he jumped, too. He loved the long moment when his body seemed to hang in the air, before he hit. Then the water took him.

So many people ended up in the day-warmed pool that when they all climbed out sometime around midnight, the water level had sunk below the slick blue tile to expose the pitted white lunar surface below. Bryan sat in the grass, dripping dry, looking at the above and below.

The night was so balmy that none of them shivered. Parents and friends arrived, ferrying the partygoers home. The high desert sky was pitted with stars that trembled in the rising heat.

In the morning, Bryan got up and put on his still-wet shorts. He jogged out to Pachea Trail with his water bottle, waiting on Quin.

Quin was late, as usual. He dragged his feet as he approached the beginning of the trail, looking up the steep grade before leaning his hands on his knees and sighing.

"I got super trashed last night with Candace and Oralia," he puffed. "Sorry."

Bryan rolled his eyes. "Where at? Your house?"

Quin shook his head. "You know that old boat Oralia's dad has in the driveway? The one with the hole he said is from sharks? We were—"

"So, are you too short of breath to do this?"

"No," Quin said, still completely out of breath. "We only have like, what? Three more weeks? Let's do this."

They jogged up together. Bryan kept his friend in his peripheral vision, slowing himself down when it seemed Quin was lagging behind, keeping a pace. He could have talked, but he knew Quin wouldn't be able to answer and keep moving. He waited.

Bryan had started before dawn, hoping to run while there was still a little fog and the sun had not yet gotten to the business of torching the day. Waiting for Quinn meant his run back down would smell like hot asphalt and look like a white, cloudless sky.

They rounded the top of the trail and Quin threw himself down on their customary log, coughing deep in his chest.

Bryan stood and put his arms up over his head, holding his elbows. He breathed deep, looking out over the city of Hemet.

Glass winked dryly as the sun rose over the valley. He could see the orange groves in the west and the decaying stretch of Old Town in the middle. The hospital lorded over it all, squat and not really tall, but still the tallest building in the city at a whopping five stories. In the east, the improbable gray shape of a castle rose above the trailer parks that surrounded it. From far away, it was impossible to tell that the castle was an assisted living facility where every year, old people somehow died of thirst despite their constant care.

Bryan and Quin had grown up in this small town, far from the beaches and glamour that come to mind when people say "Southern California." They had biked past that castle and into the same junior high, the same high school. They had had the same life. Until now.

"So, it *is* three weeks, right?" Quin's panting was almost under control.

Bryan sat down next to him. "Yeah. Yeah I leave on the 5th. My dad's gonna drive up with me and then fly back. My job starts over the summer, so I get to move into the dorms early."

Quin nodded. "So, you coming back for Thanksgiving? Christmas?"

Bryan nodded back. "My mom would probably kill me if I didn't come home for Christmas. Thanksgiving, too. I'll just drive. It only takes like eight hours."

Quinn nodded again, but didn't say anything.

Bryan broke the silence, rushing to fill it. "So is the job with your uncle a for sure thing? Like, you've got it?"

"Yeah. I mean, I've worked with him over the summers and stuff. So he's just gonna bring me on full time for the season. I start next week, prolly work until winter. Then who knows. Maybe the casino."

They couldn't see the casino from where they sat. The Luiseño band had their reservation in a piece of the flattest part of the valley, way out from town. But the boys knew it was there.

"You ever think about the curse?" Quin was squinting out at the city, already almost too bright to look at.

"It's not real." Bryan leaned in with his shoulder and pushed his friend gently.

Quin grinned. "Of course it's real." He was looking up now, to the huge white granite peak that rose above the valley, borne up by the lion-colored mountains that had suffered through another year with almost no rain. Everything looked ready to burn any second.

"You really think there's a dream demon under that rock who drags people back here? It's just their parents and their shitty decisions."

Bryan looked back at Quin, but all he could see was the white-hot shape of the rock burned into his eyes.

"You know they say that if you sleep beneath its shadow—"

"I know the story, Quin. I've heard it all my life, but it's bullshit. I'm leaving for Stanford and I am never coming back for more than a visit. I'm finally getting out of this shithole town. I'm not 'destined to return.' I'm not going to be one of those pathetic trailer people."

He hadn't meant to yell. Quin still looked up at the mountain, fixed in his place. Bryan heard the call of a red-tailed hawk before the shadow of the bird swept over them. He waited.

"I didn't mean you." Bryan said it softly.

"Oh yeah, I know." Quin's grin was lopsided, not quite a brave face.

And that was as close as they would ever come to it.

Ambling easily down the hill, their water bottles empty, they made halting plans. They wanted to spend time together, but for none of it to seem like a farewell.

"We have to go to Oryz's."

Bryan nodded. "Yeah, we do. Maybe breakfast on Sunday?"

"Sure, yeah. And we have to go boggle some oranges."

Quin was grinning and Bryan could not help but grin back. "Yeah."

"And we have to go out to the Maze Stone."

"What?"

"You know," Quin said, still grinning. "The Maze Stone. The stone with the maze on it?"

Bryan shrugged at him as they rounded the corner at the base of the hill.

"You didn't go see it with your fourth grade class, for California history?"

"We drove forever and a day to Capistrano," Bryan said. "What the hell is the Maze Stone?"

Quin opened his empty water bottle and licked the neck, just to make sure. "It's this ancient artifact thing. How have you never heard about this?"

Bryan had his phone out and Google was showing him the basics. "It's out past Warren, right?"

"Yeah. We should do that. Your last Sunday here, we go to Oryz's, then the Maze Stone." Quin closed the bottle and pitched it between two massive aloe plants on the side of the road.

"What about after?" Bryan went and found the bottle and picked it up, reaching around the thorns.

"I dunno. Do we have to plan everything?"

They said a brief goodbye and parted at the top of Bryan's street. He went home to his packed boxes and rolled posters. Quin walked a long way until he was home.

It seemed pointless to see one another in the intervening weeks. Bryan texted Quin that he couldn't go running, then went on his own. Two of Bryan's other friends were preparing to leave, as well: one to Cal State San Marcos and another to UCLA. They talked a little about leaving. How it felt like winning and betraying all at once.

Bryan biked all over town, past the trailers and fake castle. He sought out the high places where he could see over the path from the hospital where he was born to the freeway that would take him away. He thought it would feel like saying goodbye, but he only felt anxious to get on with it. He thought about going to the Maze Stone on his own, just to ruin the surprise, but he didn't.

On his last Sunday, Bryan sat at Oryz's drinking coffee, waiting for Quin to show up.

Quin was late.

On the wall, Bryan spied a black and white photo of a kid about his age, with a set of dates and "In Loving Memory" printed in a curlicued script across the top. The gravity of the photo was at odds with the kid in the picture; a ring-er t-shirt and a ball cap on his head, laughing with his arms spread wide. Bryan was used to seeing memorials like this in Hemet; kids got killed driving drunk right after graduation, or just disappeared with boyfriends. They shipped out with the military, hoping for escape and only finding more exotic ways to die.

Bryan shook his head slightly, thinking that at least they got out for a little while. Even becoming a vinyl sticker in the back window of a Camry was better than being stuck here.

Quin slid into the booth opposite Bryan, startling him a little. Bryan looked Quin over. His eyes were bloodshot and circled with a sinking brown that made Bryan think his friend had not slept for weeks. His clothes hung off him and he smelled bad. Not teenage boy bad, but like a cat that had been locked in a garage without water all this deadly summer long. As the smell hit him, Bryan felt the bitter black rising in his throat as his coffee begged to leave. He tried not to visibly recoil.

"Are you okay, bro?" It came out shakier than he expected.

Quin smiled and Bryan saw that one of his teeth had gone as gray as a dead fish.

"I'm fine."

"Are you…" Bryan's mouth went dry but he didn't dare take another sip of his coffee. No restaurants served tap water in Hemet, since it tasted strongly of industrial farm runoff and no one could tolerate it. He dropped his voice low, looking around. "You look like you're on meth."

Quin laughed and Bryan saw thick white fuzz on his friend's tongue and throat. "No, dude. I'm fine. I just didn't shower this morning, jeez."

Bryan thought to argue again, but stopped himself. If this was going to be his last day in an old friendship before everything became hopelessly different forever, he didn't want to fight.

They ate huge, fatty breakfast burritos, like always. Bryan wrapped his in a napkin and watched the runoff grease and salsa drip from Quin's elbow onto the knee of his chinos.

"So you excited, bro?" Quin's eyes seemed too bright, like he was running a fever.

"About Stanford? Yeah, definitely. It's gonna be—"

"No, to see the Maze Stone. Your first time and all. Probably your last time."

Bryan watched Quin take another huge mouthful and try to swallow it almost unchewed.

"Yeah. I mean, I guess. I looked up some of the theories about it, what it means and stuff."

Quin shook his head, reaching over to steal Bryan's coffee and taking a messy gulp. "Doesn't mean anything. Just some guy wanted to carve a maze into a stone. Not everything is like, symbolic."

Bryan had no answer for that. He did not take his coffee back. He paid their check without waiting for even a token protest from Quin; he knew there would be none. They got into Bryan's hand-me-down Volvo station wagon and headed out east.

There seemed to be nothing to say. They passed the Bowl where they had graduated. Bryan thought about Stanford and how different he was going to feel coming home in just a few months. When he looked over, Quin was staring out the window. They passed the red, hairy smear of something dead in the middle of the street. More mini-shrines on the side of the road.

They parked in the dirt beside the trail. The day was hot enough to fill the car with heavy, drowsy air. Getting out, they could hear bees droning in the foothills. Bryan had remembered to bring a ball cap to keep the sun out of his eyes.

Quin led the way. "It really blows your mind, standing there, thinking of how old it is," he said. "Imagine some dude, chipping away at the rock with another rock, or with a really old tool maybe. Iron. A piece of a meteorite."

Bryan looked at him, startled. That was more reasoning than he had given Quin credit for in a long time.

"A meteorite would make sense," he said thoughtfully. "Big chunk of metal, just laying out on the ground."

"Exactly."

The ground sloped up gently, dead grass and thorny desert growth tromped flat in the middle, but curving up around them like a hand about to close.

"Exactly," said Quin again, breathing harder. "And maybe when he found it, there was lightning striking, and then maybe Tahquitz spoke and told him the secret."

"What?" Bryan looked up, squinting. "What are you talking about?"

"It's right there." Quin was standing in the path in front of him, pointing with one outstretched arm.

The stone was a table-sized granite boulder with a historical marker plaque stuck to the side of it. It sat in the middle of two layers of chain link fence, each with its own terrace of razor wire on top.

"They really want to keep people from tagging that thing," Bryan said.

"You can't touch it," Quin breathed.

They came closer and Bryan read the plaque. "The land was donated by blah blah to Riverside County in nineteen blahty-blah. Registered landmark number who gives a shit." Bryan's mouth quirked up on one side in something that was almost a smile.

This was the best Hemet could offer: an anonymous undateable petroglyph surrounded by fences; a field trip destination for grade-school kids who had never seen anything impressive before. Bryan stared at the little figure of a man lost in the middle of the maze. At least, it looked like a little man.

They didn't speak for a long time.

"This isn't really a maze," Bryan said, disappointed. "There's no way out."

When Quin didn't answer, Bryan looked around. He didn't see him at first, but after a moment his eyes tracked movement. Quin was on the far side of the fence, in the weeds a few yards away.

He was walking backward toward the stone. He was naked.

"Quin?"

Quin did not turn or answer.

"Quin! Bro, what the hell?"

Quin made a sharp 90-degree corner and kept walking backward.

"No, it isn't a maze, Bryan. It's a seal."

"What are you talking about? Are you on drugs?"

"No," Quin said, speeding up, whipping past Bryan at a skittering backwards run. "Curses aren't real. We're not real. The stone's not real. We're a dream that Tahquitz is having. That's why we're all still here."

Bryan began to back away, and cold terror flooded him as he thought, wildly, that maybe walking backwards himself would make things worse.

"Quin." Bryan forced himself to take a step forward, toward the stone. "There is no Tahquitz. No curse. It's just something people say to excuse themselves for never making it out of Hemet."

"You're just saying that because you haven't seen it." Quin's voice seemed to be coming from far away.

Bryan had that hanging feeling, like he had just jumped off a diving board and had not yet hit the water.

The day turned dark. The heat was gone and in its place was the unmistakeable pressure of an oncoming desert storm. Thunder scared Bryan so bad that he screamed a little as it crashed and rolled out overhead.

A few feet in front of him, a man banged two rocks together like a crude hammer and chisel. He was tracing lines drawn on a piece of granite with some yellow, dusty markings. The man's back was hunched and he was nude.

Bryan came closer.

The man was Quin. Older, sunburnt, with his hair grown long and matted. But the profile was the same.

On the hillside above him. Bryan saw long-extinct ground sloths, thirteen feet tall and as big as bears, with long claws they dragged behind them on the ground.

Bryan was dimly aware that all his hair was standing on end, just before lightning struck the tree nearest to the stone. Bryan screamed again in blind terror, but Quin didn't even look up. The bear-sloths lumbered away. The ozone-crackling air thickened.

It came upon them slowly, with that underwater binding feeling, like trying to run in a nightmare but not being able to move. It was bigger than Bryan could comprehend, filling the sky, impossible to behold in a single glance. It arched over them, one long finger-thing coming down to touch the stone as

Quin worked on it.

Quin looked up finally, and Bryan saw there was nothing at all in his eyes.

Quin struck the stone a final time, putting the man in the center of the seal that looked like a maze. Loudly, he said "Takwish."

The arching, looming giant shrieked like metal-on-metal, like a flaming plane crash in progress. Bryan put his hands over his own ears and wailed, unable to look away.

The huge finger came off the stone and pointed at him. Quin pointed, too.

There was a moment of nothingness, and Bryan felt relief for just that split second.

Then the heat was back, a curtain of burn dropping across his face.

Quin put his finger on the stone and looked at him.

"How?" Bryan's voice was hoarse from screams that echoed in another world.

Quin smiled at him, and Bryan saw that same awful vacancy in his friend's eyes. "In loving memory."

Bryan opened his mouth to speak, but his teeth turned to rock, his lips to dust. He was in it, flat in the stone, bodiless and voiceless, the sunlight blades falling into his open eyes. Around him spread the maze that offered no escape. Two fences between him and his eternally limited view of the world.

Quin picked up the fallen baseball cap and put it on to shade his rosy, healthy skin. He left the Volvo parked there. He walked home, giving deferential berth to the roadside shrines.

In the fall, no student left Hemet for Stanford. Or CSU San Marcos. Or UCLA.

No one leaves Hemet.

People say there's a curse.

dreamcatcher

NANCY HOLDER

NANCY HOLDER

Nancy Holder has published more than 78 books and more than 200 short stories. She has received four Bram Stoker Awards for her supernatural fiction and is the coauthor of the New York Times bestselling *Wicked* series. She lives in San Diego with her daughter. You can visit her at NancyHolder.com and follow @nancyholder on Twitter.

SO IT HAD COME TO THIS: ROCKING THE COSPLAY AT ROARING CAMP, IN FELTON, California. Dwight wanted to slit his wrists. Angelo looked like that happy cat. The canary one.

No way will I let him eat her.

He and Angelo were cats, the Cannibal Cats, international rock stars, yet here they were with these weirdos who did what, worked day jobs at the minimart and dressed up like West World extras on the weekends? BuzzinFilms had put out the word for the youth of San Jose, Santa Cruz, San Francisco, and Sacramento to show up in costume so they could be extras and hey, howdy, had they. Tatted chicks were tricked out like whorish saloon girls and guys were leathered up in chaps and cowboy hats, and okay, it all had a slightly cool vibe because you had to admit that West World was a hot show, but really, no two ways about it, this was worse than a booking for a county fair. He wanted to hang himself. He and Angelo were too old for this kind of shit.

"This is cool," Angelo said as their cute little escort walked them through a stand of pine trees to their private cabin. Everyone was searching for them. She knew a private route. Angelo was all jacked up, swaggering around as if the chick couldn't care less about the fame and the millions and actually wanted *him*. He was like three times her age, right?

Yeah, Angelo was ogling Brothel Worker #1 with devilish delight, practically licking his chops. Dwight clenched his already TMJ-to-the-maxed-out jaw. Dwight wore this thing at night to keep his teeth from cracking under the strain. He was feeling the strain right then. He had made one thing perfectly clear: no eating anyone at Roaring Camp. Period. End of story. A couple of weeks ago they had nearly gotten busted on account of some paparazzi drone that had set off the security alarm system at their Spanish Revival mansion in the Hollywood Hills. They had barely managed a cleanup before the security team arrived, a slew of .44 Magnums drawn. Angelo had hardly cared. He didn't care about much these days. That was dangerous. Roaring Camp was even more dangerous. Despite the mock-casual whirligig swirling through the trees and train tracks, he and Dwight were on stage and make no mistake.

It was time to quit. It really was.

Roaring Camp was the kind of place Dwight had dreamed about going to as a kid: An 1880s-era themed "town" with all kinds of tricked-out old-timey buildings that served as the depot for an authentic work steam train that they were going to ride during their rock video shoot. Roaring Camp was cute 1880s, not gritty like *West World* or *Deadwood*, which they both had loved. Dwight still was not clear what on the concept for the video. Was it like a joke? They were hardcore rockers, not the Teletubbies. Their manager, Malik, kept saying, "Like that Steven Tyler video," but Dwight was not seeing it. Wasn't Tyler's video about hippies? And their video was going to be about … not losing their fan base?

Oh, my God, I'm so depressed, Dwight thought. *My gut is bulging over my black leather pants. My ass is sweating. At least Angelo's still in shape. But even with all the plastic surgery, his face is sagging.*

Time indeed had passed. He and Angelo had been too young for Woodstock, which had been held in 1969. They had fled the Midwest a couple years later, before high school graduation. Gotten the hell out before Dwight's dad beat him to death. *I have to remember that. Angelo saved my life.* They rented the Grateful Dead's mansion in San Francisco. Angelo had had so much money they had just flat-out bought themselves a band, the Tokers, and bought songs and producers, and they had lit up the charts with double-triple platinum-platinums. They had already discovered the nirvana of cannibalism, and they'd drawn up a bucket list of people to eat. Everyone on that list was a female rock star (at the time)—Cyndi Lauper, Tina Turner, Madonna. They'd never actually devoured anyone on that list. "So far," Angelo liked to say. "We're not dead yet." But if they got found out, they would be.

When their cannibalistic habit became their sole source of nutrition, they dumped the Tokers and broke away just the two of them, made their mark as the Cannibal Cats, and there were years they had actually turned *down* the Super Bowl.

Dwight had to remember these things. Angelo's money had originally funded all of it. Angelo had never stinted. He had always been generous.

A little thoughtless, maybe.

Dwight balled his fists as Angelo slid another glance first toward him, then back over to their escort and grinned. It was the bat signal: *she looks good enough to eat.* She was wearing a low-cut brown leather leotard, a short fringed skirt, and a pair of cowboy boots. Dyed purple and blue feathers were wound into her blond dreadlocks and big circles wrapped with colored thread hung from her ears. She loped along on her stilty legs like a giraffe.

"No," Dwight said aloud, and Angelo chuckled. The chick turned her head with a quizzical smile and Dwight flushed and looked elsewhere. Dwight had long ago stopped flirting with women. Every time he showed interest, Angelo zeroed in and about ninety-two percent of the time, Dwight's girl ended up getting eaten. It got old.

Old, old, old.

Worried over their health—Angelo read about a disease that cannibals get, kind of like mad cow disease—they had tried to quit being cannibals by going to Alcoholics Anonymous, hiding their real habit behind the age-old, tired trope of overdrinking. Maybe it would have worked, but Dwight doubted it. They had had to fake everything, even their amends, because of course they could not tell their sponsors anything near the truth, and besides, Dwight had found it necessary to beat Angelo's sponsor to death and cover up the murder with a house fire.

Lope, lope, lope. She had Photoshopped legs in real life. Dwight made a note to point out to Angelo how stringy she would be. Angelo wouldn't care. He was no connoisseur. He just liked to piss off Dwight.

"Here we are," said their escort, as she hung another right and led them to their cartoony-Western cabin. She had a set of metal keys and she unlocked the front door, then handed the keys to Angelo. Everyone always assumed Angelo was in charge.

The three went inside. It was *tres rustique,* with pine furnishings and red-and-white-checked calico curtains. Dwight's inner child bounced on the bed while he kept an eye on Angelo, who was revving up his charm machine. Angelo pointed to a thready circle decorated with beads and feathers that was dangling from a curtain rod and said to the chick, "This looks like your earrings."

"Yes. It's called a dreamcatcher." She shook her head back and forth to make her earrings swing. Other things swung. Dwight's jaw practically cracked. Not here. Uh-uh. "To catch your dreams when you sleep."

"And make them come true," Angelo said huskily. Dwight reminded himself that Angelo's voice had sent millions of dollars in royalties their way. And Angelo had been the first one to taste human flesh—the tip of Dwight's pinkie—and discover that it tasted not like chicken, but like nothing else on the planet.

At the thought, Dwight's mouth began to water. Human flesh was psychedelically delicious. That was how they used to describe it. If more people gave it a taste, cannibalism wouldn't be so shocking.

Angelo's cell phone went off. He lifted it out of his pocket and announced, "It's Malik." Angelo connected and touched his earpiece. "Hey." He listened. "Yeah, I *love* it. Dwight loves it too. Okay. Got it." He disconnected and said to Dwight, "Everyone's coming tomorrow morning. Four a.m." He smiled at Cutie Girl. "Show time."

That meant they had tonight all alone. Angelo had stipulated no assistants or anything until he and Dwight had checked the location out for themselves. It was all BS and it made them sound like cheap dates because here they were with no entourage, but if Angelo thought that meant they could get away with anything, he was insane.

"Hey, so do you want to be in our video?" Dwight asked the chick. He whipped out his own phone and held it up to her. "Gimme a couple poses and I'll send them to our director." He was trying to give her life insurance. Angelo might think twice about eating her if there was a digitized record of her in the cloud. Maybe.

"Oooh!" she cried, and thrust out her lower lip, cute-pouting as Dwight snapped the shot. She thrust forward her dreamcatchers and Angelo got into the act, saying, "Give it to me, baby!" while Dwight took more shots. Angelo slid his arm around her and hammed it up, which, though irritating, hopefully guaranteed that while he might break her heart, he would not eat it.

Dwight stayed up all night to protect "Willow," whose real name was Kelsey. Angelo fell asleep and totally snored, rising daisy-fresh at four a.m. while Dwight could barely keep his eyes open.

Toy, their director, took note of Dwight's interest in Kelsey and showered her with coverage during the shoot. She twirled and lip-synched; she rode the steam train with them. She had been a cheerleader in high school. Now she worked at Whole Foods.

During a break, Angelo said, "Hey, you've got some X factor there, Willow. Try singing with us." So she did, and Angelo whooped. Dwight figured her husky mid-range could be auto-tuned to something good. "You *have* to come back to L.A. with us," Angelo ordered her, and she pressed her hands over her mouth, crying, "Really? Really?"

Their director of photography came over to Toy and Toy said, "Makeup, please." Dwight figured they were going to level-up Kelsey's tart makeup due to her accomplishment of moving from groupie-chick to possible backup sign-er, but instead Bonnie came over to *him* and swathed some pancake under his eyes.

She said, "So Dwight, have you heard about about colonics? Might be good for your skin tone." He was mortified. And he noticed that no one asked Angelo if he'd heard about colonics. And Kelsey, the chick whose life he was attempting to save, was hanging all over Angelo. They always hung all over Angelo.

I should just kill him and eat him, Dwight thought savagely.

Here endeth the backstory.

Less than a year later, the entire world knew who "Willow" was thanks to "Dreamcatcher," the megahit on her debut album, also titled *Dreamcatcher*. Which meant, of course, that Angelo added the lithesome superstar to the People We Want to Eat list the second as she got the Grammy. What was it about the list? Why did he keep it? After the rock video (which was a major success), Angelo started talking about the list all the time, and how they had not eaten one single chick on that list, not one, and time was awastin'. Dwight tried to keep Kelsey out of it, arguing that they couldn't add someone just because it would be easy to chomp her. Sure, Kelsey was a star in her own right, making her eligible, but she hung around them all the time.

"So there's no challenge," Dwight pointed out anxiously. Angelo had spent the entire day listening to the first of their greatest hits albums. There had been six greatest hits albums so far.

"Who cares about challenge?" Angelo asked. His eyes misted. "Listen to your voice, Dwight. You're like an angel."

Dwight sighed. He couldn't hit those notes any more.

Angelo cocked his head, keeping tempo with his pointer fingers. "Remember all our dreams? They've all come true. Except for the list."

"The list is stupid," Dwight snapped. "We invented the list when we were just kids."

"We invented the Tokers when we were just kids. We became superstars." Now Angelo was conducting an orchestra. "That list is the last item on our bucket list."

"No," Dwight said. "Dying by lethal injection is the last item on our bucket list if we go anywhere near Kelsey or any other girl on that list."

Angelo snorted. "Dude, some of those 'girls' are in their sixties now." He thought a moment. "How about this. How about we eat just one of them? Just one. Then we'll let it go. I swear." He held up his hand like he was testifying at a trial.

Yeah, at our trial, Dwight thought, *for murder.*

Cyndi Lauper.
Tina Turner.
Cher.
Madonna.
PJ Harvey
Willow.

There were twenty-six more between PJ's name and Willow's, and the Cannibal Cats had performed duets with all of them. Every single chick on it. That should have been the point of the list in the first place. Dwight argued as much.

Angelo pouted. He said that Dwight had promised. Dwight hadn't. But he would eventually give up. Give in. The way he always did. Those months he had spent in Codependents Anonymous had been a waste. He was so passive—most of the time. He had tried to kill Angelo twice. Failed twice. Third time? A charm?

Then they got inducted into the Rock and Roll Hall of Fame. Dwight smiled and sang along with his blood brother but he was in a daze. This was the ultimate achievement. He could die happy. He really could.

So if he could die … he could risk dying.

He had to think about that. Could he risk dying in the electric chair? Or being attacked in prison? Could he do something that would threaten his very existence? He did that every day, right? When he crossed a street or got in a limo or flew in their jet.

But he didn't do things that were likely to increase the odds that he would die, like sky-diving or defusing bombs or having unprotected sex. Well, except for being a cannibal. But he was a discreet cannibal. If he and Angelo killed someone on the list, they increased their chances of being caught. And if they got caught, everyone would find out that they were cannibals. Their friends and family (Dwight had cut off all his relatives, but Angelo hadn't) would hate them. Their fans would burn their albums.

But if I'm dead, I won't care.

Except there would be a span of alive-time between getting caught and dying. Alive-time meant caring time.

Maybe I should go back to Codependents Anonymous. Or try another therapist. We ate my last therapist. And I hated CODA. People chain-smoked and ate donuts and hit on me. Because of the fame.

Angelo didn't have thoughts like those. It all came down to Angelo's family of origin. Angelo's mom and dad and grammas and grandpas and aunties and uncles and cousins had loved him from day one. If they found out he was a cannibal they'd love him anyway.

If one person loved me, really loved me, I would have the self-esteem I need to tell Angelo to shove it. I'm going to wind up eating a famous female rock star, Dwight thought. And he couldn't help the fillip of euphoria—or was it mindless terror?—at the notion.

His phone rang, interrupting his reverie. It was Willow.

"Yes!" she cried. "Let's do it! It's exactly what you need and it'll be so fun!"

Dwight almost dropped the phone. Was this some meta-karmic response of the universe to his thoughts?

"Yes," he repeated carefully.

"So my manager's sending over my approved rider," she said. Her voice was bubbly. Girly. "I get the personal assistant, costuming budget, my own makeup and hair. The stuff about the food. I'm paleo, right? So tell Angelo I'm in."

"Okay," he said. Had to be about a performance. Angelo had set it up and not told him. It wouldn't be the first time. Wouldn't be the last time some chick called him and asked him to relay a message to Angelo. Paleo, that was where you ate raw stuff, right? God, what a poser.

He ground his teeth, imagining all the hairline cracks he was creating, the TMJ headache that was sure to follow. He began to tremble.

"So wait," he blurted, but he was speaking to dead air.

Dead air. Dead.

If they got caught.

If.

He found Angelo sitting in front of their wall-sized TV watching their Roaring Camp video. Angelo's dye job was excellent. His dark Italian curls were tight. They would shave all that off if they electrocuted him.

Roaring Camp was so cute.

"So hey," Dwight said, sitting down on the couch beside him. "Willow says she's in."

Angelo smiled. Nodded in time to the music blaring out of the speakers. "Righteous." Who said "righteous" anymore?

"I don't know what she's talking about." Dwight clenched his jaw. His ear bones throbbed.

"It was going to be a surprise for your birthday," Angelo said, still nodding along. "A sequel to our video. At Roaring Camp."

You got people cars for their birthdays. Jewelry. You didn't organize video sequels without their permission.

"I thought you'd be more excited." Angelo slid him a glance. "*You* know."

"You set it up we can eat her," Dwight filled in. "Eat a famous chick."

"Chick-en?" Angelo pulled out a joint. "You know what a rush it will be. You know you'll be glad afterwards."

Dwight was quiet for a moment. Then he said, "Do you have a terminal illness?"

Angelo's laughter followed him all the way into his bedroom.

And the laughter followed Dwight all the way to Roaring Camp. His life was such a freakin' one-note: Stew over Angelo in Dwight-minor. Do what Angelo said to do, then get pissed off.

Two notes, then.

Kelsey hugged him and kissed him like a brother. But she loped her stilty-walk only when Angelo was around. She had on dreamcatcher earrings that bobbed as she led them back to their calico cabin, which had a plaque on it now: *The Cannibal Cats slept here.* And below the plaque, stacked up six feet deep, were hundreds if not thousands of dreamcatchers. And notes from fans:

You can make your dreams come true.

CC's, you are livin' the dream.

Thank you for the dreams.

Dream big.

Link to my demo reel: dreamcatcherz.com.

I love Roaring Camp.

Dwight was overwhelmed. Angelo said, "Poignant, huh."

"So call time is at six a.m. Not four like before," Kelsey said, as Angelo—of course—unlocked the door and the trio stepped into the little cabin. "Not four like before," she repeated, turning it into a singsong. "Not four like before, not four, not four."

On a 70s-era coffee table in front of a patchwork sofa, a vast spread of flowers, fruit, cheese, chocolates, and very likely cocaine was artfully fronting a glittering smorgasbord of bottles of hard liquor, beer, and wine. A cutting board for the cheese and plates and all that. Bottle openers and silverware, knives and a cheese slicer.

"How sweet," Kelsey drawled as if not less ten months ago she was stealing grapes in the produce aisle. At the moment she was too busy giving Angelo the eye to really pay attention to the spread. Dwight intercepted and translated her batting lashes: Hookup. So it was coming down to the old scenario. Dwight had Angelo's faux apology scripts memorized: *I didn't realize she was that important to you. I was careful. I hid the evidence. I cleaned up. You worry too much.*

Angelo cocked his head and looked straight at Dwight. "Bucket," he said.

"Then what?" Dwight asked.

"Whatever," Angelo said. He was getting pissed off.

Kelsey's perfect eyebrows raised. "What are you guys talking about?" Before Dwight could answer—not that he knew what to say—her phone buzzed. "It's my makeup guys," she announced, and moved a few feet away to take the call.

"*Ciao*, Andreas?" This was all still so new to her that calls from makeup guys were exciting. Nobody was smearing twenty-five pounds of pancake under *her* eyes.

Dwight glared at Angelo. His cheeks burned inside and out. His head pounded. *I feel so old and fat,* he thought, but he made himself pay attention. This was a showdown. *Just like all the others.* A moment of truth. *No. It's just another lie.*

"I can't hear you. My reception's bad," Kelsey said. She walked toward the door. "It's getting better. Hold on." She opened the door, turned and waved at the guys, and went outside.

"Roaring Camp is awesome." Angelo walked to the window and peered through the cheery checkered curtains. "If we'd had Roaring Camp in Iowa—"

"My father would have still beaten my mother to death," Dwight finished. He plucked a grape, sniffed it, and turned it over in his hands as if it was a meteorite from outer space. They didn't eat grapes any more.

Angelo shrugged. "Maybe the ripples would have been different. Maybe none of this would have happened. Except I would have gotten you out of there, Dwight. I wouldn't have let him kill you."

Dwight steeled himself. He tried to remind himself that there was a difference between gratitude and servitude. And that everything that had happened to him had been the result of cannibalism. He had a fake tip on his pinkie now.

He shifted his gaze to look through a gap in the curtains. A crowd of at least a hundred people had gathered behind a chain link fence. They were holding up signs that read "CANNIBAL CATS + WILLOW! WE LOVE YOU! CC 4EVER!" and all kinds of other stuff, including a request to donate money to a local animal shelter. They were cheering and waving at the three of them.

There was a silence in the room, which was ironic, considering that he and Angelo made their living blowing out the eardrums of people such as these. A roar went up and he figured Kelsey was waving at them while she was on her phone call. He wanted to break down in tears. Everything was messed up. He was so confused.

Kelsey sauntered back in. "They love us," she said happily.

They wouldn't love us without AutoTune, Dwight thought.

Angelo got a call, connected, said, "Yo, hi, Malik. Sure. We're happy." He didn't look at Dwight to see if he agreed.

Kelsey took Dwight's hand and walked him away. She said, "Dwight, it's cool. I *know*." She gazed at him with her big eyes and turned on the charm. "I know the big secret."

His head buzzed. He went numb. He stared back at her.

"*Chicken*," she whispered. She screwed up her face into the weirdest smile. His heart thundered. Had Angelo *told* her?

He was so scared he couldn't speak. Her eyes were spinning. Did she actually know that he had eaten—

"So." Angelo was done with the call. "Malik says hi."

"Chicken," Dwight said flatly, and Kelsey giggled.

"So Angelo said you find a groupie, and …. " Her dreamcatcher earrings danced in mid-air.

"That's how we do," Angelo mugged, sounding all ghetto. "And we do it tonight."

"Oh, my God!" she squealed, covering her mouth with her hands just like that first time. She hopped on the balls of her heels. "I know you're kidding me. You're such a bastard!" She was laughing.

Dwight said, "Excuse us a sec," and took Kelsey's hand. He led her across the room, opened the door, eased her back out, and shut the door. Then he whirled on Angelo. "What the hell is wrong with you?"

Angelo broke into a smile and crossed his legs at the knee. He was wearing cowboy boots. "You should see your face. You look like you're twelve. You're so cute with your puffy red cheeks." He shook his head. "Dude."

Dwight flared. "You told her so I'd agree to eat her. So we'd be safe. But maybe she's told someone else. Maybe she's texted all her ex-cheerleader friends and her *makeup guys*."

"Maybe." Angelo kept smiling. From out of the goodie bar he picked up a white card embossed with a dreamcatcher that read WELCOME CANNI-BAL CATS & WILLOW! He dangled it and swung it lazily back and forth, as if he were an old-fashioned hypnotist. "But who is going to believe her?"

"Someone will. You know someone will." Dwight ran his hands through his hair. What there was left of it. "This is not a game."

"Sure it is." Angelo waved the dreamcatcher card back and forth, back and forth, as if on an errant wind. "And I'm playing with fire."

"With our lives." Dwight shook. A stabbing pain shot through a molar. "Our *lives*."

"So I'm leaving it up to you, Dwight." Angelo held the dreamcatcher card against his own earlobe. "You decide. What do we do? Do we eat her or do we ride the wave? Don't you feel more alive than you have in months? We have it all. And are you happy? Don't you need a challenge?"

"You are insane. You are crazy. You are—"

"I'm the only one who really knows you, Dwight." Angelo got up and came around the table. He moved in close, super-close. Nervous-making close. "And I know that you are out of dreams." He took a breath, let it out slowly. "And so am I. I'm tired of running the show. You run it."

Dwight blinked. Did he even know Angelo? Was Angelo gaming him even now? "What if we do, and *she* runs," he said.

"We catch'er," Angelo said, tapping the card. "What if we don't, and she joins us? And we have to worry about her constantly, and watch her, and whisper about her, and at any moment, bam, we can end it. End it all. Dude, that's power."

"We're too old for this," Dwight argued. But he glanced over his shoulder at the door. "We should keep our voices down. What if she can hear us?"

"That would be righteous," Angelo replied. He was practically winking at Dwight, which was too gay. "C'mon. We're big cats. It's about the hunt."

"For what? The gas chamber?" Dwight said.

Angelo just smiled. "For whatever we pounce on next." He held out the dreamcatcher card. "Make a wish."

Dwight looked at Angelo. Really looked. Then he reached down and grabbed up the cutting board. Wheels and bricks of cheese flew as he slammed it into Angelo's face as hard as he could. Angelo fell backwards onto the floor, his face all bloody, moaning, "Wha wha?"

Then Dwight straddled him, covered Angelo's mouth, grabbed up Angelo's left hand, and bit off the tip of Angelo's pinkie, just about the same amount of Cannibal Cat that Angelo had popped into his mouth lo so many Iowa school years ago. Angelo went "*Mmmm!*" against Dwight's hand, which was kind of funny because it sounded like "Mmm, good," but really? Angelo's flesh was not all that tasty.

"Hey, so my makeup guy said—" Kelsey began as she opened the door and sailed into the room. She saw Angelo, all bloody on the floor. Before she could scream, Dwight was on her in two shakes. He grabbed her around the waist and flung her backwards. She smashed into the coffee table. More cheese, more fruit went sky high, a tornado of largesse.

He didn't bite her. He just held her down and breathed Angelo-breath on her. Her eyes were freakin' flying saucers.

"So this is it, babe," he said. "Living the dream. It's *so* Paleo. Whatcha think?"

She blinked, dazed and terrified. Like so many others before her.

"Jesus, Dwight," Angelo moaned behind him. "What the hell? What do you think you—"

"Shut up," Dwight said.

And Angelo did. He freakin' *did*. He fell silent.

And Dwight didn't really understand why, but laughter burst out of his chest. Dwight started laughing so hard that he started drooling on Kelsey, who was crying. Suddenly—and again, he didn't really get it—but suddenly, everything was righteous. He was massively happy, happier than he had ever dreamed of being.

And he was even hungrier than that.

SPENCER ELLSWORTH
FIVE TALES FROM THE
AQUEDUCT

SPENCER ELLSWORTH

Spencer Ellsworth's short fiction has previously appeared in *Lightspeed Magazine, The Magazine of Fantasy & Science Fiction,* and Tor.com. He is the author of the *Starfire* trilogy from Tor.com books, which began with *Starfire: A Red Peace*, out in August 2017. He lives in the Pacific Northwest with his wife and three children, works as a teacher and administrator at a small tribal college on a Native American reservation, and blogs at spencerellsworth.com.

SOUTHERN CALIFORNIA EXISTS ON BORROWED LIFE. FOUR HUNDRED MILES OF water, sucked from the Sierra Nevada into a river of steel and rebar and concrete. It plows through hot basins of Joshua trees, up barren hills dusted with scrub oaks, through sunblasted pumping stations that roil and hiss. It traces a line along the edge of Lancaster, California, springing tract homes and strip malls, green lawns and chlorine-wet children. It is a thing that does not belong, and like all such things, there is an old story at its heart.

1.

A tired old woman decided to catch catfish in the aqueduct. She'd been sitting in front of her house for the last week, in hundred-degree high desert heat, reading mystery novels, drinking tequila and orange juice. She mourned her son, who became a Mormon when he was a teenager, served a Mormon mission in England, and moved back there to marry a girl he had baptized. He never had enough money to come visit her, or so he said. Now, when the Mormons rode by on their bicycles, she would throw rocks at them. They never noticed.

It was noon and well over one hundred degrees when she got to the aqueduct and set her rod. By the time the sun went down, turning the sky above the brown hills pink, she was thoroughly drunk.

Something yanked on her line. The woman grabbed the pole. Her hands turned the reel and pulled, turned and pulled, as if she were a puppet being moved. Somewhere in her brain a thought fluttered and died, a thought that said this wasn't normal.

A catfish the size of a Great Dane hauled himself out of the water by his sucking mouth, slurping his way up the concrete. At the top, he spit out the lure, along with a fat gob of blood that splattered across the cover of the old lady's mystery novel.

"It's about time," the catfish said. "Why didn't you come sooner?"

The old woman giggled nervously, unable to think of anything else.

The catfish grunted, sounding irritated. "You have something to ask me?"

"To ask?"

"You know." The catfish looked around. "Old story. You pull a giant fish out of the water, he offers to answer any question you have—or grant a wish, though there's no way I'm doing that again, so don't even try—in exchange for his life." He sighed. "Quite frankly, I'm tired of living. I don't really mind if you don't ask. I've been swimming this aqueduct since oughty-nine."

The old woman said, "A question."

"You really are sloshed, aren't you?" the catfish asked. "You won't even tell me that the aqueduct wasn't really here in oughty-nine. Which means I don't get to tell you I wasn't a catfish then. You won't even play along. Go on, just eat me."

"What's 'oughty-nine'?"

The catfish sighed.

She wanted to ask him if her son really loved her anymore, even though he told her over and over that he did, even when she made international calls drunk at two o'clock in the morning. She opened her mouth to tell the catfish how much she missed her little boy when he snapped, "Ask already!"

She felt ashamed and looked down at the blood-spattered paperback. "That book. What… what happens at the end?"

The catfish had quickly gotten over being shocked by the stupidity of this woman. Still, he had his pride. (Even if the answer was easy—it was the nanny, not the first nanny, but the other nanny, who had killed the little girl.) "No," the catfish said, and accepted his fate. "Nope, not going to answer. You have to eat me."

The woman looked around, as if hoping for help. "I don't really want to—" A moment later she found herself lugging the enormous catfish to her car, wheezing and sweating alcohol.

He stayed in her freezer for three months, until the Mormon missionaries knocked on her door and she felt so lonely that she actually let them in. They brought her pamphlets and videos her son had already shown her, and one day one of them, who was an avid fisherman, saw the massive catfish in her freezer. He covered it in cornmeal and cooked it up with fries.

After dinner, the missionaries and the woman fell asleep on the couch. They dreamed of an immense tunnel, stretching through the hearts of purple suns and deep, briny black water. Pumping stations rattled in the background as they fell through pipes made of light and time. For the rest of their lives they would dream homesick dreams.

2.

Seventy-nine million, five hundred thousand, three hundred and twenty years ago, give or take a few months, a pterosaur flew the length of the aqueduct, which was underwater then. She had a vision of an immense fish whose flesh tasted of the sun. The other pterosaurs envied her when she came back and cawed that she had found the fish and eaten it, but most of them suspected she was lying.

A few months passed before any of them realized that it had been the first time they conceived of lying. There were no Huck Finns among the pterosaurs.

This complicated things. The weak little pterosaurs, normally relegated to low, wet nests near the water, started to tell the high-nested ones, the strong but foolhardy, that there was better fishing further out on the water. While the high-nesters were gone, the low-nesters took over their spots. Curiously enough, she who had flown the length of the aqueduct was fooled by this very strategy, and her eggs sank beneath green algae-rich waves.

The high-nested pterosaurs were infuriated. Determined also to battle with the mind, they created a code of pterosaur conduct that declared the low-nested pterosaurs inferior and not worthy of breeding, and justified violence in throwing them out. The low-nesters refused to leave, organizing protests atop the high cliffs. A young fiery speaker arose among the low-nested pterosaurs, demanding rights to high nests. He died under mysterious circumstances, wings torn and bloody, drifting in the surf.

A new generation grew up in this strife. The children of high-cliff pterosaurs began fraternizing with the children of lower-cliff pterosaurs. They started to build a monument of calcified pterosaur shit to their infamous speaker. Had that infamous comet not hit, who knows how many monuments they might have built.

With ancient eyes, she who had flown the length of the aqueduct saw the circle of light burning, coming closer in the sky. She tasted sunlight and sweet fish flesh.

3.

Kevin has a song in his head. It is four minutes long and every four minutes it repeats. It is as annoying as the number sixteen—two to the fourth power, ugh. As annoying as when people tell him that all woolly mammoths are dead when they haven't looked in Kamchatka. As annoying as the fact that he wants to kiss a girl, and he probably never will.

He had never heard it before today. But now that the aqueduct is drawing near, he hears it over and over. It goes like this:

Frgmg.

Hrglglglg.

Frig.

Kevin, of course, knows that it translates to "My sweet, I will give you the meat from the gannengfish's head, my spawner so sweet."

But Dan, his tender, doesn't know. "Wait up, man," Dan says. "You walk so fast." Dan looks up. It's well into the hundreds in Lancaster today. The high hill of the aqueduct ripples in the heat ahead of them.

"Do you know how annoying it is to have a song stuck in your head like this?" Kevin asks. "It is probably as annoying as getting your small intestines entirely ripped from your body, which would stretch twenty-three feet, which is how long I think I can stand to have this song stuck in my head."

"Twenty-three minutes?" Dan asks, wishing he had brought water.

"Twenty-three seconds," Kevin says, after a dramatic pause.

"We need to drink from someone's garden hose or something," Dan says. "Otherwise I'll jump into the aqueduct."

"I am not thirsty," Kevin says. He feels plenty of water around him, like a mild shallow ocean. That is all the heat of the day is, really. He imagines a girl swimming through the water toward him. It sounds nice. He just needs more water for it.

The high ridge of the aqueduct grows closer to them and Kevin sees the drainage tunnel that they will take to go under the aqueduct: round, black, set into a trench of concrete. The drainage tunnel speaks of seas and stars; sucks at him like gravity wells. Kevin steps into it. *Frgmg.* He turns, spinning through the dark on an accretion disk. *Hrglglglg.*

The tunnel spits him out into the hot Lancaster sun.

Dan pops out behind him. "Jeez, Kevin! You hurry so much! You need to wait for me in weather like this."

"It doesn't matter," Kevin says. "It doesn't matter. I…" He couldn't remember what he was going to say. A video game score? A fact about internal organs? The beauty of the number twenty-seven? All he says is, "I want to see what kind of fish are in the aqueduct."

Kevin walks up the steep side of the aqueduct, bouncing from tuft of dry grass to tuft of dry grass.

At the top, she is waiting for him.

She is a little tall, a little blonde, a little brunette. She wears running shoes, gym shorts, and a black sports bra. She looks a little bit like Katie Tucker, from church, and a little bit like Mya Hernandez from school.

Kevin has tried talking to those girls. He has told them that their eyes could probably make as many winks as extinct species in the K-T Event, which was probably seventy percent of all species on Earth, and they should see if they could wink at him seventy percent of all winks ever winked. It didn't work. Not a single wink.

She smiles and says, "I've been waiting for you."

"How long?" Kevin asks.

"As long as it takes," she says, "to get from Betelgeuse to this very planet."

"That's six hundred and forty-one light-years. Did you travel at the speed of light?"

"Oh no," she says, and steps closer. He can smell her sweat, mixed with the dust. There is another smell underlying it, like a beach covered in old seaweed on a hot day. "I crawled."

"Here's the aqueduct!" Dan calls from behind as he crests the hill. "Do you see the fish?"

Kevin stares at the girl. Unlike every other girl, she doesn't seem to care that his gaze lingers on her breasts. Sweat-marked dirt hangs, like the frond-arms of nebulae, right above the line of her cleavage.

She winks.

"How long have I known you?" Kevin asks, not taking his eyes off her breasts.

"As long as it takes a star to reach supernova."

"I don't think I have known you that long," Kevin says.

"Old story," she says. "A man meets a girl in the woods who grants him his heart's desire. He feels like he has known her for ages." She steps closer to him. "What do you dream about, Kevin? Do you dream of a girl who is like a video game? Back, A, right, right? Or do you dream of a girl like a woolly mammoth, who would be the greatest treasure alive if only people looked for her in the right place?"

He is aware that she is standing very close. He looks behind for Dan. Dan is staring at the aqueduct, his tongue hanging stiff and dry and white from his mouth. "Dan, I think you should ask the girl what she wa—"

She hooks her fingers under the elastic of her sports bra and pulls it off. Her breasts are perfect and round, nipples like little black holes that draw his gaze, spinning on whirlpools of cosmic matter.

"Which girl, Kevin?"

He finds his voice. "Mammoth."

"Right answer." She lays a finger on his neck. She takes his left hand and guides it up to her right breast.

"Can't—" Kevin stutters. "Can't. Can't. Cannot."

"You can," she says. "You're just a polynomial and I'm simplifying you."

With that, Kevin realizes that it is okay to lie down. His T-shirt and his shorts and her gym shorts and his sandals and her running shoes are all simplified and gone. Their position—two people separate—is simplified and they are stuck together. The tightness of three cubed instead of the sprawl of twenty-seven.

Her breasts hang over him, red, radium-rich stars. His sperm comes flooding out of pumping stations, rattling and shaking pipes, and swims into a dark sky. He groans,

Frgmg.

Hrglglglg.

Frig.

4.

Edmund G. Brown, who went by Pat, was the governor of the Golden State from 1959 to 1967, and he was determined to irrigate the brown lands of California. He watched the aqueduct rise, threading its way through four hundred miles of brown dust, a blue ribbon tying up the state.

He remembered being seven years old, cranking an old water pump on his grandfather's ranch in Colusa County. Creak. Creak. The water slurped its way out, shimmering in the sun, faintly brown like milky coffee. Young Pat grimaced. He hated drinking muddy water. His mother had suggested that he make it better by imagining it was the red-dust-choked water of the canals on Barsoom. Pat did not appreciate the way his mother was appropriating his imagination for her own.

Creak. Slurp. The water beat against the sides of the bucket. Pat turned the crank and looked down into the water.

Three curtains of shining, clear water rose from the dim mucky stuff. Wet, cold, ice-clear, catching the light, it formed into the fins of a beta, its black eyes staring up at Pat out of the clear water.

"Pat," said the fish, "I have to wonder why there are so many canals on Mars and not in California."

"What?"

"Pat," the fish said, "imagine canals that could wrap around this world. Constrict it like rubber bands. Keep the world from expanding too much."

This made perfect sense to young Pat. He would question, much later in life, why it never stopped making perfect sense.

A few days later as he pumped the water, a koi slipped out of the faucet, torpedo-sleek, mouth questioning in a perfect O, "Pat? No canal yet? The red planet will be blue soon! This blue planet is brown, really!"

"I don't know how to build a canal," Pat said, in the manner of all fools chosen to do great things.

"Follow the path," the koi said. "Walk the entire path. You'll see it."

The third messenger did not come for years, not until Prohibition, when Pat was watering the whiskey they sold out of the back of his father's cigar store. The faucet was new and shone, and it put clear, cold water into each sinus-clearing jar. Pat poured himself a glass of water after he was done, took a sip, and stared at it.

Enormous and tumescent, a catfish birthed itself from the jar, beard of water trailing to the floor and soaking it. The catfish fixed him with eyes that gleamed dark and deep. The catfish's mustache raised itself trembling into the air and traced a wet tentacular path along the map of California on the back room wall. "Canals, Pat!" he said. "They were too late to save Barsoom. Would you see California descend into that kind of anarchy? Canals! Wrap the world up like a present."

Later, Pat Brown never did walk the entire length of the aqueduct, but he would draw it in on maps and globes. "Just like the canals on Mars," he was heard to mutter.

"You know, sir," one of his gubernatorial assistants said after many muttered statements, "there are no canals on Mars."

That assistant was an idiot. Of course there are canals on Mars.

5.

Seventy-nine thousand, four hundred ninety-eight years from now, give or take a few weeks, an explorer will die in what was once California.

Its ship will lose orbit, hit the curve of the Earth just wrong, descend just too quickly. Its fronded tentacles, worm-fingers, will scramble over switches and levers, seeking to arrest its descent. Its dark, old eyes will open wide in panic. A tiny crack will tear in its fuselage. The soft, warm water in its cockpit will boil in the heat of the atmosphere. Its gills will burn and it will burp cries of terror.

Its ship will crash on a dusty, wasted world we would hardly recognize as our own. It will tumble and break, tracing a path among thousands of useless, waterless miles, among the few survivors who try to cling to life on the world their ancestors used up.

In its last moment, it will remember dark, warm seas, the sweet meat of a gannengfish's head, and of spawning with a bearded mate, their whiskers drifting in seed-rich water.

That thing will not belong, as water does not belong in the desert. And like all things that do not belong, it will be the heart of an old story, a story of catfish, koi, a girl unique in all the sea. Stories of water in dry places.

EZZY G. LANGUZZI
NARANJAS
INMORTALES
CALIFORNIA
GROWN
ORANGE Co.
AN BERNARDINO CO., CALIFORNIA.

EZZY G. LANGUZZI

Ezzy is a Latinx writer of speculative short fiction and contemporary MG/YA. She was born and raised in Southern California, the daughter of Mexican immigrants. "Naranjas Inmortales" is her first short story to be published. Her second story to be accepted for publication, "Viva La Muñeca," will appear in the Upper Rubber Boot Books anthology titled *Broad Knowledge*. She's an MFA candidate in Popular Fiction Writing and Publishing at Emerson College and a 2017 Las Dos Brujas Writers Workshop participant. Her contemporary MG novel *Where Hazard Meets Newhope* was chosen as a finalist in the 2016 Pitch América competition. Ezzy holds a MEd and works with middle school students by day. She lives in MA with her husband, son, and two crazy Labradoodles.

LOS ANGELES 1968

SIXTY YEARS HAVE PASSED SINCE WE FLED A REVOLUTION THAT, BY ITS END, claimed the lives of more than two million people. Now that I'm an old woman, I remember Abuela and how she'd promised our ancestors would save my life one day.

SOUTHERN CALIFORNIA 1910

The cantankerous truck we'd purchased at a junkyard in a town called San Diego protested and backfired as it lurched up the California coast. We drove past pastures, ravines and hillsides, while the air thickened with a citrusy scent that made my mouth water.

"¡Papi, mira! MENDOZA ORCHARDS," I said, pointing to a sign at the side of the road. "It says they're hiring."

Papi straightened his fedora and turned onto the dirt road shaded by entwined trees.

The sun had begun its descent into the Pacific and stained the sky violet. I kissed the dragonfly ring made of hammered gold that Abuela had given me before our journey. Its two tiny eyes cut from green stone twinkled. She'd said, "One of our ancestors created this anillo, made it before the plague poisoned our land and people with Nueva España."

I remember how she'd stooped over our wood stove, stirring sticks of cinnamon in milk and chocolate, white shawl draped over her frail shoulders. Her words have remained with me these past sixty years.

"One day you'll hear our ancestors in the ocean breeze and leaves and trees. Blood spilled to earth is the secret. From dust we all come and to dust must return."

She had died in her sleep that night.

We bumped up the dirt road toward a verdant hillside that spilled into a canyon. On either side of the road, orange trees grew as far as the eye could see. A man perched near the top of a three-legged ladder clipped an orange from a branch with a pair of short, curved shears, then dropped the fruit into a burlap sack hanging at his side.

"Que barbaridad." My father stopped the truck. "Where are all the workers? The fruit will spoil if it doesn't come off those trees, soon."

"Clip, don't pull!" the man in the straw hat said to a pregnant woman, working alongside him. "You don't want to damage the fruit."

Upon seeing us, the man waved hello.

"¿Agua, Señor?" A boy in overalls offered the worker a cup of water.

A woman on horseback approached our truck.

"Bienvenidos." She carried herself with the confidence of a soldadera, her back straight—fierce and fearless. She was unlike any woman I'd ever seen, both rugged and elegant. She looked strong, like she should've been picking alongside her workers, but proper enough to live in a hacienda. "I was on the hillside and saw you come up the highway," she said.

The boy abandoned his water jug to take hold of her horse's reins. He steadied the beast for her dismount.

She removed her gloves and strode toward my father's side of the truck.

"I'm Gimena Mendoza. The proprietress of Mendoza Orchards."

My father tipped his hat. "Buenas tardes, Señora."

"How can I help you?" She peered into the car and studied my mother and me with her hazel eyes. Her chestnut hair was long and braided, thick as rope, with red ribbon. I imagined her draped in ammunition, a pistol in the waist of her black riding pants. She reminded me of the wives I'd seen ride alongside husbands who fought for the campesinos' land.

"Buscamos trabajo," my father said. "We saw the sign. You still hiring?"

"I'm always hiring. My workers come and go like the Santa Ana Winds. Romero, here," she said, motioning to the boy, "is young, but faithful. He's the only one who's been with me for any length of time. Do I speak the truth?" She glanced over her shoulder at the boy.

The dragonfly ring began to bother me. I tried to remove it, but it wouldn't budge—my finger had swollen around it.

"Sí, Señora." The boy stared at his bare feet.

"Have you done any farming or fieldwork, Señor—?" A gust of wind swept through the orchard, whipping the trees' branches and lifting a cloud of soil into the air behind the horse. The man and woman teetered on their ladders. It didn't seem to bother Señora Mendoza.

"Carranza. Me llamo Ignacio Carranza." My father removed his hat to reveal a sweaty mass of black hair matted to his forehead. "This is my family. My wife, Miriam, my eldest daughter Alma, and Mimi." He pulled the blanket away from my baby sister's face. "Somos una familia de campesinos. We would do a good job for you, Señora."

"I have orange trees that need picking. It's hard work but pays well. The hours are 5AM to 5PM, six days a week. How does twenty-five cents an hour and free lodging sound?" She pointed to a cluster of colorful houses adjacent a red barn that loomed over them. "Choose any that's not occupied. You will find what you need to get started inside. Is that satisfactory?"

"You're very generous," my father answered. "We'll take it."

She mounted her horse and reclaimed the reins from Romero. "Please, enjoy las naranjas. I have an overabundance."

"Gracías, Señora. Gracías." Papi tipped his hat.

I couldn't believe our good fortune.

I sat on a milk crate inside our temporary home and cradled Mimi in my arms.

Papi placed our two suitcases inside the front door and wiped the sweat from his hands on his guayabera. He frowned.

"Imagine, a woman owning all this property—without a husband," he said.

Mami opened and closed cabinets. She inspected the cots, the blankets, the cracks and crevices—everything.

"Maybe because she knows her landowning days would be over. Smart woman, if you ask me." She leaned over a small porcelain sink and turned one of two knobs. "There's hot running water." She opened the lid on a metal ice-box opposite the sink and scrutinized the inside. "Who leaves food and ice in a vacant house? Don't you think it's strange? It's as if—as if she knew we were coming."

"Mujer, can you please stop being so suspicious?" Papi asked. "Let's be grateful we found honest work for honest pay."

She set her mouth in a hard line and felt for dirt on the concrete floor with the bottom of her sandal.

"Why don't you cook us some dinner, so we can get to bed early?" He smacked her backside with an open hand. "We have a long day tomorrow. You can be suspicious, then. Eh?"

I stared out at the barn. Its two un-shuttered windows stood sentry over us, which made me feel smothered—trapped.

"Is it okay if I go outside for a little while?"

"No," both answered in unison.

The Santana Winds, or the Devil Winds, as early Spaniards called them, blew hot and dry all afternoon. Papi said they originated in the Sierra Nevadas and gained speed and heat as they swept over the canyons and into the sea. Indians local to the area called them the Bad Winds, because they were a harbinger of evil.

By the time I went to bed, the swelling in my finger had gone down. Good thing, too, because Papi had joked he'd have to amputate it, which I didn't think was funny. I played with the dragonfly ring, twisting it around and around, thinking about my grandmother.

One day you'll hear our ancestors in the ocean breeze and leaves and trees. Blood spilled to earth is the secret. From dust we all come and to dust must return.

Above my cot, the wind groaned and pressed against one of the small windowpanes. Thank God we didn't have to worry about wandering tarantulas, here. Back home we'd gotten into the habit of placing buckets filled with water under the windows. Too often the furry spiders would turn up in one of our slippers or on a bed. Instead of killing them, Abuela would rescue them with her bare hands and set them loose outside. She'd stand at the doorway and watch the eight-legged creatures scurry to safety.

Mimi stirred on the other side of the room in her milk-crate-converted-crib, where she slept between my parents, whose sleep was so deep they might as well have been dead. As soon as she saw my face appear over the edge of the crate, she erupted into excited babbling and gave me a toothless grin. I scooped up the bottom of my flannel nightgown and crouched low to the floor in front of her.

"Shhhhhh. Duerme, hermanita." I guided her tiny thumb into her mouth. She took it and surrendered to sleep.

I cracked open the front door. The smell of burning wood took me to Piedras Negras, where Papi burned dry brush around our ranch each summer to protect it from wildfires.

In the distance, a thin layer of mist unfurled over the canyon and into the orchard. Trees heavy with oranges glimmered under the full moon and their soil appeared to expand and contract, as if it were a living and breathing thing. I was about to shut the door when a light flickered behind the barn's windows.

Out of curiosity, I crossed the well-worn path to the barn, where a single brass lantern on a hook at the entrance illuminated a skeleton of exposed beams that dwarfed our barn back home. I wondered if this was what it felt like to be inside a big fish.

Señora Mendoza brushed her horse with a thick brush, singing in Spanish. Her hair spilled loose to her waist and she wore a floor-length black dress with elegant sleeves. She looked like she could've been from a different time and place.

"No te escondas," she said, her back to me.

"I'm not hiding."

"Come in—it's Alma, right?"

"Yes," I replied.

"Alma is a beautiful name. Do you know what it means?"

"It means *soul*."

"So so lovely, my dear." She started to hum.

Hay scattered about the barn's floor, and the stalls were empty except for one, where chains hung from the ceiling. All around us rows of framed photographs lined the walls.

"You've noticed the photographs, I see."

"May I look at them? I don't get to see photographs, often."

"Of course."

I drew near the wall closest to me. The photographs in sepia were of people—what appeared to be families, hundreds of them. All stood before the orchard, and each person, whether man, woman, or child, stared ahead with startled eyes.

My ring finger began to throb.

"You know all these people?"

"I know every one of them by name."

"But there are so many." Seeing their frightened faces planted a seed of suspicion in the pit of my belly. "Who are they?"

She turned to face me.

"It's every soul who's ever worked at Mendoza Orchards. Many, like your family, passed through. I honor their memory, as I'll honor yours when you leave."

"Thank you." The idea of my picture hanging in her barn did not sit well with me. "Do you have a family?" I wondered aloud.

"I did, many years, ago. Before—before I came from Spain and started the orchard."

A chill shot from my nape down to the small of my back, when her radiant smile transitioned to one of a mouth lined with razor-sharp teeth. I blinked and her smile returned to normal.

"Are you okay?" she asked, a glint of concern in her eyes.

"Yes, I'm sorry. I didn't mean to stare." I fell back a step.

"Well, I am done, here. Don't you have to be up early to work?"

"Yes, I have to go." I turned to leave. "Good night, Señora."

"Please, call me Gimena."

We started work at 5AM and were the only pickers in the section of orchard we chose. After an hour my hands ached, my back hurt and my neck was stiff. I had so much trouble keeping my balance on the tall ladder that every time I reached for an orange, it teetered—so I only climbed it halfway. We had another eleven hours to go.

Mami worked quickly, even with Mimi slung across her back. She'd emptied her burlap sack in the bin between her and Papi's trees several times since we'd started.

Papi didn't try to keep up with her and seemed lost in thought.

"It's not as easy as it looks. Is it, Hermano?" said the man we'd seen picking oranges the first day. He and the woman who'd worked alongside him set-up their ladders at a tree near my parents.

"Buenos días," my father greeted them. "I'm no stranger to hard work."

"I see." The man sized him up and jutted his chin toward the woman who dragged her feet behind her in what had to be exhaustion. "That's my wife, Ofelia. I'm Ernesto."

I didn't know how much more I could take.

"¿Agua?" Romero had materialized out of nowhere and stood by my ladder. He looked like a rag doll, his clothes too big for his small frame, his sandy brown hair sticking up in the back. He offered me a tin cup filled with water, which I took and guzzled. I thanked him.

"Papi, can I take a break?"

"Tired, already?" He glanced around. "Go ahead. Just a few minutes."

"Don't wander far," Mami said. "¿Entiendes?"

All I could see were the branches move where she worked.

"Sí, Mami."

"Can you help me refill my water jug?" Romero asked, timidly.

"Sure. Let's go."

We walked several minutes in silence, took a left, then a right, then a left, and continued until we skirted the orchard where it ended at the canyon. A hawk swooped down and glided in wide circles over us.

"Do you know where you're going?" I asked, impatient.

"I know my way."

"My parents would never allow me to walk this far unaccompanied."

"My parents are dead."

We walked the rest of the way in silence. I wanted to ask Romero what had happened to his parents, but feared I'd say something that could hurt his feelings.

I followed him for what felt like a mile, until we stopped near a well and a hole in the earth the size of our pick-up truck. Rope-like roots stitched the area around it and fang-like branches fringed the opening. God help the unfortunate soul who might stumble into it in the dark.

"That's an odd looking hole." Its alabaster soil contrasted the dark brown earth below my huaraches.

"It's not just a hole. Look closer."

Aside from the roots and branches, bits of white in all shapes and sizes protruded from the soil.

"Your abuela—she wants you to be careful, Alma."

The hawk shrieked and swooped into the orchard. A cloud of monarch butterflies followed close behind it. They descended on us and fluttered about before they disappeared into the trees, too. The few that remained became tangled in my hair and several sat atop Romero's head, slowly flapping their wings, but not taking flight.

Mariposas, Abuela had told me, were the souls of ancestors who visited you—sometimes when you were happy—other times when you were not.

"What about my abuela?" I grew frightened.

"Your time is short, Alma."

"Romero!" Señora Mendoza's voice carried over the trees and echoed in the canyon.

I didn't repeat to my parents what Romero had said, for fear they wouldn't allow me to talk to him. They were already so strict! And I was lonely for a friend. Three days I accompanied him to fetch water and listened to him speak cryptically about my abuela, whom he'd never met, and the orchard. Three nights the lights flickered behind the barn's watchful windows, soon after my parents had fallen asleep. I didn't dare step outside after dark.

As tired as I'd become from picking oranges all day and babysitting Mimi after work, sleep didn't come easy to me. Every time I closed my eyes, I imagined myself tumbling from the sky into the gaping hole in the ground, where I was eaten alive, and witness to my bones being spit out onto the white soil. Twice I'd jolted awake with Señora Mendoza's razor-sharp smile and piercing green eyes hovering over my cot. Once, I'd heard my abuelita humming, dreamt of las mariposas, and awoke the next morning with my ring finger throbbing in pain.

"¿Alma, qué te pasa?" my mother asked, as she quartered a chicken with a meat cleaver. She set the cleaver down and pressed her palm against the small of her back and stretched. "You've been quiet all day. Are you not feeling well?"

"It's this ring. I can't take it off."

I leaned over the sink, running cold water over my swollen finger.

"Here, use some manteca." She slathered the ring with lard and massaged it.

It still wouldn't budge.

"Raise your hand above your head," Papi said. "That should help the swelling."

So I did, and it throbbed more.

"You know, your abuela tried giving me this same ring, when I married your father. Look at how small it is! It would've never fit me. I told her to save it for the daughter I'd have someday."

"What do you know about this ring?" I asked, fearing I'd grown allergic to its metal.

"According to my mother, it dates back hundreds of years," Papi replied.

"She told me a spell was put on it," Mami added, shaking her head, then, glancing over at my father, who peeled potatoes. "Ella estaba loca," she whispered in my ear.

"I heard that."

"You know your mother and her cuentos."

"You shouldn't talk ill of the dead. Besides, how do you know none of them are *true*?" He grinned.

"Why all the questions, mi amor?" She scooped up the chopped potatoes, carrots and onion and dropped them into a pot of boiling water with the chicken.

"I don't like it here. I don't—I don't think I like Señora Mendoza, either. Being around her makes me nervous. You should see the pictures in her barn. Who takes pictures of their workers? They're creepy! What if she's a bruja?"

"What pictures?" My mother frowned.

Papi pounded his fist on the table he sat at. "I don't want to hear that nonsense. Do you hear me? Gracías a Díos we found work—that we're not starving."

I couldn't answer. He rarely yelled at me.

"Ignacio, déjala. She's had a lot to adjust to in a short time, a strange place, far from home. Of course, she's not comfortable. I'm going to tell you something—" she rested one hand on her waist and waved the cleaver at him with the other, "I'm not comfortable, either. I haven't been since we got here. Where are all the workers? Someone's harvesting those oranges."

I picked up my sister from the milk crate and squeezed her chubby hand, hoping I hadn't just started a fight.

"Did you know the couple we worked with this morning is leaving tomorrow?" Papi, who never liked conflict, clearly wanted to change the subject. "Today was their last day."

"Oh? Where are they going?" Mami peeled an orange she'd picked up from a basket overflowing with them near the front door.

She split the wedges, giving half to my father and splitting the other half with me.

I'd lost my craving for the fragrant fruit and its smell upset my stomach. I set the orange wedges aside.

"To work the orchards further north past Los Angeles, near a town called Santa Barbara, where there are vineyards, too," he said between bites of orange. "The husband told me it pays ten cents more an hour. Hey—these are sweet," he said, licking his fingers.

"Good for them," Mami replied, the fruit's juice running down her arm and dripping off her elbow. "I'm sorry we didn't get to work with them longer. His wife is nice. She's so close to having that baby. I was hoping Mimi would have someone close in age to play with. Hopefully we'll get to say good-bye."

While my parents and sister slept, I stood at our door for a long while, feeling the breeze. I waited forever for the barn's windows to glow. Something about the photographs kept bothering me. I needed to see them, even if it meant running into Señora Mendoza, again.

The inside of the barn was cold and damp, not warm like it had been the first night, and instead of smelling of fresh, clean hay, it stank of mold. It was dark, except for a corner in the back near some bales of hay, where the floor glowed green.

"Alma?"

It was Romero, whose profile I could barely make out in the moonlight. His dark silhouette stood in the middle of the barn's open entrance.

"Are you following me?"

He did not answer. Instead, he walked past me toward the green light. The frayed bottoms of his overalls dragged hay behind him.

I followed him. As we came closer to the green light, a large square outline in the wooden floor slats became visible. He pushed hay away from it with his bare toe, uncovering a large knob.

"Open it," he said.

"You open it."

"I can't."

This had to be what it was like to have a younger brother. Shaking my head, I pulled the knob, expecting resistance. Instead, the door swung open to a spiral staircase carved from stone. It corkscrewed into the ground.

"¿Qué diablos?"

"Follow me." He took the first step.

"I don't know. That doesn't look safe."

"Please."

Romero descended and I trailed behind him, taking the wide steps, one-by-one, feeling the temperature drop as my heart thrummed faster. My parents would kill me if they woke to find me gone. The deeper we went, the green light grew brighter. We continued down and around, until we stepped into a circular room cut from the same stone. The room reeked of sour oranges and opened to a narrow passageway, where thick roots laced the earth above our heads.

He took my hand in his and led the way.

I had no business snooping around Señora Mendoza's property, but the pit lured me into its depths. The passageway sloped so that I had to lean back to steady myself against the damp walls.

"I want to go back." The further and deeper I went, the more it felt as though I was being swallowed alive.

"We're almost there."

A briny mist replaced the stink of sour orange and coated my lips with salt. A few more steps and I heard a sound I now know well—that of the ocean crashing against rocks.

The passageway ended at the entrance to a sea cave, where the ocean was visible through a giant opening in the sea wall, in the shape of a keyhole. The green light emanated from inside a copper bowl sitting atop a pedestal in the middle of the cave.

"What is that?"

Green tendrils of mist billowed from it to the ground.

"It's her eyes."

On the ground before the copper bowl rested a coffin-like box that gleamed of gold, and behind me towered gargantuan bookcases enclosed with glass. High above between the monoliths, suspended from the stone ceiling, hung a tapestry that told a three-part story.

The frayed and faded cloth illustrated an ordinary man who cast a horned shadow behind him. He wore a dark, hooded cloak and stood at the mouth of a cave. A woman with outstretched hands knelt before him and cradled an orange he handed to her. On the landscape behind them were scattered pyramids, the sun, moon and shooting stars.

The image directly below it was of a fleet of Spanish galleons crossing an angry ocean from which tentacles larger than the vessels themselves sprung and waved. One tentacle shot straight to the sky wrapped around a sailor.

The last set of images sent ice through my veins. Families of faceless Indians in shackles and with their bodies painted blue marched to a golden altar, where a figure that looked more like the root of a tree than a person siphoned with its mouth the life from a heavily-wrinkled body that lay lifeless before it.

My ring finger had started to throb the second we descended the stone steps, now it burned.

"What is all this?"

"It's her secret."

I backed away from him.

"The truth is more frightening than anything you could imagine, Alma. Thousands have died, so she can live."

"Who-is-she?" I didn't want to believe him. "Don't lie to me."

"She was an aristocrat with a lust for immortality, whose darkest wish was granted by a demon that heard her thoughts one day."

"That's impossible."

"Are you blind? Look around you."

"But—but—how could she live *forever*?"

"By feeding her lust for immortality with blood."

I shuddered at the thought of the photographs lining her barn's walls—that she could name each person by name—the children.

"The orchard is a ruse. She's consumed families of Indians and migrants. She swallows their souls then feeds the orchard their bones."

Like my dream!

"Why haven't you tried to stop her?"

"I'm under her spell, Alma. You are not. Kill the orchard and you kill her," he replied.

I slid to the ground to keep my legs from buckling out from under me and leaned against the altar. My gaze went to the tapestry.

"You see it for what it is," he said, regarding me with the eyes of a wise, old man who'd endured years of solitude.

"It's about her, isn't it?"

"Yes. She came as a stowaway to the New World with the first conquistadores. You will find this all written in her journal," he said. "It's in there—inside the bookcase."

I searched for a way to open it, but there were no doors, hinges, or handles. The glass protected the leather-bound books in a single, solid sheet. "How do I get inside?"

"There's a spell. You must hear her say it. I cannot repeat it."

My frustration mounted.

"That hooded figure—is the demon?"

"It gave her the sapling of an orange tree containing its blood, the symbol of their pact. She came aboard one of those galleons with it protected under her clothes, pressed to her heart, until she made her way north to find a place to plant it."

I became light-headed.

"You sound crazy!"

"I wish I were crazy." His gaze had grown tired. "Crazy would be better than damned."

"Who are you in all this?"

"I'm not a ghost, if that's what you're asking. I'm flesh and bone, like you. My family fell into her trap fifty years ago, when the gringos took our land. We'd lived on this side long before there was a border. She killed my parents and brothers, but spared me because I reminded her of the son she'd had in Spain four hundred years ago." He hesitated. "You have to stop her, unless you want your picture hanging in the barn, too."

I shuddered at the thought of ending up all shriveled like a prune. "There has to be something I can take to show my parents."

Romero was gone.

The corner of a gilded picture frame poked out from under several maps on a table littered with nautical instruments. I lifted the maps and gasped. Señora Mendoza's emerald green eyes stared back at me. She clutched a key to her heart and wore the same elegant-sleeved black dress she'd worn in the barn the first night. Her hair spilled over her shoulders in fiery red tresses and her flawless skin was the color of cream. It was dated 1519 and had GIMENA

MENDOZA scrawled under the date in black paint.

Something moved behind the bookcase and the sound of clinking metal echoed throughout the cave. I panicked and bolted for the passageway from where I'd come, when the bookcase creaked and began to swing open. I'd never make it, so I veered toward the keyhole opening, where stone jutted from the sea wall. I shrank into the darkness to catch my breath.

The couple we'd worked with during the day emerged from behind the glass-enclosed bookcase, one shackled behind the other, staring straight ahead. They slept, but with their eyes open. Señora Mendoza, wearing a black cloak, emerged last.

I brought my aching finger to my chest and noticed the dragonfly's tiny gem eyes pulsated with white light.

One day you'll hear our ancestors in the ocean breeze and leaves and trees. Blood spilled to earth is the secret. From dust we all come and to dust must return.

The man sat on the edge of the gold altar and then lay on his back, his eyes still wide open. The wife did not blink, did not move. She just stood there like a puppet, waiting for her strings to be pulled. Señora Mendoza drew a key from inside her sleeve and unshackled him from his wife and a ball of wind, clouds and lightning formed over the man's immobile figure. The whites of Señora Mendoza's eyes turned black as ink. She leaned over him, placed her hands on his cheeks and her lips over his, as if to kiss him but, instead, inhaled.

I clasped my hands over my mouth to stifle my screams, as I watched the man shrivel away in a matter of seconds under her lips, until there was nothing left of him but a pile of skin, bones and clothes.

Señora Mendoza swept the man's remains from the altar with her arm to make room for his pregnant wife.

I considered escaping through the keyhole opening, when the sound of a squeaky wheel echoed through the cave. Romero entered from behind the open bookcase, pushing a red wheelbarrow. His deathlike stare and stiff movement frightened me. He approached the pile of remains on the floor and slowly collected them with his bare hands. The man's skin folded and stretched like a sheath of rubber as he scooped it up. The bones clanged against metal, as he dropped them into the wheelbarrow.

I skirted the cave toward the passageway, my back plastered to the rock wall like a fly. I prayed with every shaky step that Señora Mendoza would not notice me, as she sucked the life from the woman.

And I'd almost made it, but for stones that came loose in a small avalanche from the wall near the passageway entrance.

At the sound, Señora Mendoza whipped around with the ferocity of a cornered animal, her hands out before her, fingers splayed like claws. She looked rabid with her teeth bared. She released a slow and guttural growl, as she stared at me with her darkened eyes.

I leapt into the passageway and ran. I scrambled up the narrow passageway, never once stopping to look over my shoulder, certain that if I did, I'd die underground. When I reached the spiral stone staircase, I jumped over the steps two at a time and took a second to catch my breath inside the barn, to listen for footsteps behind me, but there were none.

The brass lantern hung on the hook at the entrance, its glass enclosure ablaze. I took it and instead of running to warn my parents, I did the thing I believed would save us, and ran as fast as I could into the orchard and toward the mouth-like opening in the soil that had been fed the bones of thousands. *Kill the orchard and you kill her.*

The soles of my feet sunk into the orchard soil. It was as if it could read my mind. Something pulled me back.

Behind me, the trees, sky, and the roof of the barn were swallowed by a dark, viscous void that expanded and spiraled. The black hole was trying to suck me into it, but my parents' faces, my baby sister's gave me the strength to dig my heels into the soil and push. I kept the lantern before me to protect its flame.

I reached the edge of the orchard and stopped short of the hole in the earth. The wind howled down from the canyon, past me and into the spiraling void. A cracking noise, like that of branches breaking, filled the night air, as the hole in the ground opened and closed. It expected to be fed.

I shuddered in horror.

The opening's roots surfaced and pulsated red, extending toward the trees in the orchard.

"You're a silly, silly girl, Alma." Señora Mendoza emerged from the darkness, beautiful, her cheeks rose ripe. The wind blew her red mane into a halo of snakes around her.

"You're nothing but a murderous bruja. Selfish! All those people trusted you. We trusted you. And instead of helping us, you want to kill us?"

"There's no reason why you must suffer the same fate as your family," she said, coming closer to me. "Wouldn't you like to stay here with me—with Romero? Live forever?"

"Noooooooooo!"

I hurled the lantern into the hole with all my strength.

"Stop!" Her scream pierced my ears.

One second she leapt through the air toward me like a lioness, the next the Santanas brought with them a cloud of monarch butterflies that swirled through the air and attacked her. The beautiful black and orange winged creatures whipped around and covered her from head to toe, as she screamed in rage.

Whooshhhhh

The open wound in the earth burst into flames, the roots carrying the fire over the surface of the soil to the trees. The fire spread through them as if they were dry nettles.

The butterflies ate away at Señora Mendoza's flesh, until they exposed muscle; then they ate muscle until all that remained of her was a calavera in a dress that plummeted to the ground in a cloud of dust.

My finger burned and hurt so much I thought it might burst into flames, too. The band glowed and the dragonfly's emerald eyes flashed white before it dissolved, leaving nothing but a warm sensation on my finger.

"Abuela," I cried. "Abuelita, gracías."

The wind blew the flames away from the canyon and the sky over the orchard glowed red and orange. Everything in front of me smoldered. It was so hot sweat dripped from my forehead. The wall of fire trapped me with no means of reaching my parents.

"Alma! Alma!" Mami and Papi's cries echoed through the trees, not from the other side of the orchard, but from within it. "¿Mija, donde estas?

"Mami! Papi!" I choked on thick clouds of smoke. "I'm over here! Oh, my God. No no no—Mimi."

"Almaaaaa!"

An enormous ball of fire mushroomed over the orchard and consumed the remaining trees, sending red embers drifting into the night sky.

I lay curled up in a ball at the foot of the canyon the entire night, as the wind fanned the flames. At dawn, all that remained were plumes of smoke that rose from ash and Señora Mendoza's dress. Romero was nowhere to be found, and I was terrified I'd discover my parents' and sister's charred remains in the orchard.

I wanted to cry, but it was as if my tears had disappeared.

The workers' brightly painted houses and barn stood undamaged. I stumbled in their direction when a baby's cries drifted over the blackened land. The crying grew louder the closer I came to the house we'd only slept in barely a week.

Inside, Mimi lay on her stomach inside her crate-converted-crib. My parents had left her when they'd gone out looking for me. She'd turned on her own and Mami had not been there to see it—would never see it.

My tears finally came.

I picked her up and held her to me, hugging and kissing her so much she became upset and started to wiggle in my arms.

"I'm sorry, Mimi. I'm so sorry."

Mami and Papi were dead because they'd gone out looking for me.

I sat on the front stoop with her in my soot-covered arms under the barn's watchful eyes, unsure of what to do, when fire engines and police cars traveled up the same road that had led us to Señora Mendoza.

The years have slipped by at an unforgiving pace. I am older, wiser, as I sit with my wrinkled hands folded on my lap, watching the sunset over the Pacific. I long to see my parents and abuela, who knew with the certainty of a curandera that fate is plotted in the stars. I miss my Mimi, who stayed by me all these years. She passed away, yesterday.

One day you'll hear our ancestors in the ocean breeze and leaves and trees. Blood spilled to earth is the secret. From dust we all come and to dust must return.

Today, I join them.

salt
in her
hollows

E. CATHERINE TOBLER

E. CATHERINE TOBLER

E. Catherine Tobler has never found a portal to a magical world, but she sure keeps looking. Among others, her short fiction has appeared in *Clarkesworld, Lightspeed,* and on the Theodore Sturgeon Memorial Award ballot. The fourth Egyptian steampunk adventure in her *Folley & Mallory* series is out now. Follow her on Twitter @ECthetwit or her website, ecatherine.com.

JOSIE SAID SHE SAW ONE UNDER THE ROTTING LENGTH OF MANHATTAN PIER, trailing bright through the mussels and up the pilings, but Cassie said no, they only went to Big Sur. Lola promised they had called to her at our very own Black's Beach—thrown up into the shallows from the underwater canyon—but Nicole said no way no way, it was *only* Santa Cruz. Didn't we know about Santa Cruz? Vampires, she hissed, laughing, and we pelted her with sand-crusted tar balls. Cassie came closest—somewhere near Big Sur— because she went and never came back. Josie, Lola, and Nic and me were all still looking, but Cassie never came back.

Wasn't like you were going to find a headline, "Southern California Girl Devoured By Mermaid Off Big Sur." How many girls without families went missing in those waters, in those years? Wasn't like they were mermaids at all, either. They *weren't* mermaids and don't even get me started about vampires. No.

It wasn't a selkie that would drop its skin on the beach and leave it un-guarded, and it wasn't a mermaid that would give up her tail. Selkies and mer-maids had to be smarter than fuck—they knew better than to give up their means of escape. Same way you leash a board to your body before you go into the water—don't give up your main means of evacuating another organism. And make no mistake, the ocean is its own being.

Straddling my board off the coast at Pfeiffer Beach, I closed my eyes and listened. The sound that clawed up the dawn sky was that of a flock of loons, or foxes screaming in desperate need. The cry flowed as the water did between the craggy rock formations that loomed out of the water a ways off shore and the shore cliffs themselves. It made my skin prickle, though I convinced myself that was only the colder northern waters. Goosebumps scattered up my wet legs and my board wobbled the way it did when a wave was coming in. I just wasn't used to it up here yet—needed a full suit and not the shortie I wore. I opened my eyes to look over my shoulder; the morning ocean was flat; you could set a tea party on its surface. Farther out, the usual morning crew. We gave them plenty of space and they gave us the same, even if they didn't have to. These were their waters, though they murmured in appreciation when I mentioned Black's Beach—they knew it, wished they lived there sometimes. The underwater canyon did make the surf awesome, I couldn't lie.

I didn't ask them about the sounds, none of us did. Lola and Josie floated in silence beside me, heads tilted in a perfect mirrored reflections of the other. The scream came again, the water rolled beneath my feet, and I jumped. Neither of them did.

"Jesus, Kit—this water ain't that foreign."

"Didn't you—"

Was going to ask if they'd heard it but the way they looked at me—me who seemed about to jump out of her own wetsuit and skin—I knew they hadn't heard the sound. As the cry came again, echoing over the cliffside before it rolled back across the water, the pair of them had no reaction at all and my skin goosebumped itself all over again. I paddled away from them, pointing my board toward the ocean that was beginning to swell, as if some great beast stirred beneath its surface. Soon enough, the rest of the world fell away—when the wave rose, that magical dance between water and distant moon, the entire world tipped sideways. But the world didn't matter, not when I was flying, the ocean polka-dotting my browned skin, the sea air raking my sun-pale hair.

Later, in the parking lot while we stripped our wetsuits off, I wanted to ask them again, but they were laughing and rinsing suits and skins, shoving their boards in the back of our rented van. Wasn't like the vacation was a complete loss, Josie said; the waves were fucking fabulous—we'd get our handful of morning waters even if we didn't find Cassie's mythic beasties.

I watched the restless water, the beach beginning to crowd with those who'd come for the sun and not the surf, and wondered what the hell the sound was. Cassie hadn't ever been able to say—no one who remained really could and Cassie had speculated that was part of the point. Some things didn't want to be found; some things lived far away and wanted to stay that way, but then humanity had to encroach and mash things together that shouldn't have ever been mashed, and well, maybe this was that, Cassie had said. Maybe, I'd echoed.

That night in the cottage, I heard it again. Foxes screaming. I pushed the deck doors open and stood, cool breeze twisting around my bare legs. The night was black and thick with salt, beach grass throwing strange shapes against the star-pricked sky. I looked back at the cottage, but the windows of the other rooms were dark; the girls were still asleep.

The cry came from closer to the water so I left the deck behind, padding barefoot to the sand, to the point it became soaked with water. The heavy moon traced everything with a strange, pale light, the water running in a silver line up the beach. It looked like an eel towing a thousand glowing creatures in the rush of the tide. The minute the moonlit water licked my toes, the cry shook through the world again, shadows fleeing up the beach. I followed.

Shadows lit by moonlight—that was all it was—but beyond the sound of my own feet hitting the wet sand, there were others. Swift and fleet, these shadowed bodies loped up the beach and I with them, and we ran so fast my heart was like a fist in my throat. I caught the eyes of one—impossible, glowing like lightning—but it looked at me, its mouth split in a wide, toothy grin. Not a mermaid. Not a fox. Something el—

"Kit!"

I woke in the living room, having no memory of returning to the cottage. Only running. I felt like I'd run all night, every joint protesting when I sat up. Sand crusted my feet and one ankle was tangled with seaweed. I pulled it loose and peered at Josie; her sea-blue eyes were narrow, angry.

"Have you already been out?" Josie sank beside me on the couch, sounding betrayed.

A glance out to the deck showed it was still plenty early, plenty of time to get our boards and go. I shook my head. "Just a little run—still good to go."

"Well, you're sweeping that mess up later, not me."

Josie pushed off the couch and I saw the sand strewn over the hardwood floors, looking as if it had paw prints in it. By the time I'd swept, the girls were ready to go and we headed back to the break, the usual morning crew already in place. They gave us upnods, not frosty just respectful; they'd run this beach longer than any of us had been alive—it was theirs, we were in their space. We respected it by surfing the only way we knew how: the best. Meeting them on the beach later, they didn't say we'd done good for girls; mostly, they said "fuck!" a lot, asking if the waters off Black's Beach influenced our style. I thought it did—that underwater canyon, pulling the water up, cycling it out. It changed the way the ocean breathed; all that water hovering over a great absence.

Burrow, Dane, and Talon, three of the locals, invited us out that night, to come back to the beach because there'd be a bonfire and a band and beer. Burrow and Talon high-fived each other when we said sure and asked what we could bring, but Dane watched only me, his eyes strangely familiar the whole while. I couldn't get them out of my head even on the drive back to the cabin—blue, but not. In their depths, something more silver.

The beach was transformed at night, a different kind of gold under the wavering firelight. From a distance, people were transformed into shadows—*the swift thump thump of feet falling beside mine in the wet sand as we ran*—and only up close did features resolve from the dark. Dane could have been any of the figures around the fire but, with a bottle of beer warming in my hand, I didn't immediately find him as I wandered. Josie and Lola and I danced, long moments where the three of us just tangled and swayed, oblivious to anyone else; this was how surfing was sometimes—the way you moved as a part of the world but also slightly outside of it. We kept our own motion then, until the song ended and the spell broke. That was when I saw Dane, standing on the far side of the fire, as if intentionally making himself visible. The fire lit him up, made him look a little too tall for his own body, pliable like golden taffy.

I grabbed two cold beers and hip-bumped my girls before leaving them to join him. By that time, he'd turned his back to the fire, but I still found him, illuminated around the edges as if he were the sun in eclipse. I offered him the beer and he took it, giving me a swift smile in return. His silver-blue eyes lingered and I didn't mind because the way I looked—all sand-scrubbed and salt-tossed—I knew he'd never see the actual me. They never did.

He took a long swallow from the bottle, eyes never leaving me, and he smelled like beer and browned coconut. "Thanks," he said, fingering away the hint of beer that lingered on his lips. "You guys looked good out there this morning—been surfing long?"

"My mother took me out soon as I could stand, Daddy hollering the whole time," I said. It was true, but people seemed to make more of it than there was; didn't mean I'd been born to the water—I was born in a hospital like most folks. But Dane shook his head a little.

"When did you go out on your own, then?"

So he was a little more clever than the others. I drank my own beer, considering. "Must've been fifteen?" I finally said. "High school. Didn't much care about it until then—the ocean wasn't going anywhere, right?"

"Three years?" he asked.

Laughter broke from me and I kicked sand over his feet. "Ten."

I might've said more, but Burrow and Talon and Josie and Lola joined us, Burrow throwing an arm around Dane's shoulders. He looked high, his eyes as wide as saucers.

"These girls *actually* came for the water," Burrow said, leveling an accusing finger at we three. "They didn't come for the goddamn legends, you believe that shit."

My eyes flicked to Josie and Lola, wondering what they'd been talking about all this time—because while we had so totally come for the water, we were also deeply curious about the goddamn legends—one of us more than the others. But Lola smiled at me and narrowed one eye in an almost wink, and it was a look I knew. Getting high and/or drunk boys to tell stories was one of the easiest things ever.

"Legends?" I asked. The know-nothing blonde.

It was almost like Burrow and Talon had a script. Where one left off, the other picked up, young men well acquainted with the strange story they told.

Burrow started, his hands framing the night sky. "Picture it: early morning beaches across the world. Just you and your board and the whole of the fucking sky."

"And well, the *ocean*," Josie murmured even as Lola gave her a gentle elbow to the ribs.

Talon took over the story. "Ordinary day, ordinary waves, but then you hear it, a sound that ain't quite a sound you heard before. It does something to your body because you can feel the sound in your bones—someone walking over your grave."

It hadn't been like that at all—though I had felt it in my bones. Like something in me had woken up at the sound of it. I crossed my arms, holding the beer between the index and middle fingers of my right hand, trying not to shiver. The fire was warm enough but the stories they went on to tell— Dane was watching me the whole time and I didn't want him to see anything in my face; I didn't want him to know.

"There was this girl, see," Burrow said.

"Pretty thing, they say," Talon added softly. "Smelled like salt deep down in her hollows."

"This girl, she came to the water with a board, but she wasn't quite good enough—still learning, still having trouble remembering to leash the board to herself."

"They say it was a tragic mistake, right? But they never found no body. She paddled out one morning and poof. Never came back out."

Remember, I'd told Cassie; *always remember the leash. You don't want to get separated from your board; your board is your way back. Either one of you could just float off otherwise.*

But she never quite remembered every time. It was a plausible explanation for a girl going missing, but not entirely.

"Are you saying," Josie pressed, "that she heard this sound? And what, the ocean swallowed her?"

I looked out at the waves, trying to ignore the way Dane's eyes hadn't left me; the tide rolled in and then back out and when I looked at him again, his gaze hadn't budged. I tilted my head at him, silently demanding that he look away, but he didn't, and some part of me was okay with that. My eyes snapped to Talon, waiting for him to answer Josie.

"Not saying that. I'm saying—*they* did."

"They are of the ocean, but not from the ocean," Burrow added.

"What the hell does that even—"

"Can you take me where she went?" I blurted the question before the conversation went further.

Talon hadn't paid me much attention until then, but his eyes narrowed in on me as if he'd found the perfect wave to ride. He was lean as a board himself, browned by the sun, and I wondered how many girls he had lured with this story. Had he known Cassie? *Like salt deep down in her hollows.* Had he taken her out there?

"*Hell* yes." Talon answered before any of the others could.

I didn't dare look at Dane and neither did Talon—he was too busy high-fiving Burrow—but I could feel Dane's eyes boring into me. Could feel him seeing all the things he shouldn't be seeing. I was just a surfer girl. A pretty, air-headed blonde with a body too round and soft for surfing. They all said so, didn't I just want to wait on the beach until they finished their ride, and then my sun-warmed body could warm them up.

Talon wrapped my hand in his and pulled me away from the group. I felt Dane's eyes on me the whole way, burning the way that silver line of water had along my toes the night before. Talon laughed and tugged me closer to his side; he smelled like wood smoke and beer and gestured toward his car, still loaded with boards. But these boards were lined with LEDs, he said—night surfing always contained an element of danger, he said, but the lights would keep us perfectly safe and I shouldn't worry about a thing.

The thing about the ocean was, it was never perfectly safe, even in the daylight. The ocean was its own perfect thing and we were just interlopers. Visitors who might enjoy a slice of it for a moment, but could and would never know every single depth.

We stripped our clothes off, down to the suits we weren't surprised to see the other in. When you lived at the beach, suits were practical, and after a lingering glance at my body, Talon offered me a board. It was heavier than my usual, but he didn't ask if I needed help carrying it to the water. The lights that lined it were bright green, and they made a strange but not unwelcome glow about me as we paddled out.

"It's not too far, see," Talon said.

He gestured toward the nearby rock formations, the golden lights on his board bathing him in a surreal light. I followed where he led, my arms beginning to tire the farther we went; "not too far" was deceptive at night, the ocean always larger and hungrier than one could know. Closer to the rocks, the moon was hidden, the water darker than ever. We seemed like two glowing gummi worms as we straddled our boards and waited. All I heard was the lick of the water and the bump of our boards when Talon maneuvered closer. A little chill crept down my spine. In the dark, his eyes looked like holes, places in which to vanish. He rested one rawboned hand against my thigh

"Did you know her?" I asked.

He frowned, his focus on me alone, but then he shook his head. "Nah, dude." He laughed, a startling sound in the night. "They're just legends, right? Girls vanish all the time—it's always a monster in the water, ain't it?" He squeezed my thigh and slid his hand a little higher. "You are so goddamn beau—" He broke off, startled, his board knocking into mine again.

"What is it?"

I hadn't heard the sound and wondered if he had, but then— Something sleek and silver and glowing moved beneath our boards, and from the nearby rocks, that scream. Talon's hand tightened on my leg, but he didn't move it higher or pull me close.

"What are you doing?" I asked. "What *is* that?" Together, we peered below our boards, the water brightening as if someone had turned on a dozen lamps.

"That's not *me*—what are you talking about— Is it *you*?" His head snapped up and he stared at me, terror having filled his eyes. "This is *bullshit*—it's all talk to get girls out here, right, but this—"

The silver light pulsed upward, occluding the candy-colored lights on our boards, and as quickly as Talon's hand had been on my thigh, it was off. Something grabbed his board and pulled him off and down, under the water and into the light.

"Tal!"

Shrieking his name did no good. He flailed in the water, tried to grasp his board, but was already deep beneath the surface, his board left behind. I was torn between paddling the hell out of there and diving after him—was this what had snatched Cassie? Taken all those other girls? Was this the thing that screamed in the night?

Thinking of the scream brought it to bear; it raked the sky like claws. In that moment, Talon's board leash pulled taut, and I grabbed the board in return, foolishly thinking maybe I could haul him back that way, that I could reel him in like a fish, but whatever had him was strong, so strong it pulled the board out of my hands. When the board hit the surface of the ocean, it snapped in two, the half still attached to the leash—

and Talon, oh god Talon

—reeling down into the water. The golden LEDs went out, leaving me in a pool of green light that solidified as the silver glow began its retreat.

I grabbed for the remaining half of Talon's board and tried to breathe, but the scream rose around me again, and the world was drained of all its air. The lights on my board flickered out and I felt the silver in the water again, its nebulous form ghosting along the bottom of my feet. The silver light burned cold, but at the same time, it was like a hand inside my bikini bottom, warmly cupping me, hauling me closer. I shuddered and the sensation fled as quickly as it had come.

My board lights stayed out the whole way home, the ocean flat and calm until I came closer to shore; there, my board tumbled over the ankle biters, dropping me onto the cold, wet sand still clutching Talon's broken board. It was Dane who found me, Dane's warm sweatshirt that enfolded me right before the others got there. I didn't want to meet Dane's eyes, because I knew what I would find—the same thing I'd seen the first time I looked; that deep silver light burning inside.

They hauled me to the fire and sat me down—asked me what happened and I couldn't explain. I offered the broken board to Burrow and his jaw was tight.

"Shark," Dane interrupted and no one argued with that tone. I supposed if one looked at the board right, it had been bitten—but I knew it hadn't.

Dane shoved a hot mug into my hand and I drank, the alcohol-laced tea like a hammer between my eyes as it went down. But it had the intended effect, calming me and erasing the terror and confusion of Talon's sudden loss. Authorities came—Dane called them? I didn't know, couldn't say, but when they saw the broken board, they took it as all the answer they needed. Idiot kids, surfing at night, what did we expect? They didn't expect to find a body and I knew they wouldn't—just like they'd never found Cassie.

Josie and Lola wanted to go, and I let them. Given how Dane was looking at me, I wasn't about to leave, not when he might tell me what he knew. He topped off my boozy tea and promised the girls he'd get me home when I was feeling more steady, and I hunkered closer to the fire. Buried my feet in the sand and watched Dane shoo everyone else away, and when it was just he and me, he sat beside me, hands clasped between his bent knees.

"What're you doing out here, Kit?" he asked. "You surf, but that's not it."

There was a lot he didn't say. I watched his mouth grow tight, cheeks sparkling with golden stubble as the fire guttered beside us. He was as pretty as me, someone who fit too well and passed without much actual notice and maybe didn't like it at all. I let the silence deepen, unsure of what to say until I said it.

"There's something out here. Not hunting, but *living*." It was part of this world same as we were; we strayed into its space. Every living thing had a hunger, every living thing ate another living thing to survive. "Cassie found it, because she never came back. I ran with it. I see the same hint of it in your eyes."

Dane's chin came up. "The same thing I see in your eyes? What I saw in hers?"

Despite the heat of the fire, I shivered. He'd known Cassie? "That silver thing that took Talon straight off his board. That thing that screams and doesn't want to be found."

Dane's mouth lifted in a quick grin. "Legends about mermaids."

"It wasn't a goddamn mermaid, Dane. Legends, sure, the ocean will never be wholly known, but this—does it want something? Or is it just living the way we do? Feeding when it needs fed?" Another shiver, fear cold in my gut. "And what the hell do you mean, the thing you see in *my* eyes?"

He didn't say anything to that, only looked at the dark ocean that slushed against the beach behind us. Eventually I followed his gaze but saw nothing in the shadows tonight; saw no silver thread in the spume that washed ashore.

"They won't come back tonight," Dane said. "Morning's too soon, too. We'll surf tomorrow—unless they close the beach because of Talon. The morning after that…we'll go. I'll show you."

There was a resolve in his voice I didn't fully understand, not until he looked at me again. The silver thing in his eyes, it was there, but small, a fragment of what it could have been. I had only a few days before I had to go back home, return to the job, and postpone the search once more.

"You didn't come all this way because of Cassie," he said. "You came because it's already inside you—was probably in you before it was in her. Has been in you since you were fifteen and first went into the water alone. When you dared the ocean to take you, and when she didn't… You kept on trying, yeah? Every time, there's part of you wishing you didn't come back in."

Always remember the leash. You don't want to get separated from your board; your board is your way back. Either one of you could just float off otherwise.

It was my turn to crack a quick smile. "That sounds a death wish."

"But it's not death, is it? It's…something else. That's not what you feel out there, not what you felt when you ran with the shadows."

It wasn't death, he was right about that. A different way of living, but it went even beyond that. But how could I want a thing I couldn't even put into words? I felt like the airhead everyone mistook me for, the suntanned surfer girl who couldn't possibly have ambitions beyond marriage and kids.

But how long had Dane been out here? How long had he been looking? Or was it more than that? He said he'd show me. Show me what he already knew? In the shadows of his face I caught a familiar toothy grin, the grin of the beast that I'd run alongside on the beach.

"Are you—"

"Nah." Dane looked back to the black ocean, exhaling. "I'm just like you, Kit, wishing half the time I didn't come back in with the tide."

They closed the beach, but Dane said he knew a way—there was always a way and he didn't want to put it off another day—so while Josie and Lola were distracted finding a new beach to conquer with Burrow and the boys, Dane and I vanished down an old goat trail he knew. There was a gate at its end, but he was tall enough he could lift the boards and me over, one by one.

"Talon almost took you to the right place, but he had the wrong rock," Dane said.

We paddled farther north, to a looming rock that appeared to have a door carved in its belly. The rock gaped in a rough rectangle, a portal from one side of the rock to the other. Dane said we needed to go around, to watch the sunrise through the door; sunset didn't work half so well—too many people on the beach then and this was old, a thing that didn't want to be disturbed.

Straddling our boards in the unlit ocean, the sky arced huge above us, oppressive and watchful. Dane didn't light the night with LEDs the way Talon had, and didn't leash himself to his board. I plucked the trailing leash from the water, and turned the looped end over in my hands. I didn't ask him why—I knew why and when the first hint of sunrise pricked the horizon, my stomach fluttered.

"Almost every morning, before they all get here," Dane said low, "I try. There's stories that say the time of year matters, alignments in the sky, but alignment is just point of view—isn't it? These stars don't look like this from anywhere else in the galaxy."

"What matters, then?" My voice was just a whisper above the slosh of the sea.

"Wish I knew." He looked down at me, searching my eyes—maybe for that strand of silver I saw mirrored in his. "Wish I goddamn knew."

When the ocean began to swell, we did the only thing we could—we rode the waves inward. Dane angled toward the door in the rock and my heart skipped to watch him do it. If alignments mattered, his was dead on; when the sun broke the horizon, Dane slid through the door, and for a second, the world blinked out.

Black like night, until all I could see were those sharp and toothy faces running alongside me; like they *were* in the waves, were the waves—pushing me closer to where Dane had gone. The closer I got, the more he resolved, a shadow in the middle of a spilling liquid gold. Water and sun combined, and from within them Dane reached for me, but my fingers only glanced his. His eyes flared silver, his face eclipsed in joy and then he was gone.

I stumbled against my board, blinded by the sun shattering through the stone door. All around me the world compressed, until there was only the water, only the door. The wave licked the door like a lover before it plunged through, and me after it, through a shower of sunlit water that scalded my skin. I cried out—but it wasn't Dane's name, and it wasn't from pain—it was the sound of the beasts in the dark, coming from my own throat. I cried the way they did, but nothing carried me away. The board dipped down as the wave lost power to the rock, and I flipped over, into the water head over heel. I came up sputtering, looking for Dane. There were others on the beach—they cheered when I reappeared—but there was no sign of Dane, only his board stuttering riderless to shore.

I didn't have to explain to any of them where he'd gone—they knew. Dane had been looking for years, they said, and each touched his board before paddling out to catch their own waves. Josie and Lola tried to get me to paddle out, but I sat on the beach beside Dane's board, feeling emptier than I ever had. As the sun rose higher, the rock and its door didn't look so special—certainly didn't look like a place people vanished.

I went out every morning, circled the rock, and waited for the sun to carry me away. It didn't carry me away. Vacation came to its end and we headed back home, to the southern beaches we knew best of all, but not even the canyon felt right to me when I got back in that water. The water didn't gleam silver and the shadows at night were only shadows. No one was surprised when I took a job up north and moved; Josie and Lola just looked at me. Nic had gone up six months before.

I never told Nic what I knew—I saw her, but she went her own way, following her own memories of Cassie and the cries she pretended to hear. I knew she didn't really; she hadn't been marked, didn't shine silver in her eyes the way Dane had. Every morning after touching Dane's board, propped in the corner by my door, I went to the rocks—ruined countless boards when the waves washed me into the stones; that liquid gold water never carried me away no matter how I cursed it.

At the water's edge, time has a way of not existing for impossible stretches; the world is fluid and never seems to change. You never see the grains of sand washing out because you're too busy watching the waves rush in. I was as old as Dane had been when Mackenzie found me. Slim and burned brown from the sun, her pale hair braided in a long tail. Mackenzie found me standing by the bonfire at a party and I knew she hadn't come for the water alone. She looked at me and I found that quicksilver gleam in her eyes. She'd heard the sound; she had run with the shadows.

Nic was at that party—laughed when she heard Mackenzie asking me about the legends. Said she would take Mackenzie out, but I curled my hand around Mackenzie's wrist and kept her by my side. The memory of Talon taking me out when he hadn't heard the voices was something I kept close even after all this time. It couldn't be Nic, and she was drunk enough not to argue.

"Tomorrow morning," I told Mackenzie. "I'll show you."

We paddled out in silence, me on Dane's old board for the first time ever, Mackenzie nearly bristling with eagerness. It made me smile, made me remember *me* when I was her age. She looked at me with admiration and respect, not like I was a damn fool for still getting on a board at my age. In the predawn dark, we waited, floating and silent, until Mackenzie saw my board leash trailing in the water. She lifted it, concern creasing her young face.

"Sometimes, you can't be anchored," I said. In the east beyond the stone, the sky had begun to brighten, looking like the softest peach I ever did see. Then, I gave her the words Dane had given me. "Almost every morning, before they all get here, I try. There are stories that say the time of year matters, alignments in the sky, but alignment is just point of view, isn't it? These stars don't look like this from anywhere else in the galaxy."

"What matters, then?" Her voice was stronger than mine had been and I knew she'd keep on, long after I had gone.

"Wish I knew." I laughed as the sea swelled up beneath us, as the time came to paddle toward the door in the stone. "Wish I goddamn knew."

The water swept us up and the air prickled with another consciousness. When the cry came, I let it fill me up, let it overflow. I tipped my head back and called back to them. The water curled up, pushed us out, and the sun broke the horizon. In all that liquid gold light, I flew, giving myself up to whatever it was. Maybe I had to show another the way, as Dane had shown me, before I could go—at my side, Mackenzie screamed.

"Kit! You can't go—*Kit!*"

But I could go—and finally did. The wave swept me up, tongued me through the door, and my world ran silver and salt.

MELISSA MONKS

THE HANGING TREE'S SHADE

MELISSA MONKS

Melissa Monks is a horror writer from Sacramento, California. A transplant, she spent her childhood in Utah studying fairy tales. Eventually she went on to study English and anthropology at the University of Utah before moving to California in her early twenties. In college she taught herself beadwork and knitting, crafts that turned out to be useful in clearing her mind for work. Melissa is a late bloomer and wrote as a hobby for years before she decided to attempt publishing her stories. She is currently a mom and works with special needs children. She has published short stories and flash fiction in *Quantum Fairy Tales*, *The Literary Hatchet*, and *The Molotov Cocktail*.

WHEN I WAS A LITTLE GIRL GRANDMOTHER TOLD ME THAT THE SKY HAD CRIED all it could cry for us. "Die or move on. That's what we used to do. Gonna have to live that way again, Mim, die or move on," she would say, her dark eyes the only glistening things around for miles. Grandmother chose to die. Her spirit left her body lying under a cornflower blue quilt shortly after the scientists said she was right, the sky was done crying for us. We couldn't cry for her either, we couldn't spare the tears.

Grandmother also told me that when she was young no one noticed the drought much. But by the time I was born, whole towns were being abandoned because their wells had gone dry. Shopping malls were emptied of their contents, becoming mansions for sparrows and rats. People left their homes, most with only what they could pack into their cars. Fields of thirsty cattle lay down to rot in the punishing sun. Neighbors stole each other's rationed water, not for the sake of their hydrangeas, but for their children. And so many died. I was born when the rest of country declared our land a lost cause and opened its wary arms to refugees. Millions of refugees. Not all of us left, though. Some of us pulled dirty hats over our eyes and learned to squeeze blood out of the new desert. Why? Because the world didn't want refugees any more than we wanted to be refugees. Maybe we were wrong to stay. Maybe there is no right anymore.

Most of us who stayed were just stubborn. We figured life might be bad here, but it would be bad somewhere else, too, so what was the point in leaving? We'd take the wind-delivered grit in our oats for the sake of living with a little solitude for a change. For a change we'd belong to the land instead of the land belonging to us. We tore down the fences in our back yards and worked the land with our neighbors. We called it Perseverance Rancheria.

"There's nothing new about that," the old ones would tell us, "once we lived and died just like all the other animals. The land belonged to us in the same way the rabbit belonged to fox and wild rye belonged to the rabbit." It was new to me though and I liked the new way of thinking. The new way of being part of something.

We might have been ok, those of us who stayed behind, but we didn't count on the farmers staying. Not those little family farms, they all went dry and bankrupt, I mean the big multi-million dollar farms. Pistachios and pomegranates, crops people back east would pay a lot of money to get. The big farmers dug deeper and deeper wells and built pipelines that crisscrossed the land like hardened veins. They channelled water from the dwindling lakes, diverted rivers, killed what little life remained. They left dry riverbeds choked with dead fish and set the time bomb ticking for most meager subsistence farms. Sometimes they even trucked water in. We'd see tankers as big as whales delivering water to a green, leafy mole on the sepia face of the desert.

The second time the big farmers brought in water, some men were waiting. They blocked the road and threw flares and firecrackers at the driver to force him to stop. Once he did they dragged him out and stole the truck. I tried to go with them but my mother locked me in my bedroom.

"Do you think any of them will live through this?" She screamed at me through the door. I could hear the inherited knowledge of oppression in her voice. The fear of losing one more thing.

She was right, though. The men drove the truck to an empty swimming pool and filled it. Then they ditched the truck behind the rubble of an old Walmart. The farmers and their security men were waiting at the pool when our people returned. We woke in the middle of the night to cowboy whoops and gunshots as the farmers pulled up to our Rancheria. They rolled our men, bound and gagged, out of the back of a pickup and onto the cracked pavement. Sleek black rifles told us to shut up and pay attention. A leafless, tortured valley oak stood in the middle of what used to be my front lawn. The farmers hanged our heroes from its branches and threatened to shoot anyone who cut the bodies down.

Day in, day out was so hot and dry that after a week the bodies mummified right on the tree. Dehydration pulled their lips back from their teeth in ecstatic smiles. When stray breezes blew through, the mummies bumped and rubbed together. The sound reminded me of the whispering strings of dried chilies Mom sometimes hung on the porch. From then on, the farmers hanged anyone that crossed them. Soon mummified bodies dangled and twisted from every tree in the barren landscape, like long, grinning strips of beef jerky.

The dead have lives of their own, that's another thing my grandmother told me. Eventually the oak in front of my house gave up clinging to the dust and fell over, seventeen corpses hung from its branches. My mother sprinkled bootleg whiskey over their graves and prayed to Santa Muerte that their thirst be quenched. I swallowed hard, standing next to her in a swirl of dust.

The farmers came for my mother when they found out she'd given our dead a proper burial. We shuffled after them to another hanging tree and watched with grim faces and dry throats as one of the men climbed the tree to tie up a new rope. In the tree something grabbed him. His eyes widened and the front of his jeans went dark with urine. He screamed for help. Something held him, we couldn't see, but we could hear it sucking and slurping even over the hangman's shrieking. We said silent prayers of thanks to Santa Muerte as he fell from the ladder, a desiccated hull. With grins as wide as the hanged we told the farmers that the dead got thirsty, too. They shot my mother in the back as they drove away. I was fifteen and there was nothing I could do but promise her spirit I'd make it right, for everyone.

I met Bo when I should have been off to college. Bo's father had designed fireworks in Liuyang, China. Her mother was a doctor and they moved to our wasteland because she wanted to open up a non-profit clinic to help the people who had stayed behind. Bo should have been in college, too, but she was afraid for her parents so she moved with them. Even though she liked helping people, Bo took after her father. She liked blowing stuff up. And California had become one of the emptiest places full of stuff to blow up. Empty shopping malls, abandoned homes, toy stores. Once we spent an afternoon in a yarn shop igniting bamboo wool, bison wool, regular wool, silk, mohair, and every other kind of wool to see how they burned . To me they all burned the same and all smelled awful. Bo noted burn times and whether they melted or just ignited. "You can tell so much from the color of a flame. I need to know if any of them will make a good fuse," she said. The most beautiful thing I've ever seen was the reflection in Bo's dark eyes of the old drive-in movie screen engulfed in flames. It took five minutes for the screen to collapse and Bo said the flame reached two hundred feet up into the black night. Captured in her eyes, I thought the flame reached more than just the night.

"My heart stops when the black powder ignites," she said once, holding my rough brown hand in her delicate ivory one. "But when the energy releases, it's like my heart explodes, too."

I told Bo about my mother and about the slow smolder of my promise. Her delicate hand went to her mouth, her eyes wide.

"What does it feel like to always burn?"

"It feels like I'm dying, but I'll never be dead."

"We could set the water free."

So we did. We blew up the rich farmers' water towers and pipes and siphons. We watched the life flow and overflow back into the lakes and rivers. We watched the people we knew, the desiccated and hollowed-out people, bathing and reveling in cool running waters. We cried, because we could. We swallowed without flinching at the pain of a gritty dry throat. Children splashed in the water without being scolded for wasting it. On the banks of the Feather River I heard an old man I knew got swept away with the surging current, a wide, wild grin splitting his dry lips. No one tried to save him, it was right for him to die quenched.

I don't know what Bo thought, but I thought the joy and relief we brought would devastate the farmers. I thought they'd see how wrong they'd been. I pictured them falling to their knees in the dust, defeated and repentant. What they did was drive around strafing riverbanks with gunfire, killing dozens. Wounding more.

Where Bo and I are now is running. We planned releasing the water, the type and strength of the charges, the timing. But we didn't plan for getting hunted like a couple of man-eater coyotes. The hunters have ATVs and SUVs, we have the thick skins and hard eyes of creatures living in a barren land. We know the cracks, the crevices, the dark places where light can't tread. We know pinching thirst and aching bodies. We know we've been running for too long.

We've had to leave the city and are stuck in a wasteland of fallow fields. Pieces of stranded farm equipment, fallen windmills, a broken highway, all of it stands as a monument to arrogance. All of it makes me wish Bo could blow up the past.

It's afternoon, when the land is hot to the touch. Bo lays a chapped golden-ivory hand on my shoulder, it's time for a break. A hanging tree is the only shelter in sight and we fall into its embrace. The hanging tree's shade is cool and dark, even though it has no leaves and never will again. Bo lays her head in my lap and I lean against the tree's rough trunk. Above us blackened bodies twist and the shade seethes, a cold dark tangle of love, revenge, anger, and honor. The tree whispers its stories in a voice like those dried peppers strung up on the porch. Thirst winds through every story like a dry riverbed.

Bo and I haven't seen water in almost three days. The tree knows it and in its whispers we begin to hear our story, too. We liberated the water, brought reprieve to what was left of the land and the people. We caused death and pain, too. And we'll die for it. Our thirst is powerful. My heart has never beat so fast and I swear I see the mighty American River flowing at my feet. Bo sees a bar. She says it's funny that we met over drinks and we'll die over the lack of them. Her voice rattles like the dead seeds in a dried-out gourd. It is funny though, how I can still taste the bootleg whiskey she bought me, burning with a lick like gasoline. Funny that I'd take that over water now if I had the choice. She had what passed for a beer and wrinkled her nose every time she took a sip. The next day I took her to meet my people at the Rancheria. The old ones said that two people brought together by tragedy would never part.

Justice and enough water are two things this land will never see again, Grandmother said that on her deathbed. I hope she knows I tried. I hope my mother forgives me.

"Mim," Bo's paper-like skin brushes my cheek, "am I crying?" I brush my thumb under her eye, worried my rough skin will rip through her.

"You don't have any tears." My tongue sticks to the roof of my mouth when I talk and my heart feels like a hummingbird trying to escape my chest. As death closes in, I suddenly feel the need to explain myself.

"We're dying for justice," I tell Bo. She shakes her head in my lap. She's the smart one. I'm the crazy one. I tell her I'm sorry for the millionth and probably final time. She tells me again that she knew it would come to this. She's glad we're dying under the hanging tree where so many others have died for wanting something no one should own. I've never seen her look so beautiful, dry shriveled skin, dry sunken eyes. I can't explain it. She looks like the burnt-out fuse of the sun.

"Mim," her voice sounds like a willow in the wind, "the tree is reaching for us." She's looking up through the seething branches, her eyes wildly zipping back and forth.

"You're delirious." I'm also the blunt one.

"It's reaching," she says again. Her eyes are so wide now. My heartbeat isn't strong like a hummingbird anymore. It's like a lone cricket chirping. I decide to tell Bo I love her, but it's too late. The tree has her now.

I stroke Bo's hair and I feel the tree's cool embrace squeezing out my last breath. And then I'm not on the hard red dirt anymore. I'm in the tree, lots of us are in the tree, our spirits are the shade, our voices make it seethe. Bo is there, sitting in the branches, swinging her legs, grinning at me. She looks whole and really, death doesn't look so bad.

"I'm not thirsty anymore, Mim," she says. Then her grin twists the way it would whenever she set a charge and she says, "not for water anyway." I know what she means and I look out across the hard, shimmering landscape. A plume of dust with metallic flecks glinting at its center is racing toward us. I look down at my body, which is a stranger thing to do even than dying. My body's hand is resting on Bo's cheek. The plume arrives.

There are eleven men in dusty trucks, jeeps, and ATVs. One wearing a baseball cap and a shoulder holster kicks my body's foot. He nods, a smirk spreading across his wet lips.

"Told ya they'd wouldn't make it far. Idiot resisters."

Another claps him on the back. Hard. "Maybe you're the idiot. They ensured this year's crop will fail, which may have brought down the farms altogether." The man pulls a pistol from his hip holster and points it at my body, "I say we make sure they're really dead." My body is leaning against the tree, not harming anyone. A shot rings out, the sound lasts forever in this empty land. A black hole spreads across my forehead. He pulls the trigger five more times, the others join in. My body and Bo's body jerk and dance with each bullet. Bo whispers my name in the cool, swirling shade. I can feel her wide smile, as wide as the desert. Her shade mingles with mine. I feel the tree release all of us and we leap from its branches. We fall upon the men and slake our thirst with their blood. They belong to us now, like the rabbit belongs to the fox.

ACKNOWLEDGEMENTS

STRANGE CALIFORNIA WAS MADE POSSIBLE BY THE INCREDIBLE SUPPORT OF OUR KICKSTARTER BACKERS. TO EACH OF YOU, WE SAY "THANKS!"

Backers are listed according to the backer-level they supported *Strange California* at.

ANGEL'S CAMP
Minnie Olson
Tasha Turner
Darin Kerr
Jeremy M. Gottwig
Mike McMullan
Samuel Montgomery-Blinn
Joshua Temple

OAKLAND
Neall Price
Julienne Cunningham
Tahmi DeSchepper
Pat Knuth
Michael Burnam-Fink
Dan Sundberg
Carol J. Guess
Evan Jensen
J.R. Murdock
Travis
Gary Hoggatt
Sai
Aidan Doyle
Theresa Glover
Gabriel Cruz
Bryant Durrell
John Carter McKnight
Misha Dainiak
Scott Drummond
Phil Skents
Ann Lemay
Nils Hedglin
Lauowolf
Chris 'Warcabbit' Hare

Trace
Floor Senda Boerwinkel
Simo Muinonen
Sharan Volin
Josh McNair
Gavran
Michelle Murrain
Bruce Patton
William 'Beej' Carson
Rebecca Bennett
Nathan Primeau
Shaun Kronenfeld
Paula L. Fleming
Max Kaehn
T. Kaplan
Jake
Bob Smith
Regis M. Donovan
Chad Ceccola
Ronnie Bailey-Steinitz
Lisa Shininger
Lily V.
Bridget McKinney
Jay
Elsa Sjunneson-Henry
Lyrrael
Keshav Sapru
Kara Beal
Scott Fitzgerald Gray
Holly Daugherty
Pat Hayes
Beth Cato
Ryan Idryo
Cliff Winnig
Sarah Liberman
Rachael K. Jones
Judith Tarr

Liz Courts
Jennifer McGaffey
Casey Sharpe
Georgina Ballantine
Gail Z. Martin
Joshua Kidd
Shiyiya LeCompte
Merav Hoffman
Herman Duyker
Julie Steinbacher
Jim Ryan
Alyssa Hillary
A.P. Barton
Fen Eatough
Tibicina
Kayliealien
Alex Bacon
Erica Frank
Glennis LeBlanc
Atul Joshi
Storium.com
John Roberts
Jennifer Day
J. V. Ackermann
outlawpoet
Marguerite Kenner and Alasdair Stuart
Smashingsuns
Stephanie Wood Franklin
Carol Elaine Cyr
BerryK
Carmen Maria Marin
Larisa LaBrant
C.N. Rowen
Jen1701D
Matthew T. Stapleton
Christopher Nickolas Carlson

Caitlin Jane Hughes
SwordFire
T. M. Tomilson
Traci Honda
Cynthia Kim
Molly Forman
Michael Choi
The Strix
Marielle Kaifer
Amber Scott
Erin Hoffman-John
Gene Ha
Ashley R. Morton

SACRAMENTO

Misty Massey
Michelle Smith Keil
Dawno
Jack Hillman
Andrew Hatchell
Chelsea Shelton
Michael Warnock
Dana
Megan E. O'Keefe
AJ Sikes
Lisa Ellis
Jacob Carson
Steve D
Kate Cowan
Elaine Cuyegkeng
Ashton MacSaylor
Theresa Mecklenborg
Lola McCrary
Stephen Gordon
Andrew Louis Marnik
Dino Hicks
"Dramliz, Green Dragon of
the AGL589"
Jerry Pierce
Nicole Lindroos
Kerry aka Trouble
"Cho"" Yee"
Araceli Esparza
Anon
V. Hartman DiSanto
Catherine Pahia
Christopher S. Sanders
John Shannon
Brendan
Ian Monroe
Tiffany Bridge
Elizabeth Kite
Kendra Hillman Chilcoat
L Shapiro

Jesse T. Alford
Danica Morgenstern
Katharine Bond
Anne Hamilton
Mark Schynert
Maya Eckhardt-Polanco
Amy H. Robinson
Mark Tygart
Renee
Pulp Literature Press
Kristin Taggart
Beth Lewis
Laurette Dagorn
Tina Connell
Jean Marie Ward
Amy Goldman
Alan Blaine
Aynjel Kaye
Amber Coney
Kristina Lawton
Liz Drachnik
C. C. S. Ryan
Lisa Christensen
colt
Loren Rhoads
Tatiana
Mikaela
Lily Connors
Kitty Lanning
Jacob & Rina Weisman
Haley Bartels
A.C. Wise
Lauren Parker
Carolyn Charron
Ariel Lee
Dana Duffield
Craig Knedler
Ian Daw
Taylor Whelchel
Randy P. Belanger
Danicia
Jennifer Miller
Jude Rossell
Sarah Lemler
Angela Rega
Heather Harris McFarlane
Michael Satran (F'tagn)
Chris Brant
Jeremy Zimmerman
Michelle Iannantuono
Rebecca Roycroft
Cheryl Preyer
Florence Ion
Knut Martin Hoel
Forrest Dylan Bryant
Michelle Francl-Donnay

Deborah Sue Rowan
P.
Rita Lewis
Samantha Henderson
Emily Leverett
Shawna Jacques
Jennifer Powell
Andrea Blythe
Jennifer Brozek
Jon Lasser
Ilana
Silence in the Library LLC
Jaime Mayer
Roo Wezel
Crossed Genres
Chip Houser
C.C. Finlay
Scourger
Harley Jebens
Jonathan Korman
Simran S. Sabharwal
Rachel Tougas
Tara Shepersky
Alex Claman
Andrew Fox
Sara C
Eric Portner
Eric Asher
Felicia Lubecki
Susan Sutton
Madelyn Jirasek
Emilie
Sam Fleming
Kyle Crivello
Jentry Rodgerson McGee
Edward Harry

HALF MOON BAY

Sheryl R. Hayes
Anonymous
Rayne Banneck

SAN JOSE

Fidel Jiron Jr.
Logan Z. Liskovec
Sally Novak Janin
Erykah Fassett
Jocelyn
Patti Short
Stuart Rodriguez
Sarah Fuentez
Shauna M. Ratliff
Lord Pony's Human
Michael W. Robins
Ilsa Coleman
Cathy Green
Anthony R. Cardno
Marion Deeds
Dianne Hackborn
Meghan Elison
Kaila Stevenson
Aaron Wood
Anne D
Brandon K. Kirkham
anonymous
Saturday
Mary Kay Kare
Terry Weyna
Marta Randall
Elisabeth Oosterman
Kerry Malone
Bethany Herron
Jasmine Chiong
Steven Brunwasser
Nina Zumel
Kary English
Susan Hensley
Vincent Jorgensen
Danielle Burkhart
Figgy O'Connell
Mark Jacobsen
Jake Miknuk
Christian Stubø
eric priehs
Crash Wrysinski
Jack CJ Stark
Charlie Reece
Knees O'Fringe
Katherine Malloy
Kirstin Sims
mdtommyd

ALAMEDA

Lauren O'Brien

MARIN

Matt McCoy
Katherine Vanyai
Dalia
Karlo Yeager
Eric Damon Walters
W!
Michael Picco
Brandy Leigh Mow
Mark Cristofori
John A Pitts
Chivvis Moore
Heather Disco
Julie Gallaher
Jane Lybecker

TAHOE

Jenny Dunbeck
SPC BURGESS
PJH
Lynn Kramer
Gayathri Kamath
Christine Swendseid
Jenna E. Miller
Dion Ridley
Katrina Angelique Storey
Andy Dost
Karen Taylor
Alires Almon
Kimberly Unger
Jenn Whitworth
Lindsay Thomas
Cheryl Juliano Facas
Kayo Yoshikawa

ANAHEIM

James Mackiewicz
Laura Blackwell
S. Otto Johnson
Jacqui Piggott

SAN FRANCISCO

Patricia Sweeney
Ezzy G. Languzzi
Sandro Mingardi
Patricia Blackwell
Tom Bridge
"Erica 'Vulpin the Ponyfox'
Schmitt"
Patricia Lundy
Robert Sweeney
books4women
Faith Hunter
Mark Griffiths
Carey Gates

PALO ALTO

Donna Hutt Stapfer Bell
Jane Niemeier

HOLLYWOOD

Chris McLaren

SAN DIEGO

EC

LOS ANGELES

Patricia Sweeney

ABOUT THE COVER ARTIST

GALEN DARA

Galen Dara has created art for *Uncanny Magazine*, *Fantasy Flight Games*, *Lightspeed Magazine* *Fireside Fiction Magazine*, and *Strange Horizons*. She won the 2016 World Fantasy Award and the Spectrum 24 Silver Award in the Editorial Category and has been nominated for the Hugo, the Chesley, and the Locus Award. She's @galendara on Instagram, Facebook and Twitter and her website is galendara.com

ABOUT THE EDITORS

JAYM GATES

Jaym Gates is an editor, author, and public relations specialist. She has edited a number of anthologies, including *Eclipse Phase: After the Fall*, *Genius Loci*, *War Stories*, *Broken Time Blues*, and more, and is an editor at Falstaff Books. She grew up in the foothills of California, where things get strange indeed.

J. DANIEL BATT

J. Daniel Batt is an editor, writer, and designer. He serves as the Creative and Editorial Director for 100 Year Starship and is the founder and organizer of the annual Canopus Award for Excellence in Interstellar Writing. His novels include *Young Gods* and *Tales of Dreamside* and his short fiction has appeared in *Perihelion*, *Bastion*, *Bewildering Stories*, *A Story Goes On*, and other periodicals. He's most recently edited the science fiction and fact anthology *Visions of the Future* published through Lifeboat Foundation. He lives in California, where he has had firsthand experience with its weirdness.

STATE OF

CALIFORNIA

BY PROF. H.D. ROGERS & A. KEITH JOHNSTON F.R.S.E.

Scale $\frac{1}{1560000}$ of nature, 24½ miles to 1 inch.

Scale of English Miles

0   10   20   30   40   50   60   70   80   90   100

STRANGECALIFORNIA.COM

www.ingramcontent.com/pod-product-compliance
Lightning Source LLC
Chambersburg PA
CBHW030850030726
47495CB00005B/1456